Shayne Collier has worked as a journalist for almost four decades. She has written several romance novels that will never see the light of day. In 2014, she changed tack and started to write the novel of her heart. Her other passions are ocean swimming, walking in nature and doing her bit for the planet. She lives in Sydney with her partner and a Kelpie.

Return to Desiree Bay

Shayne Collier

First published by Shayne Collier in 2022
This edition published in 2022 by Shayne Collier

Return to Desiree Bay

EPUB: 9781922389732
POD: 9781922389749

Cover design by Red Tally Studios and Lisa Chandler

Publishing services provided by Critical Mass
www.critmassconsulting.com

*To my mum Josie, my sister Cheryl and my
dad Earl, who would have been proud.*

CHAPTER 1

Skye Summerhayes pulled into the car park opposite the beach in Desiree Bay, between a camper van with the number-plate 'shag69' and a restored Kombi with a hula doll affixed to the dashboard.

She'd left Sydney in the pre-dawn darkness for the eight-hour journey along the coastal freeway. Before closing the door to the apartment she shared with her boyfriend, Beau, she'd checked on him to make sure he was still breathing. That is, not dead. His snore, a 'putt, putt, putt' sound that reminded her of an idling Vespa motor scooter, usually made her smile. But today a vast emptiness opened out before her gritty eyes and sleep-deprived brain.

In the two years she'd lived with Beau, she'd never asked that much of him. But last night at afterwork drinks a work colleague at the online newspaper Skye joined three years ago pulled her aside and told her some great news. Skye had made the shortlist for real estate editor and the odds were in her favour.

She didn't want to get too excited, it wasn't like she had the gig, but it was still an achievement that gave her the feeling that, yes, she could have a successful career in Sydney.

She'd sent Beau a text message with the news but didn't hear back. On her way home, she stopped at the bottle shop and bought a bottle of champagne. It would be nice to celebrate this small win together, Skye thought, as she imagined Beau lifting her off her feet and twirling her around while raining kisses upon her face. Maybe they wouldn't even get to open the champagne? That would be the perfect end to a perfect day.

Instead, she'd arrived at their apartment to find Beau and three of his work mates totally inebriated. Blotto. Stonkered. Drunk as skunks. Worse still, evidence of the use of 'illegal substances' was scattered from kitchen to bathroom to bedroom.

After cleaning up the mess, flushing the pills down the toilet, organising taxis for the mates and getting Beau showered and into bed, Skye had tossed some clothes and toiletries into a backpack and jumped into her old BMW.

She couldn't pinpoint exactly what made her drive, white knuckled, foot almost pedal to the metal, away from the glittering harbour city and back to a place she wanted so hard to forget. She wasn't an impulsive person. Usually, she thought carefully before making a decision about anything.

It was as though a ghost had pressed cold lips against her ear.

'Go home,' it breathed.

During one of several 'revive and survive' stops along the freeway, she messaged Beau with, 'Home to sort out family stuff, cyu tmw♥'.

And to her estranged sister she typed, 'Coming home'.

It was unseasonably warm for the middle of June and people were out to make the most of it. Backpackers, couples, groups of teenagers and families were having fun on the beach.

Skye's bottom lip trembled. She squeezed her eyes shut and pressed her lips together to force back stinging tears. Fun equals pleasure equals joy. She had none of that in her life.

You have to open your eyes Skye, her annoying inner voice chided her. *Stop being a blubbery baby.*

She reluctantly checked her watch, two-fifty-five pm, sighed and whispered to the universe, 'What am I doing here?'

She rested her forehead on the steering wheel. It would be nice to stay there. It was comfortable. Maybe she could have a nap followed by a leisurely drive back to Sydney? Her head weighed more than a bowling ball, it took a huge effort to lift it. Then reality struck. This wasn't a bad dream. She was home. By narrowing her eyes to a squint, she could dial down the intensity of a vibrant blue sky and sand that shimmered under the afternoon sun.

Home. A 'Tidy Town' winner for six consecutive years. The main drag led to a mecca for surfers on the edge of a coastal rainforest, which the locals had fought long and hard to save from developers.

'What am I doing here?'

Then the voice message from her sister from a week ago blasted at full-volume in her head. At the time, Skye had quickly deleted it but she couldn't un-hear the plea in a hoarse voice edged with desperation: 'Skye, you've gotta come home. We need you here, it's urgent.'

Skye's chest tightened. Her sister had literally ordered her to leave Desiree Bay three years ago. How dare she demand that Skye return. Without any explanation. How dare she send a message three years after everything that had happened.

Skye laughed a humourless bark of a laugh.

'What am I doing here?'

CHAPTER 2

The urge to reverse out of the car park almost overwhelmed Skye. Her skin prickled and her pulse quickened but her inner voice knocked a quick retreat on the head. It told her to get out of the car. Standing, she put on sunglasses, dragged a peaked cap low over her forehead and filled her lungs with fresh, salty air straight off the back of the ocean.

But not even a beautiful day could move the heaviness that sat in her chest like a lump of sticky clay. It had lodged there as she drove past the 'Welcome to Desiree Bay' billboard, a collage that promoted the benefits of a life on the coast.

Lanky tanned boys carried surfboards towards the surf and shiny girls in string bikinis played with a striped beach ball on the beach. A fisherman hauled in the catch of the day and a couple raised champagne-filled glasses against a sunset back-drop. Everyone smiled, bright and white.

Growing up, Skye dreamed about her own billboard but it didn't take long to realise real life was more complicated than an advertising campaign poster. And that being born into the Summerhayes' family added yet another layer of complexity.

Nearly everyone in Desiree Bay knew Skye's family. Skye was the youngest daughter of Jonno and Donna Summerhayes. A middle child, she was flanked by her older sister Sun and younger brother Airen.

Nearly everyone knew Skye as the sporty nerd at school and the daughter being trained to take over her father's newspaper business.

Skye drove past *The Northern Sun* office on the way through town. It was where, under her father's mentorship, she learned the importance of meeting a deadline and the value of clean, concise copy.

Next door to the newspaper office stood three identical shops with the date '1938' inscribed on a shared parapet facade. Karmarama Surf Shop was one of these. The art deco premises with curvaceous shopfront windows and double timber doors had always been and remained a destination for surfers. Skye bought her first surfboard there. Behind the retail outlet, a 1960s fibro garage had been converted into a surfboard factory. Her brother Airen worked there as a board shaper - when he wasn't at the pub drinking himself under the table.

Blake and Sons Butchery came next, the business name painted across the window in an old-fashioned navy-blue script. The display cabinet showed off various cuts of meat and Barry Blake's award-winning sausages. Skye grimaced at the childhood memory of Barry's scrawny son Justin rushing up to her in the school playground to plant a sloppy kiss on her lips. She never recovered from the humiliation and avoided him from that day on.

It was better to think about twins Anastasia and Katrina Papadopoulis, whose parents George and Eleni ran their eponymous fruit and vegetable market next door to the butchery. Skye used to play handball with the sisters and was often invited to the family's modest timber home for sleepovers.

She drifted past other businesses, feeling like an audience member watching a slow-motion video with a 'greatest hits of the '80s' soundtrack.

Desiree Bay was its own little world, rotating lazily on a wonky axis. Smitty's Fish 'n' Chips, Bay Town Delicatessen, Digby's Pharmacy and post office, Bryant's Hardware and Fishing Supplies.

Recent additions included a four-storey mixed-use complex, with apartments plonked on the upper levels like carelessly assembled cardboard boxes. The ground floor contained a supermarket, gift and homewares store, two cafes, seafood restaurant, cake shop and a real estate agency.

Rubbish like that would never have been built if her father was still alive.

But he wasn't and it had been, so forget about it Skye.

The town had expanded during Skye's three-year absence. One day, the fibro-clad and double-brick single-storey homes would be outnumbered by McMansions built to property boundaries, while subdivisions gobbled up hinterland dairy farms.

But this ugly development evaporated at Two Mile Beach. A breeze tickled Skye's cheeks and lifted her hair. It tempered the afternoon heat but the sun still warmed her back through a white cotton t-shirt.

As surfers do, she observed the conditions. The waves were full of chop, unmanageable and colliding at odd angles, but that didn't stop the tragics from having a go. She spotted several older blokes on long boards out the back of a messy break.

Once, her dad Jonno would have been among them. His rough-hewn features formed before her, a blurred portrait of a man with a deep penetrating gaze and a hard assertive jawline.

She swallowed hard. This was not the time to get sentimental. *Get a grip girl.*

That's what Jonno always told her. And she obeyed him without question, hiding the fear, while it burrowed a hole deep inside her and curled up there. Skye felt it now, squirming in her belly, disguised as a tummy ache.

But then she saw him.

As if he'd leapt out of the billboard, a surfer she didn't recognise ran up the beach with his board tucked under his arm.

A pleasant flutter replaced the sore tummy and Skye scoped the other women in close range. If they could stare, so could she. Nothing wrong with that.

For Beau, checking out 'babes' was something of a hobby. 'Don't worry, Babe, you're still the one,' he'd reassure Skye when they were out at a café or bar, giving her bottom a squeeze while he watched other women stroll by. She absent-mindedly rubbed the often-fondled spot as she assessed the surfer from behind dark glasses and nailed his type. She decided on 'Modern Viking'. Thor with a Rastafarian twist.

His taut skin glistened as water droplets from his thick brown shoulder-length dreadlocks meandered down a muscular torso, over a smattering of chest hair. Skye's eyes wandered to calf muscles, lean and sculpted like an athlete's. As he jogged towards the car park, his features became clear. Wide forehead, distinct cheek bones and squarish jaw that, she guessed, had not been shaved for a couple of days. It could have looked affected, curated even. But on Thor, it appeared au natural and unselfconscious.

Everything about him seemed perfect, except for a broad long nose that skewed slightly just below the bridge, like it had been broken and reset. But she could live with that. It added to his sexiness. To make matters worse, or better, the hint of a smile hovered like sunrays on sensual lips.

Goodness. It had been a long drive and she was hot, tired, hungry and thirsty. And obviously careering towards 'bonkersville'.

She checked behind her. Was he smiling at her? The heat on her back intensified and blitzed her body in shimmering electric streaks.

Thor stopped at the beach shower to rinse off his board... and his body.

God, the heat was getting to her. Skye fanned her face with one hand, chewing at her cherry lip gloss, and leaned down to open the car door to check the temperature on the dashboard.

Metal gashed at metal.

'Shite.'

She pulled the door away from the vehicle parked next to hers and fingered chipped duco. It groaned and so did she. The corner of her door pleaded guilty. It was covered in burnt-umber car paint.

'Whoa, what's the damage?'

Double shite.

Thor stood there, no longer smiling.

Skye almost tripped over her feet, her mouth filled with marbles.

'I'm sorry, I can pay for this, get it valued or whatever you have to do, and I'll get the money into your account or wherever you want it to be...'

She pulled off the sunglasses and bent low, failing to suppress a whimper attached to 'oh no' as the extent of the damage became apparent.

He placed his board on the ground, crouched on his haunches and examined the flaw in the Kombi. More duco flaked off as he gently ran his hand across its surface.

Skye stifled the urge to cry. What an utter klutz. She pulled her bottom lip over the top lip but a small hiccough escaped. The long day was catching up with her.

'Hey.' He sprang up to face her in the narrow space between the two vehicles. 'It's not as bad as it looks. Nothing that can't be fixed.'

She gave a lame smile. If she spoke, the tears would explode and she wasn't sure she'd be able to stop them.

'It's easy to fix,' he continued. 'Klaus'll bang out the hole and patch it up so it'll be as good as new. It won't cost you a cent.'

'But I have to pay you something,' Skye blurted out. She knew Klaus. He was the local mechanic, good at his job. 'It's gotta be worth a couple of hundred dollars or even more. I can go to the autoteller, get cash out and...'

'Buy me a drink instead.'

Skye blinked. 'What?'

'I said, buy me a drink. Then we're square.'

'But I can't, I really want to make this up to you...'

'Okay, then.' The smile had returned, revealing straight white teeth. 'I can see you need convincing. Either buy me a drink or settle on five hundred bucks. What's it to be?'

'Er, I...'

'Done. Your shout. Give me a sec to change and we can walk to the pub from here. It's up the road.'

He lifted the board and brushed past her on his way to the back of the van. Skye caught her breath as he smiled even wider. Blue eyes. She'd always been a sucker for blue eyes.

CHAPTER 3

The Last Post Hotel stood opposite the new supermarket on the corner of Sinclair and Sutton Streets, Desiree Bay's two main streets. Built in the late 1940s, the two-storey cream-brick building with a terracotta-tiled roof was one of the town's iconic structures. It was a solid reminder of the community's connection to the post-World War II years when diggers returned home with a strong thirst, a pledge to forget the horrors they'd witnessed at the front and to uphold their commitment to courage and mateship.

Life was different back then. Working-class families lived on the coast in perma-clad fibro homes on quarter-acre blocks, their employment secure in the fishing, logging or mining industries.

The hippies rocked the status quo after they arrived in the '60s to set up communes in the hinterland, to surf and grow organic veggies and illegal marijuana in the rich organic soil.

In the late '70s, Desiree Bay had another influx of outsiders. Disillusioned tertiary-educated, well-connected sea changers converged on the town. They brought money and influence. They supported the arts scene and worked with the more entrepreneurial members of the counterculture to fund galleries, music festivals, regional theatre and farmers' and craft markets.

Those left behind from the early years, intransigent old timers, welfare cheats and junkies who never quit the habit, either propped up the bar or languished in nursing homes well away from the coast. Those million dollar-plus views now belonged to those who could afford the price tag.

An Australian flag with a tattered edge was hoisted next to the main building in front of the pub's drive-in bottle shop. It blew in the easterly wind, a reminder to any outsiders that they had entered the heart of parochial Australia.

Skye's chest constricted as they walked through the main bar. She slid her sunglasses up the bridge of her nose, as if that would somehow help her remain incognito.

Before Thor could stop at the bar for a chat, she grabbed his arm.

'Let's go out the back, to the beer garden.' She led him across well-worn maroon carpet with a swirling yellow pattern, past the main bar and a bank of about a dozen poker machines, to the relative haven of a paved courtyard.

Thor retook possession of his arm. 'You've been here before?'

Skye pretended not to hear the question and sat at a timber table in the corner. She pulled her wallet from her handbag and took out a Fifty dollar note. Expediency was the key. It was crucial that she leave before someone recognised her.

The pub held too many memories of drunken teen escapades and kissing boys she didn't like. That's what young girls did in Desiree Bay on the weekends back in the day because there was nothing better to do.

Thor watched her with what could have been mild concern.

'Are you all right?' he asked.

Skye stared at him. He was truly exquisite. She closed her mouth, which had dropped open as she took in the sparkling blue of his eyes that crinkled at the corners and generous lips. He *was* the billboard so it was crucial that Skye put up that wall between them as high as she could. She was in Desiree Bay for one reason and one reason only. Thor was nothing more than eye candy and he would have to stay that way because she planned to be back on the road in twenty-four hours.

She gave her head a little shake into sensibleness. 'What would you like to drink?' She tried to make it sound like she didn't care but it came out more like a cranky command.

He sat down opposite and regarded her with what was clearly puzzlement.

'No rush.' He picked up a drink coaster and tapped it lightly on the table while observing her through those damn blue eyes that were, she hadn't noticed until now, fringed with dark lashes.

'We don't know each other's names. I'm Fletcher King.'

Skye wriggled in her uncomfortable seat. She liked his name but she'd taken a fancy to Thor, not that he would ever find out about that.

'Skye.'

She shook his hand quickly, feeling the rough hardness of it through a firm grip. Her palm tingled in the nicest of ways. She had to rub it on her thigh to stop it.

This man, Thor… Fletcher made her feel totally discombobulated, a bit like a love-struck teenager. She was not here to flirt. She still had a boyfriend in Sydney and a job promotion on the cards.

She had come to Desiree Bay to deal with her family's melodrama and to alleviate the guilt brought about by a three-year absence.

Although Fletcher got her hot and bothered, she would be totally grown up about it. There was no other option. He would be a fantasy she could tap into whenever she needed a quick pick me up.

Skye waved what she hoped was a casual and dismissive hand in the air. 'Get whatever you like. I'll have a pale ale.'

He plucked the money from her hand and fluttered it back at her, a whopping grin across his face. 'Cash. I like that. Old school.'

Skye crossed her legs. This was not what the doctor ordered. She needed a cup of tea with a shot of whiskey and a good lie down. Alone.

As the heat rose in her cheeks, his grin grew wider.

'Don't go anywhere. I'll be back.'

Cheeky bastard. She was so not flirting with him but sure as hell, he was flirting with her. As he walked away, Skye couldn't help but admire the toned body under a plain white t-shirt. Nice and tight fitting enough without being too showy.

So different from Beau who wore brand-name polo shirts in block colours with chinos or dark denim jeans. Or a suit with a sensible shirt to work as a TV sports presenter.

Fletcher still wore boardies but had slipped on a pair of thongs to adhere to the 'no bare feet in the bar' rule. On his way across the room, he stopped briefly to talk to an older man feeding his pension payment through the pokies.

Fletcher must live locally, Skye thought, though she couldn't remember him being around when she left town three years ago.

Skye got her head back to the business of her visit. She furtively scanned the courtyard, feeling like a 1940s comic book character on high alert for assassins. All she needed was the cream trench coat, belt pulled tight at the waist, to complete the impression. Her mission was to get in and out as quick as possible.

She didn't recognise any of the hotel patrons. It was too early. The regulars would start to roll in around six in the evening for the Saturday dining room special of burger, chips and salad. Washed down with a coldie or two. Or more.

Fletcher sauntered back with a glass of beer in each hand, placed them on coasters and sat down, as if he didn't have a care in the world.

He raised his glass. 'Here's to the Kombi – may she have a complete recovery from the trauma suffered today.'

Skye gave an apologetic smile as their glasses clinked.

'Whoa, be careful,' he said, as the frothy head slurped over the rim of his glass on impact. 'You really don't know your own strength.'

Skye smiled. A lot of people commented on her physical resilience, which she attributed to her middle-child status.

'That comes from having to fight off my brother and sister when we were kids, especially my little brother. There was always a bit of the biff. I got used to punching hard to save me from being rumbled.'

She laughed and Fletcher smiled. He slurped the remaining froth from his beer and raised dark expressive eyebrows.

'You're from around here?' He squinted at her over the top of the glass.

Overcome by a strong thirst, she took a swig of her drink. Leaning back, she considered her next move with Fletcher. She'd already shared too much information with this stranger who could, for all she knew, be a murderer with a penchant for tall 32-year-old women with dark shoulder-length hair, hazel eyes and, if she had to choose her best asset, long legs.

She checked the room again before settling her gaze on him. 'I used to live here but I'm back for the weekend, on business. Then I'll head home, to Sydney.'

As Fletcher leaned forward, those eyes that reminded her of a Whitsunday Island holiday pierced through her sunglasses.

Skye pulled away with such force that she'd knocked her head on the wall behind her.

'Ouch.' She rubbed her skull.

'You okay?'

'Fine. I'm fine.'

Maybe Fletcher knew about her already? Her reputation as the spoilt brat who abandoned her family during their time of grief had spread around Desiree Bay faster than a grass fire fuelled by heavy winds. But that was old news and the good people of 'Dezzy' as it was known, had probably moved on to someone else's family saga.

Fletcher placed his hands on the table, his long fingers splayed, and appeared to size her up.

'So, is this a guessing game where I slowly discover your connection to Dezzy, or are you gonna share so I don't have to work so hard?'

'I don't even know you.' Her attempt at flippancy failed.

Fletcher's eyes weren't sparkling or crinkling now. They were narrowed below eyebrows jutted downwards by a frustrated frown.

'Fair enough.' He took a long draught of beer before holding it between them and observing her through the glass. 'Conversation over.'

He put the glass down and leaned back in his chair.

Skye sighed. It wasn't Fletcher's fault that she felt sick to the stomach about having to rock up to her sister Sun's place to deal with a family issue.

'Look, I'm sorry, I didn't mean to be snarky, but...'

'Don't worry about it, we'll share our drinks in mutual silence and then you can go to wherever you have to go.'

She cocked her head. He would be easy to like.

The late afternoon sun's rays lit the back of his head to create a silvery aura. Somewhere behind her ribs swallows took flight, dipping and diving with dizzying speed.

Stop it Skye, a voice in her head shrieked. She crossed her arms over her body. Maybe that would stop the fluttering. She never got fluttery with Beau. She just got comfy, or was that complacent? Whereas Fletcher made her feel uncomfortable and unsure. He was like the sparkling sea beckoning at the bottom of a cliff.

She didn't want to dive off that cliff.

'What about you? What are you doing in Dezzy?' she asked.

He seemed to think about whether to answer and stared into the distance before choosing to throw her some crumbs.

'About three years ago I came here on a surfing holiday and decided to stay. That's pretty much the end of the story.'

'Three years ago. That's when I left. We just missed each other.'

'Yeah,' he said, his lips lifting in a tempting curve, 'like ships in the night.'

Skye had to smile back, she was enjoying herself too much. She didn't blame him for keeping it brief. She'd been nasty and unreasonable for no good reason.

'Is there anything else you'd like to add?' she asked, trying to sound casual when, in fact, she was starting to get curious.

But Fletcher wasn't about to give anything away. He raised his hands and fitted his palms together, elbows on the table, as if he was about to pray. Possibly for assistance to help him escape from this convoluted chess game of a conversation.

Finally, he said, 'Nope, that's about it.'

They both laughed and Skye noticed Fletcher's had a rich lilt that warmed her right through. With his head flung back, she caught a glimpse of dark bristles under his jawline, tapering out to the smooth curve of his neck and horizontal lines of tactile collarbones.

She dragged her eyes to her watch. It was time to go. She had to get out of here. She had a deadline to meet and sadly the beautiful man sitting opposite her would be but a memory this time next week. She would never see him again.

As she searched the area for a clock to synchronise her watch, Skye's heart sank. At the bar stood the last man she wanted to see - the last man she'd had sex with before leaving Desiree Bay.

CHAPTER 4

'Skye?'

Maybe by clamping her eyes shut and wriggling her nose like a TV witch she could catapult the man who stood before her into oblivion.

But that was never going to happen.

'Cal,' came out on a sigh.

She'd half expected to bump into him during her brief stay but not on an old stomping ground. Not when she was unprepared, with no clever speech or throw-away line planned to show him how wonderful, sexy and mature she'd become in the past three years.

Lordy lord, the beer had gone straight to her head. Skye couldn't believe how light and floaty she felt.

Fletcher saved her from what would have been a bumbling introduction.

'Cal, how's it going mate?'

He stood and extended a hand that Cal Sturgess gripped lightly. But Cal's gaze remained glued to Skye. Of course, she should have known Fletcher would be mates with everyone in town.

'Well, eff me dead.' Cal's eyes were trained on Skye then he slowly turned to Fletcher, clearly puzzled. 'How do you two know each other?'

Fletcher filled the silence. 'We met this afternoon, on the beach.'

The commotion within her subsided as Fletcher threw her a sturdy blanket in the form of a reassuring smile.

She cleared her throat to avoid an attack of nervous giggles. 'I accidentally scratched Fletcher's Kombi when I opened the car door too fast. I'm buying him a drink to pay for the damage though it won't cover it.'

She trailed off as she realised how Fletcher's intentions could be misinterpreted. Of course, she knew his motives were totally innocent but Cal may have thought otherwise. He raised his eyebrows in what could have been mild disbelief.

'Right.' He pulled out a chair. 'Mind if I sit down?'

Skye wanted to say, *'Leave now because I don't need to have my life made more complicated than it already is.'*

But she murmured, 'Sure.'

Fletcher remained standing. 'Mate, no worries. Feel like a beer? I'm up for another one.'

'Thanks mate. That'd be good.'

Skye wished she could go with Fletcher to get the drinks.

If this was the start of her weekend, how it would end?

As Fletcher's back retreated, Cal leaned forward conspiratorially and said in a loud whisper, 'It's great to see you Skye. You look different. You look... great.'

Skye gave a perfunctory 'Thanks' even though she wondered what made her different, apart from the fact they were both three years older. Maybe it was Skye's city persona shining through, a brisk take-no-prisoners attitude she developed to make herself seen and heard in a competitive marketplace.

She held her head a little higher and pulled back her shoulders. She'd definitely toughened up in Sydney and gained more confidence in her skills as a writer and communicator.

Mmm. Maybe Cal could sense her aura shining, not that she believed in any of that rot her mother espoused.

'What brings you back to Dezzy?' he asked.

Skye watched a droplet of condensation slide down the side of the schooner glass, before lifting her head to meet a gaze once so familiar.

Cal's blue-grey eyes stared into hers and she stared right back. She suspected he knew more about her family's latest crisis than she did.

She tried to recall the way she used to feel about him. She'd always imagined that meeting him again would rekindle the strike-of-a-match flicker of passion that sustained their on-again off-again relationship.

But something was wrong. She didn't feel a thing. Not even an initial flare, and especially not passion. Maybe it was the realisation that came after the end of their relationship that she'd been a pawn in Cal's property developer family's game to get intel on the enemy. Cal had used her. Now, her limbs softened into relaxation intuitively knowing that her heart no longer gave a hoot about Cal. What a relief.

'It's a family matter.' She took a slug of beer and let its refreshing iciness sear her throat. She couldn't remember the last time she'd had a beer. In Sydney, she stuck with Sav Blanc or Mojitos. But what difference would a couple of pale ales make to the calorie count she vigilantly monitored in Sydney?

'Yeah, well, there's always a lot going on there.' Cal accentuated 'there', and added with a soft chuckle, 'You never get a dull moment with the Summerhayes' family.'

Skye inwardly cringed. Her family could be guaranteed to provide fodder for small town gossip. In Skye's opinion, gossip was a form of currency. It changed hands often and accrued value as the item of gossip became embellished in the retelling. For sure, bets had been won and lost over what would happen next in the Summerhayes' family melodrama.

Skye observed the small changes in Cal. He was still a good-looking man with an even tan coating his skin like an ice-cream dipped in caramel sauce.

It came from spending hours with real estate clients on the golf course, chipping away at them like he would the green as he moved in for the sale.

Skye suddenly understood what her mother meant when, all those years ago, she described his face as an 'over-ripe peach'.

Cal's face had always been a smooth surface. His plump cheeks were those of a little boy's, tinted pink and pinchable. His face hadn't altered much but his body was looser than she remembered, the muscles turned flabby, a small bulge resting above his hips like a half-inflated swim ring. It struck her that he was slowly but surely morphing into his bigwig real-estate agent father.

'What about you, Cal? Have you settled down?' she asked.

Cal blushed under his juicy-fruit skin. 'Nah, nothing too serious.'

He rubbed the tops of his knuckles as if he was feeling uncomfortable under her scrutiny and Skye wondered if a wedding ring had been hastily removed, though there was no tan line.

'How's Krystle?' It was a question she had to ask.

Those ripe cheeks turned pinker still as he nervously checked the time on his chunky gold watch.

'Good, she's pretty good,' he mumbled and ran two fingers around his collar as if to loosen a noose.

Touché. Skye experienced the sort of satisfaction a kid must get when shooting a basketball through a hoop without it grazing the backboard. One perfect shot. It was fair enough to ask about Krystle simply because Cal had sex with her the week after he'd got down on bended knee to propose to Skye.

The old anger and heartache that used to come with her recollections of Cal cheating with Krystle had well and truly receded. A bit like Cal's hair, Skye thought, lips quirking.

At the time, she hadn't found anything funny to smile about. His infidelity crushed her. The hurt doubled when she discovered that her family suspected Cal of being unfaithful but hadn't shared their concerns with Skye.

But now it didn't matter. She'd made her point. To pursue the topic would be cruel, and malicious intent was never her bag.

So, she changed the subject. 'How's the real-estate business? You've got a competitor. I saw the new shop. Is that something to worry about?'

Cal guffawed but it seemed forced. 'Nah. There's enough to go around. We've got the runs on the board and the locals won't touch the newbie. It's all about trust, Skye. And what about you? How's your life?'

Skye didn't miss a beat. 'I'm in a solid serious relationship. His name's Beau Ferguson. He's incredible.'

The words tumbled out like rubbish scattered from a bin by an alley cat. She inwardly kicked herself for sounding like a try-hard, tripping over her own insecurities.

But Cal didn't seem to notice.

'Beau Ferguson? The TV sports presenter?'

'Yep, that's the one,' Skye answered.

Cal seemed to consider this with a long pause and a crinkled brow until he finally nodded towards her, all sombre and serious, 'Well then, Beau Fereguson's one lucky guy.'

The compliment, corny as it was, surprised Skye. Maybe the adage was true, that her absence had made Cal's heart grow fonder. Or possibly, it was his realisation that Krystle meant business – she wanted a ring on it – but Cal wasn't yet ready to make that commitment.

'You know, I missed you Skye,' he added earnestly. 'You're not heading back to the big smoke straight away, are you? We never got a chance to talk. I wanted to explain. Ah, here he is. Thanks mate.'

Cal switched from confiding to blokey camaraderie as Fletcher returned with their beers. Fletcher planted two of the beers on coasters and passed a glass filled with amber liquid to Skye.

He nodded towards her empty glass. 'Thought you might like this After you'd drained the dregs of the other one.'

Skye slapped her thigh like a country hick as Fletcher's presence cast a warm glow over her. 'Why not?'

Sunshine, he's warm like sunshine, she thought, and then, *Stop it you crazy bitch. You have a lot to sort out and Fletcher is a distraction.*

Fletcher eased himself into his chair and gestured to Cal and her with his beer glass. 'How do you two know each other?'

Cal pushed his bottom lip out as though this would help form a compact answer but nothing emerged except a small belch. Beads of perspiration popped up on his forehead.

Maybe he was worried she was going to spill the beans and share the details of their final acrimonious moments together? Those moments where she accused him of being a lowlife scum whose wedding tackle ruled his head, and that he'd slept with nearly every girl in Dezzy. Including Krystle. Cal's response had been to accuse her of going off the rails since her father's death. He'd finished with, 'At least Krystle likes a laugh.'

But Skye had no ill feelings towards Cal. Not anymore.

'We've known each other since we were kids, we lived next door to each other for a long time, went to school together...' Skye trailed off.

Fletcher's eyes narrowed. 'So, you're a true-blue Dezzy local?' he asked her.

'Mate, Skye's family used to run this town.' Cal patted his moist forehead with a serviette, his relief at not being dobbed in was palpable. 'Mate, she's a bloody Summerhayes.'

* * *

Fletcher knew all about her family. Skye saw it in his widened eyes and the comprehending, 'Oh, right' roundness of his mouth as he raised the glass to his lips and leaned back in his chair to assess Skye, as if for the first time. In a new light. And possibly not a positive one. She squirmed under his scrutiny.

No one who came to Dezzy left without learning about the tragedy that befell the Summerhayes' family. How her father, Jonno, was the driving force behind the campaign to save the huge swathe of prime real estate at The Point from self-serving greed driven developers. Their goal was to amass millions of dollars by turning Dezzy into a mini-version of Queensland's Gold Coast.

Erecting high-rise towers that cast doomsday shadows across golden sandy beaches from ten am to three pm, cluttering the streets with tourists looking for action, including hordes of marauding twenty-something males filled to the gills with piss, and self-entitled blow-ins from the city who drove FWDs crammed with hot-housed children glued to their devices.

Her father Jonno had been larger than life, an environmental warrior, a huge man with a whooping laugh and a take-no-prisoners attitude. If her father didn't like someone, they knew it. Every Tuesday night, when the next day's edition of *The Northern Sun* was put to bed, he held court from the pub. Perched like an eagle on his 'reserved' bar stool, Jonno bellowed from a pair of robust lungs his disdain for the capitalist morons running the country into the ground. The power and eloquence of his condemnation held those present in his thrall.

Her father was an orator with a dramatic flair that could silence the room and elicit rowdy applause when he'd finished his damning indictment of his targets. And the few he deemed worthy to bestow with his tough love fell into line as acolytes who'd do anything to please him.

Fletcher would also know about her. The middle child and successor to the editorship of *The Northern Sun* that rallied to the cause of the underdog and exposed corrupt councillors whose pockets were lined with tainted developer money.

Skye stuffed her sunglasses in her bag. Cal's offhanded remark about her family shook her into action. She needed to go to Sun's place, sort out the meaning behind the phone call, and get out of town.

'I just realised the time, I've got to go.' She rose from her chair with a little wobble. She hadn't eaten since breakfast and her stomach gurgled with the heavy yeastiness of the two ales.

Cal shot up from his seat and placed his beefy footballer's hand on her arm. The heat of it warmed her skin beneath her white shirt.

'Hey, don't leave yet.' The pleading note in his voice transported her back, but not to the good times. A ripple of unease ran through her.

The way Fletcher appraised her from his comfortable vantage point made her feel like an abandoned puppy. Now he knew who she was, he'd switched off. Like the mystery was gone and she was a puzzle solved. She gave herself a mental pinch, annoyed with herself for wanting him to like and respect her. It shouldn't matter. She didn't come back to Dezzy to impress anyone.

Fletcher stood up and offered his hand again. This time she noticed calloused palms like a labourer and long fingers like an artist. Definitely not a rugby man. Definitely not a real estate agent. Skye's father always said you could tell the calibre of a man by his handshake and the size and shape of his hands. He'd never liked Cal, and made his displeasure clear.

'It disappoints me that you would even consider getting involved with a real estate agent,' he'd told her. 'And what's more, the son of that lower-than-a-snake's-armpit bastard, Don Sturgess.'

Had he still been alive, her father would have despised her boyfriend, Beau, whose family, the Fergusons of Vaucluse, had made their money through massive apartment developments across greater Sydney.

'Guess I won't be seeing you round, if you're heading back,' Fletcher said coolly, his expression unfathomable.

As she wished him good luck with the rest of his life, she thought, *Dad would've liked this one.*

It shocked her so much that she turned away quickly, only to collide with Cal who planted a beery kiss right next to her mouth.

'Hey, let me know if you need anything.'

Skye pulled away. Maybe it was her imagination, but she could have sworn there was an invitation in his tone and manner. A bit too close, it bordered on sleazy. Before she could open her mouth to tell him she was in control of her destiny, two raised voices inside the pub diverted everyone's attention.

A sustained murmur among the patrons grew into a beehive hum. Seated pub patrons rose as the word 'fight' punched through the wall of voices and surged towards the action which, as far as Skye could tell, was on the move.

Cal's eyes lit up with anticipation. 'Who's in strife tonight?'

A sense of impending doom descended on Skye as she scooped up her bag and headed through the pub's dimly-lit interior towards the swing doors that opened onto the street. The dispute had toppled outside and a three-deep crowd blocked her exit, everyone trying to push through the doors at once.

If Skye stood on her toes, she could see the commotion through a high-set window next to the doors. A group of spectators had gathered on the footpath where two men were locked in a fierce embrace.

A woman in a white crop top, short red skirt and cream stilettos shrieked, 'Get off 'im ya bastard' and attempted to break them up, her thin ponytail swinging like a whip as she sliced red talons into one of the man's arms. She screamed as she was hurled away when the men broke apart. Her girlfriend, who wore a similar outfit, dragged her back to safety as she yelped out her distress in melodramatic gulps, sounding like a circus seal.

One of the men was bald, his head glowed like polished marble under the energy-saving lighting. Skye strained her eyes into close-up and the shock of recognition sent her blood pressure into free fall. The other man in the tussle, blood streaming like tap water from a cut somewhere on his head, was her brother. Airen.

Skye shuddered and shouldered her way through the on-lookers, oblivious to the abuse, 'Get out of it', 'Let 'em fight' 'F*** off', and stumbled onto the footpath like a stunned rabbit in the path of an oncoming car.

A brawny security guard grabbed her arm and yanked her back. Skye winced and clutched her arm.

'Get real lady,' the man said.

'It's my brother,' she whimpered, making a pathetic effort to pull away.

The security guard, a massive Pacific Islander with a sleeve of totemic tattoos on both his arms, glared at her.

'Don't budge.'

He moved to the centre of the action, where the two men were swinging wild punches at each other. The mostly male crowd was well into it, the scent of bloodlust in their nostrils. They cheered as Airen's knuckles landed on the other man's jaw with a crack and, just as quickly, they turned and roared their support for the other man as he hit back, his hand a tight fist, missing Airen's cheekbone by a millimetre.

One bystander had his phone raised to video the whole sorry brawl. Skye tried to reach him to get a hold of the damaging footage but his hand lowered and he disappeared out of view.

The crowd booed when the security guard entered the fray. Like an umpire in a boxing ring, dressed in a white shirt with black trousers and dress shoes, he lithely circled the two dazed fighters. But instead of remaining at a discreet distance, he grabbed the bald man by his bloody T-shirt and somehow managed to wrench his arm behind his back.

As Airen veered towards the guard and the man, Skye's voice streamed out at ambulance-siren volume. 'Airen. Stop it. Now.'

He swung around to face her. 'Skye?' A lopsided grin broke out on his blood-streaked face and Airen Summerhayes crumpled to the ground.

CHAPTER 5

Skye and Airen ended up in Fletcher's Kombi van because it was the best available option. Cal sheepishly withdrew his offer of a lift after Krystle arrived. She must have witnessed the tail end of the fight, spotted Skye on the fringe and subsequently morphed into a green goblin.

Skye glimpsed a simmering resentment in the other woman's eyes. They glistened like black pebbles in a tanned face encircled by magic silver white-blonde hair teased into a static whirly gig. She couldn't blame Cal for turning into a wimp. Krystle, who 'liked a laugh', wasn't in a good mood.

After the fight, disappointed patrons shuffled back inside while Skye sat cross-legged on the footpath, nursing Airen's head on her lap.

Cal stood in front of them. 'Sorry, Skye.'

He glanced nervously back to where Krystle stood tapping her silver stiletto-clad foot. To Skye, she resembled an agitated kitty-cat squeezed into a thigh-high black dress covered in scratchy black sequins that shimmered under the dull light. Skye knew what Cal was going to say. But she didn't mind. His presence would be more of an encumbrance than a comfort.

'You don't have to stay, there's nothing you can do,' she said to help him out of an awkward situation.

As Cal walked back to a livid Krystle, Skye stroked her snoring brother's damp hair and examined the tips of her blood-smeared fingers, morbidly fascinated by the blood's warm stickiness. Leaning in close to his blood-caked ear, she whispered, 'Why do you always do this to me? Why am I always the one who saves you?'

* * *

Seconds later, Fletcher pulled into the kerb in the desert-orange Kombi.

'Here, I'll give you a lift, it'll be quicker than the ambo.'

He was right. Earlier, the town's one ambulance had been called out to a car accident in the hinterland. The emergency call centre told Skye it would be at least an hour's wait for the ambos to reach the pub. Airen was breathing normally and it didn't look like any bones were broken so Skye took up Fletcher's offer.

Three belts were on the front seat of the Kombi that stretched its width. While Fletcher eased Airen up and onto the passenger side, Skye raced around to the driver's side, hopped in and slid across to the middle. Fletcher closed the passenger door and Skye secured Airen's seatbelt before fixing her own. Airen's head lolled on her shoulder, his breathing deep and relaxed.

'Like a baby,' Fletcher commented as he revved the idling van. Skye wasn't sure if her was talking about Airen or the

Kombi. It rattled and belched like an old codger woken from a nap but once it stretched out and scratched its bits, it clattered along the main street with a soothing 'rata-tata-rata-tata', towards the winding coast road.

Despite her anger at her brother for his irresponsible behaviour, she rubbed his limp cold hand with both of hers and prayed to the cloudless night that everything would be all right. Whatever that meant. It was a general request Skye occasionally threw out to the universe. She got nothing back because she never had the conviction the 'great beyond' was anything other than infinite space expanding somewhere and shrinking somewhere else. What else was there? What else could there be? Tonight it was awash with stars.

Airen stirred slightly and his mouth made a soft popping sound as he started to snore again. Skye wiggled into a more comfortable position, roughly folding Airen's hoodie jacket and placing it between the window and the side of his bloody face.

She observed his features softened by sleep and became aware of a frown that gripped her own forehead.

Three years ago she abandoned her little brother to save her sanity and his. Airen needed to rebuild his own life without having her around to remind him of the dreadful night their father died and the recrimination-laced words that hung heavily in the air between them. Harsh horrible words that swelled inside her until they were overripe and rotten. Never spoken but never far from being spat out.

It's your fault, you self-obsessed boy. You fucked up our lives that night. If it wasn't for you...

She shouldn't have come back. She didn't think through the potential consequences when she closed the door on Beau and the familiar almost comforting routine of her life in Sydney.

If only she could blink herself forward twenty-four hours to Sunday night. Maybe she could leave the car here and, early tomorrow morning, hop on a Sydney-bound plane at the regional airport. But who would deliver the car back? Maybe Fletcher? She snuck a glance his way. Nope, that definitely was not a good idea.

His eyes were focussed on the country road. The van's lights on high beam bounced over the rough surface to briefly frame fragments of a monochromatic landscape. The only other light came from the pale glob of moon above a dense black ocean, a heavy brooding presence that set off a shiver that crept spider-like across Skye's scalp. The last thing she needed was to be reminded of the ocean at night.

A hollow ache in her belly signalled hunger. She remembered she hadn't eaten since breakfast.

'Are we friends yet?'

Fletcher's voice made her jump. 'I think so,' she said. 'Thanks for the lift. I couldn't have done this by myself.'

Fletcher glanced at her and she caught the edge of his smile. It warmed her slightly. 'Airen's a good bloke,' he said.

'Yeah, well, you know the saying. When he's good he's very good and when he's bad he's horrid.'

He chuckled. His silhouette showed off the broken nose, so in profile he looked more like a boxer than a surfer. More street-smart and urban than sun-kissed and green. She guessed he was too polite to start the conversation about her family. Maybe he was scared about how she would react, though his relaxed shoulders and steady gaze on the road ahead gave nothing away.

Skye sucked in the cool night air and talked over the top of the Kombi's engine. 'I suppose you know about my family.'

It wasn't really a question. She took his silence for a 'yes'.

'Yeah, well, we're famous in Dezzy. Or maybe that should be infamous.' She laughed as the urge to fill the night and the universe with words overwhelmed her. Even if Fletcher hadn't been there, she would have started talking.

He flicked on the indicator, urged the Kombi down to first gear, eased to a halt at the 'Give Way' sign and turned right turn onto the brightly lit hinterland freeway that led to the regional hospital.

As he cranked the Kombi back up to fourth, Fletcher's brow furrowed. 'I'm sorry about your father. I've heard the story from various people. It changes, depending on who's doing the telling.'

Skye's throat constricted and her eyes stung. She pressed her fingers either side of the bridge of her nose and closed her eyes. This was no time to lose it.

'It's been a few years.' Her voice came out all croaky. 'You'd think I'd be over it but it doesn't get any easier.'

She glanced at Airen, who was still out to it. Fletcher must have noticed.

'It's not easier for him either.'

Skye pushed away the guilt. Airen wasn't her problem. 'I didn't know he was this bad.'

'Yeah, it's not good. He almost lives at the pub, dreaming about that first beer of the day. Three o' clock sharp.'

'How do you know?'

'I know your family.'

'Really?' Skye wondered how much this perfect stranger knew about her family who had become strangers to her.

She twisted in her seat. 'You know Sun?'

'And Lou.'

'Lou?'

'Sun's girlfriend. Louisa.'

'Oh. Really? What's she like?'

'Nice. You'll like her.'

Skye waited for more. He seemed to be about to add something but hesitated and gave a light shake of his head as if he was silently telling himself to shut up.

'We're nearly there,' he said.

Skye should have felt anxious but there was no way they could have arrived at the hinterland hospital any faster. The smell of clean leather seats and the touch of cold hard metal, the 'rata-tata-rata-tata' of the engine, calmed her. And her gut told her she could trust Fletcher. His large hands lightly gripped the steering wheel like a professional long-haul truck driver who instinctively anticipates each bend in the road and always reaches his destination on time, with his cargo intact.

The Kombi headlights glowed across a red-lettered sign that directed them to the emergency department. As Fletcher pulled into the parking bay, the glass doors of the hospital glided open and a petite woman with waist-length dark hair in a plait strode out to meet them. Just behind her came a giant of a man, also with a plait, though the top of his head was bald as a badger. More noticeably, he wore a kilt.

Skye's insides twisted like a wrung-out dishcloth. She swivelled around to face Fletcher.

'What's my mother doing here?' A coldness covered her like ice across a lake.

'Did you tell them we were coming?'

Fletcher didn't reply. His expression was unfathomable and his silence intolerable.

'I can't believe you told them we were coming. It's none of your business.' Her feet stomped out a military tattoo on the tinny floor of the Kombi causing Airen to stir beside her.

'You're right, it's not my business,' Fletcher said on a drawn-out sigh. 'But it is your mother's. She and Jimmy have every right to be here.'

Skye bit her tongue on a terse but really stupid reply, something like, '*You sound like my bloody mother.*'

She slumped back in the seat, the anger dissipated in a well of hopeless resignation. Not one thing had gone according to her plan to drive in and drive out of Desiree Bay. The universe had let her down, big time. Her prayer for a speedy resolution had gone unanswered. And there was nothing she could do about it.

* * *

As the medics moved Airen from the Kombi to a stretcher and wheeled him away for cursory checks, their mother trotted along beside him cooing like a pigeon, her bird-like features creased in motherly concern. She didn't acknowledge Skye, but she did touch Fletcher's arm lightly as she passed by.

Skye flinched at the gesture. It was almost too intimate, a feather-light caress from one person to another, as though they'd known each other for a long time. It looked like Fletcher had grown close to her family in her absence. And now he chatted to the Scotsman Jimmy Trout like he was a best mate.

She heard Jimmy's Scottish brogue. 'Aye,' he murmured. 'The lad is in a bad way. Absolutely upside down with drink.'

His accent was so thick, she had to strain for fragments of sentences and vaguely familiar words. It was too hard. Skye needed food or else she would say things to her mother and Jimmy that could not be taken back.

She emptied loose change from her coin purse and homed in on the vending machine. It was in the corner of the waiting room that housed a dozen chairs covered in a purplish grape-coloured fabric impregnated with the dried sweat, grime and stench of the thousands of bodies that had sat - waiting, waiting, waiting. For news of loved ones. Good and bad. Life and death.

She knew the place well. She had once sat on one of those greasy chairs, fingers gripping the armrest, uncaring about the number of stressed and desperate people that had been there before her. Waiting, waiting, waiting.

She inserted the right number of coins into the machine. Mesmerised, she watched as a chocolate bar was released from the metal gates that held it in place and then thrust over the edge. It fell with a satisfying thud into the collection tray at the bottom of the machine.

Skye wriggled her hand through the flap and withdrew the small prize in its silver wrapping. A tiny whirlpool of saliva formed in her mouth as she tore it open with the edge of her teeth and bit off two pieces in one go. Usually, she sucked chocolate so it melted on her tongue but the need to chew and swallow the compounded sugary treat took precedence. She consumed the eight pieces in record time.

'Barely touched the sides.' Jimmy's voice in her ear like a bagpipes' drone. 'How's it going Skye?'

She tried to think of something civil to say but he saved her from having to respond.

'It's good to see ya Lass,' he carried on. 'I speak on behalf of the family when I say, we appreciate it, ya coming at such short notice on such urgent matters.'

Her eyes flew to his as a raw nerve was pressed upon, lightly touched in a too intimate fashion. 'What do you mean by urgent matters?'

Jimmy's dark eyes widened under bountiful eyebrows. 'You don't know? Have ya not talked to Sun?'

'No, not yet.'

'Well then.' He paused and rubbed his bearish hand roughly over a stubbled jaw. 'I don't know if I'm the one who should be tellin' ya.'

Skye's eyelids were heavy, her limbs loose and elastic with fatigue. She narrowed her eyes and observed Jimmy through veils of eyelashes. She could sort of understand why her mother hooked up with him. He was like the stray Golden Labrador Skye's family adopted when she was a kid. Barney had been everyone's friend, ambling up to anyone on the street, always hopeful of a tummy rub.

As was common with the breed, he'd bound up to any other dog, certain he would be accepted as one of them. Unfortunately, this led to several dog fights, with Barney coming out of the melees the worse for wear.

Jimmy had that same gullible disposition. Eager to please, Mr Nice Guy, heart of gold. But not exceptionally bright.

On the other hand, her father Jonno glowed with a brilliance second to none. A star blindingly bright in a galaxy of dust and dirt.

Skye's vision blurred. She forced herself to speak. 'Sun called me so I'll wait until I see her to find out what all the fuss is about.'

Jimmy 'harrumphed', half smiled and nodded. 'I understand, totally. Go to ya sister. Hear her out.'

He stood there, as though waiting for a prompt, his doggy eyes large and brown in a shaggy face. His expression was sad and reproachful as though he didn't understand at all.

'Is there anything else I need to know?' Her tone was softer than intended.

Jimmy looked behind him to where Fletcher sat on one of the chairs, head in hands, and back to Skye. He went to say something but seemed to change his mind.

'Nah,' he said. 'Don't worry ya smart head about it.'

The plastic doors that Airen and her mother had earlier disappeared through flapped back open. Her mother emerged in a flurry, her rainbow print kaftan adding a spray of hallucinogenic colours to the grey-walled room.

Jimmy rushed over to her and they embraced like two molluscs suctioned together. Skye squirmed at the ridiculous display of public affection between two ageing hippies, even with Fletcher the only other witness.

How revolting, 'Kilt and kaftan clash in a cacophony of colour.' She laughed to herself. The night couldn't get much worse yet she was still throwing together headlines like a hack journo.

Fletcher stood, pulled up his jumper to scratch his middle and stretched. It was a totally unselfconscious movement. The sugar from the chocolate must have kicked in as she bore the full brunt of Fletcher's Neanderthal sex appeal. It ran like a lit fuse across the room, up through Skye's feet and to every dormant erogenous nerve ending in her body.

At least he was a distraction from her mother and Jimmy.

When the couple finally fell apart, Fletcher approached them. But Skye stood rooted to the spot. No way in hell would she make the first move, even though it annoyed her that her mother hadn't bothered either.

'How is he?' Skye heard genuine concern in Fletcher's voice.

'He'll live,' her mother said, her usually melodious voice a monotone. She flicked her plait over her shoulder. 'The doctor said he was lucky it wasn't worse. A few more punches to the head could have caused...' She stopped and gulped, her thoughts obviously flying to the worst possible outcome.

Jimmy placed an arm around her waist. 'There there Oceane, Darlin', Oceane.' He murmured the name her mother, formerly known as Donna, gave herself after she and Jimmy officially hooked up.

Oceane smiled waveringly at Jimmy and continued. 'For all the bleeding, it's turned out to be a superficial cut that needed four stitches on the opposite side of the old stitches. He's to be kept in overnight for observation and they'll call me tomorrow.'

She shuddered and Jimmy held her close, enveloping her in his hugeness.

Something like relief rinsed through Skye.

Fletcher inclined his head towards her. 'Would you like a lift?'

'That'd be great.'

Oceane stepped towards Skye and cleared her throat.

'Skye,' she spoke softly, 'Thank you.'

She didn't wait for Skye's response. They both knew a waiting room that held so many awful memories was no place for a conversation. And anyway, Skye had run out of words. She could barely keep her eyes open.

As Oceane reached the sliding doors, holding Jimmy's hand, she paused and turned back to Skye, who didn't know if she had the energy to make it that far without falling down.

'We'll see you at the pre-intervention meeting,' Oceane said.

The doors slid open and Oceane and Jimmy walked out while two men staggered in, supporting their drunken mate between them. As Oceane disappeared with Jimmy glued to her side Skye's question, formed loosely on her lips, missed its target. 'What the? What meeting?'

CHAPTER 6

Skye refused Fletcher's offer of a free bed at his place in the hinterland. Instead, she booked into a backpackers' lodge, the only accommodation left in town.

'You've already done too much,' she told him after apologising for her earlier outburst.

He dropped her at her car but insisted on driving behind her to the backpackers. 'Just to make sure you're okay.'

Her head hit the pillow at around one am. She slept like the dead until, somewhere outside, the ruckus from a group of backpackers who'd been out all night, 'on the cans mate', woke her with a jarring jolt.

She checked her phone and moaned. 'Argh, seven.'

Her phone rang shortly after she shoved her head under the pillow, desperate to return to that soundless dark place uninterrupted by the monkey mind that had plagued her for the past three years. She stretched out a reluctant hand from beneath the sheet and held the phone aloft to check the caller before pressing 'answer'.

'Sun.'

'Skye.'

The silence hung between them. Skye fervently wished the new day was over and she was back in her car on the freeway to Sydney.

Sun talked first. 'Did I wake you? You sound groggy.'

'No, it's fine. I'm tired, that's all.'

Silence again.

'Where'd you stay last night?'

'Backpackers, it was all I could get at short notice.'

'Really?'

'Apparently, everywhere else was booked out by hundreds of middle-aged women attending a romance writers festival at the town hall.'

'Yeah, we wrote that up in the paper, it's good for tourism and all that.'

Sun, seeming to realise she'd veered off into friendly chat, cleared her throat and started again. 'Anyway, that's not what I'm calling you about. I heard about the fight at the pub. Mum told me you and Fletcher drove Airen to hospital.'

'News travels fast in Dezzy.'

'Yeah, well, that's Dezzy. We need to talk.'

Skye detected a hint of annoyance in Sun's voice, which, in turn, had the effect of making Skye bristle like a toilet brush.

'I can be at your place in an hour.' Her officious tone matched that of her sister's. 'But will Mum be there? With Jimmy?'

A sigh from Sun. 'I thought last night, seeing Airen like that, seeing Mum and Jimmy at the hospital, I thought it might have made you more...'

Skye leaned on her elbow and frowned at a wall that a former backpackers' guest had tagged in indelible marker with '*Jez has the munchies*'.

Here we go. The poorly concealed accusations were already rising to the surface and she'd barely uttered more than a dozen words to her older sister.

Skye helped out with, 'Forgiving?'

She imagined Sun shaking her head like a weary school principal dealing with a wayward student. 'Possibly.'

Silence.

Sun relented. 'Mum won't be coming over today. But we planned a get together at Grandma's early next week because her place is sort of like Switzerland. You know, neutral ground.'

Skye bolted upright. 'Hey, hey, slow down. I won't be here next week. I've got to be back at work tomorrow. I'm in line for a promotion. I can't afford to take any time off. Why can't everything be sorted by close of business today?'

Sun snorted derisively. 'This is family we're talking about, Skye,' she snapped. 'It's not something you can have sorted by COB as if we're a chore you get to strike off on one of your anal to-do lists.'

And then, out of the blue, she hung up, which was what Sun always did in order to have the last word, while at the same time adding dramatic effect to make her point.

It worked, and for the next hour Skye stressed like crazy about seeing her sister again. She showered and dressed in the only other clean clothes she'd brought with her. Skinny jeans, emerald-green cotton shirt with three-quarter sleeves, black calf-high leather boots. Gold hoop earrings, hair pulled back in a no-nonsense ponytail and minimal makeup except for the lips. Her hand shook as she applied a pale pink gloss.

Then she checked out of the backpackers' lodge, threw her backpack in the boot of her car and went to the hole-in-the-wall cafe next door.

After a brief read of the menu, she threw dietary caution to the wind and ordered a freshly squeezed orange juice, flat white and 'awesome surfer's brekky' of two vegan rashers, two poached eggs, field mushrooms plumped with butter from the pan, fried tomatoes and two thick slices of sourdough toast - with butter.

She was beyond caring if anyone recognised her. Of course, they did. The barista had been in the year behind her at school while the middle-aged waitress knew her from her newspaper days when, as she told Skye, 'everybody read *The Northern Sun*'.

'Those were the days,' the waitress said with a sigh, picking up the empty plate that Skye could have licked clean.

The waitress ducked her head and gave Skye a sympathetic smile.

'Your dad was the best,' she said, voice lowered. 'He stopped those bastard developers from screwing us over and made sure Dezzy stayed a real coastal town without any of that high-rise shit. Jonno Summerhayes was a dead-set legend.'

With an unsteady hand, Skye passed her cup and saucer to the waitress. She knew the comment was well meaning but hearing her father's name and the reverence in the woman's tone shook her equilibrium.

In Sydney, Skye blocked out the past with the skill and efficiency of a master plasterer, patching up the cracks and presenting a smooth veneer. Nobody in Sydney, including Beau, knew her story. The real story. She didn't give herself time to ponder the train wreck her life had become as she threw herself headlong into getting a job promotion.

She paid the bill at the cafe counter and stepped outside into the bright morning sunshine. It was as though a painter had climbed a ladder to the sky, dunked a roller into a tray swimming in matt-finish blue and rolled it in smooth swatches across a never-ending canvass. It was unmarked but for a chalky-white slash caused by a fighter jet, seemingly on a vertical trajectory. Fascinated, Skye watched the jet as it inched its way towards the stratosphere like an etchasketch line, before banking off to the right to follow a conventional horizontal path.

She wondered what it would be like to fly that high. The pilot wouldn't have clocked her existence. She was less than a speck. Microscopic. Almost invisible.

Sun's place was within walking distance, a flat above The Old Bakery. It was down the road from the pub, on the corner of Sutton Street and Sinclair Avenue.

The main street, Sutton St, was quiet this early on a Sunday morning, with the exception of the occasional van loaded up with surfboards heading towards the beach. No sign of the burnt-orange Kombi with the hula girl doll bobbing on the dash and flaking duco from a gash on the driver-side door.

Skye slipped on her sunglasses, walked away from the beach end of town and turned left into Sinclair Avenue, a wide street lined on either side by crepe myrtles smothered in pink flowers.

The awesome brekky started to make its presence felt, gurgling in her stomach like a kettle on the boil. But Skye knew that was nerves. The thought of seeing her sister again was terrifying. What could they possibly say to each other after all this time? Skye never meant for the void between them to grow but the longer she stayed away, the easier it was not to talk. Now the hole was so big that closing it seemed like an insurmountable task.

The smell of sourdough bread, fresh from the commercial oven in The Old Bakery, was enticing even though Skye couldn't squeeze in another morsel.

Several customers sat on a pergola-covered tiled verandah attached to the front of a whitewashed stone building. They chatted and ate pieces of warm flaky croissants dipped into big mugs of milky coffee. An ornamental grape vine grew up the side of the wall and across the pergola. In summer it formed a cool green canopy of leaves and tendrils. In winter, the leaves fell off to expose gnarled earthen-ware brown vines.

The building had been there for almost a century, placing it among the oldest in the town. Skye remembered it had been granted special conservation status by the council, spurred on by the Desiree Bay Historical Society, once led by her father and now Sun.

She cast a cursory glance inside and noticed locals whose faces she recognised waiting on tables and serving behind the counter. She could have walked through the bakery to get upstairs to Sun's place via an internal staircase but instead veered off around the corner to a courtyard out the back of the premises, where a set of exterior timber stairs ran to the second storey.

'Skye?'

Skye turned to face the owner of an unfamiliar voice. The woman was at the clothesline, white bed sheet held high and in her mouth two pegs, which was why Skye's name came out muffled. She grunted and signalled, frantically with her head, which Skye took to mean, 'Wait a sec.'

Deftly flinging the sheet over the line, she pulled it taut at both ends, removed the pegs from her mouth and clipped them to it.

'G'day, I'm Lou,' she said, wiping her hands across her oversized flannelette shirt and jeans before extending one to Skye as she closed the gap between them.

"It's nice to meet you," Skye said. She reached out and almost cried in pain at Lou's vice-like grip.

'Whoa, are you OK? You're real pale.' Lou's expression was one of genuine concern.

Skye flexed her fingers. 'All good, just a bit tired,' she mumbled as she regained her composure before taking in Lou's slender frame, pitch-black hair cropped to a perfectly round head, pale complexion and dark brown eyes.

'Excellent.' Lou beamed with good will. 'Come up and have a cuppa. Sun's been waiting. Nervous as hell.'

'Really?' Skye asked in disbelief as she followed Lou up the stairs. Paint flecks from the handrail caught under her fingernails. From what she could see, the place was a jumble of stuff, the courtyard filled with pot plants and fairy lights haphazardly draped over shrubs whose roots were no doubt wrapped tight like balls of string in their too-small tubs. Suffocating from a lack of attention.

The whole scene clashed with Skye's obsession with order and symmetry. She couldn't believe people could live effective lives in a cluttered environment.

The home unit, or 'flat' as Skye would classify it in her real estate stories, because apartment referred to luxurious and usually new accommodation, was 'comfortable and compact'.

Skye used these euphemisms for 'cramped and tiny' when describing cluttered living spaces in her real estate writing. Sun had rented the flat since leaving home at the age of sixteen. Skye had rented the second bedroom for a while. She'd been living there when their father died.

She and Sun had lived together in relative peace, with the unspoken understanding that it was Sun's flat and Skye was not to rearrange one item in it.

At the time, she considered Sun's eclectic collection of 1960s retro kitsch as a load of garbage.

'Why can't we clear it out and try minimalism?' she once asked her sister, who immediately launched into a tirade against cheap furniture that took the patience of a saint to assemble and wasn't made to last.

Now, she admired Sun's good eye for quality second-hand items scoured from op shops, roadside throw-outs and garage sales. In Sydney, many a collector of retro furniture would envy Sun's black-glass-topped kidney-shaped coffee table, original 1970s lava lamp and sleek mustard-coloured leather lounge with polished timber armrests. A Danish timber sideboard contained a cocktail cabinet that slid out for easy access. It was opposite a dining table made in the same style with the same pale wood and came with six matching chairs with black vinyl seats.

Resting against a stand in the corner of the room was Sun's old acoustic guitar. It looked like it hadn't been used for a while. Shoved to the background but still visible enough to act as a reminder that life sometimes doesn't roll the way you want.

'Sun, Skye's here,' Lou called out as she strolled to the galley kitchen and picked up a purple kettle from a swirly red-and-white patterned Formica bench.

'Sun's in the bathroom. She shouldn't be too long.' She lifted the kettle.

'Cuppa?'

'Thanks.'

'How do you take it?'

'White, no sugar thanks.'

Skye watched Lou take three cups from the kitchen cupboard. 'I don't know anything about you,' Skye said and realising she might have sounded accusing, added, 'You're like a surprise package.'

'Geez, I hope I'm a nice surprise and not something you'd want to regift.' Lou laughed heartily as she placed the cups on the bench, picked up a canister of loose-leaf tea and scooped a heaped spoonful into a pale pink teapot that used to belong to Skye and Sun's mother.

'Here's the gist of it. My parents run the East Meets South Bistro at the Dezzy bowlo. I manage the place. You'd know them. Catherine and Frederick Cheng.'

Skye nodded. The Dezzy bowlo had been a takeaway favourite when she was going out with Cal. The Chengs had run the club's restaurant for as long as she could remember. 'Of course, but I didn't know about you.'

'That's because when I turned five I went to live with an aunty in Sydney and then to boarding school when I turned twelve. My parents didn't want their precious daughter exposed to a rough and tumble public school on the coast.'

Skye recalled the bullies who'd hounded her throughout her school days. It would have been hell for the smart-as-a-whip daughter of the local Chinese restaurant proprietors. Dezzy didn't embrace diversity when Skye was growing up. It was mostly blue eyes and freckles. A smattering of Indigenous students were grudgingly accepted because of their sporting prowess. Skye reckoned they were lucky to survive the system unscathed and was sure many hadn't.

'I did everything my parents expected of me,' Lou continued. 'I excelled at my studies, I played violin and piano, learnt Mandarin and Cantonese.'

Skye was impressed. She sat down on a bar stool behind the bench. 'Why on earth did you come back here?'

Lou grinned. "Good question. I wasn't supposed to. I went to Sydney uni to study law and endured the whole boring-as-bat-shit five years.'

Skye felt Sun's presence behind her. No warmth, more like an iceberg.

She turned slightly. There would be no embrace. The distance between them had grown more than physical since Skye left town.

'Finish the story Lou,' Sun said in the crisp authoritative tone Skye knew too well. This abruptness didn't seem to bother Lou.

'To cut a long story short, I loathed every minute of law,' Lou said. 'Hospitality is my calling. That's why I came back.'

Sun gave Lou an affectionate squeeze of the shoulder.

'Lou won the university medal - *the* university medal,' she filled in the gaps in Lou's story, a note of admiration in her voice. 'Did it to keep her parents happy. Then she came back to Dezzy, at the 'right' time when the bistro was struggling. She took it from the red to the black in less than a year. Everyone who's anyone in Dezzy goes there. It beats the pub grub you get at The Last Post.'

The kettle whistled and Lou poured boiling water into the pot. Skye itched to turn it around three times clockwise, never anti, for good luck but restrained herself. Lou filled a cup with the fragrant black tea and added a dash of milk before passing it to Skye.

Skye sipped her tea, which was far superior to the teabags she used at home in Sydney. The last time she'd seen Sun, her sister had been going through her 'butch dyke' phase, her hair tormented into a mohawk and dyed a furious red, piercings in every orifice and wearing a flanno shirt, overalls and Doc Martens. Her hair was now its natural auburn and worn loose down to her shoulders.

She was shorter than Skye but Skye always believed her sister was way more striking, with her amber-coloured eyes and cute nose splashed with freckles.

It seemed like a lifetime ago that Sun had stood up for Skye at school against the bullies - the queen bees with a coterie of sycophants who targeted Skye for her nerdy and athletic ways. Skye surfed when it was still totally uncool for girls to pick up a board and give it a go. The girls waiting for their boyfriends on the beach found her threatening and some of the boys who surfed resented her because she was better than they would ever be.

Nobody bullied Sun, they wouldn't dare. Not only was Sun an extraordinary athlete but she knew how to party. She ran faster than anyone else and played harder. Sun had the street smarts well before Skye knew what the term meant. She also knew who she was. Sun was fully formed while Skye always struggled to define herself.

That Sun liked girls never surprised Skye because her sister understood her own sexuality way before Skye even checked out a boy as an object of desire. Unfortunately, the sisters were no different in their choice of partners. They both lamented their poor track records.

But Skye had a good feeling about Lou. She appeared to be as mentally tough as Sun and not the sort of person who would allow herself to be manipulated. She was far too clever and self-aware for that.

She turned her attention to Sun, who was extracting several homemade biscuits from a jar. She placed them on a plate and offered it to Skye. Their eyes met and Skye knew that time had not healed any wounds.

'No thanks,' she said. 'I ate a huge breakfast.'

Sun frowned. 'It's obvious you've starved yourself for three years. You need filling out. Take one.'

Lou almost dived on the plate and grabbed a biscuit. 'I made them yesterday. I call them choc-chip hipsters because that's where the weight goes once you've eaten one.'

Skye appreciated Lou's attempt to calm the pulsing line of tension that ran between her and Sun. Her big sister was as bossy and opinionated as ever and it drove Skye crazy. Taking a biscuit, despite herself, she wrapped it in a serviette and put it in her handbag.

Pointedly, she said, 'I'll save this for when I head back to Sydney later today.'

Sun's lips formed a hard line and she plonked her cup on the bench with such a bang that even Lou winced. 'Then we better get to the point.' Sun's voice had a diamond-cutter edge to it. 'I'd hate to be the one who makes you late.'

* * *

Later on, Skye wondered if Lou dug her hand into the jar for another biscuit in a futile attempt to diffuse the sisterly tension. At the time, it never occurred to her that the poor girl was struggling to keep the peace.

'Starving.' Lou widened her eyes in mock horror as she bit down on the biscuit. She showed Skye what remained of a chunk of embedded chocolate as she chewed happily on the rest.

Skye envied Lou's carefree attitude to food. She worried about her own weight constantly. If she got the promotion to editor, she would be required to file a weekly real estate news roundup via an online video. It was crucial to keep off the kilos.

If she got the promotion, she would be more in the public eye, a celebrity of sorts, under the scrutiny of a hyper-critical audience that liked its reporters neat, stylish and slim.

She'd learnt to control her cravings for food the way she'd managed to contain her thoughts around family. Food was to be avoided and it was the same with family.

Sun's voice cracked in her ear. 'I didn't call you for nothing, Skye.'

The way her sister eyeballed her and intoned her name with clipped disdain made her sit up straighter. She hated it when she was made to feel like a kid again. The younger sister by three years at thirty-two to Sun's thirty-five.

'I'll admit Airen's appearance shocked me,' Skye said. 'I thought he'd given up drinking for good. Can't he get checked into rehab? Or something?'

Sun threw her hands up in the air and slapped them to her cheeks. 'This problem isn't going to go away, Skye. This is the second relapse since, since...' she breathed in deeply and so did Skye and Lou, 'Dad died.'

Skye double blinked and sipped the last of her tea, noting distractedly that a few stray tea leaves had worked their way into her cup. She pulled one from the tip of her tongue and wrapped it in a serviette. She didn't know how much longer she could handle being here. Especially if Sun insisted on bringing up their father. Skye's heart physically hurt for the first time in three years.

Sun continued, 'We thought Airen was back on track for another shot at a footy career. He was playing at the local club and people in high places had started to notice. He was in top form on the field. Talent scouts from Sydney came to watch him play and talks started with a couple of the big-name clubs.'

Skye's throat constricted. She swallowed hard. 'Wow. I didn't realise he was going so well.'

Sun's cheeks flushed, her eyes were bright. 'Yeah. But then he got in with those hinterland dickheads. About three months ago, I think it was around the end of March. At first, I didn't get it. Why he'd let himself fall back in with those creeps when he'd been so motivated. Everything was looking up.'

Skye braced herself. She knew and Sun knew.

Sun got in first. 'Of course, it was all to do with Dad.'

For the first time, Skye noticed dark smudges under Sun's eyes. She was exhausted, worn down, defeated.

'He got totally off his face on the anniversary of Dad's death. Slipped into his bad habits. Maybe it was the pressure from having to perform. You know, to stay sober and play good footy. Maybe he started thinking too much about Dad and all that. I don't know. This is the second time we've almost lost him Skye. I don't know if we'll be able to get him back again - unless we do something about it as a family.'

Skye bit her lip, her heart going out to her baby brother.

Airen Summerhayes. Promising rugby league fullback originally picked up by a big AFL club. And dropped like a hot potato not long after Jonno's death. The media went berserk and turned on Airen, with the headlines flicking from glowing to damning.

LEAGUE'S SHINING STAR GRABS POT OF GOLD
to
LEAGUE'S BAD BOY LOSES GOLDEN TICKET

'Before I called you, we talked about our options,' Sun pushed on. 'And we agreed to try an intervention.'

Skye needed chocolate. She reached into the jar and pulled out a biscuit studded with big chunks. 'Are you serious? That's so... so American. So 'talk show'. Airen's always hated that crap. What makes you think he's going to cooperate? There's no way in the world he'll agree to this. I can picture it. All of us sitting cross-legged, holding hands in a big lovey-dovey circle telling Airen to get his act together. You. Me. Mum. Grandma. One big happy family. I can tell you now, it won't work.'

Sun snarled. 'You're always the first to condemn anything that's left field.'

Lou placed a firm hand on Sun's arm and gave Skye a consoling smile. 'We see an intervention as a starting point made more concrete, validated by your presence and endorsement.' Lou sounded like she'd rehearsed the spiel.

Sun squeezed Lou's hand as if it was a stress ball. 'Airen still feels incredible guilt about Dad. He won't go to counselling or even sit down with one of Mum's more spiritual contacts.'

Skye's eyeballs almost disappeared into the back of her head. Her laugh came out as a 'Huh!' and her voice rose by an octave. 'Like a tarot-card reader? Palmist? Psychic? The crystal lady with the runes and sparkly angel sitting on her shoulder? Or do you mean Jimmy Trout?'

Sun glowered at Skye and let go of Lou's hand. 'You should know that Jimmy's a qualified shaman with impeccable credentials.' She poked a finger at Skye. 'But this isn't about Jimmy, though he was the one who suggested we gather to 'tackle', excuse the pun, Airen's issues full on.'

Skye dispassionately observed the cookie and bit down hard, her teeth clattering together. It tasted heavenly, bitter-sweet and rich. She could feel her ravenous fat cells jumping for joy. She chewed fast and coughed as a shard of chocolate scraped the back of her throat. Between coughs she managed, 'Do it without me.'

Lou raced around to the kitchen sink, returned with a glass of water and handed it to Skye. Taking a gulp, Skye cleared her throat and stared directly into her sister's amber eyes. Petrified wood.

'You know I can't be a part of this Sun. I can't. I'm too close.' Another hasty sip and a splutter. 'When Airen sees me he sees the ghost of Dad. You of all people know Airen was the main reason I left Dezzy. You told me to leave for Airen's sake.'

Sun's eyes seemed to cloud with the memory, their maple-syrup clarity momentarily dimmed. 'To be honest with you Skye, I think we all need to talk about Dad. Get it sorted for once and for all.'

Skye ran her tongue around her teeth, clearing away every last remnant of her chocolate orgy. She hated herself for what she was about to say but her tenuous connection to reality depended on her getting out of Dezzy asap.

'You can't make me sit through a namby-pamby, bullshit, feel-good pow-wow where we pick over the past like it's some sort of archaeological dig.'

She plunged her hand back into the jar and grabbed another cookie. 'I'm done with the past.'

Sun bowed her head as though defeated and then, like a pugilist digging deep for that last vestige of energy, lined up Skye with a steely gaze.

'You might be hunky dory with your cushy life in Sydney but Airen isn't coping with his life.' Sun's voice was soft but determined. 'The past is blocking any way forward for him. I'm not going to beg you to stay, Skye, but now, more than ever, Airen needs you. So do I. Even after all that's happened, we're family. That's what matters most. And you should never forget that.'

Sun, helped by a beseeching Lou, finally convinced Skye to stay around to pull Airen through this latest dark turn. Her sister had played her into a corner where she felt powerless to protest. Somehow, she'd been sucked into two meetings - a pre-intervention meeting followed by a formal intervention.

Sun then went further and added another good reason for Skye to postpone her return to Sydney.

'We're worried about Grandma,' she said, flinging arrows of guilt at Skye. They'd hit her with an alarming regularity since her return to Dezzy.

'Grandma's health's gone downhill since Airen got back on the piss,' Sun explained. 'He moved into her place after his yobbo hinterland mates kicked him out of the share house so she's borne the brunt of his bad behaviour. We would have let him stay at our place but there's not enough room.'

Sun faltered and exchanged a glance with Lou, so deep and personal that it made Skye feel more like the outsider she'd become.

'Why can't he move back in with Mum?' she asked.

'Oceane is already well into stage one of the intervention process,' Lou chipped in. 'She won't let Airen come home until he acknowledges his issue with alcohol and initiates positive change.'

Sun finished for Lou. 'Put simply, Mum told Airen he was banned from staying at her place unless he sobered up for good.'

* * *

Afterwards, Skye sat on the front step of The Old Bakery, closed after a busy morning, and made two calls. The first was to Beau and the second to her boss Jasper Raison at *The Hunch* that she would be taking compassionate leave.

Beau didn't seem to mind that she wouldn't be back in Sydney for a week. He was more interested in her reason for extending her stay in Desiree Bay. Airen.

'What's going on? Word's out your brother's in a bad way. Drinking, causing trouble, got into a fight outside the local pub. Is that right?'

Skye's hackles went up. 'You seem to know more than me.'

Beau never asked after Skye's family so this new avid interest made her suspicious. Obviously, Beau's mates in the office were sniffing around for some juicy gossip to fill a hole in the late-night sports news.

'Hey, hey, hey, no pressure Babe. But he is your brother so I thought you'd know. After all, you said you were dealing with a 'family matter' so you can't blame me for thinking Airen was the 'matter'.'

Skye cleared her throat and crossed her fingers. 'Well, he's not. It's more complicated than that.'

'Sure.' He didn't sound convinced but Skye didn't care. Her priorities were to get the family issues sorted and leave.

Skye had ended the call with an unconvincing 'love you' and pressed a hand to her forehead to ease the building pressure there.

Next, she called her editor who didn't pick up so she had no choice but to leave a voice message: 'Jasper, it's Skye here. I'm so sorry to bother you on a Sunday but I won't make it into work this week because of a serious family matter. I'd like to explain why so call me when you have a moment. Thanks. Bye.'

CHAPTER 7

Skye walked back to her car in town for the ten-minute drive to Grandma's house, south along Shepherd Street, which ran parallel to the main beach.

As she drove out of town, she made a conscious effort to ignore the surf rolling in beyond her peripheral vision. She knew what the conditions were like out there. She could describe the white caps out to sea and, further in, row after row of storm-trooper breakers pounding the beach with barely a breathing space between. Growing up, the ocean had thrilled her when the surf was pumping and comforted her when it was becalmed.

But now Skye couldn't think about the ocean without panic rising. Soon after moving to Sydney she'd forced herself to visit Bondi beach every weekend. Little by little, she'd coached herself to hold it together whenever she heard the surf, caught a whiff of its briny body and turned to face its threatening presence.

After several months, she was able to manage the fear that had overwhelmed her since the day her father died.

On a sunny day, when the conditions at the famous Sydney beach were more like a municipal swimming pool than surf beach, she waded between the flags with thousands of other beachgoers. She occasionally swam there but only when the waves tickled at her knees.

Today, she kept her eyes steadfastly on the road as it wound around the coast before curving slightly inland to run past The Point with its pretty lighthouse that, from a distance, resembled a toy.

It took a moment to realise that her hands gripped the steering wheel and her teeth were clenched.

Don't look Skye, don't look at the ocean. Her insides roiled and her lungs seemed to fill up with water from a tap turned on full bore. It took several minutes to get into a positive rhythm as she breathed through a potential panic attack without having to pull over to the side of the road.

Around another bend was Iluka Street. Skye indicated right, drove up the hill and turned right again into a driveway in the small cul de sac. The neighbouring property was owned by Cal's parents, Dawn and Don Sturgess.

Skye's late grandfather had never got around to sealing the driveway that led to the white timber cottage where he and Grandma had lived since their marriage in 1955. Whenever it rained, the driveway dissolved into a bog but a recent bout of continuous sunny weather had dried its surface to a hard undulating crust.

Skye parked in the carport next to a faded red Holden Commodore that had seen better days. So too had the house. With a sinking heart she noted the corrugated- iron roof, much of it spotted with rust. Paint flaked off the walls, what could be seen of them behind a row of overgrown shrubs that used to be a neat hedge.

Skye tugged open the torn wire screen door, raised the brass doorknocker and tapped three times. She silently counted to thirty and tapped another three times. The curtain in the front window shifted slightly and from within came a squeal of delight followed by a yappy bark. The door opened and Skye was engulfed in a soft-pink angora hug infused with the scent of damask rose.

'Skye,' Grandma warbled. 'My dearest, darling, youngest granddaughter. It's so good to have you back.'

Skye pulled away, rubbed her waist and waved an accusing finger. 'You pinched me.'

Grandma, wearing a pink angora jumper, stretchy pants and fluffy pink slippers, ran probing eyes over Skye. Then she reached up and placed her hands either side of Skye's face.

'You haven't an inch of protective fat on your body my girl. What on earth have you been up to in Sydney? Starving yourself, that's what,' she answered her own question, a habit that used to drive Grandpa nuts. 'I don't like the way you're shrinking like all those TV types who survive on the whiff of a rice crisp and black coffee sucked through a straw to stop their teeth from getting stained.'

Skye didn't want to talk about food, eating, dieting or the unnaturally white chompers on display on reality TV and game show hosts so she changed the subject.

'Where'd you get the dog?' She unclasped Grandma's warm hands from her face and nodded to a creature the size of a large rat with ridiculous bulging eyes and a trembling body.

Grandma rolled her eyes and Skye almost laughed out loud. The resemblance between Grandma and the dog was uncanny.

Grandma was tiny, her skin darkened and weathered from years in the sun. Her eyes were her most arresting feature — honey-brown orbs that appeared too large for a heart-shaped face with a delicate nose and mouth. Her hair, natural silver grey, was cut into a neat bob that framed her small face and pointed chin.

Grandma bent down with amazing agility for a woman her age and scooped up the dog with one hand to cradle it against her chest.

'His name's Dougal but I call him Pepe because he's a Chihuahua, not a blasted terrier, and that's what you call Chihuahuas. Pepe. Pepe. Pepe. Dougal my foot. Don't you think Pepe makes better sense? Of course it does.'

The dog snuggled in closer to Grandma, staring up at her with adoration and, Skye could have sworn, a degree of comprehension.

Skye had forgotten that talking to Grandma could be exhausting. Grandma talked at a ridiculous pace, hardly pausing for breath so her sentences streamed into each other and she assumed everybody understood what she was talking about.

'Is Pepe yours?'

Either Grandma hadn't heard Skye or she chose to ignore the question. Knowing Grandma, it was the latter. Pretending to be deaf had helped the elderly woman win arguments with all and sundry.

'Come inside Love, come inside.' She took Skye by the arm and led her into the lounge room. 'You need something to eat. We'll have you fattened up in no time.'

Skye tried to protest but was firmly deposited on the lounge. Dougal aka Pepe ended up on her lap, wrapped in a multi-coloured crocheted knee blanket, while Grandma brewed a pot of tea.

The room was cluttered with Grandma's 'antiques', really an assortment of bric-a-brac. Nonetheless, it was neat as a pin because of her twice-a-week dusting regime. However, the green fabric two-seater lounge, with two matching chairs, was worn and faded as was the green carpet and walls painted a dull buttercup yellow.

Skye picked up a photo with a filigree frame from a round timber side table with ornate legs. The faces of her parents beamed back at her. It was a wedding day photo. Her mother's sleek dark hair, studded with tiny fabric daisies, was twisted expertly into a chignon and long dark mascara-ed lashes fringed hazel eyes in a pixie face. Her lips were a moist pale pink. It embodied 1970s wedding chic.

Jonno's eyes were chestnut brown in a face defined by a broad nose and firmly delineated lips parted slightly in the suggestion of a smile. His usually tousled brown hair that touched his shirt collar had been tamed with a comb dipped in water and his sideburns trimmed for the occasion.

That photo must have been taken when her mother was twenty years old and her father thirty. By the time Oceane was thirty she already had two daughters. And then along came Airen, the surprise baby.

Skye sighed. She was thirty-two and not even close to having a baby. The window seemed to be shrinking, especially as she'd started to question her reasons for staying with Beau.

She placed the photo back on the side table as Grandma returned, carrying a tray laden with scones, lamingtons and Skye's favourite childhood treat, shortbread.

Skye tried hard not to think about the awesome brekky and Lou's choc-chip cookies. She didn't know how much more she could consume without having to undo the top button on her jeans.

'I love that photo, don't you? Just love it.' A wistfulness infused Grandma's voice as she lowered the tray onto the dark wood coffee table opposite the lounge. She passed Skye a cup of tea and a piece of thick crumbly shortbread, which Skye held above Pepe, whose trembling under the blanket had subsided to the occasional shudder.

'Baked them this morning. You must eat some more. Do you realise how thin you are? You're a stick insect. It's Sydney and the Sydney set that's done it, and how on earth is Whatshisname?'

Grandma poised on the edge of one of the smaller lounge chairs and placed a piece of shortbread on the saucer of her own cup of tea.

Here we go again. Skye braced herself for an avalanche of questions. 'His name's Beau Ferguson and he's good. Thank you for asking.'

Grandma held the porcelain hand-painted teacup the old-fashioned way, by the handle with her pinky finger crooked at the joint.

She raised the cup to her lips and paused. 'Tell me all about this Beau fellow. What's he like? Is he worth it? I hope he's worth it.'

The question was simple enough but Skye struggled to find an answer. She hadn't given much thought to a character description for Beau. He wasn't a complicated human being. On the contrary, he was easy to read. She compiled a mental list and cancelled out 'demonstratively affectionate' along with 'sensitive' and 'insightful'.

Gosh. Why hadn't she done this before? Why had she allowed herself to fall into a relationship without knowing anything about her boyfriend beyond the fact that he was undemanding and had access to influential people who could help further her career?

After a minute of stops and starts, with Grandma offering no help at all, she grasped at the little knowledge she had.

'Beau is, um, sort of likeable. I guess he's a glass half-full person. Um, he's easy-going, a team player with lots of friends, I guess...' She paused, embarrassed that the accolades hadn't poured forth. Then, grabbing at another point in Beau's favour, she added quickly, 'And he's handsome. Sort of like Shane Warne, but better looking.'

Shifting back in her chair, Grandma took a sip of tea, her expression quizzical, and observed Skye over the rim of her cup. 'Handsome, is he? Shane Warne?' She smacked her lips together. 'Where's a photo then?'

Skye's embarrassment doubled. She didn't have a photo in her wallet or even on her phone. 'I don't think I have one. Not with me anyway. But you'd know him from the TV. I'm sure Airen would know him. Beau's a TV sports presenter on...'

Grandma waved a hand. 'I don't watch the sports unless it's the Olympics or State of Origin. God bless New South Wales. I hold my breath the whole game, I swear, until eighty minutes is up. It's such a worry.'

'Well, then. I could find a pic on the internet on my phone.'

Grandma shook her head side to side. 'Describe him to me Love, don't worry about a photo, describe him.'

Skye sucked air back through her teeth as she tried to imagine Beau in his element. Wearing an expensive suit, seated behind the desk in the TV studio, commentating on an international golf tournament or tennis match. From this, she cherry picked a 'Best of Beau' features.

'He's got blondish hair, cut very short at the sides and sort of puffy on top, which is the fashion, a nice smile, no facial hair and pale blue eyes. He's not quite as tall as me and he's a bit stocky, sort of like a rugby union player.' Skye had run out of good points. 'Is that enough?'

'For the moment.' Grandma put her cup and saucer on the side table, reached forward and patted Skye on the knee. 'I would like to know if he's the one. Is he? Because from what you've told me, I'm not so sure.'

Skye's cheeks heated. Her premium fertility years were rushing away from her. Her ovaries screamed at her to get a move on. But with Beau?

'I think, maybe, I don't know,' Skye said, with both Beau and Cal crossing her mind and neither causing so much as a blimp in her pulse.

And then there was Fletcher King. Skye was relieved Grandma knew nothing about her meeting him and that she couldn't see the huge spike on Skye's internal electrocardiogram chart. Skye scolded herself inwardly. She must stop thinking about Fletcher King.

Grandma leaned back in her chair. 'If this Beau fellow is the one, we'll have to meet him one day soon.'

It appeared that Grandma's curiosity about Beau had been satisfied. Her encouraging smile disappeared and her lips curved downwards to accentuate the tiny tributaries of lines on either side of her mouth.

'I'm sorry to be changing the subject Love, but Sun tells me you're back for the thingy with Airen and I'm grateful because we're all feeling desperate for dear Airen. Dear little Airen.'

The guilt again, nibbled rat-like at Skye's insides, along with the dreadful weight of responsibility she'd spent three years attempting to negate.

'Yes, he's obviously not coping.'

Grandma's big eyes seemed to expand, reminding Skye of those weird greeting cards with dogs and cats that had computer-enhanced eyes double their normal size.

'I don't think anyone latched onto that fact early enough. We thought he was doing just fine and when it came to the anniversary of Jonno's passing we foolishly let him do his own thing. But, as it turns out, it we should have kept more of an eye on him. No one saw it coming. Not his mother, Jimmy, Sun or Lou. Or me. He'd been training and playing footy just like the old days, like before. It seemed like things were getting back to how they used to be.'

She pulled out a pink handkerchief that had been stuffed up the sleeve of her jumper and dabbed it around her eyes. Skye noticed the worry etched into her features so they appeared worn out and faded, like the lounge. Poor Grandma.

'We're having a pre-intervention meeting here to organise the main intervention, and Jimmy has kindly volunteered to coordinate the whole thing.'

Skye's cup and saucer clattered as she leaned forward and placed them on the coffee table. She'd forgotten about the dog on her lap. It whimpered the way small dogs do, like she'd tried to murder it.

'This stupid dog. I nearly squashed him Grandma. He's too small, what on earth possessed you?'

She lifted the shivery bundle from beneath the blanket and moved it next to her on the lounge.

'Yes. Too right, that silly dog.' Grandma ogled the tiny bundle and a smile quivered on her lips. 'I'll kill Jimmy, I will. I didn't want a dog and definitely not a dog that's not really a dog but a sorry excuse for a dog. But Jimmy gets it into his head that I need a companion because of my angora problem so he goes to the animal shelter and picks out Dougal, I mean Pepe.

'I now have this huge responsibility to make sure this vulnerable creature isn't gobbled up by one of the local brush tail possums or, god forbid, taken by a kookaburra or a sea eagle when my head is turned for a second. That's all it takes is a second, and it ends up all over the internet that I left my dog unattended in the presence of present danger.'

Skye raised her hand like a stop sign and Grandma's rant came to a halt mid inhalation. 'Let's backtrack here,' Skye said. 'I'm hearing lots of things. How Jimmy is to blame for Dougal or Pepe, or whatever it's called, and that you have an angora problem. What's that mean? If it's an allergy, why wear it?'

Grandma shoved the remainder of the shortbread in her mouth and smiled sadly as she chewed and talked at the same time. 'Love, my problem is nothing compared to Airen's. It's nothing to worry about.'

'But what is it? What is an angora problem? I've never heard of it.'

Another wan smile and a quick lick around the teeth to clear away shortbread remnants. 'I'm perfectly fine, Love. It's this little problem I've been having lately with leaving the house.' She shook her head ruefully, her big eyes mournful. 'I can't seem to get past the damn front gate without feeling giddy. So, I come back inside and everything's fine again. It's the strangest feeling. I have a bad case of angora-phobia.'

Skye wasn't sure she'd heard properly. 'I'm sure there are people who are afraid of goats... or rabbits...' she began but Grandma interrupted.

'Love goats, love 'em, no it's not that...'

The penny dropped. 'Do you mean agoraphobia?'

Grandma clapped her hands and jiggled in her seat.

'That's it. Ag-or-a-phob-i-a. Such a long name for a small problem, don't you think? I don't know how it started but it's been coming on slowly since your father, since Jonno passed. He was my only child, my baby...' she trailed off and stared out the window before starting up again. 'I'm getting on, you know. And I love my house, it's my safe place and I don't feel the need to leave it. Ever. As long as people keep coming to me and I have the bare essentials, I'm happy. I don't have to go out.'

Skye moved from the lounge to kneel at her grandma's side, taking the cup and saucer from her and placing it on the side table. She held her grandmother's soft finely veined hand.

'We can fix this, Grandma. It's about getting your confidence back and overcoming your fears. This is a treatable problem. A good doctor can help you find a psychologist. I want you to be able to leave the house to come and visit me in Sydney. That means you'll have to leave the house. No excuses.'

Grandma squeezed Skye's hand tight and glistening hazel eyes stared hard into her own.

'But how can these problems be solved if you're going back to Sydney so soon, Love? Please think about staying a bit longer.'

CHAPTER 8

If Skye wanted to, she could stay the night at Grandma's. The bedroom she knew intimately from her teenage years hadn't changed. The blue satin doona cover with a dolphin print covered the single bed and Skye's swimming and surfing medals were strung like a festive banner on a string along the picture rail. Posters of Kurt Cobain, Pink and Australian surfing legend Layne Beachley adorned the walls. The dressing table contained a glass menagerie of exotic fish and around half-a-dozen trophies inscribed with the details of her triumphs in the pool and surf.

Grandma insisted she keep these 'dust collectors' though Skye had managed to slowly sneak a dozen or so into the garbage bin.

Grandma's place had been an orderly retreat compared to the mayhem that had defined Skye's home life as a child. Her father's acolytes were forever dropping by unannounced to the Summerhayes' hinterland property to help organise strategies for numerous causes.

Chaos reigned when they got on the pot and the piss. More often than not, Jonno's 'comrades' ended up staying over, dossing down on the lounge or lounge room floor, or setting up tents in the sprawling backyard.

It was fine when Skye was little, even exciting, but the constant noise and frequent carousing interfered with her studies when she started high school. And she didn't want to be around when her mother asked her to help clean up the mess left by her father's mates.

Above everything, Skye hated mess.

She liked everything to be in its right place. Every surface at her parents' house had been crammed with books, magazines, ring-bound folders filled with notes, loose sheets of paper, unopened mail, dirty plates, cutlery, coffee cups, wine and beer glasses, bottles and takeaway containers licked clean by the dogs, clothes baskets filled with dirty clothes and clean clothes, sometimes both. The ironing board was always set up with the iron on it. But Skye was the only one who ever used it, until one day it short fused and gave her an electric shock.

She had to admit the mess wasn't anybody's fault. There was never any time, not a second it seemed, to tidy up, and her mother and father couldn't afford to hire a cleaner. Even if they had, it would have been impossible to clear a space to vacuum or dust.

By the time she turned fifteen, Skye rebelled against the chaos and clutter. Although she knew her mother was upset with her decision, Skye moved from the rambling farmhouse to Grandma's.

For the last few years of high school, she lived with Grandma and populated the spare room with her favourite things. Order ruled with an iron fist clenching a dust cloth. Skye cleaned her room every weekend, frequently sorted through her belongings, disposed of items she deemed obsolete and generally maintained a spotless domain.

Home was meant to be a 'haven', 'sanctuary', 'retreat', not a hedonistic playground crammed with sentimental mementos and ceiling high with junk.

Skye had declined her grandmother's invitation to stay overnight. Although she loved her room and cherished the mostly happy memories, at some point Airen was bound to turn up.

She wasn't ready to deal with her brother.

And her mother and Jimmy would drop by too, checking in, Jimmy fussing about like an old woman. Crystals would be set out under the beds and near the front and back doors to encourage positive energy flow and whatever other mumbo jumbo he carried on with.

Like it made any difference. She couldn't believe her grandmother and siblings were so accepting of Jimmy, so welcoming, even eager to have him replace Jonno as the son and father in their lives. For goodness sake, the man was certifiable. Couldn't they see that? He leapt around in a bloody kilt and feigned the ability to communicate with people's ancestors. He was a snake-oil salesman.

And what the others may have missed was the way he entered their lives. Even before her father died, Skye had seen that something more than friendship had developed between her mother and Jimmy.

Too often she'd seen Jimmy's car parked outside the house her mother and father moved into after the hinterland property was sold to fund Jonno's fight against the property developers.

It was during that tumultuous period that Jimmy Trout and her mother started working together. Oceane's home-based crystal wholesale business Crystal Spirit Journeys was gaining momentum. She brought Jimmy onboard because of his own extensive knowledge of quality crystals.

Like her father, Skye was immersed in the battle to protect Desiree Bay. As soon as she graduated from high school, she went to work as a cadet journalist at *The Northern Sun*. One of her roles was to co-research and write breaking news stories about the property developers circling the town like vultures.

The stories exposed corrupt Desiree Bay councillors who courted developers and accepted payola via their back pockets to get shonky development plans fast tracked for approval.

They were heady days, exciting days, glory days when Dezzy's residents pulled together to 'fight the powers of evil'. Even now Skye smiled as she remembered her father holding court at the pub, surrounded by an adoring crowd of true believers. They were prepared to sacrifice everything to stop the construction of three twenty-two storey residential towers at The Point.

With a painful clarity, Skye recalled the moment she saw Jimmy and her mother enjoying more than a strong working relationship. Much more.

It happened the day her father died.

The news that the Land and Environment Court had overturned the approval for the multi-storey tower development at The Point had spread like a bush telegraph and the townsfolk were out to celebrate.

Her father 'retired' to the pub for a celebratory schooner. Skye was half running half skipping to The Point to interview the locals at the forefront of the David versus Goliath challenge. On the way, she decided to stop off at her parents' place to grab a cold drink.

She turned the corner and saw Jimmy's olive-green Holden Leyland P76 parked in the driveway of the single-storey red-brick house. Then Jimmy and Oceane walking towards it, Oceane laughing at something Jimmy said.

Skye slowed down, her legs rubbery, and stopped behind a native brush box tree, one in a row that ran along the edge of the footpath.

What she saw next caused her stomach to lurch.

Jimmy leaned over to kiss Oceane on the cheek but her mother turned her head so his lips were on hers.

Skye swayed as the ground slipped from under her. To steady herself, she clutched at the tree trunk. Even though she wanted to, she couldn't tear her eyes away from the kiss that seemed to go on for a horrendously long time. Shock bore into her, a whirring drill into a well of despair.

Cheeks flaming and heart beating like a box filled with bats, she flicked her head one way and the other. Was anyone else around to witness her mother's insane behaviour? Oceane's fall from grace. Her betrayal of Jonno, Skye's father and local hero, in the middle of the day for the world to see?

At that crystalline moment, Skye's thoughts turned murderous. She was delirious with hate for her mother and Jimmy.

Jimmy reversed out the driveway, but not before rolling down his seagull-poo stained window to reach out and take Oceane's hand.

Skye shrank behind the tree, seething with revulsion. She tried to get her head around what she had just witnessed and find excuses for her mother. But it was 'crystal' clear.

Her mother's open infidelity stung her to the core.

How could she have done this to her husband of thirty-five years? Her father was a brilliant man, the best dad ever, the one who gave his children every opportunity. Sure, home life was chaotic and unpredictable, no one could ever predict who Jonno would drag back to their place. And when he went bush, which was frequently, he never bothered to tell anybody.

But he didn't deserve this.

Skye had continued the rest of her walk to The Point in a daze, her thoughts like too many clothes in a tumble dryer, banging around in the void. She didn't know how she made it through the rest of that day.

And she had no idea of the horror that was to follow that night.

Enough. Enough. Enough. Block it Skye. Move to the present.

The Now.

In 'The Now' she had to deal with her darling grandmother and the crushing guilt that came from seeing how frail the elderly woman had become in her absence.

Skye could help with the agoraphobia. It was a condition she felt she understood as there were often days when she found getting out of bed an ordeal.

But the rest of it, dealing with her brother – the initial meeting, then the main intervention where she would have to be in the same room with Jimmy and her mother – was another story.

* * *

Afternoon tea at Grandma's stretched towards twilight. The sun was setting in the hinterland by the time Skye made it back to town.

The thought of another night in the small room under the cool LED lights made her feel nauseous. And besides, she'd already checked out.

She was stuck. It would be rude to call on friends she hadn't seen for years, Sun and Lou's place wasn't on offer and staying with her mother and Jimmy was out of the question.

On autopilot, Skye ended up back in the car park at the beach, sitting behind the steering wheel, gazing at the remnants of a strawberry-gelato streaked horizon.

A fisherman stood at the water's edge with two large rods, a tackle box and bucket set up on the sand. He held one rod at his shoulder and expertly flicked it back so the line flew across the foaming wash and into deeper water beyond the breakers.

A few stragglers wandered along the sand, an elderly couple holding hands and a man with his dog off-leash.

Her heart went into a triple flip when she saw the runner. As he drew closer in the fading light, she blinked back the disbelief that he had again popped unexpectedly into her line of vision.

With no good reason to avoid him, Skye hopped out of the car, locked it, and walked down the sandy path, removing her boots and socks to dig her toes into the fine sand. It struck her that this was the first time she'd set foot on Two Mile Beach in three years. She could cope with this. It was just a beach. And she wasn't going to get close to the shoreline.

She put down her boots and swung her arms above her head. 'Hey, Fletcher.'

He'd stopped to pat the dog, a Border Collie, with a ball in its mouth. Seeing her, he waved back and walked her way.

'How's it going?' He seemed pleased to see her, a smile tugged at his lips and the corners of his eyes. 'I thought you were heading back to Sydney?'

Skye marvelled at the slow rise and fall of his bare chest as though the run along soft sand had been a stroll on a level pavement.

'Not yet unfortunately. There's some unfinished business to tidy up so I'm here for another week.'

'Where're you staying?'

Skye shrugged. 'I'm not sure. I checked out of the backpackers. I didn't want to stay there another night. I'm showing my age.'

'I don't blame you.' Fletcher pressed his lips together and gave her a measured stare as though he was making up his mind whether to speak or not.

Slowly, he said, 'I've got a spare room at my place. It's yours if you want it.'

It was a genuine offer, coming from nowhere else but a place of goodwill that Fletcher seemed to inhabit 24/7. He seemed like a genuinely good person. Skye reasoned that his place had to be better than the backpackers, which smelled like a dreadful combo of disinfectant, dirty socks and rotting potatoes.

As she considered her response, Fletcher took the sweatshirt that had been wrapped around his waist and slipped it over his head. His appearance suggested a hippy lifestyle with outdoor showers and no hot water. Baggy floral board shorts and a holey shirt with the brand 'Golden Breed' scrawled across the front in a stylised font did not give her the impression of a luxe set-up at home.

He smelled of salty sweat and lime. Pour over tequila and lick with enthusiasm. Skye's lips twitched and her belly contracted as she held back a big belly laugh at her adolescent mind and thirst quenching analogy.

'Are you okay?' Fletcher seemed sincere in his concern.

Maybe she looked like she was in pain and not about to laugh her insides out. She was grateful Fletcher couldn't read her mind.

'A tummy-ache. My family's been feeding me heart-attack food since I got here. Everywhere I go, there's another plate of lamingtons or a jar of choc-chip cookies. It's never ending.'

'You've been feasting on Grandma's lamingtons and, let me guess, Lou's cookies?'

Skye wrapped her arms around her as a chill that signalled the arrival of dusk settled across the cooling sand. 'You know my family better than I do.' She hoped she sounded mock accusing.

Fletcher laughed. 'I guess I stepped in when you stepped out.'

She stopped short of correcting him with, *'When I ran away.'*

'Back to your spare room – are you sure?' Skye prompted.

'I have a room, and you're perfectly welcome to use it. There's only one rule. And that is, we make peace over your family. I don't want to hear a bad word about them. They've been good to me since I came to Dezzy. I've got nothing but respect. They're great people.'

Fletcher pressed his hand over his heart before he extended it to Skye. She reluctantly unknotted her arms and placed her cold hand in Fletcher's warm one. They shook.

'About my family,' Skye muttered. 'I don't mean to be mean but there's a lot going on there that you don't understand...'

'So, it's a deal?' he interrupted.

He might as well have stuck his fingers in his ears and hummed loudly, Skye thought, feeling thoroughly grumpy and defeated. 'Yeah, it's a deal. I'll do my best to be nice but I have got a reputation to uphold as shit stirrer extraordinaire.'

She tried to make a joke of it, but his request to talk amiably about her family would be impossible to meet.

* * *

Driving her trusty Bimmer, Skye followed Fletcher in the Kombi van along a familiar route. They turned off the coastline road and drove towards the hinterland, along a reasonably straight but hilly road bordered by pastures and large old homes tucked behind hedgerows, high walls and established native and imported trees.

Ahead of Skye's car, the Kombi's headlights flicked to high beam like a wide-lens camera to take in smaller items such as letter boxes, dry stone walls and flashes of green hedge.

They passed several small villages that owed their existence to wealthy individuals who, tired of the rat race in Sydney and seeking a tree change, relocated to the lush backwaters of Dezzy.

Her father used to say, 'There's money in them there hills. Let's go milk it.'

Of course, the new arrivals and city blow-ins who visited during the school holidays didn't want Dezzy to change any more than the locals.

They wanted to keep their piece of turf exclusive and free from the human detritus that flowed in and out of other coastal towns like a dank tidal pool. They had given freely to her father, not just money but also their connections; their power and influence often stretched to the political sphere.

Many were in awe of and even fearful of Jonno's blunt earthiness and his disrespect of authority. They liked that he was the loud-mouth, the spokesman with a crazy glint in his eyes.

The media's focus on Jonno allowed his private donors, amongst them specialist doctors, barristers and even bankers and 'entrepreneurs', to remain anonymous in their multi-million dollar properties in the hills. It was better for them that their Sydney property developer mates didn't know they were rooting for the nimbys and their madman leader.

On their way up a particularly steep hill, they passed the Summerhayes' old farm. Skye's childhood home, it was a 1970s colonial-style brick-veneer house on acreage.

The property had also been home to her mother's twelve chickens, four geese and two donkeys rescued from a cruel owner.

Selling it to a Sydney businessman, with a trophy wife a third his age, and moving to a smaller house on less than a quarter-acre block in town, had been a wrench for Skye's mother.

Oceane had loved the freedom of the farm and hated leaving behind a big vegetable garden and her animals.

Skye sensed that her mother felt suffocated in town. Back then, she ran a gemstone stall at the weekly markets and had only just started to explore an online wholesale and retail business.

Not only had her father poured his benefactors' funds into the anti-development campaign, he'd also dipped substantially into his family's savings.

Those were stressful times, made even more difficult by her father's refusal to give the family truthful answers.

He chastised Skye if she asked a hard question.

'I ask the questions, Skye, that's my job," he'd say sternly. 'I'm the one who interrogates. I don't like being interrogated.'

Her mother had shrugged off Skye's concerns by giving her a light kiss on the cheek and dishing out one of her positive affirmations like a sage or 'goddess' as she liked to be called. It drove Skye to distraction.

'Everything happens for a reason my darling,' she'd say. 'Life is a constant mystery for us simple souls to figure out.

Sometimes we don't get what we wish for and that can be a good thing because, to quote Mick as in Jagger, you can't always get what you want.'

* * *

Fletcher's property was further away from town than Skye expected. After a good thirty minutes, he indicated left and turned onto a dirt driveway on a gentle incline. They drove for another couple of minutes before reaching a more formal gravel path almost at the crest of the hill.

As they pulled up in front of Fletcher's house, her car's headlights washed against it. The flat-roofed timber-clad structure was the typical design of the 1960s beach shack. It was slightly elevated, with floor-to-ceiling windows protected by eaves that also protruded over a central timber stoop that led to a white front door.

Skye chided herself for her impulsivity. She was usually so circumspect. By coming to Fletcher's place, she was stepping into uncharted territory. Skye preferred to stick to a concrete walkway, not into rocky off-road territory. Yet here she was, getting herself into what could be a potentially tricky situation.

It wasn't that she didn't trust Fletcher. She didn't trust herself.

Fletcher must have sensed her reluctance to leave the security of her Bimmer. He tapped on the window.

'You coming in? Where's your gear?'

Slowly, she opened the car door and stepped out. She hadn't noticed it before but he was a couple of inches taller than her. She was used to being at eye level or taller than most men.

'How many bedrooms are there?' she asked. 'I mean, I can sleep on the lounge if there's just one bedroom.'

Fletcher's laugh reverberated in the emptiness of the night.

'There's heaps of space,' he said. 'Looks can be deceiving.'

She grabbed her backpack from the boot and followed him to the front door. He pushed it open and flicked a light switch. A soft golden hue from half a dozen down lights illuminated the open-plan space with a high ceiling. Thank goodness they weren't the nausea-inducing prison-cell white of the LEDs at the backpackers.

A dog barked somewhere out the back.

As she peeked over his shoulder, Skye's mood brightened. The room had been refurbished and was larger than it appeared from the outside. At one end stood a kitchen fitted out with a commercial stainless steel bench and sink that ran the length of a wall.

Pale green polyurethane cupboards with slim silver handles were affixed above it and a retro refrigerator in a matching colour hummed in the corner. 'Streamlined' and 'functional' popped into her head.

She spun around and ran her real-estate writer's eye over the other end of the room. It was sparsely furnished with a timber dining table that had six non-matching chairs, and two three-seater chocolate-brown leather lounges separated by a timber coffee table. A deep-red throw over the back of one of the lounges matched the colour of the floor rug under the coffee table. The flooring was black butt polished to a matt finish.

Skye nodded her approval which also extended to admiring Fletcher's smooth muscular upper arms as he slid open tall timber-framed glass doors that revealed a covered back deck. She didn't have a clever way to describe hot and sexy arms. 'Hot and sexy' would have to do.

Phew. Fan the flames Skye, she warned herself. *Keep it real.*

The barking dog bounded inside.

'Hey, hey, hey, Occy fella, calm down.' Fletcher ruffled the dog's ears as it collapsed on the floor for a tummy rub, wriggling on its back in pure ecstasy. He stopped and the dog righted itself, shook its thick black and grey coat in a shimmy and skidded across the lovely timber floor towards Skye, landing at her feet.

Fletcher pulled the panting dog away though Skye didn't mind at all. She'd love to own a dog like this but it wasn't an option in Sydney. Occy was a real dog, not a windup toy like that ridiculous Mexican rat. What was it called again? McDonald?

She patted Occy's wine-barrel torso and murmured, 'Good boy. What is he? Blue heeler?'

'Yeah, he's getting on, about seven years old now. That's late 40s in human years, so he's not as fast as he used to be.' Fletcher held the dog firmly by the collar. 'I'll get him some dinner. Have a squiz at the place. The spare room's next to the kitchen.'

At mention of the word 'dinner', Occy lost interest in Skye and followed Fletcher to the fridge.

She carried her bag past the kitchen. Tucked in behind it was a bathroom with a deep freestanding bath and separate shower, and next to that a bedroom. She turned on the light. It contained a queen-size bed and men's clothing was scattered over the turquoise rug that covered much of the floor.

She returned to the kitchen and cleared her throat. Fletcher turned around from the bench, where he was pulling apart thawed chicken necks and placing them in a metal dog bowl.

'Um,' she gestured over her shoulder with her thumb, 'is that where you usually sleep?'

He squirted liquid soap on his hands, rinsed them in the sink, wiped them on a paper towel and grabbed a small torch from the top of the fridge.

'Yeah, but I'll move into the other room. Let's take a tour of the house.'

Fletcher picked up the dog bowl and Skye followed him on to the back deck. He walked down three timber steps to a backyard and placed the bowl down for Occy, who chomped on the raw necks and swallowed each of them almost in one go.

Fletcher switched on the torch and shone it at a walkway, not far from where Skye stood. It connected the front of the house to a 'box' shaped addition at the back.

'We were in the front pavilion and this is the back pavilion,' he said, joining her. 'They're connected by the walkway. Out the back there's two bedrooms, a small living room, a second bathroom and another deck.'

Skye squinted into the darkness. 'From where I'm standing it doesn't look like it's finished.'

'I'm still working on it. The wiring hasn't been done yet so there's no lights. The plumbing's in but there's no toilet or shower. I've got to organise the waterproofing for that. There's some things I'm not going to muck around with, you need a pro for bathroom, plumbing and electrical work.'

The night was still, the only sounds the distant occasional 'woo woo' of a tawny frogmouth seeking out a mate and the 'bock bock' of a few hopeful frogs.

Skye took a deep breath in and slowly breathed out.

'It's so peaceful here, you don't get this in Sydney.' She stretched her arms up and craned her neck to take in the starry sky. 'The light pollution blocks out this awesome show.'

Fletcher nodded in agreement. 'It's incredible. Makes me feel small. Puts me in my place.'

They both laughed and stared upwards at the universe.

Skye squealed and grabbed Fletcher's arm.

'Hey. Did you see it?'

A streak of molten silver. A millisecond of brilliance. A moment.

'Yep. Beautiful.'

Skye let go of Fletcher's arm, feeling a sudden need to fill the silence.

'Wow. I've never seen a shooting star before, ever in my life. This is a first.'

'Stay here for a while and you'll see them most nights.'

His tone was neutral but still Skye felt breathless. She couldn't look him in the eye. It was bad enough that he was so close to her.

Keep talking, Skye. Change the subject.

'So,' she attempted to slow everything down including her words, 'where will you sleep if I'm in your room?'

'Tonight the lounge'll do. I've got a sleeping bag and I can drag the blow-up mattress out of the Kombi.'

Skye found the nerve to lock eyes with him again. He looked so relaxed. She bet he could sleep anywhere in any position, even standing up. Like a horse.

Skye was the opposite. She needed routine and clean sheets. Order and cleanliness walked hand-in-hand in Skye's world. Damn her parents and their scant regard for tidy people, disinfectant and clean sheets.

'I hope you don't think I'm being ungrateful but I can't sleep in sheets that have been, um, used.'

'You mean you don't like dirty sheets?' There was a smile in his eyes and voice.

Skye could relax again. Her imagined romantic moment was over. Now they could banter like old friends again.

'No, I don't think your sheets are dirty at all, it's just, I have this thing about sheets. I know it's ridiculous but I wash my sheets every couple of days. It's wasteful. Sometimes I think I've got OCD but I've done a bit of research on it but I'm not quite there yet.'

Fletcher leaned close to her and she felt his warmth in the cool hinterland air and smelled his woody scent. It gave her a heady sensation and she leaned away.

'I wouldn't expect you to sleep in soiled sheets,' he said without a hint of irony. 'My Egyptian cotton sheets are five-star-hotel clean, washed today and line dried.'

He bowed low, one arm across his waist and the other along his back. When he stood back up, his eyes twinkled with good humour.

'But before you hit the sack, you've gotta try my five-star pesto pasta,' he said. 'It's fit for a queen.'

CHAPTER 9

Skye ended up sitting opposite Fletcher at the dining room table. He threw together a salad and spaghetti with home-made pesto, green olives and grated parmesan. Skye sucked on the al dente pasta, her cheeks hollow as the pine nut, basil, garlic and olive oil blend slipped off the spaghetti and flicked onto the edges of her lips. She licked it, wiped it with a paper towel and burped like a truck driver.

After they stopped laughing, Fletcher made organic hot chocolate, presented in large ceramic mugs with a marshmallow melting on the surface. Perfect.

As they chatted, Skye tried to dig a little deeper into Fletcher's life.

"You obviously know more about me than I know about you," she said, grasping the mug in two hands. "So, I challenge you to tell me three things about you that I don't know."

Skye had expected resistance but Fletcher was obviously relaxed. He took a sip of hot chocolate and started to talk.

On a superficial level, she discovered that Occy the blue heeler was named after Fletcher's hero, the Australian surfer Mark 'Occy' Occhilupo.

'Put simply, Mark Occhilupo's a legend,' he said. 'Life threw a pile of shit at him. He battled depression and addiction. His weight blew out to a hundred kilos but he came back, lost weight, stopped the drugs and rediscovered the joy of surfing. That pure soaring high that being cocooned in a mother of a wave brings you.'

Fletcher's face was flushed with excitement.

'The world gave up on him, no one believed in him. But he proved them all wrong. He came back at the age of thirty three and showed the grommets what true courage is by winning the world title.'

Next, she discovered that Fletcher was head baker at The Old Bakery, downstairs from Sun and Lou's flat.

'No wonder the bread smelled so good yesterday.' Skye sniffed the air in appreciation of the memory of freshly baked bread.

Fletcher smiled. 'Old Tom Cocks helps out but I do all the bread varieties. Customers can come in at dawn and get a loaf of something, guaranteed. Then Tom and I move onto the sausage rolls and your basic meat pies and pasties.'

Even more interesting was fact three, which as more like a stream of little factoids about Fletcher's childhood: Fletcher was Sun's age, thirty five, he grew up in rural Western Australia, his parents were 'no longer around' and there were no siblings.

'None whatsoever?'

Fletcher seemed to think hard about this. A concerned furrow dragged his eyebrows inwards before he answered. 'None that I know of. As far as I know, I'm an only child.'

Skye couldn't imagine growing up without her brother and sister. Sure, their adult relationship was distant and glacial, basically screwed, but as a child and well into her teens she had done just about everything with Sun. And then with Airen.

From an early age, Airen had followed his sisters everywhere, especially Skye. God, she missed that. Not the being worshipped by her baby brother but the companionship. Knowing that when she turned around on the way to high school, Airen would be traipsing along behind her, dragging his feet.

Fletcher wasn't going to give her any more that night. The little she learned wasn't near enough to satisfy her curiosity.

By the time her head hit the pillow in the bed made up with the promised crisp white sheets with a mild eucalyptus scent, she concluded that Fletcher King was the master of subterfuge. He had the knack of being able to turn an interview around so she felt like she'd given away more than she would have liked about herself.

But not about her old life. Whenever Fletcher tried to trespass into her past, Skye skilfully sidestepped his questions, bringing everything back to the recent past that included numerous references to Beau and their potential future together in Sydney. It even sounded flimsy to her own ears but she needed to keep the lie alive to protect herself from someone as charming as Fletcher King.

* * *

Skye stretched luxuriantly in bed after an excellent night's sleep. She reached out her fingers and toes, and pretended to be on a rack. Being pulled from her hands through to her toes by some invisible force, wishing she could grow stronger and taller on the inside. Infallible, unbeatable and most of all, in control of every situation. She wasn't going to give herself a moment to feel exposed to the emotional blackmail from her family.

Her thoughts turned back to the elusive Fletcher King. It had been impossible to extricate anything but superficial details. Surfing was obviously a passion of his but Skye wasn't interested in exploring that any further. Surfing talk would lead to questions about her own surfing history. And she didn't want that.

Slipping out of bed, she grabbed the thick emerald-coloured bath towel Fletcher handed her before they said their good nights at around eleven pm.

After a hot shower with water that came straight from a tank in the back yard, she changed into her last pair of clean undies, a plain white tee shirt and the jeans and boots she'd worn the day before.

She squirted a liberal amount of orange-oil liquid soap into the bathroom vanity sink, filled it with warm water and tossed in her used undies, bra and socks for a soak. The smelly shirt would have to wait.

As she walked into the living room, the big hand on the retro clock hanging on the wall shifted to ten past eight.

Skye let Occy in and spent several minutes rubbing his belly before she made it to the kitchen. A note from Fletcher in black pen was propped up against the kettle. *'Come to bakery for breakfast.'* Underneath in red pen, as if it was an afterthought, he'd scrawled, *'Bring Occy. Leash on back deck.'*

As if on cue, Occy's warm body pressed against her leg. Skye stared down at the dog. He stared back up at her with dark trusting eyes.

'For goodness sake,' she said, irritated about being irritated because a smelly dog was about to dirty her pristine car, 'stop being so cute. I never usually allow animals in my car but I guess you're the exception to the rule.'

It was the least she could do. She was eternally grateful to Fletcher for letting her off so lightly after she damaged his Kombi, giving her a bed for the night and, not only that, sacrificing his own extremely comfortable bed.

A blow-up mattress was still on the floor, a crumpled navy sleeping bag on top of it.

Followed by Occy, she returned to the bathroom to rinse her smalls. After wringing out the excess water, she carried them out to the back deck and draped them over an Adirondack chair painted a zesty lime green.

She'd come back later to collect her gear. She'd have to find somewhere else to sleep tonight. Surely there would be a vacancy at a nice hotel in town?

Back inside, with Occy still at her heels, Skye decided to take a self-guided tour of the garden before leaving.

The results of Fletcher's hard work could be seen everywhere she turned. Along the fence line of the front yard, plantings of native lilly pillies formed a pretty hedge of glossy pink and green leaves. Fertilised mulched beds contained a mix of native grasses, tree ferns and other rainforest plants that Skye didn't recognise. A couple of established flowering gums guarded each end of the house, far enough away not to pose any threat from falling branches.

The two pavilions were painted pale taupe. Skye reckoned it was so the buildings would blend in with the environment.

Out the very back, she stopped in gobsmacked amazement. She hadn't realised it last night, but Fletcher's place was on the edge of the escarpment and had a 180-degree view of the coast. In the distance, the township of Dezzy hugged the edge of Planet Earth and the ocean shimmered like a mirage. In the backyard, native trees planted in neat rows acted as sentinels to protect the house from high winds.

Skye's mood brightened as she considered the ways she could 'add value' to Fletcher's vision.

'Water features,' she announced to Occy. 'I'd put in a fountain and a fishpond filled with koi in the courtyard and something bubbly near the front door to encourage good feng-shui. What do you think Occy?'

Returning to the main pavilion, she flopped down on a chocolate brown lounge, picked up a surfing magazine and flicked through it before strolling back to Fletcher's bedroom.

Apart from the bed, two bedside tables were the only other pieces of furniture in the room. On one, presumably the side Fletcher slept on, was a reading lamp and pile of books. You could tell a lot about a person from the books they read, Skye thought.

Beau didn't read much at all, unless the topic was sports' related. He owned about six books, all of them biographies about sports stars. She encouraged him to read thrillers written by men for men but it had been a waste of time.

Trent Dalton's *Boy Swallows Universe* sat on top of Fletcher's stash, and underneath it Tim Winton's *Breath* and, of all things, Hilary Mantel's epic *Wolf Hall*. Gosh, who would have thought it? Impressed, Skye smiled and flipped open Mantel's monumental novel based on the life of Henry VIII's main man, Thomas Cromwell. It was as heavy as a doorstop.

As she flicked through the pages, a photo fell from between the pages and into Skye's lap.

Last night, Fletcher had been frustratingly elusive when she'd asked about his relationship status and infuriated her no end when he diverted the conversation away from himself and bounced the ball back to her. He'd answered her with, 'Not a lot to report on the relationships front.'

And that had been the end of it. It was exasperating. Somehow Fletcher deflected the focus away from his private life. Before heading off to bed they had discussed life, the universe and everything but him.

'I really couldn't care less about Fletcher's personal life,' Skye said to a supine Occy. She could have sworn his lips twitched in response.

Occy's heavy breathing was the only sound in the room as Skye studied the photo of a baby no older than four weeks with alert dark-brown eyes and a head of disconcertingly thick black hair. Unlike some newborns that were downright ugly, this baby was cute and curious, staring unblinkingly at the world with both total unknowingness and wisdom.

Skye searched for signs of Fletcher in the tiny features. She could find nothing in the eyes that were shaped like delicate leaves. But the full well defined lips were definitely Fletcher. She'd bet her bottom dollar on it.

She turned the photo over. On the back in Fletcher's scrawl were some details: 'Nat Brand aged five weeks'. Brand?

Skye examined the contents of her mental fact file on Fletcher. If he didn't have any siblings it was highly likely the baby in the photo was his. Unless it belonged to a cousin or distant relative.

Guiltily, she placed the photo back into the book.

'It was an innocent discovery,' she explained to the dog, feeling as though she'd crossed a privacy line without gaining permission.

Occy stood up and did his downward dog pose before plopping his head on Skye's lap. While she stroked his coarse fur, her mind wandered.

Why hadn't Fletcher mentioned a baby? Maybe because it wasn't his.

Was he in a relationship or even married? Were there other children in his life?

There was probably a logical explanation for the photo, which she could easily extract from anyone on the street in Dezzy. Or easier still, her family.

'C'mon dog,' she said to Occy. 'Let's get outta here before I get myself into more trouble.'

* * *

If she could have, Skye would have dropped off Occy at The Old Bakery and gone on to *The Northern Sun* office. But Fletcher was oblivious to her squirming discomfort at being in his presence so soon after her accidental discovery of the photo. He insisted she stay for breakfast.

She couldn't bring herself to ask about the baby in the photo.

'I was casually checking out your books when a photo of a baby fell out from one of the pages' would sound pretty suss, like she'd been snooping through Fletcher's belongings. Which was definitely not the case.

Occy laid down on the front step at the bakery entrance so customers had to step over him to get in and out of the place. She could have sworn the dog winked at her before closing his eyes for a nap. As though the discovery of the baby photo was their secret.

Skye sat at a small table nearby, inside the entrance door. The waitress brought over a cappuccino and complimentary breakfast of toasted quinoa sourdough with small triangles of local butter and home-made apricot jam.

The sparsely decorated space was abuzz with customers, some popping into grab a takeaway coffee from the barista, a local lad working the espresso machine with calm confidence. The fresh-from-the-oven loaves of different varieties of bread that included gluten-free were flying off the timber-framed shelves that lined the old stone wall. A selection of scones, pastries, pies and pasties were on display in heated trays in a glass cabinet.

Skye watched Fletcher engaging with customers, obviously enjoying their exchanges. He placed a plain white loaf through the slicing machine for an elderly woman. She must have chatted to him for at least five minutes while a local teenage boy and girl served the other customers. He could have brushed off the woman to one of the other wait staff but instead he listened as she talked about the weather and a range of ailments that plagued her husband. As she was about to leave, Fletcher stopped her and gave her two scones.

'Take these home to Reg,' he said. The woman glowed. This small gesture of kindness had made her day.

Fletcher was dressed in the classic baker's uniform of white trousers and a white short-sleeved shirt protected by a black apron. His dreadlocks were tucked into a white baker's cap so his wide square jaw and neat flat ears were more exposed. It made it easier for her to see the resemblance between Fletcher and the baby in the photo.

There was no doubt in her mind that Fletcher King had a son.

Skye sipped on the cappuccino and sniffed the warm nutty aroma of crusty oven-baked bread.

Fletcher joined her at the table, carrying a latte and a date slice.

'I need a break,' he said, nodding a greeting to a customer who was loaded up with bags of bread and a box of pastries and cakes.

He broke up the crumbly pastry stuffed with a date filling and placed half on her plate. Beau would never have done that.

'You know you're perfectly welcome to stay at my place for as long as you like,' Fletcher said unexpectedly. He looked like he'd surprised himself with the offer.

Skye felt herself blush. On the winding drive down the hillside, she'd considered this possibility, wished he'd ask her to stay.

Her rational voice knocked the idea on the head. It wouldn't be smart to accept for several reasons. Fletcher was a rather attractive man and she was rather attracted to him. That was the main reason. Numero uno. Skye had to keep slapping herself, figuratively speaking, to stop herself from licking her lips when she was anywhere near him. Now she was so close she could see a scattering of pale freckles across his nose, the healthy glow of his skin, the sensual curve to his lips and the warmth that could easily spark into fire in his eyes.

Secondly - here she didn't want to flatter herself too much but - last night he gave the distinct impression the feeling was mutual.

Not as important as it would have been two days ago was the fact that she still happened to have a boyfriend. And his name was Beau Ferguson. That was the third reason.

And finally, number four, a new complication had arisen. Fletcher probably had a child and that child had a mother who could feasibly still be a part of his life.

Still, she hesitated. She loved his house, the warmth and ambience of it made her feel snug, like being held in a warm embrace. It was one of those rare houses she wrote about that didn't need big statement rooms or opulent fittings and fixtures to impress. Its restrained minimalist design gave its inhabitants the freedom to be themselves. To add their own personal touches to enhance character. And the location was magnificent and far away enough from town to ease Skye's own introverted reclusive leanings.

'I don't think it's a good idea,' she said. 'I don't want to be a burden. It'll be for a few nights and I don't want you to feel like you have to look after me or entertain me, or even feed me.'

'That's it then, you're in,' Fletcher said decisively. 'If you're worried about me sleeping on the floor, I can move to the bedroom in the back pavilion. Then it'll almost be like we're in different apartments. We can be flatmates.'

'But I just told you why I can't stay, I'll be a burden.'

What she didn't say was the truth. *'And I could do something I will regret.'*

'Rubbish,' he said. 'Case closed. You're staying at my place. You won't get a room anywhere in town. Every year, about ninety nine per cent of the romance writing festival crowd extends their stay. They make it their annual holiday to escape life's realities like work, kids and partners, and whatever else.'

Skye stirred the froth off her cappuccino. 'You're being very nice to me.'

Fletcher pointed to the date slice on her plate. 'Try that. It's one of Lou's creations. She comes down here after the lunch shift at the bowlo and whips up a selection of cakes, biscuits and slices. I don't know how I'll manage when she takes a break.'

'Why's she taking a break?'

Fletcher seemed to hesitate, inclined his head to one side and narrowed his eyes. 'I thought Sun and Lou would have told you.'

It was almost a question as he scanned her face for some sort of comprehension.

'Told me what?' She wiped her fingers on a serviette, silently admonishing herself for devouring the slice in two quick bites. And that was after toast smothered in butter and apricot jam. What did that add up to in calories or kilojoules? She'd have to skip lunch.

Fletcher finished his part of the slice in one neat bite.

'I think you need to chat to Sun and Lou.'

Skye thought about her last 'chat' with Sun and Lou but refrained from sharing the painful details.

'What about?'

'About where we're all heading. Down the road less travelled.'

Skye frowned and pouted but took it no further. She planned to see Sun later on at *The Northern Sun* newspaper office to go over the criteria for the intervention.

If Fletcher wanted her to ask Sun about Lou's impending travel plans, that's what she'd do.

CHAPTER 10

Skye climbed the concrete stairs to the first floor of the newspaper office. She pushed open the glass door which bore the mast head in red, italicised Times New Roman font: *The Northern Sun*. Underneath was the catchphrase in black in a smaller size: *truth trust transparency*.

The whirr and clunk of a small printing press downstairs was barely audible through the carpeted concrete floor.

The office space hadn't changed at all since she'd left town. It was open-plan; one vast space with tube lights casting a deadening glow overhead, making all who entered resemble vampires in desperate need of fresh blood. It was airless and sunless.

Nonetheless, Skye loved it. She closed her eyes and inhaled the aroma of ink on newsprint, worn nylon carpet and old cigarette smoke.

Her father had smoked Winfield cigarettes for many years until his doctor gave him a stern health warning. The smoke used to make her feel sick, and goodness knows what it did to her lungs. But today it aroused a longing in her. But for what?

To have her father back, of course. To walk up the stairs to see him marching back and forth with intent, gesticulating to the ceiling and walls, throwing instructions at the staff in a way that brokered no argument.

She missed her father so much. But she hadn't expected to miss the paper.

Every bench space was covered in a mess of newspapers and the walls plastered with yellowing blown-up headlines like

BAN TOWERS IN DEZZY
DIRTY MONEY TAINTS COUNCIL
HOW WE SAVED OUR TOWN

The editor's desk was at the far end of the room, directly across from the entrance. Sun tapped at her computer keyboard set up on a tallowwood table that easily weighed a couple of hundred kilograms.

Skye knew how heavy it was because it had taken four men, her father, Airen, deputy editor Col Spence and local board shaper Brad Cherry, to get the thing up the stairs and into the place it would stay forever. Or at least as long as *The Northern Sun* existed.

It was odd seeing Sun there. It used to be their father's desk. Sun appeared uncomfortable, perched behind it on the edge of the chair as if about to take flight.

The other two people in the room sat where they always sat, at small chipboard and plastic workplaces. When he saw Skye, Col Spence leaped from his swivel chair. His ruddy face split into a grin and, behind thick silver rimmed spectacles, cheerful eyes sparkled.

Skye had known Col since she was a kid. He co-founded *The Northern Sun* with her father and remained a loyal friend and hard worker. He'd stuck by her father through good times and bad, happy to remain in the background while Jonno played hardball with corrupt developers and councillors.

After her father died, Col somehow managed to keep the paper rolling off the presses.

Col's voice boomed across the room. 'Well, look what the cat dragged in. If it isn't Missy Skye.'

Ad manager Deb Bonofacio trilled in delight and moved at speed towards Skye, her limp from an arthritic hip momentarily absent.

After hugs and kisses that seemed to go on forever, Deb dabbed at eyes weighed down by mascara as she and Col quizzed Skye about her love life.

Yes, she was seeing Beau Ferguson, yes, he was the sports journalist son of the incredibly wealthy Ferguson family of Vaucluse, yes, she met Fletcher King and their relationship was purely platonic despite the rumours, yes, she was sleeping in his bed but not with him in it, no, she had no interest in getting back together with Cal Sturgess, no, she didn't plan to stay in town for longer than a week.

Skye finally made it to the other side of the room where Sun's greeting was less than enthusiastic.

Sun gestured to a white plastic bucket chair.

'Take a seat,' she said, and added, 'Thanks for coming,' like it was an afterthought.

At least she had the decency to drag her own chair around to sit opposite Skye so there was no table separating them. Skye's nerves clattered, nonetheless. Her sister was a no less formidable presence than their father had been. No-nonsense types who liked to do things their way. Stubborn and driven.

'Let's get down to the business of the preparation for the intervention.' Sun tucked an auburn lock of hair behind her ear and strained around to the desk behind her to grab two loose sheets of paper. 'I know you like lists so I've put together a calendar with the details.'

Sun handed her one of the sheets that mapped out Skye's commitments for the rest of her stay up to and including the dreaded main intervention scheduled for her last day in town, Saturday. It was marked up into the days of the week, every single one filled with an activity.

Sun peered over the top of black-rimmed reading glasses to check that Col and Deb were preoccupied. Not that it mattered. Skye reckoned the grapevine had been activated and the usual suspects had disseminated the news far and wide. The whole town knew the details of her arrival back in town, her chance meeting with ex-fiancé Cal, her involvement in Airen's drunken brawl outside the pub, her meeting with Sun and Lou at their place and, the juiciest titbit of all, her overnight stay at Fletcher King's house.

It wouldn't be long before chins wagged about Skye's meeting with her sister at *The Northern Sun.*

Sun cleared her throat and Skye realised she wasn't the only one feeling ill at ease.

'Today is Monday so we have the working week to get organised.' Sun said.

She removed her glasses and polished them on her shirt sleeve before putting them back on to finally meet Skye eye to eye.

'Airen's gonna be hard to pin down. And he won't cooperate if he smells a rat. We scheduled the intervention for Saturday because he's got work on during the week. He's shaping a long board for a mate.'

She wriggled in her chair and craned closer to Skye as if to block out Col and Deb. 'I have my spies and they say he's usually at the board factory. After that he hits the pub until they chuck him out at closing time. Go to Saturday on the calendar,' Sun wafted a hand and Skye immediately glued her eyes to her copy, 'you can see the intervention is planned for Saturday afternoon. He usually starts drinking at three, sometimes earlier. But if we can get him before that, we could have some success.'

Hearing Sun's practical approach to the intervention reminded Skye of a military manoeuvre. Strike the target at its most vulnerable. She imagined them dressed in flak jackets and khaki camouflage gear, steel capped boots and hard helmets with little bushes on top. Using their elbows to shimmy on their stomachs across thick jungle terrain until they alighted upon Airen in a clearing and fixed him in their sites.

Skye still couldn't believe she'd agreed to be part of this conspiracy. It was cowardly, but having to face a sober Airen made her head buzz with static. She couldn't picture herself ever talking to him again, especially in a situation that had the potential to turn into a confrontation.

She squeezed him out of her focus, she was used to doing that, and tried to give her full attention to Sun's calendar of 'events'. Maybe everything would work out if she pretended to be a tourist visiting Dezzy for the very first time. She extended that fantasy. In order to remain sane and in control, she'd treat Sun like a travel agent going through her itinerary. Distance didn't just have to be physical. She could float above this scenario and all the others to come. All care and no responsibility. That's how she'd do it. That's how she'd get through this.

Sun started to talk again. 'If you go to Monday night on the calendar, today, I've got you down for dinner at our place.' She tapped the date and time on her copy of the calendar.

Skye's arrival time was seven pm. Sharp. She didn't mind having her life organised. It would make the week pass faster.

'Can I bring anything? Drinks? Nibbles?'

'No. Lou has everything under control.'

Without raising her eyes, Sun continued. 'Tuesday night is a casual get together at Grandma's place. Grandma will cook for that one, with Lou's help, but it would be good if you could grab some stuff from the supermarket. Grandma's going to phone in a list or you could collect it from her, in person.'

Skye interjected, suddenly remembering the other problem. 'Grandma told me she was agoraphobic or, as she mispronounced it, angora-phobic.'

Sun allowed herself a small wry smile but it would take a blast from a furnace to crack her icy veneer.

'Mum and I have done our best but Grandma won't leave the house,' she explained. 'It's the last thing we need on top of the trouble with Airen and all the shit going down with the coal seam gas drill proposal and...'

'CSG?'

For the first time, Skye's eyes alighted upon newer headline posters tacked to a cork board behind Sun's desk:

COMMUNITY LOCKED OUT OF CSG TALKS
CSG GROUP'S DARK PAST REVEALED
DEZZY FIGHTS CSG
COUNCILLORS IN BED WITH VENTE

Sun's face fell and Skye noticed her exhausted features, mouth drawn tight and forehead creased with worry.

'It came from out of nowhere, virtually without community consultation,' Sun said. 'Vente Gas is a multinational company. The government gave it a coal seam gas exploration licence and we're fighting it, the town is fighting it, to the death. It barely rates a mention in the big smoke.'

'I didn't realise...'

'You weren't to know,' Sun grudgingly conceded. 'But it's not easy being so short staffed and not having Dad's supernova personality to cause a bloody commotion.'

Skye's heart pressed inwards. No one could cause the boat to rock like their father.

Sun shoved her glasses up to the bridge of her nose and folded her arms across her body as though in an attempt to stop them from waving around.

'After you left, I got stuck with a job no sane person would want. Here I am, defending the rights of a disenfranchised, disempowered and disenchanted community. They've been done over so many times by dickhead politicians and councillors that all the hope and trust has been squeezed out of them.'

Resentment flared in Sun's words. This meeting wasn't just about Airen, it was much more than that. Impotency washed over Skye.

'I didn't realise...'

'Yeah, well, you know how it goes.'

Skye sighed. 'You've got your hands full here. I'm sorry about that but we both knew I had to leave...'

Sun hugged herself tighter. 'Yes, but we thought you'd come back.'

Sun had never wanted to be the editor of *The Northern Sun*. A talented musician, she taught guitar to local students and at night performed a slew of original folk songs at the local pub.

But in the days following their father's death, Sun and Skye both joined a frazzled Col and Deb to help keep the paper afloat.

Nobody could imagine *The Northern Sun* without Jonno Summerhayes at the helm. Jonno was *The Northern Sun.* He was the reason for the paper's success, his big personality and 'hail fellow well met' attitude bringing small advertisers on board. They were like paying passengers on a train, with Jonno in the engine room stoking up the fire.

But there was no other paper in town. And without their local newspaper, the residents of Dezzy had no way of knowing the full extent of what was going on in the community.

'After you left, I had no choice,' Sun said. 'Someone has to do this job.'

Skye didn't know what to say.

She noticed two empty desks next to Col's. 'Don't you usually have two junior reporters?'

'We're down one.' Sun said. 'And the junior's new and inexperienced so he's being spoon fed. He's basically full time on sport and putting all the news online. Dad never had to worry about the online stuff. We need to be across that and social media so we can reach the whole community, not just the same loyal mob.

'We need young people to join the fight. I've got Col working almost full time on the CSG story. I'm covering council, lifestyle and all the feel-good stories we need to counterbalance the doom and gloom.'

Skye put a padlock on her mouth. Say nothing, offer nothing. She didn't want to be sucked into yet another torrid battle. The last one against the developers ended in her father's death.

She avoided Sun's gaze and referred back to the calendar, to the matter at hand and the reason for her visit. 'You don't have a pre-intervention meeting scheduled,' she said flatly.

Sun's sigh was so loud that both Col and Deb turned around, their faces lined with concern. 'Tuesday at Grandma's place should cover that.'

Sun stood up and returned to her desk, rifling through a pile of papers. Finding what she was looking for, she returned to her seat opposite Skye.

'Here,' she said, handing Skye a print-out of an article titled: *How to Perform an Intervention.*

'Read it before the intervention.'

Skye slipped the article into her bag.

'Who's coming to Grandma's then?'

The question was innocent enough but Skye could hear the unnecessarily hard edge returning to her voice. She saw the answer in the straight line of Sun's lips.

Running a hand through her hair, Skye snorted with derision. 'Come on Sun, give me a break. Jimmy is not family.'

Sun inhaled sharply and bristled like an angry echidna. 'Grandma's casual get-together is an icebreaker, an opportunity for you to get your problems with Jimmy sorted before we sit down, Jimmy included, with Airen at the formal intervention.'

Skye tried to interrupt but Sun mowed down her objections.

'I don't want to have to deal with your hang up about Jimmy on Saturday. You have to remember why, after three years of hiding from us, you came back. It's to help Airen.'

'But I can't...' Skye trailed off, a desperate tremor in her voice.

Sun was asking her to accept Jimmy into their family. Sun didn't know the truth about the day her father died. Skye wanted to shout at her sister, to tell her about the real Jimmy Trout. But by now, Col and Deb were totally switched into the two sisters' heated discussion.

Skye pressed her eyes closed and wished herself away. When she opened them, Sun was leaning forward in her chair, her hands on Skye's knees as though she was attempting to tie Skye down.

'Of course you can.' The sharp knife edge in Sun's voice sliced into Skye's mental fortitude. 'As far as I'm concerned, Jimmy *is* part of our family. You only have to see him on two occasions. How can that be so hard?'

CHAPTER 11

Skye walked out of *The Northern Sun* building and went in search of a metaphorical brick wall on which to bang her head. How had her sister done it? Skye caved into Sun's demands that Jimmy attend both Grandma's casual get-together and the intervention. To top it off, she also promised to write a couple of real estate articles for the paper. Sucked in.

'It's about value adding, keeping the clients happy,' Sun said earnestly of the paper's biggest advertisers, one being Cal Sturgess and his father's real estate agency, that took out double-page spreads in each edition.

Sun had gripped Skye's knees so tight that Skye worried she might pass out from loss of blood flow to the brain.

'The real estate agents' advertising and the classifieds are our bread and butter.' Sun kept at it, her commitment to the paper clear in every word.

It wore Skye down. She felt like a large old tree. Sun was at her base with a super sharp axe, slowly chopping away until Skye was severed from it.

'Deb's got the classifieds covered but the junior cadet who was supposed to write the real estate column decided there was more money in hairdressing. She couldn't give a bugger about people selling their homes as they head off to downsize. As a consequence, I don't have anyone to cover this patch.'

T-I-M-B-E-R.

Skye was aware of Sun's big advantage over her as the image of a rarely used guitar sprang into her mind. Her poor sister had shelved her own dreams to keep *The Northern Sun* shining.

She owed Sun and Sun knew it. Skye had to pay her back for that.

The casual get-together at Grandma's, a euphemism for pre-intervention meeting, would be hard to endure, Skye thought.

She had totally shut Jimmy and her mother out of her life from the day she saw them together. It was Skye's bitter secret, kept from her sister, brother and grandmother.

Fury and resentment slow burned in her on a long fuse, threatening to ignite into a conflagration at any encounter with Jimmy or Oceane. Skye wanted to spit at Jimmy and blame him and Oceane for Jonno's death and how it destroyed their family. It made her sick to the stomach to see them. Especially Jimmy taking her father's place.

The melodic ring tone of her mobile phone jerked her away from toxic thoughts. Her boyfriend's name flashed on the screen.

'Beau,' she snapped unintentionally, then softened, 'How are you?'

'Miss me, Babe?'

Skye did the eye roll. Whichever way you viewed it, Beau's lack of insight was, in fact, one of his strengths. Supremely confident, he had no doubt the world revolved around him.

'Of course.' It came as a shock that the lie slipped so easily from her lips.

'Miss you too,' he said.

She wondered if Beau realised the hollow ring of his own words? He sounded distracted.

'Hey Babe, I was thinking of driving to the coast to your place at...' A pause as he struggled to pluck the name of her home-town out of his head.

'Desiree Bay?'

Skye tried to correct his mistake but he talked right over the top of her.

'Yeah, thought it might be cool to meet your family, spend some time, hang out,like.'

Skye frowned. It wasn't like Beau to be so attentive.

'That's sweet of you and I appreciate it.' She couldn't sound sweeter and syrupy if she tried. 'But this week's probably not good. Maybe some other time. Then we could organise it properly, do it like a road trip.'

'Yeah, maybe. But I'd like to see you this week. I miss you, Babe. I really do.'

Skye detected something uncomfortable in Beau's tone of voice. He'd never win an award for his acting skills.

'This is pretty sudden. Don't you have to work?' Suspicion mounted as Skye caught the whiff of a rat.

'Yeah. But the upshot is work has asked me to line up an interview with your brother. I thought it'd be fun to kill two birds with one stone.'

Skye pressed the phone to her shoulder and ear as she placed her bag on the roof of her car and extracted her keys, barely able to comprehend Beau's blunt audacity.

'Really? Is that how you see it? Killing two birds with one stone?'

'Whoa, Babe. It came out wrong. What I meant was, I want to see you but I also need to talk to Airen. And since you're his sister, you might be able to help me line up a casual meeting.'

'What? With you, a cameraman and a sound guy? I'm sorry but that's not possible.' Skye's words were clipped as she stymied hurt mingled with anger. How could he sink so low? 'What are people saying? Why do they want you to interview Airen?'

She needed to know. She couldn't let anyone or anything get in the way of Airen's rehabilitation. Especially Beau and his media cronies.

'Don't get so uptight. It's just an interview, no pressure, to see where he's up to, how he's getting on. The next move. You know how it works?'

He sounded defensive now, but not guilty or remorseful.

Skye pounced. 'I don't know what you've heard but you can tell your boss there won't be an interview. Airen will contact you when and if he's ready to talk.'

'I'd do a good job, Skye.' He'd dropped 'Babe'.

He'd probably told his producers the story was in the bag, as good as done, that he was banging the talent's sister. *'Yeah, mate, it'll be good. I live with Airen Summerhayes' sister. She's a pushover, thinks I'm gonna pop the question.'*

That announcement followed by blokey laughter all round.

'I know you'd do a good job,' Skye said, aiming for a conciliatory tone. 'But this has to be on Airen's terms, not yours.'

'Here's the heads up. The other sports media have their guys onto the story too. They're onto him, Skye. I'd be fair. I wouldn't make him look bad.'

Now, he'd moved from swaggering confident to pathetic pleading.

'Then how would he look, Beau?' Skye countered. 'I can tell you what commercial TV does. He'd look like someone to be pitied. One of a legion of tragically-flawed footy players who squandered amazing opportunities because of addiction. He'd look like a loser. It would destroy his career and him.'

'I thought you would have been cool with it. An interview could swing in Airen's favour, get people talking, maybe help him,' Beau said.

Skye's wanted the conversation to be over.

'I can't see that happening. These things always end in tears. After the fanfare, everyone walks away and forgets about the broken man and his family. You, I mean, your boss, requires – more like, demands a sensational angle. You can't deliver anything less than that. I'm not stupid, Beau. I know the industry.'

Silence.

'Are you still there?'

'Yeah. Sorry I bothered you.'

'I know you are,' she said though she didn't believe him. 'You've got to support me on this, Beau. Please don't be part of any plan that hurts my brother.'

'That's not what I'm trying to do, Skye. It's my job to help him.'

Skye blew air threw her lips, anger crackling inside her. She stared at the street, at the familiar landmarks, many with a personal story attached, and sensed a subtle shift in her consciousness. It was as though she'd been sucked through a vortex. City mouse, country mouse. What on earth did she want from her own life? And the people in it?

Without thinking, words tumbled out. 'Well, it's my job to be here for my family. I'll see you in Sydney when I get back next week.'

And with that, she hung up.

* * *

By the time Skye got to Fletcher's place it was almost time to turn around and head back to Sun and Lou's for dinner.

Occy romped towards the car as she pulled into the driveway, car tyres scrunching over sand-coloured gravel.

The front door was open and Fletcher stood there in the twilight, leaning against the doorjamb, muscled arms crossed over his broad chest.

A tiny spark of something like joy propelled Skye forward. Seeing him there, waiting for her, sent pleasant tingles down her spine and radiating out to her fingertips and toes.

He wore jeans and a T-shirt. Nothing special, but Skye couldn't believe how he managed to look like a model for a surf-wear company without even trying.

He threw one of his warm grins her way. She was getting to like that, so much so that she almost did an Occy. It would have been so easy to run up the front steps and bury her nose, not quite between his legs as Occy had just done, but in his T-shirt.

'Hi there,' he drawled.

Suddenly self-conscious, she dropped her gaze.

Her hair was a mess. After the tense exchange with Beau, she'd been inexplicably drawn back to the beach where she'd sat on the sand until the northerly kicked in. It had whipped her hair around her face and stung her cheeks with a spray of fine diamond-sharp sand. Waking her back into action.

Fletcher waited at the door, totally at ease, for her to pass. She stalled the impulse to tug at his dreadlocks, and fall into his arms like a swooning silent-movie siren. Occy had scrambled through a gap between Fletcher's legs and the door jamb but Skye wasn't about to get down on her knees and crawl past to get to inside, even though it would have been fun.

She silently pushed her internal reset button to 'take control'.

'Um.' She pointed to the door. 'Can I get in, or are you holding up the building?'

He moved aside slightly and she pushed past him, inhaling his fresh salty scent. She guessed he'd been for a surf, probably at The Point. That's where the good breaks were most days.

'You coming tonight?' she asked, even though she knew the answer.

'Yep, sure am.'

Fletcher sat on the lounge and the dog flopped its head in his lap.

Skye fiddled with a stray strand of hair, feeling like a teenager with a crush. She needed to fill the pauses in the conversation with something, anything.

'I'd like to pay you for this, for letting me stay here.' She flung out her arms to take in the room.

Fletcher stroked Occy's head in a rhythmic movement that Skye found vaguely erotic. She would have to snap out of this if she was going to survive the rest of the week with at his place.

'It's usually me and the dog here, it's nice to have the company and I don't need the money.'

And then he did it again. Delivered her the gift of luscious upward curved lips that almost turned her into a hot mess on the living room floor.

Skye shakily nodded her thanks and skirted around him, better to keep her distance, and went to the deck to retrieve the clothes she washed that morning. But they were gone.

Wandering back inside, she squinted one eye and considered Fletcher and the dog.

He second guessed her. 'I managed to save the bra and knickers. They're on the bed.' He gently pushed a grizzling Occy away and stood up. 'The socks are pretty much destroyed. That might make us even.'

Occy faced her, his big doggy eyes wide and innocent.

She didn't blame the dog for chewing on her clothes. He was probably getting back at her in some Karmic way. After all, she was moving into his territory and getting friendly with his owner. Occy was definitely onto her, and probably aware of her nervousness around Fletcher.

'Occy couldn't help himself. He's a bit of a ladies' man,' Fletcher added.

Skye laughed and was surprised at how good it felt.

'No worries. This is nothing. It's been a pretty lousy day.'

'Not for Occy,' Fletcher said with a cheeky grin as he strolled to the kitchen and grabbed the keys from the top of the fridge. 'I'll drive if you like.'

Skye appreciated Fletcher taking control. Beau always liked Skye to drive so he didn't have to worry about random breath testing. She was always the designated driver and never the passenger.

After quickly changing one not-too-clean T-shirt for another and attempting, and failing, to get the knots out of her hair with a comb, she was as ready to go as she would ever be.

The Kombi did its usual cough and splutter but once warmed up it cruised down the hill towards town. Skye didn't feel much like talking. If she did, it would have gone something like this:

'Hey Fletcher, I was leafing through one of your books on the bedside table this morning and a photo fell out. The baby in the photo looks like you so I thought he might be your son.

From that, I deducted that maybe you used to be married, or you still are married or at least with someone.

'To make matters worse, this afternoon my boyfriend in Sydney phoned to tell me how he planned to totally screw up my brother's life, like it's not already a disaster zone. He wants to interview Airen about his failed rugby league comeback and his spiral into alcoholism after the tragic death of our father.

'What's more, I reckon you're totally hot, which is totally wrong.'

Instead, Skye laid her head back on the headrest, mentally blocked out the person beside her, and enjoyed the ride.

* * *

The fragrant aroma of rosemary, thyme and garlic assailed Skye's nostrils as she and Fletcher entered Sun and Lou's flat.

'It's officially winter, so we're having a baked dinner with pudding dessert,' Lou said from the kitchen where she stood before a roast leg of lamb that a team of sumo wrestlers would struggle to consume.

Sun popped up from where she'd been crouching behind the bench at an open cupboard door and placed a bottle of red wine on the bench top.

'We're usually a meat-free zone but we're eating it for a while to keep up iron levels,' she explained to Skye without a hint of embarrassment that she'd fallen off the vegetarian wagon.

Opening a top cupboard door, Sun retrieved three wine glasses and laid them out in a row. 'Smitty at the bottle shop recommended this one. It's a 2012 vintage.'

Sun opened the bottle and poured three glasses but Skye couldn't take her eyes off the lamb into which Lou had plunged a meat thermometer. The fragrant juices ran from the herb-encrusted leg and Skye dealt with a mini crisis as she tried not to reflect on the noble sentient creature chewing the cud, totally unaware of his fate. Then she calculated the amount of energy and resources that went into producing a leg of lamb.

It was an ethical nightmare.

She and Sun had sworn to vegetarianism when the family still lived on acreage. It happened after their father slaughtered and then barbecued one of the chubby sheep used to keep the grass down.

It was Skye's small gesture towards helping save the planet, which many people failed to understand, including Beau. He loved his meat and would have eaten it every night, except Skye did the shopping.

Sun caught her panicked expression and agitated fingering of the glass stem. 'Don't worry, we've catered to you and Fletcher. Homemade veggie burgers with Lou's special sauce.'

Lou appeared not to have heard Sun. Her eyes were glued to the thermometer.

'Needs to be fifty five degrees and then I'll wrap him in foil and let him rest for a while,' she said.

'To vegetarianism and the occasional lapse into an omnivorous lifestyle,' Fletcher joked.

Their glasses chimed as they clinked together.

'Cheers,' Skye said, a little surprised at Fletcher's no-meat policy, which ticked a box on her 'perfect-man' list. 'Lou's not having a glass?'

Sun placed her glass back on the bench and retrieved a tumbler from the cupboard. 'She doesn't drink alcohol.'

She went to the sink, turned on the tap, filled the tumbler with water and took it to the dining table covered in a floral batik tablecloth tinged with brown and red hues. Skye recognised Grandma's dinner set, the 1970s taupe earthenware plates with a ribbed pattern. Skye used to find them so boring and 'hippy' but now everything retro was back in fashion.

Three tall, thick cylindrical candles that had not yet been lit formed the table's centrepiece. Sun refused Skye's offer of help and lit the candles, striking a long match across the box and holding it at the wick of each. The candles flared into life, emitting buttery leaves of warm light.

Fletcher sat opposite Skye in the flickering candlelight. His eyes, clear blue in the daylight, appeared darker and less easy to read in the soft glow.

On the drive over she'd decided to start the dinner conversation with the topic of surfing in order to get it out of the way early. It would come up sooner or later. Her rationale was to nip it in the bud before the fear buzzing around the edges of her subconsciousness flashed into a swarm of European wasps.

'Do you surf every day?' Her voice came out squeaky and high.

Sun and Lou both stopped what they were doing and gaped at her like she was mad. Of course it was a dumb thing to ask. They knew where it would lead. They were worried for her.

Skye wanted to inhale the question back down into her larynx but it was too late. The ocean was out there, a swirling mass of mysteries and untold horrors scattered on its sandy floor.

Skye calmed herself. It was easier to stare at Fletcher across the table in the semi-darkness. To observe the casual movement of his hands as he tore open a bread roll and dunked it in the small bowl of olive oil and then into another bowl of Moroccan spices.

'Yeah, pretty much.' He chewed on a piece of bread he'd most likely baked that morning. If he felt the tension in the room, he didn't let on.

Skye relaxed a little. 'You've got more than the longboard?'

'Yeah.' He smiled lazily. 'I've got about six, all different shapes and sizes. In the garage. You can use them whenever you like. Sun said you used to be a gun surfer. Awards all over the place.'

Skye's heart popped and her gut contracted.

Sun had told Fletcher about her surfing?

She took a nervous sip of wine. 'I used to surf but not anymore. You must be pretty good yourself. How'd you get started?'

Hopefully, that would put an end to it.

Fletcher cocked his head and his eyes became slits.

'When I was a kid in WA. But what about you? Sun said you turned down offers to mentor young girls with pro-circuit potential. You must have been, I mean, you must be amazing.'

Vice-like grip now, strap across her breastbone and ribs.

'I don't want to talk about it. I'm not sure what Sun told you but she always talked me up. I wasn't really that good. And I don't surf anymore. It's over.' The answer shot out with the force of a hammer gun and she heard herself end it with a gruff apology.

Sun swooped to the table and placed a hand lightly on Skye's shoulder.

'Hey Skye, I didn't realise... Fletcher didn't mean to... It's just, you were, you are, an accomplished surfer.' It was the first touch. Fleeting, but still contact.

Skye felt cold and hot all at once. Shaky.

It wasn't Fletcher's fault. Or Sun's.

Skye's plan had failed. She was clearly not ready to talk about surfing. About herself. About the past. She garbled out some rubbish about being suddenly dizzy and added, 'I need to go to the loo.'

Fletcher stood up, eyes dark with concern.

'I'm sorry,' he mumbled, clearly not knowing what he'd done to upset her.

'S'okay,' she managed. 'All good.'

In the bathroom, she sat on the closed lid of the toilet seat, head in hands, and did the breathing thing.

Slow it down. Count to ten. In with the good and out with the bad.

She didn't expect her body to react with such violence to what should have been an easy conversation. Pathetic.

How would she deal with the intervention for Airen if she couldn't even cope with a friendly inquiry about her surfing?

That night three years ago was still with her. It hardly ever left her alone. It revisited her in nightmares that dragged her to the ocean floor and shoved her head-long into the swirling sand. Her father's face forming from coalescing shell grit, his mouth a gaping hole with fish coursing through it, his eyes seashells, luminescent as mother of pearl. She always woke on a death gasp, her lungs screaming for air, her body trapped in a straight-jacket sheet.

A tap on the door. 'Skye?'

It was Sun.

'I'm good. Just give me a minute.'

'We'll wait. Take your time.'

Skye stood up, went to the bathroom vanity, flicked a light switch and checked out her reflection in the old-fashioned mirror topped by a row of eight small round bulbs like those in a theatre dressing room.

She widened her eyes and pulled a silly face. Her eyes weren't the same colour as her father's. Hers were hazel and his had been brown. But she was her father's daughter. She had the olive complexion, long wide nose, full lips and dimpled cheeks, wavy dark hair and the height. She was six feet tall to her father's six feet four while her mother and Sun were both 'petite' at five feet two.

She washed and dried her hands and patted her cheeks.

Get your act together, Skye. This is no time to lose it. But what if?

She frowned, desperate for inspiration or an escape route. Her eyes gleamed more gemstone green than hazel under the artificial light.

What would happen if she told the truth?

Maybe she could confide in Sun? But what good would that do when her sister reacted to everything she said with a put down? Sun had already labelled her 'guilty as charged'.

And how could Skye even start to explain that night when the mere mention of anything to do with surfing or events leading to her father's death triggered a hyperventilating breakdown?

She loathed this juvenile weakness in her mental stamina. Therapy wasn't an option. That was not the Summerhayes' way of fixing things. Her father mocked the navel-gazing habits adopted by those Sydneysiders who moved to Dezzy to find themselves. Jonno was working-class through and through, a self-made man, from a line of Summerhayes' who settled in the town when the main street was still a dirt track. 'Shrinks' were for losers.

Sun's usual response to Skye's inability to cope with the events of three years ago was directly lifted from Jonno's book of sayings.

'Get over yourself and get on with life.'

'What are ya? A girl?' Jonno used to shout at a teenage Skye if she showed any fear, even when the ocean behaved like a howling monster. Fangs bared and poised to crush any idiot dumb enough to think they could outsmart it.

On those days, whichever way she turned, she took her life into her own hands. If she attempted to catch the wave, she risked a dumping that would hurtle her off her board like a flying champagne cork and back into the wave's collapsing glass face. If she chose the safer option, to paddle like mad and duck under and back into the wave before it broke in a thunderclap, she copped her father's sullen disappointed silence and days of being banned from his inner circle.

The Summerhayes' kids didn't like to disappoint their father. Ever.

Skye switched off the bank of movie-star lights, closed the door and returned to the small dining area. Lou and Sun were laughing at something Fletcher said. Without a word, Fletcher stood up, walked around the table and pulled out her chair.

He whispered in her ear, 'Don't worry, I won't pull it out from under you.'

'Thank you.' She sat down, grateful for the small gesture of kindness and appreciative of everyone pretending that nothing had just happened.

Everything was back to being perfectly normal.

Fletcher sat back down opposite her.

'I don't know if Sun told you about the goat that belongs to one of the bakery staff,' he said, knowing that, of course she hadn't.

"What happened was, I planted a huge patch of herbs and veggies behind Sun and Lou's fence line. It took a couple of days of hard labour. That was a few months ago, and it was coming along nicely. Until the other day, I get to work and the whole thing has been dug up and destroyed. The goat. The goat ate everything. Parsley, rocket, sorrel, sage, oregano, three varieties of thyme, mint, tomato seedlings, everything.'

Skye was grateful for the change of topic. 'I think I know the culprit,' she said. 'Brown-and-white with Dijon-mustard-coloured eyes with minus-sign black pupils?'

'I read somewhere that goats are really smart,' Sun said. 'They can be taught to carry out simple tasks and they have excellent long-term memories.'

Fletcher chuckled. 'I won't be planting anything in that spot again. Not while that clever goat's around.'

A silence fell as they watched Lou place an enormous plate on the table. It was piled high with slabs of lamb, along with a white jug filled with Lou's special sauce. Next to it, Sun put down a tray of baked vegetables - crispy potatoes, glossy skinned onions, slivers of red capsicum, carrots and fennel drizzled in olive oil. Finished with a twist of black pepper and sea salt. On another plate were four plump veggie burgers, the patties fried to a crisp golden consistency.

'Help yourselves. You first Fletch.' Sun handed Fletcher serving tongs. Skye took note of her casual use of the more familiar 'Fletch'. Up until now, Sun must have been restraining herself but had relaxed enough to use the endearment.

Fletcher offered the tongs to Skye.

'No, you go first, I can wait.'

He didn't push the point and took two of the burgers before adding a generous serving of veggies, finishing off with a hearty dash of Lou's special sauce.

Fletcher handed her the tongs and Skye filled her own plate with the vegetarian feast. It was far superior to any of her own attempts at fine vegetarian cooking back in Sydney.

She was pouring the special sauce when Lou sat down, easing herself into her chair. Skye did a double take. Underneath the extra-large black-and-white checked flanno shirt, she was certain she'd caught a glimpse of a bulge the size of a small watermelon.

Pregnant. Lou was pregnant. Skye was almost certain of it. But she couldn't afford the embarrassment if her assumption was incorrect. She'd have to wait until Lou rose from the table, and if that didn't confirm her suspicions, she would somehow have to corner Sun before the night was over.

Of course, Lou was pregnant. Red meat for iron. No alcohol. It made perfect sense. Skye found it hard to concentrate on the conversation because each time Lou jiggled in her seat, her eyes shot to Lou's belly.

Why hadn't she noticed sooner? Because no one told her. That's why. She must be imagining it? Surely, someone would have said something before now? Skye stopped her mind from wandering back to the baby bump while they chatted about the bakery and its possible expansion, before moving onto the coal seam gas project.

'The whole town's against it, except for the Sturgess family and a few of Cal's Dad's mates on council.' Sun shot Skye a sideways glance. 'They're not happy with us kicking up a stink.'

'Oh dear.' Skye remembered the Sturgess family's stealth-like behind-the-scenes support of the failed hotel development. She wanted to make it clear that she had no remaining loyalty to Cal.

'The Sturgess family are always happy to get involved in a project if there's money in it. Can Mr Sturgess do a deal with the coal-seam gas company?'

'There's generous compensation on offer to landowners who open their gates if the drilling's approved. But we're determined to stop the bastards.'

Skye couldn't help a small smile. Sun sounded just like Jonno when she got on her political soapbox.

'We're pulling out all stops, using the potential for an environmental catastrophe in the Pilliga as an example.'

Skye frowned and guilt flooded her. She used to be so tuned into current affairs when she worked for her father.

'My head's been buried in the sand for too long. What happened there?'

A scowl crossed Sun's face, 'That's what living in the city does. It removes you from the real world.'

Lou cut in, again saving the day. 'Environmental groups pounced on the operation at Pilliga after they found out an aquifer was contaminated with uranium twenty levels higher than the safe drinking water guidelines.'

Skye thought she sounded like a newspaper article, quoted word for word.

'The world's going to hell in a hand basket,' Sun added grimly.

Fletcher dared to enter the fray. 'The problem is that people no longer have a voice. Back in the '70s and '80s, there was a chance of a positive outcome if people banded together. The best example is the Franklin River blockade. People power stopped the dam and now the river's a tourist mecca. But that was a long time ago.'

Sun took up the thread. 'Big business calls the shots nowadays. Full stop. Deals are done between governments and big business behind closed doors. It's too late by the time the community finds out the real story. A fait accompli. The bulldozers are out and the drills are whirring away, boring down into the earth and contaminating the land and water with toxic chemicals. They pay lip service by offering community consultation but it's total bullshit.'

She barely paused for breath. 'People are exhausted. They're so busy trying to keep their own lives and families afloat that they don't have the time or emotional resources to oppose anything that'll lead to an ongoing battle. There are fewer Davids willing to take on the Goliaths because the Davids are worn out.'

Fletcher added, 'And they know they're gonna get screwed by governments and big business. And some elements of the media. They're taking a huge risk, putting themselves out there and being labelled greenies, socialists, cultural elites and nimbys. Ordinary people are demonised because they want to live good lives and have a future for their kids.'

And so they went on and on, around in a circle familiar to Skye. It made her realise that living in the city had made her softer than marshmallow. She'd shunned the more noble motivations that originally attracted her to journalism.

The candles melted slowly. They reminded Skye of glaciers breaking away from their Antarctic home. Wax dripped down the sides and the candles' rims slumped inwards, succumbing to the relentless heat.

She desperately wished for X-ray vision to be able to see that baby bump. But she didn't have to strain her eyes too hard. She got the confirmation she needed. Lou did what pregnant women do and rubbed her hand over her tummy, revealing a perfect hemisphere.

Sun volunteered to organise the desserts while Lou stayed put, depriving Skye of a chance to see the burgeoning belly in action.

When the steaming chocolate puddings were on the table, sitting in pools of custard like ducks in a pond, Sun cleared her throat and clinked her glass with a dessert spoon.

'I'd like to make an announcement but I think Skye already knows what it's about.'

Had she been that obvious? Of course she had. Still, she wasn't game to say anything. It could still be a furphy so she remained silent. Then she caught Fletcher's eye and, with alarming clarity, the final piece of the puzzle fell into place.

She was right. Lou was pregnant.

And Fletcher King was the father.

CHAPTER 12

Sun and Lou almost leaped out of their skin with excitement. They fizzed with anticipation. Sun started to talk and Skye thought she'd never stop. It must have taken all of her willpower to keep Lou's pregnancy a secret for so long.

'We searched high and low for the right donor,' Sun said. 'But you know what Dezzy's like? There's not exactly a platinum gene pool to choose from. A lot of the good ones have either left town or they're unapproachable because their wives and girlfriends won't have a bar of it. We asked one of our gay friends but he wasn't interested. We wanted someone with integrity, emotional intelligence and half a brain.'

Skye almost chipped in with, 'and good looks' but pulled right back.

Sun slapped her hand over her mouth, staring at Fletcher in horror, before she removed it.

'Oh, sorry, sorry, sorry Fletch. We're making it sound like you're the best of a bad bunch but that's not the case at all. You're bloody wonderful.'

'That's right,' Lou said with a grin. 'Fletcher is the whole package, so to speak.'

Lou had taken the words right out of Skye's mouth.

Shadows cast by the candlelight flickered across Fletcher's face but didn't hide a blush. Lou pressed her lips together in a failed attempt to suppress a smile, her excitement palpable.

'We got to know Fletch and we didn't approach him until we were totally convinced he was the one.'

Lou wriggled in her seat. How could Skye not have noticed the taut roundness of her belly when they first met at the clothesline?

Fletcher placed his elbows on the cleared table and crossed his arms, resting one large hand over the other. Skye had to drag her eyes away from the fine hairs on his arms glowing golden in the dim light, and absorb the fact that this man was now related to her, if only through association.

'At first, I wasn't into it,' Fletcher said quietly. 'Like, why me? But when Sun and Lou explained, it made good sense. They didn't want to approach a local. That was too close. People talk. I mean, they're talking now the news is out. But it would have been more complicated if someone from town had been involved.'

He locked his serious gaze on Skye across the table. She nodded her head too fast, pulse racing, feeling she was a fraud in so many ways. He already had a baby, didn't he? She wanted to ask if the baby in the photo she accidentally discovered was also a favour for a friend. But she couldn't do it. It would ruin this moment for her sister and Lou. And she liked Fletcher a lot. More than a lot. Way too much.

'I totally get it,' she murmured. 'But it's a huge commitment, isn't it?'

She must have pulled off the non-threatening response because Fletcher nodded to Lou and Sun, who then nodded their permission for him to continue their shared story.

'I didn't know anyone when I came to Dezzy,' he said. 'Lou and Sun took me under their wing and helped me settle in. It was through them that I got to know the locals and make connections. It can be hard in a small town. People are suspicious. You don't belong if you don't grow up here. But Sun and Lou gave me a good rap. They put their trust in me.'

Sun cleared her throat. 'Fletcher wasn't so keen when we first approached him. So we gave him a heap of stuff to read on the subject and told him to go away and think about it,' she said.

'What convinced you?' Skye asked Fletcher.

'I thought about it for a long time. I knew it was a massive commitment, that wasn't without consequences, or something I could shrug off lightly. But in the end, it came down to friendship and trust. I decided this was something I could do for them that would be life changing.

'I went into it knowing my rights,' he continued. 'A solicitor wrote up a legal document so it's clear where I stand. It's a collaboration between the three of us. And I get to stay involved. That's important to me. I want to get to know Lou and Sun's child.'

Sun stood up for what seemed like the umpteenth time, walked around to Lou and massaged her shoulders.

'With Fletcher there's no hidden agenda,' Sun said. 'He's also smart and easy on the eye. Sorry Fletch, it's true. We're not immune to hot men.'

As they laughed, except for Fletcher, whose smile was shy and self-deprecating, Skye wondered if Sun and Lou knew about their sperm donor's mysterious past? Surely, if they were going to get pregnant they would need to have Fletcher's most personal health details and knowledge of past relationships, pregnancies, etcetera?

Skye buried her concerns. She was determined to be happy for her sister and Lou. It wasn't the time to ask too many questions, especially when she and Sun were standing together in the middle of a rope bridge above a raging river. Both holding very sharp rope cutters. Their relationship was, to say the least, precarious.

Skye was intrigued. 'And it worked first go?'

'Yep,' Sun said. 'Abso-bloody-lutely amazing. All the stars were aligned. Fletcher has perfect sperm and Lou must be incredibly fecund.'

'Fecund,' Skye repeated, savouring the ripe fullness of the word on her lips.

'What's more,' Lou joined the conversation, 'the pregnancy's been a breeze, touch wood.' She rapped her knuckles on the wooden table. 'Standard twelve weeks of morning sickness, baby in the right position, head down, anterior not posterior, kicking when he's meant to...'

'It's a he?' Skye asked, finding herself slowly being drawn into their enthusiasm, despite her misgivings and the fact that Fletcher was now her de facto brother in law.

'We haven't found out so we alternate. One day it's a boy and the next it's a girl.'

'How many weeks are you? When's the due date?'

Lou stared adoringly at her tummy and pressed her hand to it. 'Mid- September, around the sixteenth.'

Skye's pulse spiked. She swivelled to face her sister's profile. 'Really? Is that intentional? Or was it a fluke?'

Sun's eyes met hers. 'You can't plan this sort of shit. It happened that way and the date's a guesstimate.'

'What's so significant about September sixteen?' Fletcher asked no one in particular.

The answer came from Lou. She rubbed her tummy as she spoke softly.

'It's Jonno's birthday. I couldn't think of a better day for our baby to be born.'

From that point on, the conversation became stilted. Skye had grown superstitious since her father's death and wasn't sure the date was auspicious or portentous. Even Fletcher appeared uncomfortable with the knowledge that this baby could be born on the same day as a Dezzy legend.

As she and Fletcher rose to leave, Sun reverted to business mode, handing Skye a list of the names, addresses and phone numbers of local residents whose 'for sale' properties were being advertised in the paper.

'All the hard work's been done,' Sun said, and folded her arms tight against her body. 'I talked to every one of them and they all agreed to be interviewed and have their photos taken for the paper.'

Sun had pulled up the drawbridge again. Skye made an effort to keep her arms relaxed as Lou changed the subject and apologised for not being able to offer her a place to stay.

'We're turning the spare room into a nursery and it's full of crap like paint tins and baby stuff. Any other time...'

Skye waved her apology away. 'No worries. I'm good. Fletcher's loaned me a bed at his place for the rest of the week.'

As if the whole wide world, or at least the population of Dezzy, didn't already know it.

* * *

On the drive back to Fletcher's, love ballads streamed out of the Kombi's radio tuned to the local FM band. Skye hummed along to The Everly Brothers' *Love Hurts*.

She should have been buoyed by Sun and Lou's baby news but there were too many questions for Fletcher she didn't have the right to ask.

After the song ended, a silence hung between them.

Questions bustled like a courtroom drama in Skye's head.

Did you, Fletcher King, have sex, with Lou in order to impregnate her? Her internal chatterbox replied. *No, of course he didn't. Lou is gay.* But that didn't preclude Lou from having sex with a bloke for a good cause.

Skye shook her head almost imperceptibly at her own naiveté and flipped the thought over again. Maybe Fletcher and Lou *did* do the deed. Maybe it worked better that way. The sperm zoomed towards their ultimate destination faster during sexual intercourse rather than the chicken-baster method where the sperm were already out, before being regrouped and shot cannon-like from a nozzle.

There was no subtle way to ask Fletcher the obvious.

The Kombi turned into the driveway, headlights flashing across the front of Fletcher's house. On cue, Occy emitted a mournful howl from inside.

'He doesn't like being left alone for too long.'

Fletcher's flat dry accent had a poetic lilt to it that appealed to Skye.

She liked everything about Fletcher King but it had to stop. Especially with the news of the pregnancy. The affairs of the Summerhayes family were tangled enough without her attempting to 'seduce' the father of her sister and her sister's partner's baby. Skye reasoned that the unborn baby wasn't technically Sun's. Strictly speaking, it was Lou and Fletcher's.

She wondered how Sun felt about this. How the choice was made for Lou to get pregnant. Had coins been flipped to reach all these complex decisions with far-reaching repercussions if any one of the trio pulled out of the commitment?

As for her own lustful thoughts about Fletcher, now was the perfect time to dampen them.

'Wanna mug of hot milk? It'll help you sleep.' Fletcher's offer snapped her back to the present.

Skye bit her lip.

Say no, Skye. This is not a good idea.

'Don't you have to be up and gone by four?'

Oh dear. You left a door open.

'Yeah, but there's nothing like a mug of hot milk with a slug of Bundy to help you sleep well.'

Say no, now!

'You're twisting my arm.'

The heat emanating from Fletcher permeated her skin. She needed to get out of the Kombi and into the house where there was enough space to avoid a close up view of his lips or to breathe in his fresh rainwater and soap scent.

She flung open the Kombi door with such force that she expected it to fly off its hinges, leaped out and almost fell over her feet as she stumbled to the side, slid open the vehicle door and retrieved a bag of clean clothes on loan from Sun and Lou.

By the time she reached the front door of the house, her weak little mind was made up. It wouldn't hurt to have a small mug of milk with a dash of rum before bedtime. And it could be a good opportunity for her to learn more about the pregnancy. Why Fletcher agreed to be the sperm donor, how he was going to be involved in the baby's life and if that life involved the other baby she'd seen in the photo.

She could approach her line of questioning like an investigative journalist.

As soon as Fletcher turned the key in the front door and pushed it open, Occy tumbled out like a rugby league player scrambling desperately for the corner of the try line, panting, and sliding into Fletcher's legs.

Skye stepped inside and placed her bag and the bag of clothes on the floor next to the kitchen bench.

'I'll take you up on the hot milk before bedtime offer,' she announced.

Fletcher scratched behind the dog's ears. 'It's good to try something new every day. Keeps life interesting, opens up your mind, takes you places you've never gone before.'

Skye laughed. 'It's just hot milk.'

'It's more than hot milk.'

'With Bundy?'

Now it was Fletcher's turn to laugh with the added bonus of the full brunt of his dark blue stare.

'And me.'

* * *

Skye cupped her hands around the swirly blue ceramic mug as the aroma of cinnamon and nutmeg stirred through syrupy rum and milk wafted into her nostrils.

She sipped and closed her eyes momentarily as the heady blend finished with a star anise floating on top warmed her right through.

Being here, in Fletcher's softly lit lounge room, she could almost forget everything from the past few days, and tonight at Sun and Lou's. Release every anxious thought about her future to the starry night sky beyond the picture window. Forgive and almost forget.

She tucked her legs further up under her on the lounge and took another sip, enjoying every moment in Fletcher's company. Occy curled up next to her, emitting the occasional muffled bark. His muscles twitched as he dreamed about running free through a paddock or nipping at a flock of pesky geese.

Fletcher sat a safe distance away from her cross-legged on the floor, which was fine by her. It helped keep her impulses in check. Now was not the time to grab those dreadlocks in her fists and tug him to her so their bodies were pressed hard together. The thought was delicious though. It curled up inside her like the swirls of steam from her beverage.

Fortunately, he sat opposite, leaning against the coffee table with legs crossed. Her 'personal guru' replete with spiritual pulling power, wisdom and charisma.

It would be so easy to give up on the niggling questions about Fletcher's motives for becoming a sperm donor.

But at some point she knew she would have to break the spell that held them in a happy talk bubble that started when Skye posed the question, 'Do you think dogs dream?'

Occy snored and they both laughed. 'He must be in a deep sleep now.' Fletcher continued the current thread of their conversation. 'I read somewhere that dogs are like us; they dream during REM sleep, often of running and catching a ball, or about their owners' faces.'

'I wonder how researchers figure that out?' Skye frowned. 'They must get the participants to fill out a questionnaire after they wake up.'

Fletcher laughed again and Skye enjoyed the spontaneity of it before she decided that now was as good a time as any to flip the conversation to babies and parenthood.

'I have a question for you about dreams,' she said, striking while the iron was hot. 'Did you always dream about becoming a dad?'

Fletcher sipped his drink and considered her through half-closed eyes as if searching for a hidden agenda behind her question. The mood in the room had changed. Mellow replaced by a nimble wariness.

'It's a big deal to become a father.' Fletcher drew out the sentence and paused again before adding, 'To answer your question, no, I didn't always dream about it.'

He blew across the top of the mug. 'I'm doing this, or more like I've become involved with Sun and Lou because I know they'll be the most amazing parents. They're two hundred per cent committed to giving this baby the best life and the best opportunities. And you can't say that about everyone. Some people have kids for all the wrong reasons.'

He sounded sad. Skye wasn't sure how far she should push it. Maybe he was one of those people?

'Do you know much about kids?' she asked. 'Are there any nieces or nephews in your family?'

'No,' he said. 'This is all new to me.'

It was an emphatic 'no'. He sounded sincere enough. Maybe she had reached a dead end? Maybe the baby in the photo had nothing to do with Fletcher? Maybe she was a big sticky beak? Maybe Fletcher was a good liar?

She tried a lighter approach.

'How does the mechanics of it work?'

Fletcher finished off the rum and milk and put his mug on the floor. He arched his back and stretched his arms to the ceiling before staring straight at her. Skye held her breath, shocked by the intensity of his gaze.

'If you're curious, which I believe you are, the process was completed with a chicken baster. It was very impersonal and carried out in a professional fashion.'

'Oh,' she breathed out. 'So, that's the traditional method?'

This caused Fletcher to give a small chuckle. 'We, the three of us, thought that was the best approach. You can read everything you ever wanted to know about artificial insemination on the internet, the instructions are pretty straightforward. I went to Sun and Lou's place and they left me alone with some appropriate reading material and, there you go.' He clicked his fingers. 'I produced the magic ingredient.'

'Oh.' Skye felt her face heating up like a tomato under a hot griller. Thank goodness the lights were low. 'I guess you'd need some sort of incentive.'

'Yeah, I like that way of describing it. 'Incentive'. It did the job. Or I did the job. God, it's hard to say anything without it sounding like a dirty joke.'

He slipped his hands behind his head and stretched out his legs.

Skye observed his easy manner. Even when he was switched on, he emitted a peaceful non-confrontational vibe. Her mother would have analysed Fletcher's aura by now, Skye was sure of that. And it would be pure enlightened white.

'Who volunteered to get pregnant?'

Fletcher gave it a moment's thought.

'Well, that was interesting because neither one of them minded if the other was the 'carrier'. I guess that's what you'd call it? So, they basically sat down together and decided that, from a practical point of view, it would be better for Lou to have the baby because Sun was the main earner in the household and it would be harder for her to take a break from the paper.'

Skye nodded, feeling a twinge of guilt. Sun was always the pragmatic one in their family. And she didn't have one jealous bone in her body. Once the baby was born, there would be no competing for the baby's love and attention on her part. Sun would always be there for Lou and the baby. Skye could see theirs was an equal partnership.

Skye ran her hand over Occy's smooth head; he didn't budge. 'He's dead to the world,' she murmured before launching into another round of questions.

'I was curious about what happens after the baby is born, when it gets older? Do you get a say in the choice of religion, schools, sport, even what he or she eats and drinks? Vegan, vegetarian, paleo, omnivorous? And vaccinations and all that health related stuff? Do you have to pay part of the medical bills if something goes wrong with the kid's health? Do you get the call if he or she has to have an operation? What about mental health issues? Are you involved in making these big decisions?'

Now she'd started, the questions seemed to be rolling out in a never-ending stream. Until she'd started, she hadn't realised how much of a responsibility Fletcher had taken on. Having a baby was a massive commitment.

'I know, it's daunting. Seriously scary,' he said quietly. 'It's been an eye-opener for us because we had to think long and hard about all that shit. It took months to get the legal documents drawn up. People about to embark on the most important journey of their lives tend not think about that important stuff you reeled off. But we got it sorted well before the chicken baster. It was epic, a massive learning curve. You've got to believe me Skye, we are ready for this.'

Skye wasn't sure about any of it but Fletcher would never know that. Like the baby in the photo, it was none of her business. Whether or not she agreed or disagreed with their decision to dive into unknown and often ethically muddied waters, Skye had to admire their bravery.

Fletcher, Sun and Lou had entered into a long-term contract that would forever tie them together and hold them to account for the wellbeing of the precious child they would soon welcome into the world.

She stared out through the window where the stars winked like diamonds flung across an unravelled bolt of obsidian velvet.

Fletcher followed her gaze. 'Amazing, isn't it? I'll never get tired of it. I love it here,' he said.

She had nothing more to say.

CHAPTER 13

As soon as she finished her cross-examination of Fletcher, Skye made her excuses and scampered to bed. As she slipped between the sheets, erotic thoughts about her host fought for screenplay rights in a head and body simultaneously exhausted and switched on.

She'd escaped before her loose lips led to a confession about the baby photo. A midnight reveal wasn't the way to cleanse her of the remorse over the accidental discovery of what could be no more than a fictional tale she had dreamed up about Fletcher's past life.

Occy woke her around seven. He nudged her with his moist snout and launched most of his torso onto the bed while she half-heartedly pushed him aside, avoiding his sloppy pink tongue and doggy breath.

She hadn't heard Fletcher leave before four am. She counted on her fingers. He would have got about three hours sleep.

Skye left the house at around eight, with a full day of interviews for the real estate section of *The Northern Sun* ahead.

Before lunch, she managed to squeeze in three face-to-face meetings with homeowners selling their properties.

The final one for the day was with Maria Montaro.

Skye got to the Montaro property at about two in the afternoon. Mrs Montaro had talked non-stop for an hour. The plain rectangular wall clock with the flip-over date and time on the wall now read: 3:05pm. Time wasn't an issue for the eighty-four-year-old grandmother of ten and great grand-mother of five.

She had all the time in the world, whereas Skye didn't. She wanted to get to *The Northern Sun* office to write up at least one of her stories before the pre-intervention gathering at Grandma's that evening.

She made a futile attempt to push her impatience, along with salacious daydreams about Fletcher, to the back of her mind as Mrs Montaro extolled the merits of double-brick houses on concrete slabs.

They stood in the living room of the two-storey house built circa 1965. Originally, the house had sat in the middle of a 2000 square metre block owned by Maria and her husband Tony since their marriage in 1955. They had subdi-vided the block a couple of years ago. They then gifted the swathes of land either side of their house to their son and daughter.

Electricity power-line towers behind the hinterland prop-erty dominated the landscape, stretching into the distance like a row of Meccano sentinels.

Skye wouldn't write about anything that detracted from the property's appeal in the real estate profile piece. Instead, she would focus on the home's biggest asset, which was...

'My favourite room,' Mrs Montaro said, her Italian accent still strong even though she migrated to Australia with her family as a young girl in the early 1950s. She made a sweeping gesture towards a cavernous room down a set of six steps.

'It was double garage but we change to rumpus for grandkids.'

'Great idea,' Skye said, her tone overly enthusiastic. 'I love it.'

It didn't matter if she liked the room or not. As a real estate writer, it was Skye's job to turn a sow's ear into a silk purse. So that's what she would do.

The hulking space still resembled a garage. The roller door had been removed, the gap bricked in, the floor tiled and several prints of the Madonna and Christ on the cross were in pride of place on the exposed-brick wall.

Skye mentally dictated a description of the room that would appear in the real estate section of the paper next week.

It would read: *Down a small set of stairs is a sunken tiled rumpus room with a textural exposed brick wall adding an element of surprise. This comfortable spacious room offers yet another discrete living zone for family members to chill out or entertain guests. Versatile in its layout, it is currently used as a media room complete with in-ceiling speakers. Other possibilities are endless including the option of reverting it back to its original use as a two-car garage with space for a workshop.*

Mrs Montaro beamed to reveal a gold-crowned molar on an upper tooth. She was short and stocky with raven hair straight from the packet. Her feet in black orthopaedic shoes and sturdy legs encased in thick flesh-coloured stockings had almost certainly carried her to and from the clothesline in the backyard day after day for more than sixty years. A sensible grey skirt and black long-sleeved blouse highlighted her sallow skin. In her ears were heavy gold sleepers and on work-worn hands a wedding band and simple diamond engagement ring. The gold chain with a fine gold cross around her neck matched her molar.

Her austere appearance belied a generous nature. She plied Skye with homemade pickles, salami and jars of tomato passata, insisting she drink a glass of fresh lemonade packed with ice cubes and mint from the garden.

Skye peered down at her from what felt like a great height, increased by a borrowed pair of Lou's black sling backs with three-centimetre kitten heels.

Mrs Montaro probably hadn't talked to anyone all day and relished the chance to complain about her husband of sixty-five years, Tony, without any fear of judgement.

According to Mrs Montaro, she had the edge over her 'lazy gambler' of a husband. She saved every cent she earned, hiding some of it in secret spots in the house and garden. (Skye interrupted at this point in the interview. She advised Mrs Montaro to retrieve the money and stow it in a safe place in case buyers at open inspections stumbled across a couple of thousand dollars under a mattress or wherever else it might be stashed).

It turned out, Skye learned, that Mrs Montaro also had an uncanny knack of spotting real estate bargains and instinctively knew the right time to buy and sell. The properties were in her name so poor old Tony had no room to move.

It never ceased to amaze Skye that people trusted her with intimate details about their lives. She was a stranger in their homes, there to write about their properties. Skye learned that an hour-long interview could lead to all sorts of revelations. These people trusted Skye to keep their secrets safe. And she did.

Over endless cups of tea and coffee, she had listened to tales about cheating spouses, acrimonious and amicable divorces, happy homes filled with joy and good fortune. Some of the interviewees unravelled their hearts, opening up to her about loneliness and grief at the loss of a loved one, who may have died last year or twenty years ago.

Skye packed her writing gear into her bag and wished Mrs Montaro all the best with the sale of her home. The elderly woman squeezed Skye's arm affectionately and leaned in close.

'Your papa, Skye. Everybody miss him. Everybody love him. And your mama too. Say my love to your mama. She is a good lady.'

Skye muttered something appropriate and blinked back the tears that inexplicably sprung to her eyes.

* * *

It had been building up all day. A compacting of her chest and an acidic fizz in the pit of her stomach.

It'll be fine, you'll cruise through it, Skye told herself.

She had to keep the good vibes coming because the bad vibes were chasing her back. She'd been through the wringer in the past few days but managed to stave off the panic that bubbled away beneath her ribs. It was coupled with anxiety that threatened to strangle her like a python wound around her torso and neck, pinning her arms to her thighs. Its grip slowly tightening in a death crush.

'These things are sent to test us,' she said aloud.

Back at Fletcher's house, she changed out of her work clothes, a white shirt and black pants that belonged to Sun, kicked off the kitten heels and checked out her options of something more comfortable to wear to the 'casual pre-intervention get-together' at Grandma's.

She tried another affirmation.

'Time wounds all heals.' Her brow creased. *Geez, that's not right.* The correct version came to her. With feeling, she said, 'Time heals all wounds.'

If she couldn't even get the old adage right, how would she be able to contribute anything meaningful to a pre-intervention gathering?

She flounced around the room, plonked down on the bed and fell back onto the mattress. Ridiculous. The whole damn thing was ridiculous. Skye would make that clear tonight. She couldn't understand how a confrontation with Airen would aid his recovery in any way whatsoever.

Saving Airen from himself?

'Pft!'

It was a pointless exercise. Her brother was a grown man. He should know how to look after himself by now. Skye stared at the ceiling. That was exactly what Jonno would have said.

'Argh.'

What was she doing here anyway? She should be back in Sydney sorting out things with Beau and nailing her career. That was where her life was now. Not here in Desiree Bay with her dysfunctional family. She didn't belong here anymore.

'Belong.'

Such an odd word.

Skye sat up, ran her hands through her hair and tugged at a knot.

'Where do I belong?'

Occy sat at the foot of the bed and gave her one of his mournful stares. If only he could talk, Skye was sure his advice would make the positive affirmations sound flimsy and clichéd.

'You'd set me straight, wouldn't you, fella?'

When Fletcher wasn't there, Occy latched onto Skye and followed her around the house. On several occasions, lost in her own thoughts, she'd almost tripped over him.

Skye guessed Fletcher had been home earlier. She could tell, just as she could tell when Beau came and left the apartment while she was out. Men left tell-tale signs. In Beau's case, it was the raised toilet seat and used cups, plates and glasses left on the poof, or even on the floor next to the toilet bowl.

Fletcher was different. He'd rinsed a spoon, bowl and mug and placed them in the sink. Using her investigative powers, she figured he'd eaten a bowl of homemade muesli and drunk a mug of chai latte after he arrived back from the bakery, some time after two. He worked an eight to ten hour day, she'd noticed.

An open garage door, closed when she left in the morning, was evidence he'd gone to The Point for a surf. Skye walked outside, poked her head in and glimpsed racks of boards of all different shapes and sizes. Just as quickly, she exited. No more snooping unless invited. Easier said than done, she reprimanded herself with a guilty smile.

In the bedroom, Skye tipped a bag of clean clothes onto the bed and sorted the items into socks, undies, workwear and casual, which were interchangeable.

Unlike Sydney, where appearances counted, in Dezzy it didn't matter if she turned up to work wearing jeans.

She logged three flanno shirts and chose the green-and-black check pattern over a red-and-black and a grey-and-black. They would keep for another day. Sun must be really low on flanno shirts. She'd loaned them all to Skye.

'Whaddya think?' Skye held the shirt to her front and posed in front of Occy.

She could have sworn his satin-soft jowls lifted in an approving smile. After getting ready, she loitered around the house. If Fletcher came back, maybe he would give her a lift. She didn't feel like driving to Grandma's and back on her own.

Although the bench top was reasonably clean, Skye wiped over it with a damp cloth, stood back, observed a blemish and wiped it over once more.

'Doesn't look like he's coming home.'

In reply, Occy nudged her thigh with his snout and, in a demonstration of affection, bestowed upon her a love nip, a gentle nibble on her hand that reminded her it was time for his dinner.

She fed the dog, cleaned his bowl, replenished his water container and scribbled a 'dog is fed' note to Fletcher that she left on the spotless bench.

Reluctantly, she left the house, but not before sending Occy, who looked pretty miserable, out to the back deck.

* * *

As darkness descended, the wind howled and heavy clouds skittered across a waning crescent moon as though harassed by a witch with a bristle broom.

Skye drove up to the speed limit with the radio blaring tunes from a local radio station locked in a 1980s' time warp. A DJ with a voice like some of the sleaze bags who'd tried to pick her up over the years back-announced *Eternal Flame*, 'That was The Bangles with their number one hit from 1989. Man oh man, were those chicks hot or not.' Reaching the main streets of town, she slowed down to the speed limit of 50 kph along Sutton St and turned onto Shepherd.

Smitty's Fish 'n' Chips shop was doing a roaring trade for a Tuesday night, with several hooded youths huddled outside on a bus stop seat sharing hot chips wrapped in butcher's paper. Their BMX bikes lay across the footpath, blocking the thoroughfare.

Apart from that, the town centre was empty. Dry leaves and other debris swirled and scuttled across the road in front of the car's headlights as she took a bend that led from Shepherd to Coastal Drive. As she neared The Point, the cloud cover momentarily cleared to give a clear moonlit view of the headland and, below, a roiling ocean, white lipped and raging. Daring anyone or anything to take it on.

For a second, the breath left Skye's body. She double blinked and gripped the steering wheel. All she had to do tonight was remain calm and focussed. That would be her mantra.

Calm and focussed. Calm and focussed. Calm and focussed.

A car that had been a fair distance behind hers caught up, its headlights blinding her every time she checked the rear-view mirror. It was just about tailgating her on a poorly lit winding part of the road.

'Bugger off,' she grumbled under her breath as Tears for Fears launched into *Everybody Wants to Rule the World*.

She indicated and turned into Iluka St. The car followed.

As she turned off the ignition, she checked the rear view mirror and cursed under her breath. Behind the wheel of the beat-up Holden Leyland P76 was her nemesis Jimmy Trout. Beside him sat Skye's mother, Oceane.

CHAPTER 14

At least Jimmy wasn't wearing a kilt. He could have passed for normal in a pair of denim jeans and a checked flanno shirt, not unlike, Skye noted despairingly, the one she was wearing.

She squinted at the rear-view mirror as her mother emerged from the passenger seat. Oceane's clothing choice definitely leaned towards the bizarre.

Skye couldn't see what she wore underneath a woollen poncho and matching helmet-style beanie. As her mother stepped beneath the front porch light the bold pattern screamed 'crazy lady'.

There was a definite Peruvian inspired theme. A row of black alpacas (or maybe yaks?) were underlined by a pink geometric pattern. This was above a row of stick-figure honchos wearing black hats, green shirts and blue trousers. The garment was fringed with long multicoloured tassels. To consolidate the 'nutty old bird' impression, the helmet hat replicated the pink and other colours in the poncho. It had large pink earflaps and a long plaited tassel sewn on top.

Her mother didn't often get the chance to wear winter garments. She must have pulled this one out for the unusually chilly evening. At least her legs were covered by conventional black knee-high boots.

Skye had no option but to get out of the car, even though she longed to reverse down the driveway at the speed of light.

'Skye, Lass, we're glad ya could make it.' It was Jimmy, extending the olive branch. Again. Her mother appeared less enthusiastic though she managed a nod and a wan smile.

Skye gave a stiff smile. 'I'm here for Airen.'

She regretted the words as soon as they were out. Too harsh. Sandpaper on soft timber. Not a good way to start the evening. She reached the front door, head down, feeling a weird combination of sheepish and defiant.

Grandma never locked the door because Dezzy was that sort of town. Its residents lived with the naive belief the world was still a safe place, and it sort of worked. Dezzy had a low crime rate; it was a town where kids could wander down to the creek or beach without adult supervision because there was always someone local keeping an eye out for their wellbeing.

'Skye, Jimmy, Donna,' Grandma trilled as they filed into the living room. Skye imagined her and her mother's glum expressions contrasted against Jimmy's permanently fixed inane grin.

'It's Oceane not Donna,' Skye's mother corrected Grandma.

'Oh, Donna, Love, you know I'll never get used to that strange name but if I must call you Oceane, I'll do my best. Oceane it is. Take a seat over here, Love.'

Under an iridescent light ensconced in a white pendant shade, the yellow walls, green carpet and lounge took on a golden glow that disguised their disrepair. The effect was enhanced by the pale circle of light from a standing lamp with a plain cream shade next to the lounge.

Grandma wore what could have been a dressing gown but wasn't. Skye recalled the 1960s' housedress, created, obviously, to be worn around the house and never in public. The synthetic fabric fell to just below her knees. It featured a bold red-and-pink rose pattern. Her feet were encased in pink terry-towelling slip ons. Around her neck was a pink floral silk scarf that had been fashioned into a sling. It took a moment for Skye to realise Grandma's arm wasn't in the sling but cupped under it.

Jimmy placed his big hands gently on Grandma's shoulders and planted a kiss on her forehead She came up to his ribs.

He drew back, arms still lightly upon her. 'How's wee Dougal?'

Grandma's brow crinkled and her lips pursed; they resembled a soaked prune. She stared at the shaking parcel of skin and bones held firm in the makeshift sling.

'Oh dear, what is it with you people and names? It's Pepe.' She blew out a sigh worthy of an Academy-Award nomination. 'And since you asked, he's a damn nuisance, worse than a two-year-old what with his demands so I had to bundle him up or he would have been hysterical, what with all these visitors.'

Jimmy grinned. 'Aye Betty, that might be the case but the wee dog looks comfortable and content-like in your capable hands.' He dropped his arms and turned to Skye. His hairline was receding but he was still able to cultivate a straggling ponytail, today woven into a plait flipped over the front of his shoulder.

'He's a wee battler, is our Dougal. I picked him up at the pound, just in the nick of time. He was on death row, number almost up. And now, here he is, warm as toast in Betty's arms, spoilt rotten. As it should be.'

He beamed at Grandma like he'd witnessed a miracle and she was Mother Theresa. 'Och aye, as it should be,' he repeated.

With a smile on his lips and in his eyes, Jimmy crossed the room to the small kitchen lit by a harsher fluoro-tube.

Grandma beamed as he passed by, which added kindling to the firewood piling up inside Skye. Her grandmother obviously adored the pompous idiot, as their light-hearted banter indicated. But seriously, Grandma should hate the man. He'd usurped her only son, Jonno. For god's sake, he was Claudius! Which made her mother not Donna nor Oceane but Queen Gertrude. OMG. That meant Skye was Hamlet!

With difficulty, Skye unclamped her grinding teeth and moved closer to the tiny creature in Grandma's arms to be confronted by Pepe's black spheres. The dog's pointy ears were too big for his small head. They poked up, on alert.

Skye kissed Grandma's warm wafer cheek and drew back.

Her mother joined them.

Avoiding eye contact with her mother, Skye asked, 'Do you still have Airen's marble collection?' She knew it was a petty question but she didn't care.

Oceane had taken off the gaudy beanie and was in the process of removing the poncho to reveal an equally blinding caftan in swirls of jaffa orange and burnt umber. Her hand went to her breast-bone, fingers splayed to reveal an array of large rings sporting big chunks of crystal. Every petite finger with orange-lacquered nails was accounted for.

'Of course I do,' she said quietly, defensively, in her sing-song voice. 'Airen threw it out a while back but I went through the bin and saved all the important stuff, the stuff he might one day value again.'

She seemed to risk a glance at Skye and decided it was safe enough to finish her train of thought. Skye was thrown. She hadn't expected her mother to have a ready response.

'One day Airen might have children and he'll ask the very question you just asked. I'll be able to give back to him those things he considered of no use when he was in a dark place.'

Their eyes locked for a moment, carbon copies, before Jimmy poked his head around the kitchen door, big lips upturned.

'Sun and Lou'll be here soon but we might as well get started. Anyone for a wee tipple? A shandy, Betty? Anything for you Skye? Betty's got a rather pleasant Chardonnay in the fridge, Margaret River 2018.'

Skye went to the dining table covered a white linen tablecloth, its edges scalloped embroidery, and opened her contributions to the evening – two store bought dips and a packet of rice crackers. She set them next to two large bowls, one containing Skye's favourite coleslaw recipe and the other a potato salad.

Jimmy returned to the room, drinks balanced on a round red enamel tray with a raised edge, circa 1966.

Skye took her glass of wine and sniffed inside the rim, aware that it could elicit comment from Grandma about how she'd become a city snob. She tentatively sipped. It was good.

She observed Jimmy over the top of her glass. He took a long draught of beer in a schooner glass and wiped off the creamy moustache.

The man had a hide coming here tonight. Walking around Grandma's house like he owned it when he'd flagrantly flaunted his affair with her mother for the whole town to see. He'd moved in with her mother shortly after Jonno's death.

She doused the small fire in her belly with her mantra.

Calm and focussed. Calm and focussed. Calm and focussed.

The door burst open and Sun and Lou brought their unfettered joy and enthusiasm for life into the room. Lou was a walking cliché. Pregnancy suited her. Her hair was black silk, thick and shiny, and her complexion smooth and plumped up with feel-good pregnancy hormones.

Sun looked as beautiful, Skye thought. They were the perfect couple.

Lou carried a bag filled with baguettes, baked by Fletcher no doubt, which she took straight to the kitchen. Sun, hands in oven mitts, held the handles of an oval cream casserole.

She followed Lou, and the fragrance of some wonderful meaty stew aroused Skye's taste buds. She was still tied in nervous knots but the heavenly aroma made her salivate. It took her back to those pre-vegetarian days on the farm when their mother would spend all day Sunday chopping and slicing and dicing vegetables to add to a huge beef casserole for at least twenty hangers on.

Lou came back into the room with the baguettes cut into manageable portions on a white plate.

'Fletcher's popping over in a bit,' she announced to the room in general but Skye had a funny feeling it was meant for her.

'Is he involved in the intervention too?' She couldn't help herself. There was already one outsider present and that was one too many.

'Just the lead up,' Sun said. 'We thought he should be here tonight. Maybe he has advice. He's one of Airen's closest friends.' Sun placed her hands on her hips, as though she was ready to draw some imaginary gun if Skye disagreed with Fletcher's presence.

So Skye sipped on her wine and shrugged. Some things in life were beyond her control. Who told her that? Ah yes. Now she remembered. An osteopath she once visited on a friend's recommendation in Sydney. He told her this seconds before sliding his hand underneath one of her buttocks - she was on her back on a massage table - and asked if she was interested in a casual 'friendship'.

'Totally after hours,' he suggested with a greasy grin midway through the 60-minute consultation.

She'd left immediately without paying and never went back.

Calm and focussed. Calm and focussed. Calm and focussed.

* * *

Jimmy thrust a piece of Grandma's hummingbird cake, wrapped in a linen napkin, at Skye.

'Will ya not have a wee slice, Lass?'

Usually Skye was a sucker for accents, particularly Scottish. But Jimmy's coo-ing and clucking sounded like an addled hen about to lay an egg.

'No thanks,' she said, lips barely moving.

She caught Fletcher staring at her across the room and felt like poking her tongue out at him like a spiteful adolescent.

Fletcher didn't get it. He had no idea what it felt like to see your mother getting it on with another man on the day your father died.

Fletcher's arrival had coincided with the end of the main meal. To foster the casual get together vibe, Grandma encouraged everyone to eat in the lounge room.

Skye slotted herself at the far end of the green two-seater couch next to Sun, who sat next to Oceane. The other two women had to wriggle closer together to fit Skye in but it meant she didn't have to directly face her mother.

Their plates were balanced precariously on their knees. The couch sagged in the middle and they rolled awkwardly into each other every time one of them leaned forward.

Grandma, Lou and Jimmy sat opposite on dining chairs.

It was an uncomfortable little circle.

Fletcher was, Skye conceded silently, a welcome distraction.

Grandma somehow managed to haul herself off the lounge. She went to the dining table and piled Fletcher's plate high with leftovers and her own vegetarian version of a stew. He made the right noises and gave the impression this was his last meal. Skye admired his diplomacy. The man sure knew how to work the room.

Fletcher pulled up another chair next to Jimmy.

The women fussed over Jimmy, especially Grandma, who clucked at his corny jokes about grasshoppers, Irishmen, Scotchmen and elephants walking into bars or jumping out of aeroplanes.

Skye wriggled her way off the lounge and into the kitchen. She opened the fridge, pulled out the wine and refilled her glass. The bottle was almost empty. Surely that couldn't have been all her doing? Rather than leave the dregs, she drained the last of the contents into her glass.

'I take it you're staying here tonight or am I the designated driver?'

Skye spun around and wine sloshed over the glass edge onto the bench top.

'Bugger.' She lamented the waste. 'What do you mean? Stay the night? I'm perfectly fine.' The moment the words blurred out in a smudge, she knew she wasn't.

Fletcher put his plate in the sink and rinsed it under the cold tap.

'What's it to be then? I'm the designated driver.'

She gulped down the wine, a juvenile gesture that made her head spin.

'Guesso.'

If she was going to be the naughty teenager, insolent and resentful of adult authority, she might as well take it all the way.

She elbowed past him on her way back to the lounge room, which seemed to be shrinking after each desperate glug of wine. She felt like Alice In Wonderland. After she drank from the special cordial in the white rabbit's house, Alice grew and grew and grew.

God, she, Skye Summerhayes, needed to be a mature adult and stop the guzzling.

Sun, Lou and Oceane were clutching copies of *'Tips for a Successful Intervention - a step-by-step guide'* that came from an American website.

'You share yours with Fletcher, Lass.' Jimmy handed Skye a spare copy and dragged a chair next to his for Oceane, who had stood up from the couch to stretch her arms jangling with colourful bangles.

Sun also moved to a single chair.

'What is this? Musical chairs?' Skye wondered aloud. She didn't add that it appeared that Sun had intentionally vacated the couch to make space for Fletcher to sit next to her.

Skye sank back down into its velvet-covered lumpiness. Fletcher landed beside her, with his second piece of cake. Cake. Didn't Alice shrink after taking a bite of cake?

'No one cooks savoury like Lou and no one bakes like Betty,' Fletcher declared to no one and everyone. He bit down into Grandma's tangy creation. Closing his eyes for a moment, he chewed slowly as if to savour every crumb. Skye watched in fascination and warded off the fantasy of wanting to become that piece of cake.

In her increasingly trashed state, she could see the similarities between Fletcher and a bust of Poseiden she'd once pored over in an ancient history textbook. His features hewn from rough stone into a smooth perfect form. God of the ocean.

Jimmy cleared his throat and Skye's eyes flew to his. She widened them and blinked. He'd caught her out. Perving at Fletcher.

What had she been doing? Smiling dreamily on the crest of lustful thoughts about Fletcher King? Where was sobriety when she needed it most at a pre-intervention gathering for her alcoholic brother? Skye hiccoughed and shoved the notes at Fletcher.

'Skye?'

Skye jerked up her head. Jimmy's dark features were inscrutable. 'Have ya caught up with Airen since the wee altercation outside the pub?'

Examining the dwindling contents of her wine glass, she chewed her bottom lip. 'I've been flat chat, flat out, flat out like a lizard drinking.'

It was a lame excuse. There had been more than enough time to visit Airen while he was at work at the board-shaping factory out the back of the Karmarama Surf Shop. It was right next door to the newspaper office. But she'd avoided it.

She didn't know what to say to a sober Airen. Drunk Airen was another matter. She could deal with that. But not Airen before those first few drinks of the day. Serious, laconic, brown-eyed Airen.

'What would I say to him anyway?'

Calm and focussed, this was not. Defensive? Yes.

Still, she relented. 'I could say, 'Hey, Airen, mate, bro', I'm back in Dezzy to watch you squirm under the swinging light-bulb of a family intervention.''

'He was only asking Love,' Grandma placated. It wasn't quite a smack on the hand but Skye felt the sting. She shut her mouth.

'Right then.' Jimmy slapped his thighs as though Skye hadn't spoken. 'Has anyone had time to read over the intervention process?'

Skye slumped further back into spongy cushion and crossed her arms. Lou raised her hand and leant forward over her pregnant belly. Dead keen.

'Sun and I read it. We're giving you our full support as moderator, Jimmy. We're doing this because we care for Airen. We want him to know we love him and we want to do everything possible to see him through this.'

Sun put up her hand to be next speaker, which seemed to be the etiquette. Skye found the formalities unnecessary but everyone else seemed to be abiding by the 'raise your hand before you speak' rule.

'This gathering is to organise our roles on intervention day. It's up to us to show a united front. We have to work together and share our thoughts on how we approach Airen on Saturday,' Sun said.

Eyes down, she ran her index finger underneath the text in the middle of the sheet of paper. 'It says here, and I quote, 'Before the day of the intervention, discuss openly with one another the subject's negative actions and how these are causing harm to both him and to his loved ones'.'

Sun paused and looked up for a moment. Seeing that she had everyone's attention, she returned her gaze to the intervention notes.

'It goes on to suggest that we plan what we are going to say on the day. We have to be super sensitive to Airen's fragile condition. We have to make our case in a gentle way. It's not supposed to be a confrontation. We don't want him to turn against us. We have to gain his trust.'

This time Oceane's be-ringed hand flew upwards. Jimmy gave the nod and placed his hand on her thigh, a sign of support that made Skye want to scream.

'I'd like to run through what I plan to say to Airen, if that's all right with everyone?'

While Skye mumbled 'whatever' under her breath, the others murmured their encouragement. They couldn't be serious about this?

In a flash, Skye recalled her mother sitting next to her on her bed when she was a child, reading to her from a well-worn copy of *Alice in Wonderland*.

'Alice said to the Cheshire Cat, 'But I don't want to go among mad people.'

The Cheshire Cat replied, 'Oh, you can't help that, we're all mad here. I'm mad. You're mad.'

Alice asked: 'How do you know I'm mad?'

The Cheshire Cat smiled: 'You must be or you wouldn't have come here.'

Skye grabbed at Fletcher's sleeve and through gritted teeth implored, 'Take me home.'

Fletcher raised his eyebrows as though puzzled by her need to leave and whispered back, close to her ear, 'When this is sorted.'

A sense of desperation invaded her as the fright flight reflex kicked in. She wouldn't do this. Couldn't. Her family was stark-raving mad and this pre-intervention gathering was the best evidence yet.

She wanted order and normality, not a room full of crazies from the coast.

Jimmy coughed behind his hand and Grandma said, 'Go ahead Donna, I mean Oceane. We're listening Love.'

Everyone turned to Oceane, whose eyes welled. She blinked and Skye watched, fascinated, as tears plopped onto her mother's cheeks like the beginnings of a storm, big globular crystal balls raining on dry plains. Rolling down her face towards her chin.

'This is what I plan to say to Airen at the intervention.' Her voice trembled as she laced her fingers together and rubbed her palms with her thumbs. 'I love you, we love you, with every fibre and it's killing me, us, to see such a wonderful human being, my little boy, Sun and Skye's little brother, who has so much to give the world, drinking himself to death.

'I have been, we have been, distressed by your behaviour of late. Just when we thought you were getting back on top of things and starting to see your way through the darkness, you let go of all hope.'

Oceane paused, her eyes bright with fear. 'Is that too negative? Can we define negative?'

Jimmy patted her thigh. 'No, no, no. That's fine Darlin'. Keep goin'.'

A delicate sniff. 'The fight at the pub the other night was the last straw. Please stop drinking Darlin'. Please come back to us. We know you can do it. And we'll be with you, supporting you all the way.'

Oceane began to sob loudly and convulsively. Jimmy fished an extremely long tartan handkerchief from his jeans' pocket and handed it to her.

'Thanks Darlin',' she said as she blew her nose. 'It's not easy.'

A pause. Then Jimmy extended a hand to Sun. 'Lass, are ya ready for it?'

Her sister's eyes streamed. She sniffled, gulped and ran a flanno sleeve under a nose as pink as a ringtail possum's.

'I'm sorry, not yet, not yet.'

Grandma was having a quiet cry and Lou was busy consoling Sun.

Skye almost suggested that they share the hanky. It was as though she was watching the whole scene from a distance. Her feet were drilled into the floor to stop her from floating off with her family. They were clearly daft.

Jimmy stared in Skye's direction. She was the obvious next choice. Her eyes as dry and arid as the outback. Not a tear in sight. She felt good. Powerful even. And definitely in control.

'Skye?'

Her eye roll came unbidden while 'okay' rode out on a sigh.

Fletcher leaned in close again, this time his lips brushing her ear. Pleasant, ticklish, mildly erotic. 'Think about it first, don't rush it.'

She slid her vision sideways to his profile. He was totally into this. Straight faced. Earnest. Invested in Airen's rehab. No one in the room was on Skye's side, she was sure of it, and all eyes were on her. Expectantly.

She focussed on her lap and wiped an imaginary crumb from her jeans. Her mother's and Sun's sobs subsided. The only sounds in the room were tiny nasal snorts and general throat clearing.

If only she could muster up emotions other than resentment, apathy and fatigue. She closed her eyes, squeezed, and opened them again to stare at one of Grandma's Australian flora plates in a collection of eight mounted on the wall across the other side of the room.

'I don't think what I'm about to say will make any difference whatsoever to Airen.' She swallowed, pressed her lips together and fiddled with the garnet ring on her middle finger. A twenty-first birthday present from her parents that she never took off. Realising she was fidgeting, she placed her hands in her lap. It was strange, but she felt her heartbeat move from a steady even beat to a canter.

'Airen,' she began, feeling like a fake, as self-conscious as a ten year old who is made to read a thrown-together poem in front of the whole class. She never handled that reading aloud stuff well.

'I haven't given any thought to this and I don't know what I feel or think about your situation. But... I do love you. We all do.'

What next? Just fill the silence Skye. Give them what they want to hear.

'I haven't been here for you lately, for a while. I hope you don't think I left just because of Dad. It's more complicated than that. Anyway, this isn't about me. It's about you.'

She raised her hands slightly. They were shaking so she slid them under the backs of her thighs. A vision of a punch drunk Airen gave her a new momentum.

'When I saw you for the first time in ages the other night I was, frankly, shocked and upset. I somehow felt responsible. I never sorted out things with you. I should've kept in touch.'

Skye bowed her head. Defeated. This was ridiculous. How could her ramblings help fix Airen? Everything was fucked up and couldn't be mended.

'Okay.' Breathless now. And exhausted. 'This is it. This is my pitch, Airen. You are not to blame for what happened that night. It wasn't your fault.'

CHAPTER 15

That night. It returned in flashes when Skye least expected it. While she buttered a piece of toast, during an interview about a house, as she pulled up to red traffic light, on the commute to work, sitting in the cinema, at the gym, on a sunny morning or a rainy afternoon.

It hit her like a small electric shock.

Out of nowhere. A macabre pop-up postcard or tableau vivant.

Her father, a death's head, hair plastered and shiny as a seal under the moon's spotlight, a tar-black ocean pouring brine from hollow eyes, nostrils and an apocalyptic roar from the hole where there used to be a mouth.

Or she would relive it in her drowning dreams, where the only way to save herself was to beat her legs and feet furiously upwards through viscous opaque fluid into terrified, sweating wakefulness.

No one knew what happened, except Skye. She held the grim truth tightly to her. It had become her personal nightmare.

It was too late to share the horror. It would only lead to untold trauma, re-open old wounds and cause more disconnection from her family.

Jonno's body was never recovered. That made it harder for everyone.

Two weeks after he drowned, Jonno's memorial was held at the premises of *The Northern Sun*. One month later, a gold memorial plaque was drilled into the red-brick wall at the building's entrance.

> ***In loving memory of journalist Jonno Summerhayes, a visionary who dedicated his life to the community as a tireless activist for the preservation of Desiree Bay.***

For some months, Skye clung to the irrational hope that Jonno had been picked up by a tanker and was stricken by amnesia in some far flung outpost. Or he'd crawled, half dead, onto an uninhabited island where he survived on coconuts and fish caught with his bare hands.

Plain dumb that. Jonno was dead. He'd never return to Desiree Bay.

Last night in her inebriated state, she almost spilled the beans. Fortunately Oceane cut in and finished her plea to Airen with 'get a life'.

Jimmy gently corrected her with, 'Maybe 'love your life' might work better Darlin'. We'll work on it.'

* * *

'Skye?' Sun leaned across the breakfast bench and clicked her fingers.

She was too close. Skye could see the dark brown flecks in her amber eyes. It was disconcerting.

'Do you need to reach out and share your thoughts?'

Skye swallowed. Her throat was a desert. She had no thoughts. She had a hangover that had sucked all the hydration from every last cell in her body.

The 'program' for Airen's intervention on Saturday wasn't finalised until well after midnight.

She could barely remember Fletcher driving her back to Sun and Lou's flat where she crashed on the lounge. Fletcher slept in the Kombi before walking the ten steps to the bakery at four am.

Woken by the histrionics of a distant kookaburra that started its mad cackle before dawn, Skye had burrowed further into her makeshift bed to shut out the noise and hide herself from the outside world. Only to be shaken into a zombie state by her sister's firm hand a couple of hours later.

Now, half awake and feeling fragile, she craved coffee and toast with heaps of butter and sliced tomatoes doused with salt and pepper. Then she might be able to think straight.

'You know Airen blames himself,' Sun said as she spooned ground coffee beans into a glass plunger.

Skye watched, her head dull and vision foggy, as Sun poured in boiling water and pushed the plunger filter down slowly. The crushed beans compressed. Her brain compressed. Water. She needed water.

'He's never been right since Dad died,' Sun continued. 'He acts weird all the time, even when he's off the booze. And he's angry. And sad. Angry and sad.'

Skye blinked furiously but her eyes remained dry.

'I blame myself for some of that,' she managed.

It must have sounded like she had mouthful of gravel. Sun passed her a glass of water before she poured coffee into two white mugs and shoved one at Skye.

Skye drained the glass, put it on the bench and gripped the handle of the coffee cup for dear life. She inhaled the nutty caramel aroma. Heaven.

Sun propped her elbows on the counter. 'You know,' she started.

Skye braced herself for what was coming.

'It's none of my business, and tell me to butt out if I'm going too far.'

Skye gingerly moved the coffee cup to her lips, blew, sipped and lowered it to the bench. Relief.

'Okay. I'm ready. Shoot.'

Sun exhaled. 'The night Dad died - you never explained what *really* happened.'

Skye closed her aching eyes and took another sip.

Sun again. Persistent. 'Skye, it's been hard for all of us.'

It hurt to open her eyes. 'I don't want to go back over this, Sun. You know what happened.'

'Really? Do I? Airen's story's different from yours.'

This was news to Skye. There had only ever been one story. Hers.

'What do you mean? Airen was unconscious. How could he remember anything?'

A sigh from Sun. 'He said he couldn't remember at first, it was like he had selective amnesia. But after a while stuff floated back, like in a bad dream. In dribs and drabs. He said you were there. In the ocean. Not on the beach where you said you found him.'

Sun paused and cocked her head at Skye, as though she was trying to figure out her next move.

'Skye, Airen said you were out there in the ocean with him. That you saved him. Somehow you managed to get out, get him on your board and bring him back in. He reckons he stopped breathing on the beach and regained consciousness with you giving him CPR. Is that right or isn't it?'

Skye gulped more coffee. It burned her throat. She needed to eat.

'I'm ravenous.'

'Skye? Did you hear what I said?'

Skye ran her fingers through knotted hair. 'I found him on the beach. Unconscious. That's it.'

Sun's nostrils flared and her eyes darkened. She could have been about to say something else, something explosive; instead, she sucked in a breath.

'Fair enough. If that's your story, that's that. But maybe you should talk to him before the intervention, clear things up a bit. You've obviously moved on, got your life together in Sydney. But Airen's still here, stuck, in a rut. And he's confused because there are two *very* different versions of the story. And he doesn't believe yours.'

'For god's sake Sun, why does it matter which version he chooses? He can believe his own version if he wants. But Dad's gone. Nothing'll change that.'

'It would help if you talked.'

'Or it could make things worse.'

Sun raised her hands, palms facing the ceiling, before slamming them down on the bench on either side of her coffee cup.

'How can things get any worse? He's drinking himself to death. Smoking his guts out. Cigarettes and god knows what else. Col saw him at the pub yesterday morning. *Yesterday morning.* He was shitfaced before lunch and you could have mistaken him for a homeless bloke. That's what Col said. I don't know about you but I don't want to lose him, Skye. He's our little brother.'

'Seriously, Sun. I have to get these stories done for the paper. Won't the intervention be enough to sort this out?'

'Take the morning off. Get the booze out of your system and find Airen. Talk to him. Sort it out, then get on with the rest of your day.'

'I said I'd go to Grandma's, give her a hand, try to get her out of the house.'

Sun shook her head in a firm 'no'.

'First things first,' she said. 'Grandma would want you to see Airen. We can sort out her problems later.'

Skye stared longingly at the pale green sleeping bag where she'd spent a dreamless wine-sodden couple of hours. All she wanted to do was crawl back inside the cocoon and go back to sleep.

'Okay, if it helps I'll do it.' She didn't know where the words came from but they were out there.

Sun reached across the bench top, placed her hand over the top of Skye's and squeezed.

'I have a good feeling about this.' Sun's eyes crinkled at the corners and her lips curved into a half formed smile. Almost convincing. But Skye knew bravado when she saw it.

Skye left her hand where it was. Wishing she was brave but feeling like a coward.

* * *

Heading in an easterly direction towards the beach, the Karmarama Surf Shop was on the right-hand side of the street, in the building that abutted *The Northern Sun* newspaper premises. Out the back was the board shaping factory where Airen 'worked' if he was up to it.

Skye walked around the block, building up the nerve to step inside to find her brother. She stood outside the shop and did some slow breathing exercises, shaking her arms and inhaling into her belly.

When a hand latched onto her upper arm, she nearly leapt out of her skin.

'Good grief, Cal. What the hell?' Skye brushed at her shirt as Cal apologised profusely.

When his eyes met hers, she surprised herself by feeling fine, yet again. No heart flutters, butterflies or wobbly legs. No instant attraction. No Prince *I would die for you* or Barry White *You're The First, The Last, My Everything* spinning in her head like a mirror ball.

If anything, her former fiancé's sudden appearance irritated her. Her agenda did not include Cal.

Cal glanced at his watch. She noted that it was different from the one on his wrist the night Airen got into the fight at the pub.

This suave time piece had a black leather band and a silver face. Cal's reddish-blond arm hairs sprung up around the band. On the other wrist he wore a thick gold-link bracelet.

'I've got time for a coffee. What about you?'

Skye slung her bag higher onto her shoulder and folded her arms across her chest.

'I'd like to but I can't.' She almost mentioned her reason for standing outside the surf shop but decided against it. Cal would definitely send a text to Krystle if Skye gave anything away about her intention to catch up with Airen. The news would be all over town like a rash on a baby's bottom.

'I have appointments,' she said. 'I'm helping Sun, writing a couple of real estate stories for the paper.'

Cal's tanned baby face creased into a grin. His teeth were so white that Skye bet they'd been cosmetically treated. He placed the palms of his hands together as if he was about to pray.

'Pretty please. Five minutes? My shout.'

Skye shrugged. Maybe another coffee would get rid of the hangover headache and give her the boost she needed to deal with her brother.

Cal ushered her into Rusty's Cafe, his hand light on her back. Skye's senses screamed invasion. The touch was way too intimate and presumptuous.

They sat at a small table near the big timber-framed front window of the cosy establishment that hadn't been around three years ago. It was neat, clean and smelled of freshly ground coffee beans. A blackboard menu with the day's specials hung behind a counter where a small cabinet displayed brought-in croissants, muffins and cinnamon and raisin scrolls.

'This used to be a bike-hire shop,' she said after they ordered their coffees.

'Yeah, it expanded.' Cal wore grey suit pants and a white shirt, opened at the collar to reveal tufts of reddish chest hair. He had the appearance of a man who was well off and well fed, Skye thought.

'Town's changing,' he said. 'Bike shop's moved around the corner, opposite the beach. It's added dive gear and kayak hire to the mix. Dezzy's not like it was when you left, Skye. More people wanna come here for their holidays and make their lives here. More businesses are keen to get involved in the place. It's booming and it's time to get in on the boom.'

Skye leaned back and assessed her 'ex' more closely, suspicious of every word of the salesman spiel.

A lanky male waiter, no older than seventeen with shoulder length, sun-bleached hair, placed their coffees on the table. Cal had ordered a scroll with his. It came, all sticky bun studded with tiny black raisins, on a white plate with a paper serviette.

Cal tore off a piece of scroll. He stared into her eyes, his lips slightly parted, and Skye wanted to laugh. It was the glassy blue stare he used to put on when he wanted something. Usually sex. But surely he couldn't be flirting with her now?

She broke her gaze from his. She needed to make her position clear. 'Yeah, things have changed. A lot.' *If you catch my drift.*

She sipped her coffee but it didn't taste half as good as the blend at The Old Bakery where Fletcher worked. She lowered the cup into the saucer and waited.

Cal washed down half the scroll with a gulp of hot liquid and winced a little.

He wiped his fingers on the edge of the serviette. 'Changing the subject briefly - you look amazing. I know I've already said it but 'hot' is the word I would use.'

Skye cringed inwardly. Krystle could have him.

'Um, thanks, if that's supposed to be a compliment. You were always so good at dishing them out.'

She hoped he noticed the sarcasm but doubted it.

As if to confirm her thoughts, he steamrolled on. 'Are you serious about this bloke back in Sydney?'

Skye hesitated. She'd only been away for a couple of days, yet life with Beau seemed like a distant memory. Since their last conversation, which hadn't gone well, they'd exchanged short text messages to each other. But that was all.

It made her uneasy that the certainty she'd built around her relationship with Beau had collapsed. All she ever wanted was order in her life and for her plans to be played out sequentially.

City Skye and coastal town Skye were caught in a wrestle hold. There wasn't a door Skye could walk through to move between the two worlds. They were vastly different.

She stirred her teaspoon across the creamy film on top of the coffee, just for something to do. Fletcher flitted across her mind.

'Beau's a fantastic human being, you'd like him,' she said but Fletcher's life-embracing smile and eyes clear as a rock pool stuck in her head like a catchy Pharell Williams song.

Her non-answer had Cal stumped, she could tell. He frowned and pouted, his big lips rolling outwards like two caterpillars, one lolling on top of the other.

'Cool,' he finally said.

'And Krystle? Are you two happily engaged? Married?' There, she'd done it. Asked the question, and it didn't hurt a bit.

'Nah.' The creases in his forehead deepened. He rubbed the back of his bull-like neck. 'Krystle's not like you Skye. Not to say she's not good value. But geez, talk about possessive. Jealous even. I said we should take a break, like time out from each other, but she's not into it. No way José.'

Skye got why Krystle wouldn't want to loosen the leash. Once Cal broke free, there'd be no stopping him. For a moment, she felt sorry for Cal. And Krystle. But then again, they did deserve one another.

'It's been nice to see you but I've got to go.' She inched out of her chair.

Cal raised a meaty hand.

'Give me one more minute,' he said through a mouth filled with the sugary pastry. 'I wanna run something by you.'

Skye narrowed her eyes and eased back into her seat. She pushed the untouched coffee to one side. Of course there was a hidden agenda. There always was with Cal.

He dipped the last piece of scroll into the coffee and finished both. Still chewing, he leaned both elbows on the table, palms down and fingers in her direction. His shirt strained against his bulky torso and his neck bulged. His hair had been longer and covered his ears when they'd been together. Now they stuck out, ruddy and shaped like two mangled abalone shells.

He cleared his throat. 'Your sister would've filled you in on the mining licences.'

'Yes. And?' Skye viewed him through narrowed eyes. So this was why he was so eager to buy her a coffee? It had nothing to do with his rekindled feelings for her but everything to do with a project that would bring huge financial benefits to the Sturgess family.

'If you want my opinion, Skye, there's been a bit of an overreaction around town. These coal companies don't just waltz into communities like ours without doing their homework. They've taken every precaution to ensure that any drilling doesn't impact on the water table in any way, shape or form whatsoever.'

Skye kept her voice steady. 'I heard a different story.'

Cal snorted out a laugh and his nostrils expanded to reveal black nose hairs. Why hadn't she noticed this when they were an item?

'Of course you have. Because that's the angle Sun's taking. She's got the whole town up in arms.' His tone was incredulous, patronising, disbelieving.

'She's doing a Jonno but she hasn't done her background checks properly. Your sister's got the greenies, nimbys, youth, Indigenous agitators and cultural elites on side, but she doesn't get it.'

Skye wondered if Cal had done any of his own research, if he'd bothered to twiddle the radio dial away from the shock jocks and check on the veracity of the information from politicians with dollar signs lighting up their eyes.

His eyes had a feverish glow and he craned forward, his neck turned bright red. He wasn't going to listen to anything she said, so she waited for the next barrage. She leaned into the back of her chair as he wagged a finger at her.

'These mining people aren't like the developers who were after The Point. They've got the government's full endorsement. They won't stop 'til they get what they want. So Sun and her followers are causing all this trouble for nothing.'

His hands whirred through the air as he wound himself up for the final pitch. Skye watched, fascinated, as his face turned a deeper shade of tomato sauce red.

Dezzy was such a beautiful part of the world, admired for its stunning pristine coastline and verdant hinterland, dotted with national parks and farming communities that grew beef and dairy and orchards and crops.

That's the part Skye didn't understand. Why put all of that at risk?

'The thing is Skye, the thing is this. This coal seam gas drilling could make Dezzy wealthy. It can only be good for the town.'

'And how is that Cal?'

He was so wound up, he could barely focus on her as he spoke. She was sure he was thinking about the new Audi, the new mansion with a chef's kitchen and butler's pantry, seven bedrooms (all with ensuites), media room, pool, spa, tennis court, ten-car garage and full automation. And a big rock for Krystle's wedding band finger.

'If coal seam gas is here on our land, and it is, the people of this town could get richer than houses. We'll be set for life. Our kids, Skye, they'll inherit this incredible wealth that's there below the surface. And our kids' kids and so on and so forth. It's a win-win situation but your sister's trying to put the kibosh on it. She's muddying the waters Skye. Confusing some of our older residents, making the farming community worried about methane, pollution, water tables, artesian bloody basins and all that crap.'

Skye tilted her head up and down to ease the tightness that had spread from upper back to shoulders to neck.

She stared directly into his eyes. 'What do you want me to do about it Cal? Wouldn't it be better to take this up with Sun, go to her directly and present your views?'

Glassy eyes blinked back at hers. 'Yeah, well, you know me and your family. We never really hit it off.'

At least he wasn't that dense, Skye thought. During their brief time together, she'd always gone over to Cal's place, never the other way around. Not even her mother, who was into Buddhism and forgiveness, invited Cal into their home.

Skye recalled an argument she had with Oceane/Donna/her mother about Cal, a year into their relationship.

Skye had asked her mother, 'Isn't Buddhism about being nice to every creature on the planet because in a past life they could have been your brother, sister or best friend? If you follow the dharma, why can't you find it in your heart to accept Cal for who he is?'

Her mother had replied, 'Because I'm not yet enlightened and as long as I remain unenlightened I cannot accept Cal as your boyfriend.'

'That's a piss-weak excuse.'

Oceane had smiled beatifically.

'He's a dickhead Skye. One day you'll realise that.'

Today was that day.

CHAPTER 16

Karmarama Surf Shop reminded Skye of happier times. In the 1980s it had been a destination shop for surfers from around the country.

As a teenager, Skye hung out there on the days the surf was messy chop or flatter than the Simpson Desert.

The shop hadn't changed much but the back section had been extended to include a wider range of surf wear and must-have accessories like sunglasses, wallets and beach-themed jewellery.

The front remained dedicated to its original core product, quality hand-crafted surfboards and windsurfers. Boards of different shapes and sizes were filed vertically into racks that lined the right and left walls from 5'5' shortboards to 10' guns - longboards with attitude.

In the middle of the floor was a large glass display cabinet that contained two Thrusters from the 1980s, iconic short boards signed by their inventor, legendary Australian surfer Simon Anderson.

Skye marvelled that they were still there after all these years. She used to dream about smashing the glass and hot-footing it down to the beach with a Thruster under each arm.

She pushed open the heavy glass door with a surfboard-shaped silver handle and stepped inside.

Fleetwood Mac's *Second Hand News* played though the sound system. Skye's spirits lifted. Fleetwood Mac had that effect.

Maybe things would be good between her and Airen. The blame game would dissipate like dew in the morning sun once they met under the dome of sobriety and newfound mutual respect.

If only it could be that simple.

The acid-coated tongue that hissed in her psyche after Jonno's death weedled its way back into her thoughts.

Dad would still be alive if Airen hadn't stuffed up.

No one was around so she gravitated towards one of the board walls along the left-hand side of the room, humming to Fleetwood Mac as she went, trying to tamp down the anxiety.

The boards were gleaming epoxy-resin sealed objets d'art, every one of them demanding her attention.

A slender longboard the colour of golden wheat caught her eye. A perfect line ran down its centre. This wasn't just decorative but a 'stringer' made from wood used to strengthen the surfboard foam. Skye guessed this particular stringer was red cedar.

Her fingers ran lightly across the rails of several more boards. She paused at a board that, once upon a time, would have been added to her list of 'Boards I Would Like To Own'.

The list was capped at twenty and Skye used to update it on a regular basis. She saved up enough to buy four boards on her list. Three of those were still around, probably under

Grandma's house. The other one... smashed to smithereens the night Jonno died.

It had been her favourite, an all-purpose board designed by yet another legend of the Australian surfing community, Mick Fanning.

A slender mocha-cream-coloured leaf shape with a pointed nose, square-tipped tail and twin fins setup, it skimmed down the face of a wave with Skye's feet dancing lightly across its waxed surface. On that board she was the Queen of the Surf, a ballerina in a wetsuit pirouetting her way across the clean crystalline surface of every perfect wave that emerged into fleeting existence.

A perfect wave was like a butterfly, she thought. A joyful experience. Over in moments. Savoured forever.

A tremor ran through Skye as a buzzing sound started up towards the back of the premises. The shaping factory was out the back in the old converted garage. Airen had picked up some work there after losing his rugby league contract.

Skye walked to the back half of the shop and spotted a shop assistant restocking a '50 per cent off' clothes rack. The diminutive woman-child wore calf-high chocolate-brown Ugg Boots, minuscule denim shorts and a white lace top that revealed her midriff and tattoo on her lower back in a calligraphic flourish: *This too will pass.*

Skye suppressed a smile. She wondered if anyone had pointed out the tattoo's unfortunate position and wording.

'Hi there,' the assistant said in a little-girl voice. She pulled her dyed silver-blonde hair into a pony-tail to reveal two huge silver hoop earrings on bud-like ears lined with stud piercings the colours of the rainbow.

'Can I help with anything?' She chewed on a piece of gum.

She had a sweet elfin face but Skye would struggle to pick her out in a police line-up if the makeup was removed.

Skye got straight to the point. 'I'm looking for Airen Summerhayes.'

Underneath the false lashes and eyeliner, the girl's eyes widened. Skye noted their colour, Bratz-doll blue. Definitely tinted contact lenses.

'Are you his sister? I mean, I know Sun but you're the other one. I can see it. The resemblance. In the nose.'

The girl behaved like she'd struck gold. She tucked stray hairs behind her ears before extending a hand. Skye stared at the wrist as fine as a swallow bone, weighed down by a jangle of red, black and yellow plastic bangles, and a little hand, each finger swamped by a ring or rings.

Chewing furiously. 'I'm Ash-Lee. That's two words - Ash and Lee. Spelt L-E-E but with a hyphen in between the Ash and the Lee. Last name's Watson.'

While they shook hands, Ash-Lee jumped up and down on the spot like she was on a pogo stick.

'I know, I got it, I got it.' She pulled her hand away and pointed at Skye. 'You're Skye. It's Sun, Skye, Air-en,' She counted off on her fingers. 'That's cool enough but like, all you needed was Moon and Earth to make it totes amaze-balls. Like, Gwyneth Paltrow and Chris Martin should've done the whole fruit thing. What's an Apple without a Banana without a... a... Cucumber! Oh. Is that a fruit?'

Skye had never had that one thrown at her before. She couldn't figure out if Ash-Lee was fifteen or twenty-five. Or if she was playing dumb. Or not.

'My hippy mother wanted something a bit different but not embarrassingly so,' Skye said with a smile, knowing she sounded like a patronising snob.

'Well, it's nice to meet you. Real nice. Airen doesn't say much about you though. He talks about Sun but you're the...' Ash-Lee chewed hard and frowned before a smile lit up her pretty features, '...the missing link.'

'Possibly.' Skye wasn't sure if she should take that as a compliment.

Ash-Lee chewed thoughtfully, rolling the gum around in her mouth as she regarded Skye. 'Now I remember, you're the surfer,' she said, nodding sagely. 'Airen said you won a couple of major comps.'

Skye blew out hard. She didn't have time for a conversation about her own wasted potential. She checked her watch and stared pointedly at Ash-Lee.

'I'm sorry, I'm in a bit of a rush...'

'Airen's not here,' Ash-Lee interrupted.

Skye had worked herself up for the inevitable and now a cement block of disappointment hurtled towards her from a great height. She desperately needed to get this over and done with.

'Do you know where he is?'

Ash-Lee cocked her head and folded her arms over the visible strip of flat-tanned stomach. Thinking again.

'Well,' she drew out the word and tilted her head. 'He could be at Grandma's. But I know he's not hanging there much because he's scared of bumping into you or your Mum, I mean, Oceane. Gotta love that name. Oceane. If she marries Jimmy, she'll be Oceane Trout.'

As if Skye hadn't already considered that unfortunate union. And merging of names.

Ash-Lee meandered on. 'Um, he might be at my place but...' She frowned at Skye, as if considering whether to share more information.

No one had told her Airen had a girlfriend. 'Are you his...?' Skye paused.

Ash-Lee twitched her cute button nose with a pierced nostril. 'I'm a friend.' She smiled. 'Helping out. Airen's nice, real nice. I'm available if he needs me.'

The sincerity in Ash-Lee's tone hit a nerve.

I haven't been available for three years.

Instead, Skye persisted. 'Is it possible to find out where he is? Can you call him?'

Ash-Lee shuffled uneasily, her startlingly blue eyes suddenly wary. 'His phone's always turned off. Maybe Brad knows.'

Brad Cherry was the local board shaper. He'd been a good friend to the Summerhayes family for as long as Skye could remember.

Brad and his wife Danielle had a son Scott, who was on the autism spectrum.

Skye recalled a story in the *The Northern Sun* about the community's efforts to raise money towards a deposit on a new house with a pool for the family. They could no longer cope with their son's needs in a two-bedroom townhouse.

Skye had spent many afternoons during her adolescence watching Brad at work. At one point, when she was sixteen, she considered shaping as a career because of the flexible hours that allowed her to surf when the conditions were optimum. But it was hard yakka and she didn't have the patience for the job.

Skye nodded at the exit at the rear of the shop. 'Is Brad out the back?'

Ash-Lee nodded a slow 'yes'.

'He should be cool,' she said. 'I can't go with you but I'm sure you know where it is. I gotta stay here in case any little shits sneak in to nick stuff.'

Skye thanked Ash-Lee, left the shop and crossed the court-yard to a separate building. It was single-storey rectangular fibro, with a corrugated iron roof. As she approached, the buzzing of the sander stopped. The plain timber front door was ajar.

Skye tapped on the door. 'Brad?'

A bald middle-aged man wearing a Hawaii shirt, board shorts and black thongs emerged from a room on the right-hand side of a short corridor. Goggles protected his eyes and a white mask his nose and mouth. Otherwise, he was covered from top to toe in a white dust from the surfboard foam. The superfine particles settled on the hairs of his burly arms and legs like a fine layer of icing sugar.

'Skye.' As he removed the goggles, Brad's grey eyes creased at the corners.

'I won't touch you,' Skye said though she really could have done with a hug from this big bear of a man. He was a friend she could trust.

Brad pulled down the mask and gave Skye an appraising glance.

'Too skinny,' was his assessment.

Skye threw back at him, 'Too bald. What happened to that beautiful wavy black hair?'

He ran a hand over his smooth dome. 'Losing it fast so I shaved off the rest. Way to go.'

'Yeah.' Skye smiled. If anything, the bald head suited him and drew full attention to his kind eyes. 'How are Danielle and Scotty going?'

The eyes lost their sparkle and, almost imperceptibly, Brad's shoulders slumped. 'Fine, all good. We've got a place with a pool. Scotty loves to splash around. It's made a big difference.'

Skye held her breath, feeling his discomfort, but he quickly recovered and pulled his large frame up to full height. She knew not to ask more personal questions.

'S'pose you're here to see Airen but he's not in,' he continued as if no awkward moment had just passed between them. 'I'm doin' one of his jobs. Not too happy about it either.'

'Sorry about that. Do you have any idea where he might be?'

Brad's happy round face dominated by a bulbous nose deflated again.

'Try the pub. He's more of a regular than your dad.'

Skye let it go. Everybody knew about Jonno's notorious drinking bouts. And everyone forgave him, especially Skye.

'It's that bad?'

Brad scratched behind his ear. 'We thought Airen was back in the driver's seat. The footy scouts from the city come to Dezzy to check him out. He was off the piss, drugs, eatin' healthy, swimmin', surfin'. He was in great shape. Like the old Airen. And he was tearin' up and down the paddock like a pro. They would have took him Skye. The blokes at the top wanted him back in the premier league.'

Brad readjusted his bread-loaf shoulders and shook his head sadly. 'But then it all went to shit again. Dunno if I can keep him on here. I done me best. We all done our best to help him through it. He was like a son to me. That makes it hurt even more. It's a shame. A bloody shame. Airen was a lovely bloke.'

Skye chewed her bottom lip. He was talking in the past tense as though Airen was dead. Her heart sank Titanic-style. Slowly, slowly, slowly, and then with a mighty plunge, to the bottom of a freezing ocean.

Her smile was bitter. 'I guess the pub's my next stop then.'

CHAPTER 17

She saw him first. He sat on a stool, his lean body a 'C' shape, elbows on the bar and head in hands. He'd moved the schooner of beer to one side.

Features hidden, Airen could have been any one of his drinking comrades. He represented each and every one of them. Drowning in treacherous waters in solitary despair.

It was mid-morning on a sunny winter's day, with storm clouds on the horizon. Her brother chose to spend it in a lightless den that stank of stale beer, cigarettes and body odour.

As though he felt her presence, Airen lifted his head and turned in her direction. He picked up his glass and raised it to just beneath his eyes as she closed the space between them.

'Only a matter of time before we met again,' he said, as Skye hoiked her bag on to the bar top and pulled up a stool. She forced herself to ignore the sarcasm and sat beside him. She dragged the hem of her black pencil skirt towards her knees and hooked her ankles around thin metal stool legs.

Several other serious drinkers were scattered across the main bar, each alone and each nursing a schooner glass of their favoured 'poison'. Their dull eyes were affixed to the midweek horse racing on a flat-screen TV with the volume down on the wall at the end of the room.

Airen was by far the youngest.

At least he's not blowing all his dough on the gee-gees, Skye thought, and immediately regretted her meanness. She had to get her 'loving kindness' mantra out before the conversation started, or she'd blow it. Big time.

'Brad said I'd find you here,' she said, relieved when the bartender approached. She recalled his face from high school. He might have been in the year above hers but she couldn't remember his name.

Usually when her memory lapsed, she ran through the alphabet for a trigger: A for Adam, Aiden, Alex; B for Barney, Bryce; C for Chris, Charlie, D for Daniel, etcetera. But she couldn't be bothered with this guy.

It was enough to focus her depleted mental energy on A for Airen.

'Skye, long time no see,' the bartender said, with way too much familiarity.

'Hi,' she answered without enthusiasm but made an effort at politeness. 'How's it going?'

He was a small stringy man with a thin goatee beard and greasy brown hair that needed a trim.

He peered at Airen as he spoke. 'Could be worse, could be worse. Gotta job at least, gotta place, gotta life.'

Skye would have liked nothing better than to wipe the idiot grin off his ugly mug but that wasn't an option. He planted grubby fingers on the bar and she shuddered at his black-rimmed fingernails.

That awful leer again. He pointed at Airen's beverage. 'Same as ya brother's?'

Skye smiled, saccharine sweet. 'Lemon, lime and bitters.'

Airen held up his glass. Hadn't he noticed goat man's lack of respect? 'Another one for me, mate. My sister's got it.'

Skye wanted to say, 'But you haven't finished this one yet,' and to ask, 'How much have you drunk already?' And to beg, 'Please don't have another drink. Please don't screw up your life again.'

She watched as goat man lifted a clean schooner glass to one of the silver taps in a row of half a dozen. He pulled the sleek lever that shimmered with droplets of condensation. It released a rush of aerated liquid gold with a creamy head. In that moment, Skye could understand the allure as she inhaled the fermented yeast and nutty hops.

Airen was around two schooners into a long day, she guessed.

Not yet blotto, hammered, stonkered, off his face or whatever you wanted to call it, but well on his way to viewing the world through beer goggles.

They were silent until goat man set down their drinks. Skye ignored him and left cash on the bar.

'Do you want to sit outside?'

Surprisingly Airen agreed and they walked past goat man, who seemed disappointed. Under her breath, Skye muttered, 'Creep.'

Entering the beer garden, she stopped and blinked in the sunlight.

It was almost empty. They had their pick of the long timber benches in the middle of the courtyard and shorter tables along the perimeter wall.

Airen placed both his glasses of beer on one of the benches, under the shade of an oak tree, and sat down. As he slurped the head off the freshly poured glass, Skye slid in on the opposite side of the bench.

The bruises on his cheeks from the pub brawl were a mottled purple. His right eye appeared to be glued shut, the maroon-coloured upper lid zipped to the lower lid. His other eye was bloodshot and watery.

Skye's eyes were hazel, Sun's amber and Airen's brown. Oceane called Airen her 'brown-eyed boy'. Large soulful pools the colour of burnt caramel. Everyone who met Airen commented on those eyes.

He was the baby of the family, the son her father always wanted. It wasn't as though her parents weren't trying to get pregnant after Skye's birth. It took 10 years that included several miscarriages.

'I was happy with two daughters but your father was desperate for an heir,' Oceane once told her. 'Though I always wondered, 'heir to what?''

Of course, Airen was spoilt. Or Skye thought so. Spoilt meaning everything he did, every move he made was regarded in awe by his adoring parents.

Airen crawled early, walked early and talked early. He picked up a footy and booted it over the fence almost as soon as he could walk. He took to the surf like a pro at the age of four and, aged six, demanded his father buy him a surfboard and teach him to surf.

Skye found herself squeezed in between confident, self-assured Sun and prodigiously talented Airen.

She had to work hard to achieve her nerdy academic reputation and practise surfing every day after school to become a competent athlete. To become as good as Sun and Airen. Good at everything.

Grandma was the only family member who had a somewhat different perspective on the topic of Airen, the child genius.

'I don't know what will become of that boy,' she confided to Skye after his peers voted the then eleven-year-old Airen into the role of school captain in year six.

'What do you mean?' Skye asked.

Airen was always going to be school captain. It was a given.

'It's been too easy love, way too easy. That boy, and don't think I don't know he's gorgeous and talented and could charm the pants off a snake, but that boy has been molly-coddled by your mother and father since he came into the world, and one day it will all go awry. I like that word, 'awry'. How do you pronounce it properly?'

Skye frowned hard at her brother now and searched for the old Airen under the bruising and self-inflicted neglect.

Airen was one of those rare beings who oozed the x-factor.

Women loved him. He was cheeky and irreverent, and there was always something indefinably vulnerable about him that made girls want to take him home.

Airen had it all. His long glossy dark hair flew like a banner as he sprinted, fleet-footed, across the rugby league field or down to the surf.

His limbs were longer and his frame lighter than those of the majority of his rugby league playing peers, yet his physical strength was undeniable.

At 84 kilograms and 5'10', he was a rippling, ripped god of speed.

His feet almost skimmed above the earth as he ran. Skye, a fan of ancient Greece at school, thought Airen had a lot in common with the Olympian god Hermes who wore winged sandals and was a messenger, thief, inventor, athlete, fighter and chief of commerce.

When Airen was sixteen, Skye attended the local high school athletics carnival to report on the event for *The*

Northern Sun and ended up writing a story around Airen's domination of the 100, 200 and 400m sprints, and the hurdles.

Airen could have turned pro surfer but the rugby league talent scouts spotted him. Already a local star, he played half-back for the Dezzy Bay Tiger Sharks. He travelled to Sydney, aged eighteen, all expenses paid, to play in the National Youth Competition.

Airen was poised to become Dezzy's first premiere league player, a star at the age of nineteen.

He returned to Dezzy to get all his gear organised for a permanent move to Sydney where he'd been recruited to a big-name team, the details still under wraps.

Skye often thought their father would still be alive if Airen hadn't turned up for that one last hurrah that coincided with the town's victory over the developers.

These days Airen was better known as an alcoholic, no longer 'functioning'.

He smiled at Skye. 'Whenever I come out here to the beer garden, I think about your twenty first and the balloon incident,' he said.

Skye would have preferred to forget the balloon incident. And her twenty first. But it turned into a family story retold so often that it became embedded in Summerhayes' family lore.

Airen finished off the first schooner. 'What a fucking excellent night that was.'

Skye thought differently. On the day of her twenty-first birthday party, to be held in the beer garden, she, her mother and Sun strung pretty Chinese lanterns from one side of the courtyard to the other. They formed a criss-cross pattern Skye had mapped out on white cardboard beforehand, along with seating arrangements and the order in which the evening's events would unfold.

Eleven-year-old Airen bagsed the job of blowing up party balloons with helium from a hired gas bottle.

She should have known the evening would end in disaster.

The three women were almost rolling around in hysterics after Airen, who had sucked on a helium-filled balloon, piped up with, 'I squeaks-es like meeces.'

Revved by their laughter, he did it again. 'I hate those damn meeces to pieces.'

And again. 'Meeces, pieces, meeces, pieces, hee hee hee, hee hee hee.'

Skye was on a step ladder, adding the final touches to her lanterns, when Airen fainted. She watched in appalled amazement as his knees crumpled and he went down like a swooning silent-film heroine.

At the hospital, the on-duty intern inserted the stitches to close a small wound where his head had clipped the side of a table.

The party went ahead but Skye didn't feel like the star attraction. Much of the attention was centred on her little brother, nursing his sore head and playing it up for all it was worth.

In a way, it became Airen's night. 'Poor little bloke', 'How's Airen?', 'Did you see it happen Skye?' 'Geez, he's a character.'

Airen showing concerned partygoers the small patch of shaved head with three neat stitches, Airen re-enacting the balloon jokes (without inhaling the helium that had deprived his lungs of oxygen), Airen doing the funny high voice.

Airen, Airen, Airen.

It was always about Airen.

Funny how history repeated.

Airen gulped the beer and examined the remaining contents of the schooner. 'Who told you I was here?'

'I met Ash-Lee then Brad.'

A thin slice of lime floated near the bottom of Skye's glass. She poked it with a straw. She hadn't given any thought to what she would say to Airen. He drew another slug from his glass and one more to drain it. He wasn't going to make it any easier for her.

'Ash-Lee's nice. Are you seeing her?' she prompted.

Airen's lip curled and he scowled in her general direction. Animosity crackled in him like live wires.

'What does that mean? Seeing her?'

'I dunno. That you're dating. That you like her maybe.'

'What you mean is, am I fucking her? The answer is 'yes'.'

'I didn't... that's not what...'

'Let's get to the point here Skye, let's not fuck around with small talk or that evasive bullshit you crap on with, like you're circling me, like a vulture or something.'

Skye raised a hand, almost in defence. His words flew at her like rubber bullets. 'I didn't want to come here today,' she managed to get in before he went off on a rant, 'but Sun thought it would be good for us to meet before the barbecue on Saturday.'

'Why did you come then? Because Sun ordered you? Not because you give a fuck but because Sun got on your back, like she always does. Some things never change.'

The words were spat out and a smirk of disgust blurred his mottled features.

Skye counted to three in her head to get grounded. Then she said, 'I came to make peace. I didn't want to have an argument.'

Airen, now more than three drinks into his day, seemed to change down a gear.

It killed Skye to see his once beautiful face. It was such a mess. No longer Hermes, he was now a skier caught in an avalanche of his own making. Out of control. But it was happening in slow motion. And he was becoming part of the whole horrific process. Caught in the maelstrom of a suffocating crystal cloud, bits of him slowly falling away into the gaping crevasse.

'Shit,' Airen said. 'And you call yourself a journalist. Peace? Sounds like cowboys and Indians. Gotta pipe? I'll have some of that.'

'Airen, I didn't come here to put up with this. You're making it hard for us to have a real conversation.'

'I didn't ask you to come back home, Skye.'

'I know but I'm here. I came to see you. You're the reason.'

His hands were jammed around the empty glass, knuckles still bruised from the pub fight.

He observed her with his one good eye and Skye flinched.

'Okay, if we're playing fair, you need to tell me the truth,' he said, suddenly serious and sounding sober.

An early lunchtime crowd started to trickle into the beer garden. Seeking shade, several backpackers sat at the other end of the long bench. The girls were both straw-blonde, the boy dark and swarthy. They were laughing and trying to communicate with each other in stilted English.

Skye lowered her voice.

'The truth has already been told Airen. Can't you let it go?'

At that, Airen slammed his glass on the table. One of the female backpackers let out a startled squeal and everyone stared in their direction, including several locals whose faces Skye recognised but couldn't place.

She kept her voice soft and even, despite the constriction in her throat. 'I'm sorry, maybe this wasn't a good idea after all. Maybe it's best if we talk about it on Saturday at Grandma's.'

Airen stood up and pushed himself away from the bench with such force that the schooner glass fell and splintered into sharp shards on the terracotta paving.

He ran shaking hands through his knotted hair.

'This is what you do Skye. You piss off to Sydney without telling anyone the truth about how Dad died. And now you're back, you still won't tell us. You're full of shit. You're as fucked up as I am but you won't admit it. You're in total denial.'

Skye stood up, her face hot with embarrassment. She hated being in the spotlight, especially when it was so large and Dezzy was so small.

People whispered behind their hands and the backpackers were too terrified to move. None of this seemed to bother Airen. He must have been past caring.

'Fuck Skye, life's not all about appearances and ticking off neat little boxes.'

Skye clenched and unclenched her fists, heart pounding. 'You don't know anything about me, about what it takes to get somewhere, to make something of yourself. I've worked my arse off to do something meaningful with my life.'

Airen snorted in derision. 'Like what? Hanging out with wankers in Sydney and writing about the mansions of arsehole billionaires?'

Skye's mouth was open and she was ready to blast Airen with her own views about his empty life when, out of the corner of her eye, she spotted goat man with his smart phone pointed in their direction.

Something inside her snapped, like a branch breaking off a tree without warning. Her boots scrunched on the broken glass as she strode towards him, Airen's taunt momentarily forgotten.

In an instant, it all came back to her. She recognised goat man. All those years ago, when she was a teenager, he and his yobbo mates had taunted her as she ran down the beach with her board.

They'd shouted, 'Show us ya tits slut, show us ya fuckin' tits.'

Enraged, she sneered, 'Give me the phone you prick. Now.'

A thrill of satisfaction galvanised her as she saw a glint of fear in his eyes.

'If you put that photo on any social media or give it to any low-life journalist to use, my family will sue your butt off and make sure you never work in this town again.'

The clichés tumbled out but she liked the sound of it. Better still was his panicked reaction. Goat man shoved the phone in his pocket and waved his hands randomly at her. Small beads of sweat huddled together like stagnant globules on his greasy brow. His small current eyes popped.

'It's a free country,' he whimpered.

Skye pounced like a lioness. 'We're not at school anymore, creep. And this country isn't as free as it used to be when people like you were allowed to get away with bullying and sexual harassment. Don't think I don't remember you and your loser mates. There's safety in numbers but you don't have that anymore, do you?'

She got as close to him as she could bear, smelling his rolled-cigarette breath. Then dropped her voice to a low monotone. 'I'm engaged to a barrister and my best friend's a cop,' she lied with ease. 'Delete whatever is on that phone right now or I'll make you pay for this, big time.'

Goat man hesitated. 'This is a threat. You're threatening me.' He reluctantly dug in his pocket and pulled out the phone.

Skye grabbed it off him and clicked on a video of Airen, who screamed like a madman at a dumbstruck Skye. She swiped 'delete'.

'That's all?' Skye demanded.

Goat man nodded fast.

'Good.' Then, using her best overarm, she hurled the phone over the courtyard garden's back wall and into, she was fairly certain, a thicket of the spiky weed lantana on the other side.

Goat man glowed red with impotent fury.

'Fark me. That's my new phone you bitch.'

Skye smiled benignly and shrugged. 'Sorry about that.'

She scanned the beer garden for Airen but her baby brother had disappeared. The wings on his sandals propelling him further out of her reach.

CHAPTER 18

Two days flew by in a blur as Sun called upon Skye to write several more stories for *The Northern Sun.*

The proposed installation of a skate park near the beach, the move to save a block of uncleared land (home to an endangered species of frog), the launch of a new small craft business 'Crafty old chooks', and a local court case that involved a group of lads who had the not-so-bright idea to start a bonfire next to a bushland reserve.

Skye hated to admit it, but she was having fun. The variety of the content invigorated her. People thanked her for talking to them and telling their stories. The Desiree Bay Council staff were pleased the messages about the long range storm forecasts were being reported in the local paper and small businesses were grateful for the free publicity.

It was rewarding work. It meant something. It made her feel good.

Saturday had come around too soon. And with it, the realisation that her week in Dezzy was almost over. Tomorrow, she would head back to Sydney to complete that part of her plan that required her to climb a career ladder. She didn't have the time to consider where the ladder went or if it ever ended. It had always been on her list. A box that must be ticked.

She shoved Fletcher in the too hard basket. For the last two days, they'd barely seen each other. He left the house early to go to work. She returned late from work, intentionally. Fletcher was too much of a good thing and she was slowly becoming addicted.

She brought her attention back to the main reason for her presence in Desiree Bay. The nervous energy around the imminent intervention arose again in Skye as she hopped out of the car and walked towards Grandma's house.

Although she'd long ago made a pledge to vegetarianism, the aroma of savoury juices running onto the coals of a fired-up barbecue brought back a raft of happy memories. Those carefree moments during childhood when her family seemed cohesive and united. She understood how people became nostalgic about childhood. Hers, she recalled, was filled with love. And meat.

She imagined Grandma's house as it appeared to her as a youngster. Soft-focus pretty with an edible garden that often provided her family with fresh fruit and vegetables.

That was then. And now?

Today it was tired and run-down, the garden long gone.

In real estate parlance it would be described as 'a tightly-held and much-loved family home in need of a makeover. Or why not knock down and rebuild your dream home (subject to council approval)?'

But Skye wasn't there to write about the house. Today was the dreaded intervention, which Airen knew nothing about. The family gathering, slash, barbecue was a ruse to lure him there for a 'grilling'.

More like the Spanish Inquisition, Skye thought.

After the gruelling pre-intervention gathering on Tuesday night, Skye outright refused to attend a 'full dress rehearsal', where Jimmy volunteered to role-play Airen.

Skye couldn't believe it when Sun backed Jimmy and argued the case for it. 'It'll prepare us better for Airen's responses and stop us from reacting negatively,' Sun said.

But Skye stood firm in her own corner. 'An intervention's not like a school play. We don't need another rehearsal. Unless you invite Airen and give him his lines. If you want to do it, go ahead. But I won't be going.'

She won that round. The role play was abandoned and a consensus reached to 'roll with it' on the day.

Sun and Lou's white ute and Jimmy and Oceane's green Leyland P76 were parked in the driveway. Airen hadn't arrived. Skye checked her watch. It was almost midday.

Fletcher had pulled out of the afternoon at short notice. Smart move, Skye thought. His excuse related to his own 'personal' stuff that needed sorting out. Skye didn't delve any deeper. She had enough on her plate, and having Fletcher attend the intervention would distract her attention away from Airen.

She also felt relief for another reason. It was becoming harder to manage her growing attraction to him. Fletcher was putting her off her goals. A little more of her resolve to leave Desiree Bay slipped away every time she saw him. She couldn't think straight when he was around and hardly stopped thinking about him when he wasn't. It was a crush, nothing more, she told herself. Sure.

She could almost convince herself that her fantasy about what it would be like to be with him in the intimate sense could be erased once she left town.

She wondered if Fletcher thought about their relationship in that way. Flirty but nothing else. He liked her, she knew that for sure. There were moments at his place where she looked up and found him staring at her with those crystal clear blue eyes and that sensual mouth curved into a smile.

It was enough to curl up her toes. She knew what he was thinking. She was thinking it too. His smile turned her on like a bunch of fairy lights.

Skye tapped lightly on the front flyscreen door and opened it. Stepping into Grandma's lounge room, she took a deep breath and exhaled. It was going to be a long afternoon.

To Skye, it was clear that Jimmy had gone out of his way to annoy the crap out of her and push her to the edge of madness. He was there in full Celtic regalia. Kitted out in a bottle-green kilt cap with a red pom-pom, pressed white shirt and a tartan kilt, as if he was trying out for the Royal Edinburgh Military Tattoo. This gave Skye permission to roll her eyes a la Bette Davis and twist her mouth into a disapproving grimace.

'What is it that are you doing?' She didn't try to hide the snarkiness as Jimmy bent over and slipped something between the lounge cushion and its base. Thank goodness the kilt was long enough to cover his man bits. His thick muscled legs were bare to the calves and encased in bottle-green knee socks with a red horizontal stripe around the border. His black Blundstone boots had a spit-and-polish shine.

Braveheart meets boofhead, Skye mused.

Jimmy stood up and turned to her, all teeth and gummy smile. 'How are ya, Lass?'

She grudgingly noted that his teeth were in pretty good nick, for a Scot.

'As good as can be expected.' Rude and insolent, that's how she sounded. Like a child who resented her new stepfather.

She knew it and so did Jimmy but, and she had to hand it to him, he took it with good grace. This non-reactive approach to her behaviour made her want to fall face first on to a bed and punch a pillow with closed fists until millions of feathers flew around the room.

If Jimmy noticed her agitation, he chose to ignore it. He opened his palm to reveal an assortment of mauve and pale green gemstones. They seemed incongruous in such a big powerful hand. If he clenched it tight, the delicate stones might crumble into minute fragments.

'I'm working with amethyst today, placing these around the room to invite in positive Karmic energy. Amethyst is the sobriety stone and it's used to ward off drunkenness and addictive urges.'

With great effort, Skye warded off yet another drama-queen reaction, her eyes were already hurting. Instead, she set her features into perplexed enquiry. 'To be honest with you, I don't see how stuffing random rocks under Grandma's furniture is going to make any difference to today's outcome.'

'Every little bit counts, Lass. We're doing what we can.'

'Whatever.' More and more, Skye reminded herself of a recalcitrant teen. All she needed was a piece of Ash-Lee's gum to complete the effect.

'Where's Donna?' she asked with a smirk. Surely that would get a bite?

Jimmy answered quietly, 'Your mother, Oceane, is in the kitchen lighting the sage smudge stick for a cleansing before Airen gets here.'

Skye puffed out a sigh. Why had she bothered to ask?

As if on cue, her mother floated into the lounge room wearing a purple caftan and under it white leggings. The outfit was accessorised with a chunky amethyst necklace and matching bracelet. In one hand, she held up a smouldering object that looked like a mini witch's broom, a bunch of dried herbs bound by a string in the middle. In her other hand she carried a small bucket with a handle, which she held under the herbs to catch the falling ash. At least she was taking precautions. The last thing they needed was a fire in the lounge room.

She wandered past Skye as if she hadn't seen her, and across the room to the front door where she turned and walked in a clockwise direction.

The smoke wafted into the air as she dipped and raised her arm in a strange balletic movement. Skye half expected Jimmy to shout, 'Let the games begin.'

She considered leaving the room before it got too weird, but how could it get any weirder than this?

Seconds later, her mother snapped out of her trance-like state and called out a greeting. 'Skye, thank you for coming today. It means so much to everyone.'

She popped the still smouldering herbs into the bucket and handed it to Jimmy. They exchanged secret smiles. He squeezed her arm and she his.

'Darlin', will you extinguish this for me?' she asked.

Skye thought she detected a trace of a Scottish accent in her mother's voice. She was absorbing Jimmy's accent. Becoming Jimmy Trout.

Jimmy dutifully took the container and left the room.

'It's smudging,' Oceane explained to Skye, who realised her own mouth was open in an 'O' shape like a funfair clown. All she had to do was shake her head from side to side to look the part.

'I combined sage and lavender in a smudging stick to cleanse the negative energy from this space. We're starting afresh today.'

'Great.' Skye closed her mouth. She didn't know what else to say because she'd forgotten how to talk to her mother. This woman with the grey plait, pixie features and billowing caftans had become a stranger to her. The gap between them would take more than a bridge to close.

She walked into the kitchen, ignoring her mother's welling eyes. If Skye had somehow hurt her feelings, then so be it. She wasn't here to make amends with her mother, Donna, Oceane, or whatever she called herself this week.

The scene in the kitchen was one of domestic bliss. Lou chopped tomatoes on a timber cutting board while Grandma poured combined cake ingredients into a round tin lined with baking paper.

It was cosy and familiar. Warm and inviting. But Skye had stepped outside of it three years ago and an invisible line prevented her from hopping back in.

Grandma used a spatula to scrape the remaining cake mix from bowl to tin. 'Skye, Love, it's all happening at HQ. That's head quarters.' She chuckled as she smoothed the top of the cake.

The earthy scent of the sage and lavender smudge stick momentarily masked the aroma of steak, sausages and onions sizzling on the barbecue in the backyard. Through the open back door Skye saw Sun on barbecue duty, using tongs to turn the sausages.

Skye opened the heated oven for Grandma to slip the cake onto the rack. 'Must be hummingbird cake.'

It was Airen's favourite. A delicious cake made more luscious by the inclusion of tinned crushed pineapple, mashed bananas and sunflower oil. Because of Airen's allergic reaction to tree nuts, Grandma omitted the walnuts.

Skye closed the oven door. 'Can I do anything to help?'

Lou and Grandma chimed 'No' but Skye wanted to stay occupied to keep her mind from wandering, usually from Fletcher to Beau, and finally to Airen.

She checked outside again where a white tablecloth with embroidered lace trim covered a plastic outdoor table.

'I can set the table.'

Lou glanced up and smiled.

'I can't see why not. You're the neat one in the family.'

Skye, grateful for an activity, collected forks, knives and spoons from the cutlery drawer.

She asked, 'When's Airen coming? Did we give him a time?'

Grandma pursed her lips and frowned, silent for once.

Lou shrugged and sighed as she scraped the chopped tomatoes from the board into a big salad bowl. 'Anybody's guess. We suggested midday.'

'I met Ash-Lee.' Skye was curious about the girl. 'She seems nice enough but very young. Is he staying at her place?'

Grandma ran frail fingers through her hair and tucked it behind her ears. 'You'd think she was sixteen but she's twenty. Two years younger than Airen,' she said, reading Skye's mind. 'Lives at Ocean Beach Coastal Park, in a caravan. One of those blow ins. Comes to town, stays a while and moves on. He could have courted any number of lovely girls and he's cooped up with her.'

She made a 'tsk tsk tsk' of displeasure with her tongue at the thought of Airen ending up with anyone less than perfect.

Skye and Lou exchanged glances over the top of Grandma's head and Lou volunteered, 'I think Skye's right. Ash-Lee's a nice girl and maybe, at this point in time, she's what Airen needs. No pressure. What you see is what you get.'

Grandma 'hurrumphed' and leaned down to check inside the oven, the palm of her hand supporting her lower back.

'We'll see, we'll see,' she muttered, slowly becoming upright. 'I'm turning into a horrible old bag, must be the nerves. All I want for our boy is for everything to be all right and today could go one way or the other if we apply too much pressure.'

CHAPTER 19

'He's here.' Oceane jerked back from the window as though she'd seen a ghost or worse still, a serial killer. She'd stood there for over an hour, waiting for her only son, moving away from the window once to go to the bathroom.

The hummingbird cake sat on the kitchen bench, pale buttery yellow icing slapped on in thick wedges like it had been trawled across with a paint spatula. It reminded Skye of the faux Tuscan residence she wrote up as a feature story for *The Northern Sun* yesterday, where the stucco had been painted on by the owner-builder in broad yet measured brushstrokes.

'Just the way Airen likes it,' Grandma said of the icing on the cake.

When Airen hadn't arrived by mid-afternoon, Lou covered the salads and placed them in the fridge. The onions and sausages were piled into an oven-proof tray for reheating.

The forced chatter faded to the occasional upbeat remark from Jimmy. 'He should be here soon, let's keep our wits about us for a positive outcome'. These were offset by false alarms from Oceane who, on several occasions, cried out when she thought she heard the roar of Airen's silver ute.

Skye's pulse leapt around like crickets in a sack. He was finally here, rolling up late like a rock star to an after party.

The outside table setting was lifestyle-magazine perfect. Hi gloss. Skye had raced around Grandma's yard and cut sprays of flowers from a copse of dwarf flowering gum trees. She'd trimmed and arranged them in an old jam tin to use as a centrepiece. Gathered in a bunch, the mass of baby pink native flowers reminded Skye of a cluster of sea anemones, their fine wavy tendrils quivering in the occasional afternoon breeze. She'd then scrabbled around Grandma's display cabinet and found a selection of coloured glass tumblers and plates with a vintage rose patterned border.

The festive colours stood out against the stark white of the tablecloth. Skye almost forgot the reason for the barbecue, half convinced the intervention would turn into a party. A celebration. She almost asked Grandma if she had any streamers hidden away for special events.

When Airen saw Skye's table setting and Grandma's cake he would relax and forget about the drink. They'd cancel the intervention and spend the afternoon reminiscing about the good times.

She checked herself. Who was she kidding?

Everyone agreed to make the intervention alcohol-free, so the Esky was filled with ice and an assortment of fizzy drinks, bottled water and a plastic tub of orange juice. Skye suggested they move it somewhere out of Airen's direct line of vision.

'If he sees what's inside this he won't be happy and he'll leave,' she said to Sun. They'd just lugged the Esky under the back steps and wandered back into the lounge room when Oceane made her shrill announcement.

Airen was about to enter the building.

'Should we all hide?' Skye suggested and immediately regretted it. It wasn't funny but she felt a tiny tick of hysteria. She pulled one arm down behind her neck, holding the elbow with the other, for a neck and shoulder stretch. And repeated it with the other arm.

Jimmy stretched out his arms and indicated like a policeman on traffic duty for those present to assemble around him.

'Okay, everybody, this is it. The plan is to have a low-key lunch first, with the emphasis on 'relaxed', followed by Betty's superb hummingbird cake. Then I'll casually comment that this gathering has provided a nice opportunity for a chin wag about the boozing and so on and so forth.'

Oceane was still perched at her lookout. 'He's getting out of the car and he's got a six pack of beer.' She turned around, the skin stretched over her face like a taut mask. Skye double blinked at the panic in her mother's eyes, absorbing it into her own skin.

'You all look like you're at a funeral,' Oceane whispered loudly, eyes wide with fear. 'Smile, lighten up, get calm. We need to be calm.'

It was like telling the passengers aboard the Titanic to relax and enjoy their final hours. Skye felt the floor tilt under her feet and grabbed the top of the lounge.

Lou clutched at Sun's hand, Oceane merged into Jimmy, Grandma scooped up a yelping Pepe from the lounge and cradled him in the crook of her elbow.

Skye edged towards the kitchen. She didn't want to be present for the tortuous 'g'days' and the pretence that it was just another barbecue.

She was starving. In the pantry she dug out a packet of savoury crackers and retrieved an unopened tub of hummous from the fridge. She removed the plastic lid, tore off the aluminium seal (why did products have so much packaging?) and plunged in the cracker until it was half covered with the stuff.

No second thoughts about double dipping. This was an emergency. And besides, she planned to eat the whole lot in one go.

From the lounge room she could hear Oceane's tittering laughter, a portentous sign. Pepe's bark was as harsh as a bike with squeaky brakes and just as annoying. Grandma's attempts to calm the dog with a series of 'tut tuts' only increased its intensity.

Jimmy's Scottish brogue rose above it all. 'Welcome Airen, Lad. Welcome. Come in, come in. We're all here Lad. So glad ya could make it.'

The crackers were stale and lacked crunch. Skye plonked another one in the dip, scooped down for maximum coverage and shoved it into her mouth. Mid-chew, she paused. Oh god, she had to stop.

What was the point of any of this?

Hastily shoving the lid back on the dip, she almost threw it back into the fridge before flinging it and the remaining crackers in the kitchen garbage bin.

Sun poked her head through the kitchen door. 'Skye,' she hissed. 'You can't hide in here all afternoon. Come and make yourself known before we head outside.'

Skye checked outside. The weather was closing in as banks of clouds drew together to form a brooding phalanx that could not be outrun or outmanoeuvred. She pushed out her bottom lip as she pictured her beautiful table setting ruined by the rain. She didn't know how long it would take for the army to complete its march before deciding to attack and dump its ammunition.

'Hi,' she said and smiled way too brightly at everyone as she entered the lounge room. She caught Airen's gaze, moved hers away, and added to no one in particular, 'I don't know how long we've got before it buckets down so we should probably go into the garden and get started on a late lunch.'

Her unintentional metaphor was not lost on Sun and Lou, who stared at her grimly. 'Good idea,' Sun said through clenched teeth. 'I'll get the salads out. Airen, could you cut the bread?'

Airen held onto a six pack of beer, nursing it in much the same way Grandma held the dog. It was his baby and no one was going to steal it from him. No one dared.

There was only one way into the backyard and that was across the red linoleum floor of Grandma's eat-in kitchen and out the back door. Everyone traipsed through with Jimmy at the rear like a Kelpie on sheep muster duty.

Skye grabbed a breadboard, knife and two crusty white sourdough loaves, courtesy of Fletcher. She almost tripped down the six back steps that were really just loose house bricks shoved together. One day someone would come to grief, she thought. Maybe she could ask Fletcher to build a new set of proper steps with a handrail for Grandma?

Everyone made the appropriate noises over her table setting.

'Wonderful Skye, just wonderful.' Grandma's smile was grateful, her eyes bigger and more mournful than ever in her tiny face. She sat down and placed Pepe on the lawn but he began to whine and bark so she picked him up again.

'You're spoiling him Grandma,' Skye said.

'I know Love, but what can I do because he won't stop barking until I pick him up.'

'Lock him in the laundry.'

Skye could have sworn Pepe edged up one side of his upper lip to reveal a set of short sharp teeth. Vaguely ferocious, a mini shark in rat's clothing, his ears pointing up and back like Martian satellite dishes.

'I think he snarled at me?'

Jimmy eased his big body into the chair next to Grandma's, his maw around a bottle of dry ginger beer. 'The wee Chihuahua is a sensitive creature, Skye, and it takes time, patience and unconditional love to gain his trust.'

He unscrewed the lid and poured the effervescent drink into a tall pink glass with a 'glug-glug-glug'.

Airen, who'd been standing at the barbecue with Lou, swaggered to the head of the table. Skye reckoned he'd already started the day with a few fortifying ales.

His eyes weren't quite focused, his hair was dull and uncombed, his navy blue shirt and jeans hung off his diminishing body. He was crumpled and unwashed.

'What's this mate?' Airen spoke his first full sentence since his arrival and pointed at Jimmy's beverage. 'Not having a beer with lunch?'

Not waiting for Jimmy to answer, he pushed a plate and cutlery out of the way and put down his six pack. He pulled out a stubby and twisted off the top, which he dropped on the ground. Not bothering with a glass, he took a swig and wiped his hand over his mouth.

Throwing down the gauntlet, Skye thought. Dare to criticise me and I will leave this joint. Never to return.

She watched as her family did their utmost to ignore the defiance that defined Airen's every move.

Oceane, seated beside Jimmy, coughed and gave him a nudge. He responded by pouring her a glass of water.

Sun stood up from her seat opposite Jimmy's, peeled the protective bees' wax wraps from the salads and popped in Grandma's white porcelain salad servers.

She gave Airen a tight-lipped smile. 'Why don't you sit down mate?'

He nodded towards her, dipping an imaginary hat, and pulled out a chair opposite Jimmy's. Skye stood at the other end of the table, where she'd organised the bread on the cutting board.

Sun had given Airen the task of cutting the bread but it would be easier to do it herself. She'd be able to get the width right. The bread would end up hacked and the slices too thick, or too thin and wonky, if Airen got hold of the knife.

Airen's eyes slid her way and he sucked on the lip of the bottle as he examined her. She placed the edge of the serrated knife lightly over the top of the crust and held the loaf stable as she sliced through it.

Airen lowered the bottle. 'Glad to see you're in control Skye. Always in control.'

Skye inhaled and stopped slicing. The air felt still and heavy. She could smell the soil, its rich mineral content rising in anticipation of rain.

'I didn't think you wanted to do it.' She held the knife out to him, handle first. Her voice sounded louder than she wanted it to be. 'Here, you do it.'

Airen rubbed thumb and fingers across his temple. 'Don't be so defensive. 'Course I didn't wanna do it. I would've stuffed up.'

He stopped rubbing and, with what seemed like great difficulty, smiled. 'Your slices of bread will be perfect in every way.'

Sun licked her lips quickly and turned her head from Airen to Skye. 'We'll get you to cut the cake mate.' She laughed and

Grandma joined in, stroking Pepe so hard across the head that his eyes bulged like ping-pong balls.

Lou called out for help from the barbecue, just in the nick of time.

Airen didn't bother getting up so Jimmy heaved himself out of his seat and trotted to the barbecue to return with the reheated meat, onions and mushrooms. He craned his head back to get a better view of the sky. As if on cue, a drop of rain as big and round as a golf ball plopped on his forehead.

'Feck.' He grimaced, placed the tray on the table and removed his kilt cap. More huge blobs splatted onto the table, spaced wide apart. 'We better get inside.'

Everybody stood in unison. At the same time, ragged lightning tore through the dense clouds, which could no longer bear the weight of their load. At the thunder's angry crack, Pepe hiccoughed frantically and shook in Grandma's arms.

The sky opened as all but but Airen, who'd already retreated inside with his beers, frantically cleared the table.

'Lou, Betty, get inside,' Jimmy shouted over the din as Skye swept up plates and tumblers into an unwieldy pile. The rain pelted down, puncturing the earth with the force of a nail gun.

Already, Skye's shirt was plastered to her back, her jeans were wet and heavy and her hair soaked through.

'Bloody Airen, he could have helped.' She swore under breath, trying to screw a lid on her annoyance.

She jogged towards the back door and started up the steps. Then a loose brick gave way underfoot. With her breathing on hold, Skye watched herself falling up and towards the back door. Just before she hit the bricks, self-protection took over from saving dinner and side plates and a couple of tumblers. She went down hard with her hands out, helpless to stop the smashing of her porcelain and glass across the outside wall and top steps.

The wind knocked out of her, Skye lay in an odd almost forty-five degree angle on her stomach for a couple of seconds, her breathing shallow and fast.

'Jesus Christ. Skye, are you okay?' Sun knelt beside her and attempted to pull the hair away from the side of Skye's face. 'Sweetie, are you okay? Are you all right?'

Jimmy's voice. 'God almighty. Skye? Lass? Are ye still with us?'

Oceane: 'My dear baby girl, my dear Skye.'

Gingerly, Skye pushed herself up into a kneeling position and held out her grazed bleeding hands as if in an offering. Jimmy gently grabbed her around the waist and hauled her to her feet.

'Here, lemme get ye inside.'

Another flash of lightning illuminated the devastation.

'Oh no, Grandma's plates.'

It was like a Greek wedding had spiralled out of control.

'The plates,' she whimpered over and over.

Thunder, a bowling ball on a crash course, rolled down the lane and hit the tenpins for a strike.

Skye's face was slick with rain and, she licked her lips, tears. How did this happen? She should have got out the old everyday plates and not worried about creating a perfect table setting for everyone to admire. What did it matter? And now Grandma's plates were destroyed. Irreparably damaged. Broken.

'Don't worry about the plates,' Jimmy said as she limped inside.

In a small sunroom that adjoined the kitchen, Skye slumped into a chair.

'Here.' Sun handed her two towels, cottonwool, a small bottle of disinfectant and a pair of pyjamas. 'They're all I could find, unless you wanna wear Grandma's gear. Go get changed.'

Skye hobbled and dripped her way into the bathroom. Shaking uncontrollably, she washed her hands, examined tender palms and swabbed her hands with the disinfectant-soaked cottonwool. Consciously slowing down her breathing, she peeled off her sodden clothes, towelled herself dry and put on the pyjamas covered in a purple print that featured the cartoon cat Garfield. They were her favourites as a teenager. Grandma had never thrown them out.

Her reflection in the bathroom mirror revealed a smudge of brown on her forehead from where she'd rested her face on the brick step. Shock reverberated in her ears like symbols being slammed together by a pre-schooler. She looked like a woman on the verge.

She turned on the tap again, cupped her hands under the running water and splashed her face. Her palms tingled and her knees throbbed.

Tomorrow there would be bruises.

As she dried her face with the towel, a knock on the door caused her to jump. It was Grandma and Pepe tucked into a pouch.

Skye sniffled. 'I'm so sorry Grandma. Your plates.'

Grandma waved a hand dismissively. 'Plates, schmates. Those bloody loose steps are to blame. Let me take your clothes. I'll run them through the washer and dryer.'

'I feel so bad.'

Small hands on Skye's shoulders. 'Please Skye, there's nothing to feel bad about. The plates can be replaced. Come and have something to eat, a cuppa and a piece of cake.'

'Is Airen still here?' Skye hated herself for it but the thought of having to deal with Airen again made her feel sick. She wished he would leave. She didn't want to deal with the issues tearing them both apart. She hated his smugness, spite, selfishness, victim mentality and unfettered anger generated mostly in her direction.

'Yes, he is. But I think we need to get started soon. The six pack is shrinking.'

A flare of anger re-ignited in Skye. Airen didn't bother to help when the rain started to belt down. He was first inside, disregarding the wellbeing of his grandmother, mother and a pregnant woman.

She followed Grandma into the lounge room in her purple pyjamas, wondering if she would have dropped the plates if it wasn't for her self-absorbed baby brother.

CHAPTER 20

Jimmy hustled everyone into the lounge room and their correct positions for the intervention. If Airen had noticed the ominous semi-circular seating arrangement or guessed at its significance, he didn't let on.

His plate was crammed with sausages, steak and bread. Obviously, salad was no longer a dietary requirement. Beer was. The six pack was down to two, with one opened and perched on the edge of the coffee table within easy reach. He wouldn't be able to drive in his condition. They had him trapped here, a victim of his own irresponsible behaviour, Skye thought.

She accepted a plate of food from Lou and sat on the lounge next to Grandma and Sun. Jimmy, Oceane and Airen sat opposite. Skye could hardly disguise her disgust at Airen as he shovelled food into his mouth. The little prick couldn't care less that she'd fallen over. The palms of her hands stung like mad and her head throbbed, whereas it seemed like Airen was enjoying himself immensely.

Skye's appetite evaporated. She cut up her vegetarian patty into teeny tiny pieces and shuffled it around the plate with her fork and knife.

Airen combined eating and drinking, taking a swig of beer quickly followed by a mouthful of sausage or steak coated in tomato sauce on a white bread roll.

He burped without apology and wiped his nose and mouth across his shirt before taking another slug on the stubby.

Skye exhaled her frustration through her nose. 'Are you doing this on purpose?' It was out before she thought about it.

Grandma nudged her in the ribs. 'Shhhh.'

Airen appraised her under heavy 'couldn't give a shit' lids. Maybe he'd snuck in a joint while she was in the bathroom.

'Huh?'

Skye gave her best smug smile. All lips, no teeth.

'Don't worry about it.' She moved her head side to side. 'Forget I spoke.'

'What the?' Airen pretended to choke on his beer. 'Like, what do you really want to say Skye? If you've got something to say, say it 'cause I'm not gonna hang around after I'm done here.'

Skye carefully rested her knife and fork on the plate.

'Airen. This get-together was organised around you, and this is what you do. You behave like an ungrateful prat.'

Jimmy whirred his arms around like a conductor who was missing a page of a musical score. The orchestra was playing too fast, its instruments at odds with one another in a discordant cacophony.

Skye had started a commotion.

'Now, now ye two, ye canna carry on like pork chops.' His tone was conciliatory. 'We're here to make amends.'

'Thanks for trying to keep the peace man, appreciate it.' Airen talked with his mouth full and stabbed his fork in Skye's direction. 'But I'm interested in what my sister has to say since she hasn't bothered with any of us for three years. Then she prances back into town like a friggin' princess and expects the world to stop for her.'

Sun stretched across Grandma to touch Skye's arm and Pepe let out a strangled whine.

'Skye.' Sun's voice was low and strained. 'Let's sort this out the way we'd planned.'

'Planned?' Airen's fork and knife clattered on his plate. 'What do you mean? Planned?'

Oceane's eyes glimmered like gems. 'Airen, Darlin', there's a lot of love in this room, surely you can feel it?' Her voice trembled with unshed tears. 'It's directed at you like a beam of golden light. An enveloping force field of affection.'

Airen slammed his plate on the coffee table and it cracked in to three neat pieces. 'For fuck sake Mum, cut the crystal healing mumbo jumbo harmony Zen bullshit.'

'Don't speak to ye mother like that.' It was the first time Skye had seen Jimmy lose it with Airen.

It was as though Jimmy's brain snap had the effect of flicking on the swinging light bulb in Airen's head that Skye had talked about. He tore the last stubby from the cardboard container and ripped off the lid.

Lou leaned against the kitchen door frame, holding a brush and dust-pan.

'Hey, mate, go light on the booze,' she said. 'How're you gonna get home in that condition?'

Airen snapped, 'Shit Lou, not you too?'

Skye's laugh was more of a yelp as the last words of Roman dictator Julius Caesar to his best friend and murderer flashed through her head: 'et tu, Brute?'

'Jesus, Airen.' Blood roared in her ears. 'Here's what I'm saying. Here's what we're all saying. Stop drinking. Stop. Can't you see what it's doing to you? What it's doing to our family? It's impacting negatively on every person in this room.'

Airen turned on her with a snarl. 'I'm 'impacting negatively'? Can you hear yourself? What are you? A psychiatrist? This 'little get together' should be about you Skye. The family's got it wrong if they think I've got a problem. All you've done is lie since Dad died. To everyone. Mum, Sun, Grandma. Yourself. And every second of every day you blame me for what happened to Dad.'

Skye flinched and her blood pressure dived as Airen flung the light bulb across her head.

Indignation heated her cheeks. 'I never lied to you.' The words were ground out of her.

Airen stabbed an accusing finger. 'You never told the truth about what happened that night. You said you found me unconscious on the beach. That's crap. Total crap. My memory's come back.' He knocked a hand on his head as if that would help, not totally sure of himself.

'At first,' he paused and breathed deeply. 'At first I thought it was a bad dream. But it's become clearer to me since you left. You paddled out to me that night, didn't you? And somehow… somehow you got me back in.'

Airen swilled more beer. His cheeks were sunken, his eyes hollow. He could have been the ghost of their father, Skye thought. She couldn't talk. The roar was turning, turning, turning into the surge of the surf, a monster three-metre swell, thick black ink in the moonlight between the clouds.

'Skye?' Her mother's voice, concerned, shocked.

Skye squinted down on stinging eyes.

Her voice emerged, a loud whisper. 'Why does it matter what happened? Dad is dead.'

'Fuck you Skye.' Airen stood up fast and drained the last stubby. 'Fuck you.'

Sun leaped to her feet, hands spread out in a placating gesture. 'Don't go. Stay. Sit down. We can sort this out.'

Outside, rain pounded Grandma's tin roof as hard as a boxer at a punching bag. In the cosy lounge room, no one uttered a word. It surprised Skye when Airen sat back down.

Skye stood up and put her plate filled with food on the coffee table.

Grandma hugged Pepe close. 'Skye, you don't have to do this.'

Skye leaned down and squeezed Grandma's hand. If Airen wanted the truth, she'd give it to him. She stood tall in the middle of the intervention circle and talked directly to Airen.

'On the night Dad died I saw you leave the pub together after the celebration. I was worried because you'd both been drinking since lunchtime.'

Skye swallowed and thought for a moment, the visual memory of the night flickering across her brain like a black-and-white silent film.

'I shouldn't have been driving either but I got in my car and followed you. I knew where you were going. Back to The Point.

'What I didn't guess was that you'd drive right down to the beach where the whale watching boats are launched. From The Point, I could see the ute's headlights facing the surf. I could see you both racing each other into the water like a couple of idiots.'

Skye hugged her arms across her chest, raised her eyes to the ceiling and rested them back on Airen.

'I felt sick to the stomach. I couldn't believe you'd be stupid enough to go out in those conditions. It was suicidal. The swell was massive and the rip ran out past The Point.'

Skye pushed her fingers hard against her eyes causing stars to form when she pulled them away. 'I got down to the beach and dragged the board out of the car.'

Skye breathed hard as though she'd been running. Like she was back there. Airen's hands hung between his legs. He closed his eyes and tilted his head back.

'And this is what I saw Airen.' In the deathly silence, she forged on. 'I saw something bobbing in the water. I called out but the wind and surf, waves crashing, were too loud. I didn't know what to do. I was so frigging scared. How could I get out past those monsters? They were coming in so fast, there was barely a space in between them. But I did it. I still don't know how I did it. I pulled off my jeans and ran in with the board. It felt like forever but it must have been a couple of minutes. And then I found you, floating face down, and I dunno how but I got you onto the board, sort of across it, and I got into the ocean and held on. And then...'

Skye gulped at the blockage in her throat but it wouldn't move.

Grandma's voice: 'Skye, Love, don't do this.'

Airen opened his eyes like a man waking from a coma. Dark and fearful, almost uncomprehending. He found his voice. 'And then?'

She saw him, their father, the mighty Jonno, sleek silver lion head bobbing like a cork, big strong arms held aloft, being carried out by the rip like flotsam.

'Dad was further out, near the rocks, waving his arms. I wanted to get to him but it was impossible. I couldn't reach him. I wouldn't be able to keep you on the board. And then it clicked. He didn't want me to come. He wanted me to leave him there. He was waving me away. So, I did it. I turned around. I let him go. And I got us back to the beach.'

Oceane stifled a sob with her fist over her mouth. Jimmy rubbed his hands on his knees and leaned forward. 'Why did ye not tell this story before today Lass?'

Now the truth was out, Skye wanted to drag it back and bury it deep inside her. Ennui descended upon her like a warm wet blanket.

'Like I said, what do the details matter? Dad's dead. You can't undo that.'

Airen stared, glassy eyed, as though Skye's final revelation hadn't sunk in.

Sun rubbed her hands over her face, crossed her arms, raised and lowered her head, and turned it slowly from side to side in a slow stretch before directing her gaze at Skye. 'You saved Airen.'

Airen's eyes flickered towards Sun. 'Saved me?'

Grandma blinked furiously. 'Skye brought you back to the beach, Love. That's all Sun meant.'

Airen's expression turned from stunned to contemptuous as though the fog had lifted and he had a clear view of the lay of the land for the first time.

He rose from his chair, shoulders hunched, fists clenched, eyes flint struck with steel.

'You kept this to yourself like a dirty little secret Skye.' Words scathing, each with a serrated edge, dug into Skye. 'It gave you a reason to blame me for Dad's death. Sacrifice Jonno to save Airen. When you would have preferred it to be the other way round because it wasn't Dad's fault that we were out there in the ocean. It had to be mine.'

Skye shrugged. 'I don't blame anyone.' It didn't sound convincing.

'Dad was your idol,' Airen said. 'The old man was perfect in your eyes. You blamed me first, then Mum and Jimmy second. You didn't want to hear our side of the story or believe Dad had any flaws. That's why you'll always be a hack journo.'

The room seemed to shudder around Skye as everyone leapt to her defence.

Sun started. 'Steady on Airen. Skye, you're a first-class journo.'

Lou, rubbing her tummy like it was a Genie's lamp, went next. 'Fair go mate, that was uncool.'

Grandma, running a hand over Pepe's avocado-sized head, pitched in. 'Please Love, don't talk to your sister like that.'

Jimmy's arms rose and fell as though trying to douse a fire. 'Quiet everyone, let's get some order in the room.'

Oceane, in between sniffles, sobbed, 'Airen Darlin', Skye Darlin', everyone's missing the point of this intervention.'

Airen's laugh rocked everyone back into yet another stunned silence, their mouths agape like a school of hunted fish the second before the net tightens. He snorted derisively. 'Fuck. That'd be right. A fucking fuck-off intervention.'

Jimmy stood up and straightened his kilt. 'Lad, it's about the drinking.'

Airen ran his hands through his hair and gesticulated wildly. 'Don't you get it? This isn't about me being on the piss. It's about blame.'

Airen threw Jimmy's hand off his shoulder, strode to the door and opened it. A gust of wind blasted in, lifting his hair from his shoulders.

'I'm sorry.' Skye heard the hollow insincerity of her words, knowing she sounded like a fake.

The door slammed like a thunderclap on Oceane's plea of, 'Don't go. You can't drive in that condition... in these conditions.'

Jimmy hugged her close. 'A bugger's muddle, that's what this is, a total fiasco.'

Oceane's sobs overrode the noise of the storm.

Grandma continued to pat Pepe as though this brought her some comfort.

'I have a feeling.' Grandma's voice cracked and she paused, for once, to consider her words. 'I have an *instinctive* feeling this has all gone terribly wrong.'

CHAPTER 21

Minutes after Airen left, Skye grabbed her bag. She made for the front door despite entreaties from her family to stay and, in Sun's words, 'sort this out once and for all.'

The room had become stifling. Skye needed to get away from her family. Her system was in overload, a computer about to crash.

She jumped in the car and rattled down the rutted driveway the rain had churned into a fast flowing creek.

Screw 'em. What did they know about pain and suffering? How dare they sabotage her and turn her into a psychological case study. The intervention was supposed to be about Airen's issues. Not hers.

Skye pulled herself up short.

Her issues.

She had issues?

After Jonno's death, Skye remained stoically, melodramatically, silent. Seriously, how could she have said anything, what with the memorial service coming up, a town in mourning and her brother at risk of being blamed for Jonno's death?

This afternoon's disastrous intervention went into rewind in Skye's head as she drove back out to the coast through heavy rain. The windscreen wipers swept back and forth with a soft thunk, wiping clear the glass for a second. It felt like they were inside her head, clearing the muck out of the way for a momentary glance of the complete landscape.

She thought she'd done the right thing by Airen. That her prolonged silence had protected him from small-town gossip ignited by those who were quick to judge and reach the wrong conclusions. She also held her truth of the night's events tightly to her to help smooth the path to Airen's career as a star rugby league player. The big clubs wouldn't touch a player tainted by controversy. The questions would always remain: Was Airen somehow instrumental in causing his father's death? Was he a coward who failed his father? Mud sticks.

Conspiracy theories had abounded following the tragedy, even without bringing Airen into the picture. The most common one to do the rounds was that Jonno was murdered by hitmen hired by disgruntled property developers.

Skye squashed an impulse to find Airen, to head to the caravan tourist park where Ash-Lee lived. Surely that was his destination, though it could also be the pub. What better way to spend a stormy afternoon than to get thoroughly tanked.

She sighed heavily. It would be stupid to try talking to Airen so soon after this catastrophe. And she needed to consider her own position. Two sides to every story. It was a basic tenet of journalism.

But Skye hadn't given Airen the space to tell his story about that night. She'd blurted out hers and that was that. He didn't get a chance to contribute.

Her disappointment in him had caused her to block a two-way conversation. She reached a guilty verdict without giving her brother a fair trial. Airen's foolish behaviour led to their father's death. Jonno would still be alive today if her brother hadn't been a willing participant that night. What was the point of more talk, excuses or reasons to explain away their father's drowning after the fact?

Her duty done, Skye could now return to Sydney. It was up to the rest of her family pick up the pieces of Airen and put them back together again.

By the time she arrived at Fletcher's, it was early evening. The rain had set in.

The Kombi van parked in driveway brought a smile to her lips. Good. He was home. She bit down on her lip as her heart did a backflip. Her mood was swinging all over the place, from despair to excitable puppy. She needed to slam a lid on her growing feelings for her de facto sister-in-law's sperm donor.

Barefoot and still wearing the purple cat pyjamas, she sprinted from the car and up the front steps. The door wasn't locked so she let herself in. Just in the nick of time before another fuse blew in the sky in a sensational flash. It was closely followed by a hard smack of thunder that, had she been outside, would have bruised her eardrums. Rain sluiced off the corrugated roof and rushed down the guttering and into the drainpipes like the onslaught of a waterpark ride. It created chaos on the tin roof.

The noise was a crazy metallic clanging like coins tumbling from an old-fashioned poker machine. The intensity increased as though floodgates in an unholy sky had been flung open and a deluge released. As quickly as it eased off, another engorged cloud dropped its motherlode to saturate the earth, penetrate to the core, fill to the brim, pelt down in a torrent.

It kept coming. Skye loved it, didn't want it to stop. Even though she knew that somewhere the torrent was causing havoc and possible disaster, bloating rivers, streaming over causeways, charging down stormwater drains, tearing up tree roots, digging out valleys. A violent force of nature, it could lift trucks and buses and send them careening into a raging waterway as though they were as light and harmless as a child's bath toys.

She felt safe here, at Fletcher's place.

A lemon-butter light glowed from a floor lamp in the corner of the lounge room. Music played. Blues and roots, John Butler Trio, an earthy blend of post-hippy blues and funk. It reminded her of The Point on a good day when the surfing gods saved the best waves for Dezzy.

Skye poured a glass of wine in the kitchen before heading to the bathroom to towel dry her hair. Moving out onto the back deck, she sipped on her wine. The rain formed a sheer curtain on either side of the covered walkway that led to Fletcher's temporary bedroom.

'Fletcher?' The rain drenched the word so she tried again but louder. 'Fletcher?'

A dim light shone through the bedroom window opposite. She stepped lightly across the walkway to be greeted by Occy, his tail wagging like a wind-up toy.

'Hiya boy.' Skye tickled behind his velvety ears. 'Where's the boss?'

Occy trotted into Fletcher's bedroom. Skye lightly knocked on the half-opened door.

'Hey, Skye, come on in.'

She peeked around the corner to find Fletcher seated on his bed, fully clothed, his back propped up by pillows. She breathed in the smoky scent of patchouli coming from an oil burner on a bedside table. Light flickered from several tall cylindrical candles set on a tray on a matching table on the other side of the bed.

'I'm meditating. Just started. Come and sit with me.' He shifted from the middle to the side of the bed.

Skye stood there, wine glass in hand, not sure what to do. Her heart thudded so loud she thought he might be able to hear it above the pouring rain.

'Occy's here to keep me honest,' Fletcher said with a smile, and Skye had complete faith in him and his intentions.

Of course, she knew she didn't have to worry about Fletcher. But could she trust herself to sit beside him? She doubted it. It would take a huge amount of self-discipline.

She hesitated. She could leave now. Should leave now. Now.

Instead, she walked around the bed and placed her glass next to the oil burner. Occy followed her and sat on the floor next to the bed while she climbed on it and sat up, legs crossed.

'Lean forward,' Fletcher instructed as he plumped up the pillows behind her.

Heat like the after-effect of a whiskey shot burned through her as his hand brushed her shoulder. It was as though he'd run his fingers lightly over her breasts and down her middle to her navel, to have them linger there.

Shite. A thought flittered into her consciousness that since returning to Dezzy she'd wandered like a sleepwalker from one disaster to another without considering the consequences. *What am I doing here?*

Fletcher was dressed in a white long-sleeved shirt, unbuttoned, and loose black pants. Feet bare. Around his neck was a leather strap threaded through a circular mother of pearl carving that sat just below the hollow of his neck. On most men this type of adornment would have been silly, on Fletcher it was downright sexy. Surfer and pirate rolled into one. Every woman's fantasy. Her fingers itched to reach out and caress his skin beneath the white shirt. She was dying to know what it felt like. God, she knew what it would feel like. That was the problem.

She grabbed for the glass of wine and gulped so fast that it made her cough.

Why don't I ever feel this way with Beau?

The heat shot into her cheeks as Fletcher interrupted her thoughts.

'Have you meditated much before?'

'A bit.' She jiggled into a position a little further away from him. 'I went through an *Eat, Pray, Love* phase in Sydney but Beau doesn't like anything 'Zen'. He calls it 'hippy shit'.'

Fletcher laughed softly. 'If you haven't done it for a while, twenty minutes should be enough today.'

Skye placed the wineglass on the bedside table. She straightened her spine and rested her hands in her lap with her thumbs and middle fingers just touching.

Fletcher pressed the timer on his deep-sea diving watch.

'Focus on the breath and we'll reconnect in twenty minutes.'

It was cheating, but she watched as he closed his eyes and breathed in an easy relaxed manner.

She nearly jumped out of her skin when he said, a smile twitching at his lips, 'Skye, shut your eyes and stop staring at me.'

'Sorry, I wasn't, I just...'

'Shoosh,' came the amused admonishment.

Even with her eyes closed, Skye found it impossible to concentrate on her breathing. Her thoughts darted to the man next to her and then hopped, guilt-stricken, to Beau, before the events of the day took hold.

How did it all get so out of hand? It was Jimmy's fault. Blame Jimmy.

Jimmy had no idea how to run an intervention. If he'd done it properly, none of those cruel words would have been spoken and the intervention wouldn't have faltered, with Skye copping the brunt.

But maybe it wasn't Jimmy's problem. There *were* two sides to every story but she'd been so self-righteous, so arrogant to believe she had all the answers. She'd stood atop the metaphoric mountain and passed judgment on her mother, Jimmy and Airen. Again.

Maybe Airen was right. She blamed her mother and Jimmy for everything that happened in the lead-up to Jonno's death. Nobody else got air-time because she was so determined to keep Jonno on a pedestal.

Airen was right about one thing. She was a hack, a fraud who could barely hold down a job as a real estate journalist. What was wrong with her?

'Skye?'

A voice in the distance.

'Skye, are you okay?'

She opened her eyes and licked her lips, wet with salty tears. Pressed fingers down hard on her eyes and cheeks.

Skye hiccoughed and pulled her arms around her waist as though she was in a straight-jacket. The deluge from outside had somehow found its way into her core. Streaming, tearing, gouging, pouring, banging and clattering. A sob tore through her and she curled up tighter.

'Hey, it's okay.' A gentle voice consoled her and melted into her bones like a salve.

But still she couldn't stop the hurting everywhere in her body.

'I... I... I...'

She was dragged into the hard warmth of him. A blanket pulled over them both. 'Let it out, let it go.'

Permission granted, Skye allowed three years of pain, guilt and grief to swallow her whole. She slipped into the belly of the whale, pitch black and terrifying. Heart torn open, throat constricted with words unspoken.

Fletcher rocked back and forth with her as she bawled, wailed and whimpered for the incriminating accusations that could never be taken back.

She ran away from home because she couldn't face the truth. Since Jonno's death, she'd convinced herself she was right and everyone else could go to hell. She'd played the blame game like a pro.

'I'm such a bitch, bitch, bitch, bitchy bitch,' she sobbed into Fletcher's chest. She pulled back slightly and examined his shirt. It was smudged with mascara.

She sniffled and, rather than ruin Fletcher's shirt any more than she had already, wiped her runny nose on her pyjama sleeve, leaving a silver snail trail.

With the maelstrom ended, she lay still in Fletcher's arms. Breathing in lightly and out lightly. She wriggled in closer, if that was at all possible, and inched her hands up to his chest.

Outside, the rained had eased off momentarily to a pleasant drumming on the roof.

Occy, satisfied that Skye was okay, wandered out of the room.

She relaxed and sighed, inhaled Fletcher's scent. Au natural, clean and oceanic. Sniffed again and pressed her nose into his shirt. *Mmm.* She needed to get closer, slide her arms slowly up to his neck and around the back of it, underneath the thick dreadlocks.

Fletcher tensed and inhaled sharply.

'Skye?'

Skye tipped her face up to his.

He frowned. 'Are you sure about this?'

All she could do was nod and raise her lips to his. She needed to do this. It wasn't on any list or in any plan. She had no idea where it would lead. Even if she wanted to stop, she had no choice. Destiny had pushed her towards this moment.

Their lips met lightly. Soft, sensual. Cool and lush. The first taste. Sweet and salty.

Skye wanted more.

They both moved away, centimetres apart, eyes locked in surprise for a heart-stopping moment.

He wanted more, too.

Outside, the rain poured down and the earth swelled. But Skye could only see Fletcher, hear his heavy breathing, feel his skin next to hers and inhale all of him.

Their second kiss was a tease, the third lingering and the fourth lips parted, tips of tongues touching. Fletcher's bristles grazed her chin and she relished the roughness against her sensitised skin.

Skye tingled all over, her body lengthened and toes stretched out like a ballerina's as Fletcher ran his fingers down her spine, lightly touching each vertebrae as though it was a precious jewel.

Without a word, she slid off her pyjama pants. Fletcher raised her arms and pulled the top over her head. Effortlessly, he removed his own shirt, pants and underwear.

Their bodies united and Skye firmly gripped and slid her hand along him in a slow measured rhythm, in time with the distant drumming.

She couldn't get enough of him, navigating her hands and mouth across his body, exploring every curve, from the soft indent where neck meets shoulder, along surprisingly soft skin on firm arms, across sharp shoulder blades, feeling springy chest hair, tips of fingers finding a round and deep belly button and then kissing it and breathing him again and again.

Later on – long after Fletcher's watch beeped at twenty minutes – torso arched and toes definitely curled, she rose and fell with him, filled with a wild ecstatic joy.

Afterwards, they lay bathed in a thin sheen of sweat, panting as though they were standing on the cliff edge about to jump.

Slowly, awareness dawned and rational thought seeped back into her senses. *Shite. What a fine mess I've made.*

Skye stared at the rain lashing at the window and coursing down the panes of glass in gleaming rivulets. What had she gone and done now?

She'd had sex with Fletcher King, that's what. She did what she promised herself she'd never do.

Oh God, Beau. She was meant to be with Beau. A sigh rose in her like a big bubble about to burst. Destiny had played her for a fool.

'It's still raining,' she said, desperate to say anything that would make this big mistake disappear.

Fletcher propped himself on an elbow and gave her a quizzical look, his lips curved into a lopsided smile. He had no idea.

He ran his fingers over and around her lips. 'How did that just happen?'

She shrugged. If she'd known how the day was going to unfold, or unravel, she would have stayed in bed with the covers over her head.

'I'm so sorry,' she half whispered. 'I didn't mean for this to happen.'

He pulled away from her, his relaxed body suddenly stiff as a board. She'd obviously said something wrong and needed to fix it fast. 'It wasn't supposed to end up this way. I've made... I think we've both made... a big mistake. I mean, you are such a wonderful person and... and I'm really, really sorry if I gave you the wrong impression.'

She sounded like an idiot, bitch, loser rolled into one but she couldn't properly explain the turmoil that churned up her insides.

She couldn't tell him, 'You weren't on any of my to-do lists and that makes me anxious and terrified.'

Fletcher blew out a sigh, hopped off the bed and scooped up his clothes. 'We can have a proper conversation when you're thinking straight and you've sorted out your agenda.' He avoided her gaze. 'You can stay here, I'll sleep on the lounge.'

Skye couldn't see his face but she got the body language.

'I'm sorry Fletcher, I really am.'

God, she sounded pathetic.

'Don't say you're sorry,' he said quietly, without malice. 'I'm glad I helped you out. If you're over it already, then so am I.'

* * *

Skye woke up, groaned and slapped a hand to her forehead as the memory of last night rose before her in all its coruscating brilliance.

Then another sort of fear gripped her. She couldn't afford to be head-over- heels in love with Fletcher. He was the opposite of a safe bet.

A huge risk.

What did she say last night?

'I think we've both made a big mistake.'

She groaned again, the sound muffled against the pillow.

Dear god. If only she could turn back time then yesterday would have had a totally different outcome. Instead, she'd stuffed up. Majorly.

The rain had stopped and she could hear slide guitar and John Butler's distinctive blues roots infused rasp coming from the front pavilion.

Morning sun shone through the window like there had never been a storm.

But there had definitely been sex. The best ever sex in an infinite universe.

She'd barely slept, her thoughts swirling around Fletcher and sex, sex and Fletcher, Fletcher and sex. It was never ending.

She dragged her pleasantly sore body from the bed and walked to the half-opened wardrobe. A shoebox tied with red string enticingly placed on the top shelf piqued her interest. Skye wondered what it contained. Maybe more photos of the mystery baby? More clues to Fletcher's past?

'No more regrets Skye,' she said and pushed the cupboard door shut.

If Fletcher wanted to share his story with her, he would. But that was unlikely after her callous rejection of him last night.

She'd perfected the fuck-up and made it her own.

Last night she hadn't given a passing thought to anything, except being with Fletcher. Unable to control her emotions, she'd flung herself at him like the end of the world was immi- nent and this was the last chance to have sex with the person of your choice. She didn't for a moment consider that she'd have to deal with the consequences of having sex with a man who was the father of Sun and Lou's unborn child. It was also likely that Fletcher could have another woman, and baby, in his life. She hardly knew anything about him.

And then there was the matter of Beau. Skye sighed. She realised she'd been chewing on her bottom lip. She lifted her finger to it and touched it gingerly. Kissed into a bruise.

Skye started as Occy scampered into the room followed by Fletcher wearing khaki pants. His naked torso caused her to momentarily forget about her promise to never ever dabble in regrettable Fletcher sex again. She was a slow learner.

His demeanour was calm and relaxed.

'I wanted us to part friends, no hard feelings and all that, so I made pancakes,' he said, his usually sparkly smile seeming a little dimmer.

The offer was friendly and nothing else. As though last night had been a dream. Before she could answer, he turned and left the room. Occy left too, obviously picking up on the cooler vibe. And choosing Fletcher.

She followed them into the kitchen and poured herself a glass of tap water, swallowed in several gulps.

Fletcher handed her a pancake stack scattered with fresh berries on a large white porcelain plate.

'Maple syrup and butter on the bench,' he said.

He went back to the stovetop and flipped a pancake onto his own plate before topping it with two others from a warming tray in the oven.

Skye sat down at the bench and trickled toffee-coloured liquid onto the golden circles of just-cooked batter. The combined aroma of butter, maple syrup and sugar made her salivate. She was beyond starving.

Must have been the great sex, would've burned a gazillion calories.

She stabbed at the stack, shoved a double layer into her mouth, closed her eyes and swooned as the delectable blend of sweet and savoury burst across her taste buds. Piercing another slice, she ran it around the plate to sponge up the maple syrup and catch some berries.

Fletcher sat beside her and pointed his fork at her dubious achievement, a mess of diminishing pancakes.

'You're a machine,' he said, mouth half-full.

Skye decided to take it as a compliment. *I am not going to ruin this*, she thought, *by saying something stupid and rash. Such as, 'It's because I ran a sex marathon with you last night.'*

Shooting him a sideways glance, she said, with feeling, 'I will remember these pancakes for as long as I live.'

The words 'these pancakes' could have been replaced by 'sex with you'.

'I will remember the amazing sex I had with you for as long as I live.'

Did she just say that or was it a shout in her head?

Fletcher chewed thoughtfully. She would have loved a penny for his thoughts but his own revelations would cause further complications.

Talk could ruin everything.

Skye continued to eat like a ravenous wolf, partly to keep her from saying something, like, *'I want to take back everything I said about mistakes last night'* or *'That sex was the best ever'* or worse still, *'I think I love you.'*

Yet again, she reminded herself that Fletcher was the father of her sister and Lou's unborn child, and he could still have serious connections in Western Australia.

And he wasn't the 'fatherly type profile' she had envisioned in her plan. Skye's future family photo didn't feature dreadlocks. It was clean cut, urban and conservative. Until now.

They finished eating in silence, Skye's crowded thoughts leaping between Beau, Fletcher and the pressing matter of the errant Airen.

Could she go back to Sydney and take up with Beau as though nothing had happened between her and Fletcher? And abandon Airen like she had before?

She jumped at Occy's bark shortly followed by a knock at the door.

'I'll get that,' she volunteered as she eased herself off the bench stool.

'Sure,' Fletcher called over the sound of running water in the sink, like everything was the norm. Like they were an old couple who knew what the other was thinking, and shared all the responsibilities around the house.

Pulling the front door open, Skye almost slammed it shut again.

'Babe.'

'Beau?'

CHAPTER 22

Their greetings, his an exclamation and hers a question, collided. They both laughed uncomfortably.

Beau's eyes wandered down, up, down and up again to meet hers.

'Nice PJs,' he said. 'I can see you've been enjoying the climate and food. Been loading the carbs.'

Skye licked her lips, tasting maple syrup and the fear of being found out. Her immediate response to his dig at her weight was to wrap her arms around her waist but she realised with a start that she didn't care what Beau thought.

In her best calm voice she asked, 'What are you doing here? Why didn't you tell me you were coming? I could've met you at the airport.'

'Yeah, well.' Beau scratched the back of his head like a dog with an itch. 'I left a message on your phone but you didn't get back to me.'

Shite. Skye hadn't checked her messages since before the intervention or after the amazing sex. *Shite shite shite.*

She ruffled her fingers through her hair. She also hadn't bothered to look in the mirror, in the real or metaphysical sense, this morning. Her lips would be red as strawberries or worse still cherries, her colour heightened and her smell would be of... Skye almost gasped. Sex.

Alarm bells went off in her head.

'How did you know I was here? I didn't tell you... did I?'

'Small town. I asked some guy, a local.'

'Really?' The question rose to a high squeak on the 'y'.

Who on earth would have known she was here? At Fletcher's?

Everybody in Dezzy, that's who, Skye thought. It went without saying. Some wag would have seen her pull into Fletcher's driveway last night and that wag would then pass it on to some else, and so on and so forth. Until it reached 'the local' who happily shared it with Beau. By now, the whole town would know Beau was at Fletcher's place and they would also know that's where he would find Skye.

Beau gave her a perplexed smile and peered over her head. 'Can I come in?'

Skye returned her focus to the present. 'Of course. Why not.'

As she stepped aside, he passed her and walked into the lounge room. Fletcher was nowhere to be seen though Occy approached Beau and waited for a pat.

Beau stepped away and Skye's annoyance meter flickered. That was one of the things that irked her about Beau. He wasn't an animal person and failed to react to Occy's obvious canine charms, instead raising his hands as though the poor dog had a disease. His attitude to animals struck Skye as being unnatural.

'Nice place.' Beau picked up a cookbook on the coffee table and put it back down again with barely a glance. He sniffed the air. 'I smell coffee. Any chance of getting a cup? I've been driving for hours.'

'You drove here?'

Beau never drove if he could fly.

'Yeah, thought I'd give the new Merc a run. Got it last week. C-class with a soft top.'

'Great.'

Skye momentarily wondered if a C was a lower score than an A or a B. Cars never really interested her. They were merely a convenient way to reach a destination. But for Beau, they confirmed his status among his eastern suburbs mates and work colleagues. He was forever changing cars; she couldn't keep up. It crossed her mind that it was probably a gift from his parents.

As she padded into the kitchen, Skye realised she and Beau hadn't hugged or even air kissed. How long had it been like this between them? This total lack of intimacy? When was the last time they'd had sex? A couple of months ago. Beau had returned from a piss up at the pub with his mates to celebrate a coup after he'd gained an exclusive with a tennis player embroiled in a betting scandal.

The sex that night wasn't particularly memorable. More like a 'lay back and think of England' session where she certainly 'came off' second best.

Skye cringed at the memory. And her lack of enthusiasm. And, now she came to think of it, self-awareness.

The coffee was already brewing in a glass coffee plunger prepared by Fletcher. She poured the steaming-hot beverage with a nutty aroma into two cups, added milk to her own and two heaped spoonfuls of sugar to Beau's. She carried them to Beau who'd made himself at home on the lounge. Occy lost interest and wandered out to the deck where he rolled onto his side to make the most of the cheery morning sun.

'Thanks Babe.' Beau took the cup and put it to his lips.

Skye sat next to him and observed his typical Aussie-lad good looks: blond hair, a little messed up (he must have had the soft top down on the Merc), cheeks tinged with pink from the coastal breeze on the long drive. His short-sleeve powder-blue shirt with a button-down collar complemented his baby blue eyes. She recognised the Armani jeans and Polo Ralph Lauren sneakers.

He lowered the cup and did a quick scan of the room. 'Nice place. Your brother's?'

'No,' Skye said, almost adding, 'if only.' She got the distinct feeling Beau was fishing for information.

The less said about Airen the better, she thought. 'This is my sister's friend's house. I'm not sure if he owns it but he definitely built it.'

Beau pouted and raised an eyebrow. 'He? So, you're here dog sitting?'

Here we go. Skye took a deep breath.

'No, he's here, the guy who built the place. I'm sleeping in the front bedroom and he's in a separate pavilion out the back. We hardly see each other. He's a baker so he's up early and gone by the time I get up. When I get home he's either surfing or out. So, it's been good. Really good. Did I say we hardly see each other?'

Beau slurped. 'Ouch. Hot. Babe, got any toast to go with this? If the guy's a baker there must be heaps of sourdough lying around.'

If Skye wasn't already sitting, she would have fallen over in sheer relief. Beau believed her story. And why shouldn't he? It was true. Mostly.

She put her cup on the coffee table and rushed back to the kitchen just as Fletcher strolled in.

Widening her eyes, she shot him a 'please help me out' look.

At least he was dressed, choosing red boardies and a black T-shirt adorned with a print of Bob Marley's face, plus two lines of lyrics from the great Rastafarian artist's song *Exodus*.

She feigned surprised. 'Hey. You're up already. This is early for Sunday.'

Fletcher's smile stretched forever and Skye hoped for a little less levity from him if they were going to pull this off. If possible, she opened her eyes wider, praying he would play along.

She spun to face the lounge. Beau rose to his feet and met Fletcher in the middle of the room. The two men shook hands.

'Nice to meet you man. Skye's always talking about you. Good things.'

Beau's eyes moved from Fletcher to Sky and back. 'Mate, can't say the same. Your name is?'

Skye cut in with, 'Fletcher King, this is Beau Ferguson, Beau, this is Fletcher.'

She quickly poured coffee for Fletcher and handed it to him with a meaningful glance. Fletcher asked about the drive from Sydney and told Beau he was lucky to have missed the bad weather. Beau said he'd stayed overnight at a small pub a little bit inland from the coast where the weather was fine and the night sky clear.

The mood in the room was not chilled but chilly.

'Sit down, sit down,' Skye flapped her hands at the lounge. But rather than sit next to Beau, she moved onto one of two replica Eames organic chairs with patchwork upholstery.

Fletcher eased himself into the other Eames. How could he be so relaxed, when Skye was as antsy as a novice adventurer about to run over hot coals?

After a torturous few seconds, Fletcher rebooted the conversation. 'It's good to be able to put a face to the name. How long are you here for?'

Beau picked up his cup from the coffee table. 'I've got to be back in Sydney by tomorrow. I don't know if Skye filled you in but I'm a journalist, a sports journo, but like at the cutting edge.'

Skye scrutinised Beau's serious expression; his tone revealed not a hint of irony.

'The job's basically twenty-four-seven. I'm not kidding when I say that mate. I'm under the pump to get stories out, exclusives, one-on-ones with superstars, up-and-comings and the rest of it. Never stops. Pressure's enormous.'

Beau checked his watch and cast a glance at Skye.

'Hey Babe, what about that toast?'

Skye leapt up, a jack in the box, and was lucky not to spill any of her coffee. In the kitchen, she put two thick slices of fruit-and-nut loaf in the toaster while the two men discussed rugby league's struggle to draw the crowds to matches compared to AFL and football, which were often sell outs at the city's main stadiums.

As she buttered the toast, she silently thanked Fletcher for keeping the focus on Beau. While she sliced the toast, she considered that Beau had always been the focus of their relationship too.

'I came here to see Skye, of course,' Beau said as she handed him the plate of toast and sat back down.

He picked up a slice, bit into it and gave Fletcher the thumbs up with his free hand. 'Like I was saying,' he said, chewing, 'I'm always searching for exclusives. The big chiefs in Sydney said I should check out Desiree Bay and catch up with Skye. But while I was here, they thought it'd be a good idea touch base with Airen, interview him for a series we're putting together on rugby league players.'

The words were spoken so casually that, at first, Skye didn't quite understand Beau's meaning.

She leaned forward, elbows on her knees, and rubbed her hands together. 'So, what are you saying? You're here to interview my brother?'

Beau finished off the slice, did a quick scan for a serviette and, not finding one, licked butter and crumbs from his individual fingers.

'I'm definitely here to see you Babe. But if Airen's around, I got the camera, the sound, and it can be done as casual or formal as he likes. I mean, we could do it here, if it's easier.'

It was Fletcher's turn to look perplexed. 'What do you want to interview him about? He hasn't played for a while.'

Beau pushed out his bottom lip, eyebrows jutting over his eyes in sincere mode. 'Life as a player, life after playing, what happens next, etcetera. All fun, nothing serious. I wouldn't want the guy to feel uncomfortable about all the shit that's gone down.'

Skye's nervous energy shifted to suspicion. She lightly placed two fingers on her neck in an effort to slow down the pulse there that seemed to be beating out of control.

'I don't want to make a fuss but I thought we already went over this when you called me.' Skye could barely recall their phone conversation even though it was only a couple of days ago. 'It was a no then and it's still a no. An emphatic no. You can't do this Beau. You can't walk in here and expect to interview my brother about his personal life.'

She never thought she'd see Beau wriggle in mental discomfort but she was certain he was sheepish. He lowered his eyes away from hers to stare intently at his designer shoes. But it was all over in a matter of seconds as if he'd given himself a silent pep talk. He raised his head and gave her his attention, like he was doing a piece- to-camera, directly at her, all fake sincerity and intimacy. As though he'd rehearsed his lines earlier, knowing his integrity would be queried.

'Babe, the big guns are pushing for this,' he said and sniffed. 'It's a golden opportunity for Airen to defend his position and get the sympathy vote from the fans who love him, no matter what shit's gone down. These people, the fans, deserve answers and I'm the best man for the job. I've got the credentials. I can give your little brother the boost he needs to get back in the game.'

Fletcher rubbed his chin. 'Mate. With all due respect, I can't see how this could help Airen. It's up to him to approach you when the time is right, and he's ready to talk.'

'Yeah, well sometimes that's not how it works, mate.' The friendly happy-go- lucky demeanour had disappeared in an instant. Skye had seen it happen before. Beau did not like to be challenged.

'If Airen steps up now, he's got a chance to redeem himself in the eyes of the true believers.' Beau's voice had a hard edge to it. 'If he leaves it for too much longer, people will only remember the bad stuff. He can save face by speaking out now.'

Skye cocked her head and frowned. 'You're not here to see me, you're here to corner my brother.'

In a nonchalant move, Beau hooked his shoulders to his ears and faced her, palms opened and fingers splayed. 'This is a deal breaker Skye. I need this gig. I promised I'd get an interview with your brother in the bag by tomorrow.'

'I'm not sure I'm following you. A deal breaker in what respect?'

'Us. Relationships are about support. I get the feeling you're not supporting me on this.'

Skye pressed a hand to her mouth to stifle a burst of the giggles. She couldn't believe he could be so arrogant. Why hadn't she ever noticed before? Regaining her composure, she fixed him with an if looks-could-kill stare.

'Here's the facts Beau. I would never betray my brother for you to get an exclusive interview that would destroy any chance of him getting back into the game, or any other profession for that matter. I don't know where Airen is and, if I did, you'd be the last person I'd tell.'

She stood up and gestured to the front door. 'I think you should go back to Sydney. We don't have anything else to say to each other.'

Beau stood up too, completely nonplussed, as though he'd fully expected Skye to hand over Airen like a lame horse to the knackery. She was sure he'd assured his superiors of her cooperation, that he'd have an interview with the disgraced former footy star locked in and done and dusted before the end of the day.

'I'm sorry it had to end this way.' He smoothed a hand over his hair, not sounding sorry at all. 'I'll have to find him without your help.'

Suddenly, Fletcher was up and blocking Beau's path so there was only a hair's breadth between them. A good ten centimetres taller, Fletcher towered over the other man.

'Mate, I don't think that's a good idea,' Fletcher growled.

He appeared to have grown in stature, swamping Beau with his height and quiet yet menacing presence.

'If you want to keep your pretty-boy television face intact I suggest you get in your fancy car and get the hell out of here.'

Beau shifted his head back, eyes glazed. 'Are you serious, mate?'

'I'm giving you good advice. No one in Dezzy will help you find Airen so if you're smart, you'll fuck off back to Sydney and tell your ratings' obsessed chieftains that your tawdry little assignment ain't gonna happen.'

Beau stepped back and dug in his jeans pocket for his car keys. In a flash it became clear to Skye that he lacked any of the traits required to make a good partner and father.

He inclined his head towards her, mouth downturned in a typical Beau pout. 'I'm not gonna stand here and take this shit from your weed-smoking, hippy-dippy boyfriend from the bush,' he said. 'I'm sorry it had to end this way Babe.'

Skye smiled weakly. He could have stolen the line from a B-grade romcom.

'Yeah, me too,' she said, without feeling and not feeling anything, as the man who had been the focus of her perfect family fantasy walked out the door.

Hopefully, it would be forever.

CHAPTER 23

After Skye showered and dressed, she checked the four voicemail messages on her phone. She deleted Beau's without listening to it. Rather than feeling a sense of loss at his departure, a weight had lifted from her shoulders.

How could she have been so dumb? Beau's unexpected appearance at Fletcher's fast forwarded the inevitable demise of their relationship. When she stopped to think about it, which she'd never done before, it had always been a casual arrangement that lacked any real commitment from either of them.

Comfortable, easy, unchallenging and lacking passion. Lazy on both sides. Both their faults. It would have petered out anyway. Maybe if she'd stayed in Sydney, it would have been a slower and more painful ending.

But that couldn't stop the tiny knife of disappointment that twisted in her back. Of knowing Beau's only motive for the drive to Dezzy. He planned to use her to get to Airen for a tell-all tale that would seal her brother's fate as a loser and has-been. Washed up in his twenties.

Beau's insensitivity bordered on mental cruelty. That and his total lack of respect for her and her family hurt. Why hadn't she noticed these things before?

For all his lack of insight, Skye had to give Beau credit for picking up on the vibe between her and Fletcher. When Beau made the reference to her 'hippy boyfriend', Skye snuck a peek at the accused whose stormy gaze remained steadfastly fixed on her ex-boyfriend.

'Fletcher's girlfriend'. It had a pleasant ring to it.

The remaining three voicemails were from Sun. They were basically the same. The last was sent half an hour ago, just after one pm.

'Please call me. It's urgent.'

Skye threw up her hands in despair. Didn't Sun know how to send a message that contained useful information, not the bare minimum that drove Skye to distraction?

An image of Lou in early labour nudged her into action. She pressed her sister's number, heart in mouth.

Sun, breathless. 'Skye, thank god.'

'Is Lou okay? Is it the baby?'

'Yes, yes, she's fine. Lou and the baby are fine. It's Airen. He's gone. Disappeared.'

Skye didn't get it. Airen often disappeared, so what was the problem?

'Have you checked with Ash-Lee? Or Grandma? Or the pub?'

'We called the pub. He's been there, and so has Beau.'

Skye's heart plummeted. She leaned against the wall and slid her back down to the floor. 'Bastard.'

'Apparently, insults were exchanged, then punches. Airen hit Beau in the face. It was a beauty, according to my sources.' There was a hint of a chuckle in Sun's voice. 'Then the gutless bastard ran to the cops to file a complaint. But I don't give a frig about Beau. I'm glad Airen belted him. He's not the right person for you, Skye. He's a scumbag, of the lowest order...'

'Yeah, yeah, yeah, but what about Airen? Where did he go? Does anyone have any idea?'

Silence. Then a cough as though Sun was trying to hold it together. 'He left a note.'

Skye's throat constricted. She swallowed hard. 'What do you mean, a note?'

'We found a note slipped under our door, like a farewell note.' Sun's voice broke but she managed to continue. 'It hasn't been there for that long. Maybe half an hour.'

'What did he say, what's in it?'

Sun, who never cried, sniffled. 'I can't read it. Wait, I'll get Lou.'

'Skye?' Lou sounded like she had a blocked nose. She'd been crying too.

'Lou, what did he write?'

''It's a bit of a scrawl. I think he was crying when he wrote it because the bottom bit's blurred.'

'What's the gist of it?'

''This is hard for me too Skye but here goes,' There was a pause. Skye could hear Lou swallowing. She drew in a shaky breath. '"To my family, I love you very much. Please forgive me. I'm not in a good way. I failed you. I'm not the son or brother I wanted to be." And then it gets harder to read. We can't make out the rest. It's like it got wet and the words smudged.'

'None of it?'

'No, well... we think your name's there but we can't be sure. But we're all so worried. We think it could be a...'

Skye finished for her, 'a suicide note?'

A strangled sob from Lou. 'Where would he go, Skye? We have to find him fast. He's not anywhere. It's like he dropped off the planet.'

'I'll come over now.' Skye hated to ask but this was no time for grudges. 'Where are Mum and Jimmy?'

'They're here. We'll wait for you. Bring Fletcher.'

Skye drew in a deep breath. 'We'll be there soon.'

She found Fletcher on the back deck, head tilted back to watch a flock of sulphur-crested cockatoos squawking like squabbling children as they streaked across a Cerulean sky.

Skye hesitated. She was loathe to break the spell; he appeared so serene. But she had no choice. 'I'm sorry to interrupt but it's Airen. He's missing. We're meeting at Sun and Lou's place.'

Fletcher snapped to attention. He placed the tip of his thumb and index finger between his lips and blew out an ear-piercing whistle. Then he strode back inside and grabbed his car keys off the kitchen bench as Occy bound into the room.

Without speaking, they left the house and piled into the Kombi van, Occy wedged between them, ever watchful as though he was aware of the grave nature of the situation.

Skye felt like she was going to explode. She wished Fletcher would drive faster. They needed to be there. Every second was precious. Airen could already be gone. He could be lying somewhere with an empty bottle in his hand, or even worse…

'You can't think of the worst outcome Skye. We'll find him. It'll be okay.' Fletcher talked quietly in a measured tone. She knew he was right. But the note.

'He wrote a note. It didn't sound like a cry for help, it was a more like goodbye.'

She turned her head to the passenger-side window and stared at the newly lush countryside, transformed by the rain from pale brown to deep green. She would usually marvel at nature's ability to repair itself, to recover from the onslaught of increasingly traumatic weather events. Maybe that was what happened to Airen. The trauma of their father's death had manifested into a monster from which there was no escape. He no longer had the strength to repair himself.

They passed a macadamia plantation where row after row of trees, that from a distance resembled huge green pompoms, hung heavy with clusters of round nuts encased in thick woody armour. At the end of long sturdy stems, they reminded Skye of the clicker clacker toys Airen used to play with as a kid, usually while she was studying.

Skye broke the silence to run through possible locations that Airen might flee to, and fell into reminiscing.

'He followed me everywhere when he was little. It used to drive me crazy. I used to take him to the shops on Mum's bike. He was four. He'd sit in the baby seat and I'd pretend he was *my* baby.'

She laughed and shook her head at her youthful naivety.

'He was the cutest kid. Everybody adored him. Tourists, especially from overseas, stopped us in the street or on the beach so they could pose for photos with him. It was those big brown eyes and that infectious smile. I could've made a fortune in photo fees if I'd been savvy.'

'And what about your Dad?' Fletcher turned to her briefly. 'How did he get on with Airen?'

Skye frowned. 'It was hard.'

She sucked on her cheeks as she tried to recall any moments of true affection between father and son. 'My mother was over the moon when Airen was born. That's not to say that Dad wasn't. He'd always wanted a son.'

Fletcher pressed his foot to the floor on the accelerator and the Kombi increased in speed to 90kph, with a slight tremor through the cabin.

'But,' Skye continued, 'when Airen was born I was ten and Sun was thirteen. Ten years is a long time between kids, and Airen wasn't an easy baby. He was colicky and demanding. Mum was exhausted and, now I come to think of it, Dad didn't get it. He expected her to carry on, business as usual. It took its toll, Dad's refusal to help any more than he had to. I think he was resentful of this difficult baby.'

Skye laughed at this new realisation. Her father had resented the attention the women in the family gave Airen.

Fletcher eased his foot off the pedal as they reached the bottom of the hill and a speed limit of 80kph, which dropped to 50kph in the town centre.

'What about when he was older?'

'Yeah, problems there too. Dad was dux of primary school and high school. Airen didn't exactly excel at academia even though his sporting prowess was extraordinary. And he got into big trouble in high school. He climbed into the school bell tower with a couple of mates and decorated the walls with manga-style graffiti. The only reason he wasn't expelled was because he excelled at sport, particularly rugby league.

'Dad was mortified. You'd think he would have been proud of his son's rebellious nature. But I think he had this dream of Airen becoming a Rhodes Scholar or prime minister, or some such palaver.'

Skye stared thoughtfully out the window, the green hedgerows giving way to an avenue of eucalypts. 'Airen came into his own when he was playing footy or surfing. Dad may have been the literary genius, chief debater and all-round raconteur but Airen, he was poetry in motion once he touched a football. And he could have been a pro surfer if he cared at all about it. He was grace itself. And everyone in Dezzy adored him.'

Occy, tired of sitting upright, draped his body across Skye, his head resting in her lap. Stroking his thick fur calmed her.

'I didn't give Dad and Airen's relationship that much thought. It's taken this long for me to really see that I was Dad's favourite. I guess it must have been obvious to Airen. He seemed to accept it. Maybe he just became resigned. And Sun didn't care. She never got on with Dad. He didn't like the idea of having a lesbian daughter even though he came across as the most liberal-minded person you could ever meet.'

She rested her cheek on the upholstered leather seat and released a big sigh. 'Shame I had to leave town in a huff and come back again three years later to get it into perspective.'

Fletcher gave a gravelly chuckle. 'Sometimes that's what it takes. Time and distance. Helps you come to terms with the shit that goes down in life.'

He slowed down as they cruised through the outskirts of town. Skye risked the question, 'And what about you? Did you get on with your father?'

Fletcher's harsh laugh was enough to make Occy twitch. 'Oh man. No. Long story short, I never saw him much. Or my mother. They were junkies. I was an accident. After I was born, they basically abandoned me. I was brought up by my father's parents. My paternal grandparents. They're good people. They gave me the stability and love I never got with my mother and father. I was lucky. Without them, who knows what would have happened.'

Skye tickled underneath Occy's chin, her heart going out to Fletcher. She waited a moment before attempting another personal question. 'Did you ever meet up with your parents later and make amends?'

That laugh again, but less convincing as though time had dissipated the anger. 'Nothing so romantic. My mother's whereabouts remain unknown. She probably died from an overdose in some backstreet in Fremantle. But a couple of years ago my father crawled out of the woodwork to congratulate me on my success.'

He stressed 'congratulate', his voice tinged with distaste. 'He wanted money. Hitched all the way from the Pilbarra to Margaret River to find me. It had nothing to do with wanting to reconnect. To check I was okay.'

'How did he know you had money?'

'One of his mates saw my name mentioned somewhere, joined the dots and told him.'

Skye stopped scratching Occy's head. 'Where was your name mentioned?'

The quality of Fletcher's laugh softened. 'Didn't the girls tell you?'

'Girls?'

'Oceane, Sun and Lou? I call them the Three Degrees. If you want to know almost everything about me, they're the ones to ask. I got the third degree before we entered into the baby agreement.'

He changed down a gear as they entered the 50kph zone on Sutton St and chugged towards the war memorial on the corner of Sinclair St, across the road from The Last Post Hotel. The Old Bakery, and Sun and Lou's place above it, was around the corner. Fletcher indicated right.

Skye had so many questions but didn't want to push too hard too fast.

'Did you give him money?'

'Yeah. He's still my father.' The bitterness had seeped from his voice.

Skye waited for the bright flash of perfect teeth. But Fletcher was in his head, dealing with his own demons, staring ahead as they pulled up outside the bakery.

CHAPTER 24

All the other words on Airen's note were blurred like the transient work of a sign writer buzzing around on the face of the sky. Eventually, they were dispersed by the wind. But Skye's name was still distinguishable, though fuzzy around the edges.

She placed the note on Sun and Lou's kitchen bench, underneath a 1960s glass paperweight, in its centre a cluster of coloured glass that resembled bright assorted lollies. That would hold it there. She didn't want to lose this connection to her brother. While there was a note, there was hope.

Oceane pulled a piece of paper and her thick purple reading glasses from a recycled hessian bag. 'I've made a list of five places Airen might consider going.' She adjusted the glasses and scanned the list.

Everyone seemed relieved that Oceane had taken control. Skye didn't mind either. She wasn't about to get petty over matters of life and death, and, she had to admit, her mother had always been a highly adept businesswoman, despite her daffy manner. She knew how to run a meeting and organise a spreadsheet.

Of course, the list was an excellent idea. Common sense really.

'One,' Oceane said in a shaky voice. 'Mt Manning. He climbed it recently. He went up there at dawn and didn't come back down 'til late in the evening. He loves the isolation and the view across the bay.'

Staring over the top of her glasses, she gave Fletcher a trembling smile. 'Fletch, would you mind covering that one? I know it's a big ask.'

Fletcher grabbed an apple from a bowl filled with fruit. 'No worries, it's getting late already so I'll leave now, if that's okay. There's no reception up there so you mightn't hear from me for a while.' He made for the door, lightly brushing Skye's hand with his as he passed. She had no idea if it was intentional, but it had the desired effect. Now Skye knew how it felt to have an electric connection to someone.

'I'll go with him,' Sun said, picking up a backpack and jacket. 'It's better to have two people out there to scout around.'

Skye knew the pang of jealousy was unwarranted but she didn't want Sun to be sharing a conversation with Fletcher that she could be having. But there was nothing she could do without coming across as a complete prat so she watched the pair leave with longing seeping into her bones.

Oceane gave her an odd look and pushed the glasses firmly up to the bridge of her nose. Its red raw tip matched the rims of her eyes.

'Two. He could be at Ash-Lee's caravan. She's not picking up her calls, so I'll go out there and check. He might be there or somewhere close by. Whatever, Ash-Lee might know something we don't. I've got feelers out at the pub and Brad's at the board factory. By the way, the pub is number three and the board factory's four. Brad'll keep an eye on both. He'll be in touch straight away if Airen turns up.'

Skye turned to Lou and Jimmy. 'So, what are we doing?'

'Well.' Oceane gave a throat-clearing cough. 'Lou's staying here, just in case. I'd like you and Jimmy to head out to The Point,' she checked her list though she didn't need to, 'which is number five.'

This wasn't fair. Why had she been partnered with Jimmy and why did she have to go to The Point? Her breath quickened as the warning signs of panic flared in her chest.

'Mum, please?' Oceane jerked up her head, and Skye realised she hadn't used the term 'Mum' since before her father's death. It slipped out before she could stop it. She needed to explain.

'I've avoided The Point all week,' she blurted out. 'I don't know how I'll deal with it, going back there...'

Her mother smiled sadly but Skye could tell she was resolute. 'You know The Point better than any of us, Skye. You used to give Airen surfing lessons there. And you'd stay with him on the beach while he built those ridiculously complicated sandcastles. You were amazing. You always kept an eye on him, watched his back.'

Skye blinked at her mother. 'I'm not sure I can...'

'Of course you can.' Oceane put down the list and grabbed Skye's hands in her own. It was familiar and oddly comforting when it should have been annoying. 'If anyone can bring Airen back, it's you Skye. You're a strong woman.'

It had been a long time since her mother had talked to her with this much honesty and empathy. And it had been a long, long time since Skye had managed to hide her animosity. But today she didn't feel any anger towards Jimmy or her mother.

'Big surf. It scares me. I get panic attacks.'

The mere thought of the ocean in all its swaggering aggression tore her skeleton from her body, leaving her soft and exposed.

'I'm not brave enough for this,' she whispered through dry lips.

Why wouldn't her mother believe her?

Oceane closed her eyes as though struck by a bad memory. Squeezing both Skye's hands tight, she opened them again and stared straight at her.

'Jimmy can swim breaststroke. If need be, he can strip off the kilt and dive in to help out. If need be.'

Skye appraised Jimmy with his pale Scottish skin that turned tomato red after ten minutes in the unforgiving Australian sun, and his big thick limbs that were more appropriate for caber tossing than freestyle.

Breaststroke wouldn't save him in a big swell.

Skye moved to the door. She had no say in this. She had to find her brother.

Her mother took the keys to Sun and Lou's car and power-walked out the door ahead of them. She scooped her red caftan up around her thighs as she eased into the driver's seat, revved the motor and shot off with a wave of a heavily beringed hand.

To say Skye felt uncomfortable with Jimmy was an under-statement. They'd never spent time alone together and she did not intend to start the conversation.

As she yanked at the passenger-side door of Jimmy's car, the Leyland P76 protested by creaking with a painful rusting-metal whine.

Jimmy winced and ground his teeth, shoulders raised to his ears. 'Gotta get some WD40 onto it. Poor ol' Duncan, he's an ol' fella with rheumy joints. A bit like myself.' He gave an apologetic smile as he slid into the bucket seat behind the steering wheel.

Skye pulled the seatbelt across her torso, inserted it into the dock with a click, and pressed the palms of her hands either side of her thighs on the milk-chocolate coloured vinyl upholstery.

Jimmy placed the key in the ignition and turned it decisively. Duncan coughed and spluttered like an old man shaken into a twilight wakefulness from a nap before falling back into a snoring slumber.

Jimmy had another go, this time flicking his wrist like he'd probably done hundreds of times before. This time it failed to convince Duncan to wake up. They jerked forward and stopped with a shudder as Jimmy eased his foot from the clutch pedal.

'This isn't the time to get all temperamental Duncan boyo.' He spoke soothingly to the car and stroked the wood-grained dash. Then, with a ferocious growl, 'C'mon ye useless old bugger. Start.'

Skye checked her watch. It was almost three. It would be dark by six. She exhaled slowly, determined not to screw up this fragile rapprochement with Jimmy.

'We could walk there, or run.' She kept her tone neutral but felt like her heart was doing its own thing in her chest. Totally out of control.

Lou, hearing the commotion, came outside to watch as Jimmy made one more attempt to start the car.

She squealed and poked her fingers in her ears after Duncan backfired with an alarming shot-gun 'pop'.

Jimmy thwacked his hands on the steering wheel. 'Bloody useless piece of crap. Bloody Australian-made rubbish.'

In several minutes, after Skye swapped her flimsier sandals for a pair of Lou's runners, they were half running half walking down Sutton St towards the beach.

As she tried to find a rhythm to her breathing, Skye thought they must look like the odd couple. Jimmy wore a blue-themed kilt and a 'Save the sharks' T-shirt and Skye, a tartan flanno shirt and overalls.

For a big man, Jimmy moved in a smooth relaxed style, large feet one in front of the other, his torso held tall. He covered a lot of ground with little effort and Skye had to focus on keeping up. It was tiring.

Over his shoulder Jimmy called to her, 'Yer aura has changed.'

'What?'

'Yer aura. The light around ye. When ye got here last week it had a nasty hue to it and yer chakras associated with feeling were imbalanced. Ye lacked self-love and, if yer'll forgive my forthrightness, ye needed to 'be with',' (using his fingers, he made the parenthesis sign around the words 'be with') 'someone who loves ye. But now the orange is back in yer aura. Glowin' like the sun. If I didn't know any better, I'd think yer'd found the right bloke.'

He slowed down and they fell into line.

'Really?' Skye's face was hot from the exertion which she hoped covered the blush.

'Och aye. I know yer not into this sort of thing Lass but even so, something has changed in ye. A bright light has replaced the dirty brown, torn ribbons that *were* flowing from ye.'

Skye didn't know how he managed to move at such a steady pace and talk at the same time. The man was a Celtic giant, propelled by a belief that the world and everything in it had redeeming features, that chakras and auras could explain away everything.

They were running, him at a jog and Skye at a fair pace, along the paved path parallel to the beach. The surf, Skye noticed, wasn't pumping. It was manageable, she thought, with a wave height of about one-and-a-half metres.

Jimmy kept on talking. 'And ye heart chakra has opened up a bit too.'

Skye couldn't help a laugh. 'Should I be worried about that?'

'Nah,' Jimmy said. 'I can see hints of green, not quite there yet.'

'So green is good, not mouldy or gangrenous?'

'Och aye. Green means yer giving and receiving love. And yer finally able to forgive.'

They sprinted up a hill. It was a mild winter's day and Skye could feel the sweat. Moisture had gathered under her armpits, across her back and on her face. She pulled up the bottom of the flanno shirt, bent her head and wiped it across her damp brow. If she could take it off, she would. Same with the overalls.

In the distance, The Point jutted out like a bony leg. Almost at the end of its dangerously elevated foot was a small white lighthouse that was still active.

In any other circumstances, it would have been a pleasant journey to the top of the hill. Skye would have admired the rare wrought iron structure with a small round window that reminded her of a space ship.

But not today. Skye pounded up the steep gravel incline. Her feet felt more like lumps of cement with every step. The land fell away to her left sand plunged into an azure sea that had the clarity of rare diamonds. The wind threaded wispy fingers through her hair, lifting it from her shoulders as she inhaled pure unadulterated air.

On the horizon, she made out several small fishing boats, yachts and whale-watching cruise boats. Humpbacks and dolphins, swordfish and sharks, turtles and sea lions, rays and octopus were out there somewhere, diving to the depths of the shimmering ocean.

Skye stopped in her tracks, doubled over and placed her hands on her thighs as she fought for breath to stave off a panic attack.

I mustn't think of the past or the future. I must be in the present.

'Can we just stop for a sec?' she panted at Jimmy. She didn't want to cry in front of him, or collapse in a heap. But, what if something bad had already happened to Airen? It would be her fault. Always her fault. She was the problem.

Jimmy turned to her and led her by the hand, his expression soft and gentle. 'Lass, don't give up now. Don't let me down. I need yer to help me find the Lad. He'll be right. We've got this in the bag.'

Skye nodded furiously. Her nose streamed and her vision blurred.

'I'm good,' she insisted, taking in small gulps of wind and sucking back the snot. 'Let's keep going.'

The Point used to be Skye and Airen's adventure playground. Together they'd watched, mouths agape, as humpbacks breached, flinging their massive bodies out of the water and smashing back into the sea.

She'd shared her 'secret spot' at The Point with Airen when he was five and she was fifteen.

'Whatever you do, don't tell Mum and Dad about this,' she'd warned him. Skye made her little brother swear on their mother's grave that he would never tell.

He'd gazed up at Skye, his big eyes swimming with confusion. 'But isn't Mum still alive?'

Their secret spot was a cave on the rock platform at the base of The Point. To get there, they followed a steep rock-strewn path worn into the almost vertiginous cliff face by generations of fishermen and surfers.

Skye remembered how she used to scramble down, as nimble as a goat, with her board to join the throng of surfers. But she left the board behind when she was with Airen.

Together, they explored tidal pools that teemed with marine life. It was like staring into mini aquariums, regularly cleared out and refreshed as the tide inched in and out, in a predictable rhythm. Star fish, crabs, barnacles, periwinkles and tiny fish, many of them brightly coloured, were swept into temporary accommodation by the incoming tide. They floated away as another high tide began its recession. The tide flushed them out to freedom.

Then there were the creatures that made the deep shimmering bowls of sea water their permanent homes. Barnacles, limpets and whelks, that reminded Skye of a Mr Whippy ice-cream, stayed suctioned to the smooth worn stone, forever attached to their little piece of paradise. Never to see or explore, ever tied to the shore.

She and Airen were free then. Happy. Airen, eyes alight with mischief, poked gently at tiny sea snails that retreated into swirly shells, prodded lightly at soft anemone that folded in on themselves, whooped in delight as he tripped lightly across the rock platform and dived in the sea for a quick dip. Skye, frantic, would shout at him to 'get out quick smart'.

How many times had she threatened to dob him into Mum and Dad? 'You could've killed yourself,' she'd shriek and haul him, a slithery fish, out of the sea. Then they'd both laugh. Lying on their backs on the platform, squinting into the blue as the sun dried their salt-encrusted bodies.

Skye had discovered the honeycomb sandstone sea cave before Airen was born. Like the rock platform, it was only accessible at low tide. It became Skye and Airen's retreat at the edge of the world. Or that's how the teenage Skye imagined it. Airen drew caveman pictures on the walls in white chalk while Skye watched the surfers through high-powered binoculars nicked from Jonno's ute. For lunch, they filled up with marshmallows toasted over a fire made with kindling gathered beforehand and stuffed into Skye's backpack, along with one of Jonno's disposable cigarette lighters.

Jimmy's lilting voice jolted her back to a hellish reality.

'Skye, Lass, I wondered if I might tell ye something that ye may or may not already know.'

Skye caught up again and saw Jimmy feeling the heat. Droplets of sweat had formed on his upper lip and brow, and his T-shirt clung to his back.

She didn't think there was anything more to reveal. No more truths to be told.

'I guess so.' The belligerence lingered so she tried to soften it with extra encouragement. 'Go ahead. I'm listening.'

They were at the lighthouse, a circular tower constructed from cement- rendered concrete blocks more than one hundred years ago and painted in nautical white with a blue rimmed balcony with black balustrade.

Jimmy slumped against the cool wall in the shade and gulped down half the bottle of water he'd grabbed from the car. He wiped his arm across his mouth, cleaned the rim of the bottle with the bottom of his T-shirt and offered the rest to

Skye. She leaned her cheek on the cool rendered bricks and accepted the offer, hesitating for a moment to consider Jimmy's germ count before draining the bottle. Thirst had got the better of her.

She walked ahead and Jimmy followed. Stopping at a scrubby entrance to the path, they observed the ocean again. The late afternoon southerly breeze had strengthened to knock the waves flat.

'I only started going out with yer mother after she and yer father agreed to, how shall I put it, call it a day.'

Skye flinched as the wind whooshed around them. Jimmy's 'announcement' had come from out of nowhere.

'What do you mean - 'call it a day'?'

His dark eyes softened around the edges, he puffed out his cheeks and expelled a breath.

'Yer mum and Jonno had been driftin' apart for a long time. They agreed to a friendly separation which coincided with council's decision to scrap the DA for the resort.'

She was about to retort with 'I don't believe you' but a collage of secret smiles, comments and actions between Oceane and Jonno in the weeks before Jonno's death now meant something different.

Separate bedrooms because of Jonno's snoring, or so Skye assumed. Oceane's crystal buying trip to India without Jonno. The uncomfortable silences between her parents whenever Skye was around.

And there were Jonno's derisive remarks about Oceane's blossoming business. At the time, Skye had thought them unfair. When Oceane began to gain kudos for her business, her father dished out personal insults such as, 'Right time right place, that's all it is. You don't need credentials to sell crystals in these uncertain times.'

Skye assumed her father's unwarranted criticisms would subside over time and his and Oceane's relationship would eventually return to normal.

She sighed and squeezed her face into a grimace. If it was truth time, she would speak her truth. 'I saw you with Mum the day Dad died. Outside their house. Kissing. I hated both of you so much for that. I was going to dob you into Dad. I thought you and Mum were having an affair, making a fool of Dad.'

Jimmy's expression was one of momentary puzzlement and then comprehension as he pulled back the curtain in time to that day.

He opened the palms of his hands towards Skye. 'Believe me Lass, it was well and truly over between yer mother and father by then. They planned to officially announce their separation to the family that weekend.'

The now familiar sting of tears pushed at the back of Skye's eyes. 'This makes Dad seem like a right royal prick, doesn't it?'

Jimmy shook his head vehemently. 'Na, no way.' His voice rose to a shout as the wind lifted its game to a howl. 'Jonno was a good man Skye, ye must never forget that. Jonno knew about yer mother and me. It was transparent. And on that go-dawful day, he gave us his blessing. A lesser man would ne'er ha' done that.'

CHAPTER 25

As she and Jimmy clambered down the path, Skye fought to remain upright against the wind. It shoved and buffeted, a massive swinging hand that attempted to scuttle her feet from under her. The path was a semi-dried mud-pie mess from recent wild weather. Tufts of hardy native grasses and the occasional stunted shrub dotted the area. There was nothing much to hold onto. If she fell, she would collide with Jimmy and they would hurtle to their deaths below on the rock platform.

Skye scolded her inner voice. 'It'll be all right on the night,' she murmured into the wind, which snatched the words away like a thief.

Jimmy kept turning his head to check on her, giving an intermittent thumbs up and grinning like he was having the time of his life.

It used to take Skye and Airen about ten minutes to scuttle down the goat track. When Skye went on her own with her short surfboard slung over her shoulder in a surfboard bag, she managed it in less.

But she'd never done it in these conditions.

Jimmy swivelled to face her and Skye, who had gathered momentum, almost slammed into him.

'A wee bit ta go,' he shouted. His large hands gripped her forearms and kept her stable. 'We're almost there but it's slippery ahead where the water runs off.'

They tiptoed around a patch of green slime where the path ended at bare rock, then stepped lightly as a pair of gazelle across the platform, avoiding rock pools.

The tide was low but turning.

Skye scanned the vast open space, on alert for any sign of Airen, in or out of the water.

She led the way and pointed to the far end of the platform.

'This way,' she called over her shoulder, skipping across the still pools filled with live gems she and Airen used to treasure as their own.

They had named themselves 'the keepers of the tidal pools' with a 'look but don't touch or remove' policy.

When Airen was older, he came to the platform on his own. He photographed many of the pools and compiled an album filled images of maroon sea anemones, slate-grey crabs, iridescent fish, luminous-green kelp and burnt-umber starfish.

She and Jimmy were almost at the end of the platform when the entrance to the cave became visible. Still, Skye had to guide Jimmy to it.

'A long time ago a rock fall partially blocked the entrance to the cave, which is why it's hard to find,' she told him, as the wind whipped her hair across her face.

They squeezed between two massive rocks into a cavernous interior space that looked like it had been gouged out of the rock face with a massive ice cream scoop. Left behind was a curved wall and cathedral ceiling streaked with shimmering golden and cream striations.

Jimmy cupped his hands either side of his mouth. 'Airen?'
Skye repeated the call, which echoed around the cave.

At the same time, they spotted the makeshift fireplace at the cave's centre. Skye inhaled the scent of medicinal eucalyptus and burnt kindling. She thought of the many times she and Airen had sat around a fire here, warming their hands, pretending to be shipwrecked on a desert island.

Jimmy crouched down and hovered the palm of his hand above the charcoal remains. 'I don't know if it's my imagination but it feels warm. Not long out.'

Skye sat on her haunches and did the same. 'It is. It must be him. He's been here.'

She bounced back up onto the balls of her feet, energy surging through her. In the dim light, she could make out something shoved against the glistening rock wall, damp from water seeping in from a fault line.

'Hey, over here.' She ran to the spot, knelt beside a backpack, unzipped the main compartment and pulled out a length of rope.

'Oh God,' she whispered and unconsciously touched her hand to her throat.

Jimmy was by her side. He placed a big mitt lightly on her shoulder. 'Not to worry Lass, rope's still in there. Unused.' He observed the smooth rock surfaces. 'I'm not sure what he planned to do with it.'

Skye's moan echoed around the cave as she dug deeper into the backpack and hauled out two one-litre bottles of vodka and a one-litre bottle of scotch. Unopened, seals intact.

Low to the dusty ground, she undid the rest of the zippers and upended the backpack's contents. Skye compiled a list. Three different coloured bottles of pills, one A4 writing pad, two black pens, one packet of three coloured highlighters, one packet of thick coloured chalk sticks, one packet of pink musk sticks, one 350g block of Cadbury Dairy Fruit and Nut chocolate (opened, the first two rows missing) and a worn paperback copy of *Occy: The Rise and Fall and Rise of Mark Occhilupo,* a biography of the famous Aussie surfer.

As she turned the book over and flipped through its pages, she wondered if Airen had borrowed it from Fletcher. Then she noticed the makeshift bookmark. It was a family photo at Sun's birthday party, taken about a year before Jonno died.

In it the three siblings grinned inanely at the camera, arms around each other. Their parents appeared more subdued. And rather than standing together, they acted as bookends to their three grown-up children. Skye shook her head ruefully. Now she'd heard Jimmy's version of events it was clear her parents had fallen out of love a long time before she noticed any emotional distance between them.

She flipped through the writing pad and found nothing except white pages ruled with fine blue lines. What had Airen planned to write to fill those pages?

They stood up, Skye struck by a sense of dread. Her breath quickened and she found it hard to speak. 'If he's not here, the only other place he can be is...'

Jimmy interrupted, his dark eyebrows drawn down. He rubbed his fingers over his whiskers. 'Not necessarily. He could have gone back up in another direction. An agile bloke could do it and Airen is a natural mountain goat. It's possible.'

They left the cave, which had been a respite from the now gale-force wind that beat the ocean into white tips that, when observed for any length of time, began to resemble shark fins flicking and disappearing from the opaque surface. Skye knew it was a trick of the eye but that didn't make it any less terrifying.

She inclined her head and squinted, seeking a sign from the roiling deep. Then tugged furiously at Jimmy's sleeve.

'I can see someone.' Her voice shrieked from somewhere out of her body as her heart galloped like a horse bolting from the start gate. 'There's someone out there, for god's sake.'

Jimmy whacked a hand to his forehead. 'Shite, I see it. It must be him.'

'What do we do? What do we do?' Skye felt faint. She grasped at Jimmy's arm with her eyes fixed firmly on the tiny speck that must have been about five hundred metres away. Out to sea. She couldn't afford to lose sight of him. If she did, she might never see him again.

She clutched harder as the speck lifted its stick figure arms and waved at them. She knew it was futile but she shouted out her brother's name and leaped up and down like a deranged cheerleader minus pom poms.

She had to let go of Jimmy, who was pulling off his shirt.

'What are you doing?' She glared at him, licked dry lips and tasted the salt. 'You can't go in there. It's not like it's a bloody twenty-five metre indoor swimming pool in some hick Scottish town. It's the bloody Pacific Ocean you bonkers idiot.'

She was losing it now, jabbing at him accusingly, letting the panic take hold. Jimmy continued to undress, removing the kilt followed by shoes and socks. He stood there in his red stretch underpants and a white singlet, his pale milky complexion luminous in the late afternoon light.

'I'll doddle on out there and have a wee chat to him.'

They both flinched and stumbled back as a white-frilled wave crashed onto the rocks and dissolved into hissing bubbles around their feet.

The tide had turned. It was on its way back in.

'A wee chat?' Skye laughed out a hacking cough of disbelief. 'Please, please, please Jimmy. You can't do this. I can swim. I'll go. You stay here.'

She'd made a commitment. There was no choice but to act. Without a thought in her head but Airen, she wrenched off shoes, overalls and flanno.

As she skittered to the edge of the platform in her bra and undies, Skye focussed on the dot in the distance before she dived into the teal-green depths of the ocean that had claimed her father's life.

* * *

Blind fear drove her forward and out to sea. Far from the safety of dry land and the firm warmth of mother earth.

The shock from the freezing water made her gasp and claw at the ocean like a rat fleeing from a sinking ship. Her stoke was uneven. She floundered. She was afraid she'd forgotten how to swim. If she breathed to the left, she copped a mouthful of briny sea, which coursed into her trachea so she had to stop and tread water to cough and splutter. She felt light-headed, as though she'd flown out of her body, which was functioning on autopilot.

The horror of the night her father died howled through her. She tried not to hyperventilate, her mouth a distorted oval vortex, hollow and ice cold as flashbacks wrenched her deeper into despair.

Back then. Jonno waving in the silver-slivered black of night. Airen floating faced-own, limp and lifeless. The wind's ululation, the ocean rising to meet its shrill cry with a swell the height of a three-storey building.

Now. She strained her eyes and fear jumped on her back her like a mugger sneaking up from behind.

Where was he? She'd lost sight of Airen. Where was he, for god's sake?

Skye swivelled her head this way and that. She almost sank with relief when his head reappeared, bobbing in the distance. It didn't feel like she was making any headway. He was too far away. The ocean would take him from her, claim him for another statistic.

Like it did to Jonno.

Somehow, another surge of adrenaline charged her and Skye's arms thrashed through the chop. Surprisingly, it seemed more manageable and she found a rhythm if she breathed to her right side.

Every few strokes she poked up her head, crocodile style with her eyes facing forward, to check his position. Closer, closer, closer. Feet beat, thrust down and up, opposite arm to leg, torso stretched and powerful.

'Skye!'

Her head jerked up, and she trod water. She was making headway.

'Airen!'

Head back down. Stroke after stroke, she closed the distance between them. Until she was there, almost beside him and, glancing over her shoulder, at least one kilometre from the rock platform.

'Airen, are you okay?'

He swam the several metres that separated them and hugged her close, almost pushing her under. She cried but her brother laughed, his usually sullen demeanour replaced by a big grin.

'What the?' She shoved him away, treading water with her arms and legs sea kelp fronds, in a weightless universe.

'I'm alive.' Airen moved in again, grabbed her tight and planted a fishy kiss on her cheek. 'I'm alive.'

Skye wriggled from the aquatic embrace. Her confusion must have been as plain as the nose on her face but Airen's gaze had shifted to the middle distance.

'Shit,' he said, euphoria abating. 'It's Jimmy.'

Skye couldn't believe it. Jimmy must have dived in after her.

'Far out! He can barely swim. We've got to get him.'

They struck out towards the Scotsman, whose hand was raised and, Skye wasn't sure if she imagined it, middle finger pointed skywards in a gesture colloquially referred to as 'up yours'.

By the time they reached him, Jimmy looked the worse for wear. Except for two hots spots on his cheeks, the colour had bled from his face and his complexion had turned from a healthy glow to dull pasty grey.

Skye gave his arm a reassuring squeeze. Even though she felt the chill of being in the open ocean for an extended period, Jimmy's flesh was unnaturally cold and he'd started to shiver.

He was seasick and hypothermic.

From her years as a junior lifesaver at high school, Skye had become familiar with hypothermia, where the body temperature drops from prolonged exposure to cold conditions. She witnessed its effects on several unlucky peers. If she and Airen didn't act fast, Jimmy's condition could become serious.

This was no time for harsh reprimands for foolhardy behaviour. 'We don't have far to go to get back to the shore. We'll swim either side of you and if you need to stop, let us know.'

Jimmy shuddered. 'I'm a wee bit under the weather.'

As Skye exchanged glances with Airen, she saw his expression change to one of firm resolution.

Airen shouted with great gusto, 'You'll be right mate, we're here.'

He resembled a wet shaggy dog, his dark hair plastered to his scalp and his cheeks bright from the exposure to the sun and wind.

It was the old Airen talking. A revitalised Airen. He hauled one of Jimmy's big arms across his shoulder and started a lop-sided sidestroke.

'Jimmy, raise your free arm and pull it through the water,' Skye coached as they set off at an excruciatingly slow pace as the swell heaved up and down.

Every so often, she called out encouragement. 'Nearly there' and 'When we're back, I'll wrap you in my flanno and we'll light a fire in the cave. See that in your mind's eye, how warm you'll feel in a soft comfy flanno in front of the fire. And whiskey, Airen has a bottle of quality Scotch whiskey in his pack. That'll do the trick.'

As they swam, with Jimmy's weight occasionally stopping Airen altogether, mother nature gave them a get out of jail free card. The ocean seemed to soften its grip as the tide flowed in, allowing them to move through its dense volume with greater ease than had been the case in the opposite direction.

But while the tide was helping out, it also caused a problem. It was on its way back in to cover the platform, to deposit new creatures into the rock pools and taxi temporary visitors back into the deep blue.

The low, exposed rock shelf was often swamped by waves so powerful they could knock a man down like a bowling pin and sweep him out to sea. They had to get Jimmy to the cave and warm him up before they could start back up the cliff.

Without warning, Jimmy's whole body twitched and he shoved Airen down hard on the shoulder. Airen went under and came up hacking and belching.

Arms flailing, and eyes lit like burning coals, Jimmy screeched, 'Shark.'

Skye's heart pumped like the bellows of a piano accordion and her ears roared but she kept it together. 'Keep your arms still. Sharks react to splashing.'

Dying in the multi-teethed maul of a shark was a visceral fear of most human beings. What they didn't know or refused to believe was that most lives claimed by the ocean in Australia were through drownings. And every year, at least a dozen hapless rock fishermen were swept into the sea compared to the average fatality rate of two persons per annum from shark-related deaths. But this was not the time to give Jimmy a lecture on the value of sharks and their importance to the ecosystem. If he'd seen a shark and it had noticed them, it was probable that curiosity would motivate it to check them out. No matter how much Skye defended sharks, she didn't fancy dying from the bite of an inquisitive apex predator.

Hoiking her legs up tightly, and hardly daring to breath, she narrowed her eyes and scoured the ocean's surface as efficiently as she could, periscope up. By her guesstimate, they were less than two hundred and fifty metres from the rock shelf. All she could see as the three of them rose and fell with the gathering swell was the whitewash from waves sloshing onto the platform in the distance.

She kept her voice hopeful. 'I can't see anything. Can you see anything Airen?'

Airen smiled benignly, reminding her of either a saint or an absolute eejit.

'It's not a shark.' His tone as serene as an oracle. 'It's dolphins.'

As confirmation, one of the creatures leaped in front of them, a glowing vision contorting its sleek torso into an effortless mid-air twist worthy of an Olympic ten. It winked at them with a gleaming eye, Skye was sure of it, before disappearing in a tidy splash. Now you see me, now you don't. The performance was over in a millisecond but they all witnessed it.

Skye was almost delirious with relief.

Jimmy blubbered like a baby.

Airen's smile was beatific. 'Hallelujah, praise the dolphins and all the awesome creatures on the planet.'

This was all Skye needed. Jimmy and Airen going bananas before they could get back to terra firma. Time was running out. The cold had started to creep through her bones, draining her of warm blood and replacing it with trays of ice cubes. Then, in the distance, she heard it. A familiar sound that rode on the back of the wind.

Skye put a finger as wrinkled as a prune to her numb lips. 'Shoosh. Can you hear it? Listen, it's an engine.'

Airen 'whooped' with joy as a boat came into view. Skye forgot about any danger from sharks; she trod water furiously in an effort to fling her arms as high as she could. 'Help, help, we're here, help!'

The small vessel bounced across the water in their direction and then decelerated. Skye's spirits soared. They'd been spotted.

As it drew closer, she yelped in ecstatic delight. Fletcher steered a small motorboat with an outboard engine and sunshade on top. Sun sat on a seat with Occy perched next to her. Both Fletcher and Sun's eyes widened in alarm while Occy barked an agitated welcome.

'Man, it's good to see you, the three of you,' Airen called out.

Fletcher nimbly pulled up the engine behind the stern and shouted instructions. 'Get Jimmy around here and I'll get him up.'

Airen and Skye dragged an almost unconscious Jimmy to the stern, where Fletcher reached down and grabbed at his brawny arms. It was a battle to get the big man aboard. Fletcher must have used sheer brute force to drag him under the armpits onto the narrow deck where he landed with a massive 'thwack' like the catch of the day.

Skye clung to the side of the small vessel, terrified it would upend and they'd all end up in the drink. After the boat stopped rocking violently, Fletcher got a shivering Jimmy upright on the middle seat where Sun tossed a blanket across his shoulders.

Fletcher gave Skye the go ahead. Teeth chattering, she scrabbled aboard as an imaginary Great White surged up from the ocean floor like a missile towards her vulnerable legs. *Jaws* had a lot to answer for, she thought.

Sun had moved to the seat near the bow. She shifted to make space for Skye beside her. Moments later, Airen clambered aboard. He sat next to Jimmy and began to vigorously rub the dazed man's big hands.

Fletcher positioned himself on the seat at the stern and flipped open a metal first aid box, white with a red cross. He handed a foil poncho to Airen. 'I've only got one of these. Put it on Jimmy and,' reaching up his arms, he dragged his jumper over his head and tossed it to her, 'Skye, put this on.'

To Airen, he said, 'Grab the towel under the seat mate, it'll keep you warm. And for Chris'sake, get the mad grin off your face. I'm not used to it.'

Occy, as if knowing his role, squeezed his plump warm body in between Jimmy and Airen.

Skye pulled the old grey woollen jumper over her head, pressed her face into it and inhaled Fletcher's scent of lemon myrtle soap, lanolin and sea spray.

Oh dear, she fell into a euphoric haze, *I'm in lust.*

CHAPTER 26

For the second time in a week, Skye found herself in Desiree Bay Hospital's emergency department.

Jimmy was suspended between Fletcher and Airen as they staggered into the main waiting room, each of the Scotsman's huge arms slung across their shoulders and his Yeti toes dragging along the floor.

He was still wrapped in the silver foil poncho with the hood over his head partially obscuring his face. The ocean had drained all the colour from him, Skye thought. His skin had the hue of pumice stone washed onto a beach and worn down by the elements. Jimmy's hairy muscular legs wobbled like jelly snakes as Fletcher and Airen helped the emergency team ease him onto a gurney. Covered in several blankets, he was whisked away into a rabbit warren of wards.

Jimmy's appearance reminded Skye of Tin Man from *The Wizard of Oz*. Or a sickly albeit slightly overweight E.T. She expected him to poke out a frail finger and utter in a Caledonian brogue, 'Jimmy phone home.'

She never thought she would get teary over Jimmy Trout but the burly Scot had risked his life to save Airen's. What could be more selfless than that?

She blew her nose with a tissue and turned to Fletcher, who insisted on staying with her while she and Airen waited for triage.

He'd raided the Kombi floor for loose change and scraped together enough to buy her a hot chocolate from the vending machine. He'd also given her the only blanket in the van, and promised her it hadn't been used by Occy.

She wasn't too sure about that as she flung it over her shoulders and caught a distinct whiff of canine eau de parfum.

'Mmm, I did smell that too,' Fletcher admitted and Skye was thrilled to see the sparkle back in his eyes. She leaned into him, telling herself that she really needed that extra bit of warmth.

'What made you go to The Point?' she asked and sipped on the hot chocolate.

Fletcher's answer was a much needed distraction from the aches in her body from running, climbing and, finally, swimming in an ocean with a temperature of around fifteen degrees.

He told how he and Sun were driving to the mountain when he recalled a recent conversation with a very drunk Airen at the pub. At the time, Airen told Fletcher his only desire was to be with his father.

'I wanna hurl myself into the darkness mate,' Airen had confided to a dismayed Fletcher. 'Get it over and done with. It would be Dad and me in the bloody deep blue forever. Forever him and me. That's the way to go.' And then he'd thumped a hand on his chest with such force that Fletcher thought he might have bruised his breastbone.

The significance of Airen's terrifying prophecy hit Fletcher square between the eyes 'like, the bleeding obvious' after the Kombi had coughed its way 'almost to the mountain.'

Fletcher cursed his lack of insight and chucked a u-ey, a stricken Sun by his side and Occy laying low in the back. He'd pushed the Kombi 'full pelt' to reach The Point. 'It was the last place Airen saw Jonno. I should have known that's where he'd go.' Fletcher slapped a hand to his head as if trying to physically punish himself for his forgetfulness. 'I should have thought about it earlier.'

Luckily, a fisherman handed over his dinghy without question after Fletcher and Sun poured out the story of Airen's probable intentions in a mixed jumble of half-finished sentences.

Sun had pointed to the horizon. 'My brother could be out there…'

Fletcher had squinted into the gloomy distance and wheeled around to face the fisherman. 'We have to search for him…'

'He has a plan, we think…' Sun had faltered on a sob.

'…to take his own life.' Fletcher had finished.

'Would you mind lending us…?' Sun's plea had come from the heart.

'It's the only way. We need to use your boat, mate.'

Skye was overwhelmed by gratitude for the fisherman. That someone could be so trusting of total strangers never ceased to amaze her. She was sure it happened all the time. But it was something about country and small regional towns' folk that seemed to be more giving, open and accepting, less cynical and distrustful of strangers than their city counterparts.

The humble fisherman didn't expect any recompense for his act of kindness. He helped save three souls from drowning in a wild ocean.

'Go home, get some rest,' Skye told Fletcher after he finished the story. 'You must be wrecked.'

He had the demeanour of a competitor who'd completed an endurance course where tasks include scaling high-rise netted walls, swinging on ropes across croc-infested moats and running a marathon over terrain slippery with stinking mud.

He smiled again, his blue eyes more aqua in his windburned face. Skye was immediately taken back to their first encounter a week ago when he ran up the beach. There was an instant attraction that pulled her to him. He emitted an irresistible magnetism that slowly broke through her force field.

'I can stay and wait for you if you like?' His question hovered like the beginnings of an offer of commitment.

Skye wanted to say, 'Yes, please stay,' but the words stuck.

Fletcher King is not in my plan.

Fletcher-King-is-not-in-my-plan.

Her plan, even though Beau's name had been erased from it, was to make it in Sydney. To be a journalist with a beautiful house on the harbour.

Awesome sex aside, magnetic attraction aside, common interests aside, she could not add the complication of the mysterious Fletcher King to an already ambitious to-do list. And she could not, at this point in time, get her head properly around the whole baby thing with Sun and Lou.

As if on cue, Sun and Airen came to her rescue and plonked down on the lino floor in front of them. As happy as two playful puppies, Skye thought, suppressing an urge to ruffle their heads.

Sun couldn't get the grin off her face. 'I called everyone to share the good news and, as you'd expect, Mum is a tiny bit hysterical. Happy hysterical with relief but nonetheless hysterical.' Sun gave a hee-haw laugh, sounding as though she wasn't that far from hysteria either.

'I'll walk Occy back to Mum's place,' she continued, 'where I'll present a calm unembroidered account of the events, playing down the part where Airen, Skye and Jimmy nearly succumbed to hypothermia. And I'll convince Mum that it's better to let Jimmy recuperate here without visitors for the night. She can visit tomorrow.'

'Good idea,' Skye agreed. 'It'd be too distressing for her to see Jimmy in his hypothermic wild-man state.'

Skye felt like leaping for joy and performing cartwheels across the floor. She knew her natural high didn't only come from relief that Airen was safe and sound. It gained an ultra-boost because she was having a relaxed non-judgmental conversation with her sister and brother for the first time in three years. Later on, she would crash as the exhilaration wore off. But for now, the brilliant buzz of endorphins kept her going. She wanted to laugh and cry at the same time. She hadn't been this happy since? It was hard to remember.

A nurse carrying a clipboard and pen entered the reception area and cast her gaze around the room.

'Skye Summerhayes? Airen Summerhayes?' she asked in a sing-song voice.

All four of them stood up.

Airen gave Fletcher a bear hug and thumped him on the back. 'Man, you're a legend. I can't thank you enough for what you did today. Thank you. I love you.' Airen placed his palms to together over his heart as if in prayer and gave a small bow. 'Namaste, mate. Namaste.'

'Namaste to you too,' Fletcher said and did the same. He chuckled, a deep warm growl, and squeezed Airen's shoulder.

Then he turned to Skye.

She didn't know where to look. Her socked feet would have to do.

'We gotta go. See you soon,' she muttered breathlessly.

She kept her eyes down when he replied, 'Whenever you're ready.'

* * *

Skye and Airen were ushered into a small examination room lit by fluorescent tube lights and populated by a standard office desk, two chairs, examination bed, vinyl couch and chip-board shelves stacked with medical journals. On the wall hung a clock and posters with detailed illustrations of the axial and appendicular skeleton.

It was almost seven pm.

They were met by a triage nurse, her severe expression heightened by grey hair pulled into a too-tight bun. For several minutes, she quizzed them about Jimmy.

How did he end up in the ocean in his underwear? How much time did he spend in the water? Whereabouts was he swimming and why didn't they remove him from the water earlier?

She resembled a cranky emoticon with her thin black brows drawn downwards and her mouth a horizontal line. Obviously unimpressed by their explanations, she stood up, tucked the clipboard under her thin bony arm and checked the watch pinned to her navy blouse.

'We're short staffed and Mr Trout needs attending to asap but as soon as his condition is stabilised I'll be back to examine you two, so don't move,' she said sternly and threw Airen a black look.

As the door clicked decisively shut behind the triage nurse, Skye turned to Airen. 'I don't think she likes you,' she said, deadpan.

Airen's mouth twisted into a rueful smile and he laid his palms down on his thighs.

'I don't blame her.' He grimaced at Skye, seated next to him on the poo-brown couch so worn that small vein-like cracks had formed in the vinyl arm-rest.

'This is like a second home to me,' he explained. 'I've been here on and off for the last few years, usually totally shitfaced. I hope she noticed I was sober this time around.'

He curled over, moaned and leaned his head into his hands. His fingers, turned to crepe paper by the ocean, catching in his knotty sea-salted hair.

Skye frowned her concern and raised her arm above her brother's curved back, covered by an apricot-coloured cotton weave blanket. She hesitated, her hand hovered there. Confusion and guilt clouded her conscience. She slowly lowered her arm and ran a hand over his back, feeling each nobbly vertebrae under her fingers along with the pain and despair of the past three years.

'So, what happened out there today?' she asked in a quiet voice.

Airen remained bent over and Skye stilled her hand. After a short silence punctuated by the electronic 'tick' of the wall clock, he sat back up and expelled a huge sigh. 'I was gonna top myself. But you already knew that.'

'Yep.' Skye pressed her lips together, emotions welling inside. 'Sun and Lou found the note but the bottom was smudged. I could see my name there.'

Airen rubbed his eyes and rested the back of his head on the lounge. 'Yeah. I wanted you to forgive me the most.'

Skye's throat tightened. 'Is that what you wrote? Forgive me Skye?'

He nodded. 'You could've saved Dad if I hadn't got in the way.'

Skye laughed but there was no humour in it. 'No mate, that's not right. Only a miracle could've saved Dad. And miracles weren't working for us that night.'

After another short silence, Airen inched forward and turned to face her, taking her hands in his. She was surprised they were so warm when hers were still icy.

'Yeah, but that's not how you felt about it, about me, afterwards,' he said.

Tears pricked at the back of Skye's eyes. 'I was a right bitch. I made everyone's life hell.'

Airen nodded thoughtfully, let go of her hands, and they lapsed into another mutually agreed lull in the conversation. She rubbed her hands together vigorously to maintain the transferred warmth.

'I didn't want to swim in the ocean that night,' Airen finally said.

Skye linked her fingers tight. Her heart broke from grief and regret as her little brother met her gaze and held it as though his life depended on it, his big brown eyes beseeching.

'I told Dad he was mad to go in but he was so charged, so sure of himself. He felt invincible after the big win against the developers. And you know what he's like... what he was like,' he corrected himself.

'He kept daring me, prodding me, pushing me. He told me he'd done midnight swims in worse conditions at my age. He said it was a rite of passage. Man up, he said. Said we were in it together. Like brothers in arms. I felt like I didn't have a choice, Skye.'

Sadly, Skye knew exactly what he was talking about. Her father loved to throw down the gauntlet to his children, daring them to go that little bit further, to take risks most parents would consider insane.

'Why didn't you tell me this?'

A sigh followed by a shudder. 'Think of the situation we both found ourselves in that night. You concealed the truth because you didn't want me to get the blame for Dad's death. I kept it to myself because I didn't want Dad's name besmirched and dragged through the mud and...'

He trailed off and stared out the aluminium-framed window at a cloudless starry night.

Skye broke the silence. 'And?'

'I didn't want to be a dobber, a snitch. Putting the blame on a dead man.'

Impulsively, Skye reached out and drew Airen close. They remained in an awkward squeezy hug, Skye's arms around her brother's neck and his around her waist. He breathed in and out in big sighs as though clearing himself of all the bad energy that had come from lugging around his own personal albatross.

A weight slowly lifted from Skye's soul but remorse cast a heavy net back over it. She flopped back and rested her head on the vinyl. Closing tired eyes against the harsh flouro light, Skye mulled over the whole sorry business. For several minutes they didn't speak.

The clock ticked.

After a while, she said softly, 'You haven't answered my question.'

'What?'

She forced her eyes open and gripped Airen's arm. Anguish gnawed at her guts.

'What happened out there today?'

'Today was meant to be my last on Earth,' he said gruffly.

Skye shivered and Airen squeezed her arm reassuringly. He frowned in concentration, like he was mentally filing away the least important stuff and compiling his best version of the events.

'I got down to the cave pretty early and lit a fire, had something to eat, fish and chips with salt and vinegar, thought a lot about drinking myself to death but forced myself to hold off for a bit. The plan was to go quietly, without doing anything that would upset anybody, or not too much.'

Skye held down the sourness rolling in her gut at the thought of finding Airen dead. Because of her.

'I waited until the fire went out, it reminded me of our pirate adventures when we were kids. I was going to have that first drink but then I thought I'd go outside and say a final goodbye to the world.'

He wriggled on the couch, his features becoming animated.

'And guess what happened? Guess what I saw?'

He paused and his face lit up as all tension and stress seemed to drain away.

Skye shrugged. She'd never been good at guessing games. 'Dunno. A rainbow? Um, a paraglider? A drone? Seabird, like, um, oh gosh. I can't think.'

Airen gave her a thumbs down each time she answered incorrectly.

Skye felt the pressure mount. 'A bolt of lightning?'

Airen stared at Skye as though she should be able to read his mind. 'Here's a hint. One of the largest mammals on the planet, can be spotted off the east coast as it migrates north in winter, heads back to the Southern Ocean in summer. Eats krill...'

Skye wished there was a big red buzzer in the room because she would have thumped it hard, like a desperate game show contestant. 'A...'

But Airen stole her moment of glory. 'Humpback whale. Or more like two humpbacks. I saw whale spouts, not just one, two.' Airen's eyes were wide with wonder as he threw the full force of his blazing smile upon her.

He was on his feet now, almost floating. 'So I walk to the edge of the platform to get a closer look. And guess what?'

Skye shrugged again, impatient to hear the answer, latching onto his excitement, a faint smile tweaking her lips.

'I have no idea. What?'

'I see a mother humpback and a smaller whale, her calf. They're close to me. So close. I figure it's about a hundred metres, the length of two Olympic swimming pools.'

He stretched his arms as wide as possible and shook his head slowly, as though still not sure what he witnessed was real.

'And then the mother whale breached.' He ran one arm in an arc over his head. 'Most of her massive body rose out of the water and she flung her flippers out wide, showing off, asking me to join them. She said, 'C'mon in, come and hang with us for a bit'.' He fizzed like a just-lit sparkler and slapped his hands together. Skye almost leapt off the couch. 'And then she smashed back into the water like it was a fluffy pillow, sending up a flurry of feathers.'

Airen re-enacted the explosion of sea spray, fluttering his fingers up above his head and back down to his waist like an interpretive dancer. He drew in a deep breath, not yet finished. 'I thought they'd leave but they kept moving closer, lolling and lazing, waving at me, 'Come in, come in'.' He imitated the voice of the character of Dory in the film *Finding Nemo*.

He grinned again, grabbed Skye's hands, let go and twirled to face the window. 'It gave me hope Skye. It made me happy for the first time in a long time.'

Skye sniffled, cried and laughed in tiny gulps, tears spilling down her cheeks in big splashy drops. Joining him at the window, she shoved an arm around his waist and gazed at the big night sky.

'And that's when you decided to dive in, I s'pose?'

''Course I did. I swam out to them, to about the fifty-metre mark. I swam around them, not too close. Mum and bub didn't mind. Mum totally sussed me out. I got closer, and she got closer too. I dived further down and we made eye contact. I stared right into her eye Skye. I know this sounds fucking dumb and for god's sake don't tell anyone. But she sized me up and down, from top to bottom, with that one wise eye. She checked me out. Thoroughly.'

He laughed in disbelief and hugged Skye to his side.

'What did she say?'

'Don't give up. And then her song boomed out. But it didn't hurt my ears, it vibrated through me like a healing. I've never heard or felt anything so amazing. It was ethereal. It was a song for me and the planet. It filled me up.'

It was totally corny but Skye could have sworn a shooting star streaked across the sky at that very moment.

Airen smiled at her. 'I knew that I wanted to live; that I wanted to be in the world again.'

CHAPTER 27

By the time Skye and Airen emerged from a thorough examination, mostly a tongue lashing from the triage nurse, Sun, Lou and Oceane had turned up.

Obviously, Sun had not succeeded in her attempt to keep their mother away from the hospital for twenty-four hours.

The three women swarmed around Airen and Skye like a bunch of fusspots, Skye thought. Oceane, anxious and teary, rained kisses over Airen's face and hugged him to her for so long that he was forced to gently detach himself from her grasp. Still not through with him, she pinched and stroked his cheeks like those of a baby.

Tentatively, she moved to Skye and they fell into a light embrace. As she pulled away and met her mother's enquiring hazel eyes, Skye was reminded of Airen's encounter with the whale. Her mother was sizing her up, trying to figure out what changes had taken place in her daughter in the past week. Transforming Skye from antagonist to pacifist.

'I'm fine Mum, it's all good,' she murmured, not wanting the others to hear.

Her mother removed a necklace with a quartz crystal pendant studded with a line of coloured gemstones from her own neck and handed it to Skye, pressing it into her palm.

'I want you to have it. It's a chakra sword.'

'Thank you,' Skye said, with a big swallow to get rid of the stupid lump followed by tears that, once started, kept coming.

Oceane inclined her head and gave Skye an all-enveloping 'I love you no matter what' smile and turned back to Sun and Lou who, being the pragmatic couple, were giving Airen the third degree about his life-changing epiphany.

'Ah,' Skye said, finally figuring out what Fletcher meant when he'd called the women the 'Three Degrees'. She fingered the pendant and felt its warmth, imagined its empowering glow, before slipping it over her head and around her neck.

She wondered where Fletcher was. She needed to talk to him. To sort things out about last night. So much had happened since then she could hardly believe it.

Sun summed her up and read her mind. 'Fletcher had to leave suddenly.'

Skye couldn't control the rush of blood to her cheeks and the disappointment that tempered her new-found contentment. 'I guess… I thought he might have been with you.'

Sun narrowed her eyes as if it helped place Skye and Fletcher's relationship into focus. Skye thought she was going ask her about Fletcher, but then Airen swept Sun into an almost life-threatening embrace and the moment was lost.

They trailed into the intensive care unit where Jimmy sat on a trolley bed, propped up by plumped pillows encased in crisp white pillowcases. He sipped on a steaming beverage in a white mug.

Oceane gave him the death-by-a-million-kisses treatment. His black button eyes twinkled with mirth. 'If that's the reception I get, I'll have a go at drowning meself every weekend from now on.'

Jimmy revelled in the attention from the hospital staff. The nurses, he explained, placed hot water bottles over his 'gonads', abdomen and neck in order to raise his core temperature that had fallen from the normal 37 degrees Celsius to less than 35 degrees.

He'd obviously recovered; it was as though the years had fallen off him. His skin was no longer waxy, but glowing with the brightness of a man half his age.

Sun said what everyone was thinking.

'There is absolutely nothing wrong with you, you look amazing.' Her tone was mildly accusing.

They all laughed, a little awkwardly. They'd never been together like this, in total harmony, with Airen sober and Skye happy to be in the same room as Jimmy and her brother.

'This feels odd,' Sun said, again picking up on the vibe.

Lou rolled her eyes and touched Sun lightly on the arm.

'It's fine,' Skye said. 'She's right. This must be a first.'

Jimmy grew sombre. 'I'd like to thank ye Lass. Ye saved my life today and I put yer and Airen's lives in jeopardy.'

'Well,' Skye said, feeling expectant eyes upon her, 'I think we all saved each other. All that matters is everyone's safe and in good nick.'

During the next half hour, Airen talked about his meeting with the humpbacks in minute detail, describing the ridges on the mother whale's torso as being like 'vertical isobars on a weather map', and her 'perfect almond-shaped eye' and how 'she spoke to me. She said, 'Stay here Airen, stay'.'

Skye suppressed a giggle but everyone was entranced. The story was bound to grow to epic proportions on each retelling.

Grateful to have him back, the family probably would have sat there and listened for the rest of the night but were asked to leave by the hospital staff just before midnight.

Airen went back to Oceane and Jimmy's for the night. Skye got a lift back to Fletcher's from Sun and Lou.

She sat in the back of the car, barely able to keep her eyes open. She was exhausted and starving. And, if she cared to admit it, looking forward to being at Fletcher's.

From the driver's seat, Sun asked with a forced flippancy, 'So, what does the future have in store for Skye Summerhayes?'

'Sleep,' Skye murmured, hoping that would be the end of it.

'It'd be great if you could stay on for a while, help out on the paper,' Sun pushed on. 'The coal seam gas story is major. I'll need a lot of help to get the right information out to the community. We could work out something and give you a title like, 'associate editor' or 'roving editor'. And I could become 'publisher'. I like the sound of that.'

Skye laughed. 'You've given this some thought.'

But Sun knew her better than she knew herself. She had taken a punt that the prospect of staying in Dezzy was far more appealing to Skye than it had been a week ago. And that was true, more or less. She definitely wanted to spend time with Airen, to reconnect with her mother and get to know Jimmy.

She wanted to ask Oceane about love, and how and why it fades away. When did her mother and father know it was over? When did they decide to sever their connection and split from each other permanently?

It made her feel terribly sad. Those damn tears started up again. Maybe not crying for three years had something to do with it. At last, her surplus of tears was being used up.

Outside the car window, the world hurtled by. And time with it.

And what about Fletcher? Where did the father of Sun and Lou's unborn baby fit in with her change of heart? Skye mulled on this as the Milky Way cast a luminescent spritz across a molassess ocean.

Lou swivelled in her seat to face Skye, gripping the seatbelt. It must have been terribly uncomfortable, Skye thought, and wondered if the baby was kicking his or her dissatisfaction at being thrust into a corner of the uterus like a child sliding to one side of the seat on the fun fair ride, the Cha Cha.

'We want you to be here for the birth,' Lou said. 'Even if you decide to go back to Sydney, we would love it if you could come back to Dezzy for that.'

'Yeah,' Sun said, eyes on the road. 'It's gonna be huge.'

Lou squeaked in mock horror. 'I take it you mean the birthing gathering and not the size of the baby?'

Skye wondered if she'd heard right. 'Birthing gathering? Do I dare ask what you mean by that?'

'We're having the gathering at the hospital's natural birthing centre and, naturally, a date can't be confirmed until I go into labour. So watch this space.' She awkwardly patted her tummy.

'But the whole family will be there.' She counted off on her fingers. 'Sun, Oceane, Jimmy, my parents, Grandma, Airen, Fletcher. And you.'

Skye wanted to make sure she understood the exact meaning of 'birthing gathering'.

'So.' Skye drew out the 'o' and paused, wondering why her family couldn't just hold a celebratory barbecue after the birth, like a normal family.

'We, our dysfunctional family, is in the birthing suite during the labour and birth. Have I got that right?'

Sun raised one hand from the steering wheel and gave the thumbs up, adding, 'Every family is dysfunctional, Skye. When it comes down to it, we're pretty ordinary.'

Still facing her, Lou gave one of her star-studded smiles, the sort that made people love her instantly.

'Yep, our dysfunctional family is getting together to celebrate a momentous occasion. Our take on it is, the more the merrier,' she beamed.

CHAPTER 28

The lamp in the corner cast a warm light over Fletcher's lounge room. Calmness descended upon Skye like a balm as soon as she saw it. The room seemed to gather her in a welcoming embrace to dissolve the stress of the past twenty-four hours.

She loved this place; the simple spacious layout, earthy tones and natural recycled materials used in its creation, and floor-to-ceiling windows that let light pour in during the day.

All that was missing was Fletcher. And Occy, of course.

'Helloooo,' she called out tentatively. 'Fletcher? Occy?'

Well, what did you expect Skye? A welcome party?

That inner voice was at it again. And it was totally right. She'd basically given Fletcher the flick, and now she wanted the decision reversed?

Fletcher had to be at work well before dawn. She couldn't expect him to wait up for her. It wouldn't hurt to check though, to confirm he was safe and sound, tucked in for the night. It would be reassuring to see his handsome face in sleep, his naturally sculpted arms flung above his head on the pillow, his legs so long that his size-12 feet reached the end of the mattress.

Guided by the light of an almost full moon in a clear starry sky, she slid open the door to the deck and tip-toed across the connecting walkway to the rear of the house. The door to Fletcher's room was partially open. Skye gave it a gentle push with the palm of her hand and squinted into the silvery darkness.

Empty. The room and the bed, which was neatly made up.

'Fletcher?' Skye asked the room.

Silence, except for the constant 'bock bock' of a frog army that had taken up residence in the courtyard garden.

Her heart dropped with a plonk, like a stone chucked into a river, and drifted to the bottom of her stomach.

Hugging her arms around her, she walked back into the main house, flicked on the kitchen light and went straight to the freezer section of the fridge.

Armed with a tub of ice cream and a spoon, she sat at the bench and bit into the creamy frozen treat. She winced as the nerves in her teeth pinched at tender gums and the dessert-spoonful momentarily lodged in her throat like a glacier.

She had considered adding hard liquor to the tub but the brain-freeze from pure unadulterated vanilla ice cream had a similar numbing effect.

It finally occurred to her why romcom-movie heroines often binged on the frosty confection. It was momentarily gratifying, a sweet fix that filled the void left by the absence of the hero. And, in this case, his dog.

She scooped out a chunk of ice cream as big as her fist and ran her tongue over and around it. 'Mmm.'

And then there was the desperate running scene towards the end of the romcom, Skye thought. The one where the hero or heroine sprinted through the traffic, along an empty street, across a bridge or through an airport, barely drawing breath, to reach his or her lover.

To utter those three loaded words.

Would she run after Fletcher? She wouldn't run after Beau. But Fletcher?

Another big lick. Another brain-freeze.

Through the masochistic haze, she noticed clutter on the usually clear bench top. She hesitated before she put down the tub and spoon and wiped her sticky mouth with the back of her hand. Did she really need to know anything more about Fletcher's private life? Then again, Fletcher wouldn't have left his personal belongings lying around if he cared who saw them.

Skye was over second guessing.

Picking up a photo on top of the pile, she recognised the baby from the pic slotted into the book on Fletcher's bedside table. This photo was different, though still a tight head and shoulders shot. The baby was older, more animated, a cheeky smile adding personality to his blue eyes. He really was gorgeous.

She turned it over and examined neat writing on the back before putting it down and picking up a print-out of an email confirming a one-way flight to Thailand for 'Mr Samuel Fletcher Brand'.

Samuel Fletcher Brand? Skye was confused. Who the hell was Samuel Brand?

Fletcher? Had he been going by his middle name instead of his first? This wasn't uncommon but what was it with the last name 'Brand'?

Logical Skye told her Fletcher would have a perfectly logical explanation for using a pseudonym, and that he never intended to deceive her or anyone else.

Skye snapped herself into alert mode and checked the date on the email. Today. It had arrived at six-forty-five pm. The flight departed tomorrow at nine-ten am from Sydney airport.

She went to the lounge room window and dragged the curtain aside. No Kombi. He must be on his way to Sydney. He most likely took the dog with him and dropped it off on the way, at a friend's place maybe?

She visualised Occy sitting upright on a seat on the plane next to Fletcher, sipping a cocktail with a novelty paper umbrella stuck through a chunk of pineapple.

She returned to the bench and saw another piece of paper, scrunched into a ball, on the floor. She picked it up and smoothed it out on the bench top. It was another email printout of a short note received at six pm.

'*Dear Sam,*' it began, '*I call your phone but off. I sorry to tell bad news. Samorn passed away, maybe yesterday. The nuns find her today. I am in shock to lose my sister. My number at home is 284-7000. I am grateful for you to call me.*
With blessing,
Kiet Thongprasom'
Underneath this, the numbers '0011662' rushed across the page in red pen in Fletcher's familiar style.

That's an area code, Skye thought. She picked up the photo of the baby again.

'Dear little thing,' she said out loud. 'Where do you fit into this?'

She carried the photo to the lounge and lay down. Arms extended towards the ceiling, she stared up at it. Sitting up again, she picked up one of the cushions at her feet. Its cover was a pretty batik cotton patchwork in teal blue. From Thailand, she thought, as she popped it under her head.

The act of lying down after almost twenty-four hours with-out sleep hit her like a speeding train. She stood on the tracks, powerless to stop it.

As sleep bore down on her, she clutched the photo of the baby to her chest and murmured the words written by Fletcher King, or should that be Samuel Brand, on the back. 'Nat Brand aged 16 weeks'.

* * *

It took Skye a moment to compute that her phone's alarm tone had infiltrated a potentially erotic dream with Fletcher about to apply sunblock to her flat as a board tummy. She re-luctantly dragged herself away from the beach and glaringly blue water and forced her eyes open.

Another few seconds were spent in a fug trying to figure out where she was. Not in a bed but on the lounge at Fletcher's, dressed in the tracky dacks and t-shirt provided by Sun at the hospital.

Skye had barely moved during a deep sleep of exhaustion so the photo was still intact, thank goodness. Morning sun streamed in though the lounge room windows. The wall clock ticked over to seven-fifteen am.

Skye felt like she'd gone the rounds in a professional cage fight. Every muscle throbbed with fatigue. Every part of her was sore. Her head pounded. It was more than a headache, more like a nutcracker and her head was the walnut.

She tugged at her earlobe to try to ease the pressure. 'Ouch.' How could an earlobe possibly be affected by yester-day's ordeal? Her earlobe hadn't done any heavy lifting or played a role in the marathon swim in fifteen-degree waters to rescue Airen.

Skye gingerly got to her feet, found her phone in her bag and turned off the alarm. In the kitchen, she shakily filled a glass with tap water and drained it in one go. Maybe her body was in delayed shock. It felt that way. Feeling unsteady on her feet, she leaned against the kitchen bench.

She half expected Fletcher to stroll through the door with Occy at his heels and sighed at the twinge of longing in her.

Stop it Skye. There is nothing more to be said or done. He's gone. It was a one-way flight. This isn't a romcom.

She was sure her detective work was correct and Fletcher was at the airport, soon to board a flight to Thailand.

Skye needed to get real. Fletcher was the father of Sun and Lou's unborn child. He was, in effect, her brother-in-law.

She thought about calling him but let it go. The man obviously had other things on his mind. He wouldn't be up for a deep and meaningful with Skye about that one night of incredible sex and whether she had totally misread his nuanced words and actions at the hospital.

It wouldn't be the first time she'd done the crossed wires thing in a relationship. No way would she screw up again.

His name change was a whole other topic around deception. Maybe Sun and Lou could fill her in on the gaps in her knowledge around Fletcher's past?

She picked up the flight details and flipped the page over. The red pen Fletcher used to scribble down a phone number was still on the bench.

Skye picked it up and drew a line down the centre of the page. On the left-hand side she wrote: *Reasons to stay in Dezzy* and on the right-hand side, *Reasons to leave Dezzy.*

She started with reasons to stay:

1. Family
2. *The Northern Sun* and the fight to keep big business honest and accountable
3. Fletcher

Next, she contemplated reasons to leave:

1. Career prospects
2. More money
3. Fletcher

Skye sat still as a statue to calm her breathing through the wild commotion of her galloping heart.

Slowly, the distant sound of cockatoos squawking and screeching grew louder until a flock of what sounded like hundreds, but was probably only a dozen, flew straight over the top of the house and away again. Like in a dream. There and gone.

What was her next move? What did she want to achieve in her life?

She would have to go back to Sydney to clear her belongings out of Beau's apartment. Skye never wanted to see Beau again. That was the one thing she knew with certainty as strong as steel.

She rested her head on her arms atop the cool timber bench top and tried to imagine life back in Sydney. But her thoughts kept returning to Dezzy, the people she loved and bloody Fletcher King aka Samuel Brand.

That was one mystery she had to get sorted.

CHAPTER 29

At the office of *The Northern Sun,* Skye failed to fend off the mad rush of hugs and kisses from deputy editor Col and ad manager Deb.

Sun rescued her and they embraced. Skye didn't feel like letting go. It had been a long time coming and she surprised herself by getting all teary.

'Don't.' Sun held Skye at arm's length and frowned in mock anger at her damp eyes. 'You'll get me started, and Col and Deb will want to join in.'

They wandered downstairs to the cafe across the road with the aptly themed moniker of 'Coast'.

Inside, two surfboards covered in swirling psychedelic patterns hung horizontally as artworks on the walls. They were above framed collectible posters promoting surfing competitions that starred 1970s Australian surfing legends like Nat Young, Wayne 'Rabbit' Bartholomew and Mark Richards.

Maybe it was a coincidence that the baby in Fletcher's photo was named Nat?

She and Sun sat on distressed wooden stools at a high table with a recycled metal top affixed to a wall. They ordered flat whites from a young waiter. He wore the uniform of classic Reeboks, skinny jeans, Metallica t-shirt, horn-rimmed glasses, and sported a shaved head and trimmed beard.

After joking that Dezzy had finally found its cool vibe since the hipsters moved in, the conversation between Skye and Sun became more intense.

No point putting off the obvious question, Skye thought, stirring her coffee. First things first. 'How's Airen?'

A smile hovered at Sun's lips. 'I called Mum this morning. He's still at her place.'

'Good.' Skye released a relieved breath. Although Airen had pledged a change for the better, nothing could be guaranteed when it came to addiction.

Sun read Skye's face. 'Yeah, I know how you feel. Anything could happen but this time he's determined to follow through. He's going to need some help so he'll spend a couple of weeks with Mum and Jimmy. Mum'll do the mornings with him so Jimmy can fit in his regular clients, and Jimmy'll do the afternoon shift so Mum can manage the business. I'll go around when I can. He's going to the doctor's this morning to write a rehab plan. Mum said he was pretty shaky but in good spirits, so to speak.' She paused and laughed at the unintended alcohol-related pun. 'The main thing is, he's excited about getting well.'

Skye relaxed her shoulders, which had been hunched up.

'Do you think he'll want to see me?'

Sun leaned across the table and placed her hand over Skye's. 'Of course. We're through the worst of it. In a strange way, the intervention worked. We're back together as a family and Airen's regained his love of life.'

A week ago, Skye would never have imagined she would be sitting in a café enjoying her sister's company.

'What a week it's been.'

The warmth of a smile shone through Sun's eyes. 'Feels more like a year. But I'm so glad you're here. That you came home. I don't know that Jimmy's ambitious plan would have worked without you.'

'Yeah, well, we all needed to sort out our shit.' They laughed together in the intimate and raucous way that might grate with other café customers, left out of the secret. Skye felt sunshine in her bones and the world turning once again.

The waiter delivered their coffees and they talked about Airen and his future for the next half hour before Skye tentatively broached the other subject that had her stomach in knots.

She fiddled with a paper serviette and met Sun's eyes. 'I know I'm switching topics. But I wonder if you could throw some light on the mysterious Fletcher King whose real name, I discovered last night, is Samuel Brand?'

Sun shrugged apologetically, knowingly, her demeanour shifting from totally open to arms folded and closed.

'It's a long story but we all know him as Fletcher King.' Sun spoke hesitantly as though she had been drawn into an agreement with Fletcher to keep everything about him a big secret.

Then she did that annoying thing the Summerhayes' family specialised in, turning to one of a politician's favourite evasive tactics by changing the focus to the person asking the question.

'More importantly, what happened between you two?'

Skye pressed her hands to burning cheeks and whined, 'C'mon Sun, that's not fair. I asked you first.'

Sun's eyes were wide and round as she clapped her hands at staccato speed like an excited schoolgirl.

'O.M.G. Something did happen. You did it. You and Fletcher.'

'Shoosh.' Skye's heart pounded as she checked left, right and behind.

She swung back to Sun, leaning her elbows on the tabletop, talking in a fast raspy whisper. 'For your information, yes, we did. But it meant nothing. We're just good friends. Like, with benefits. That sort of friends.'

Sun could have been opening her mouth for the dentist to have a dig around inside. It would have been possible to shove a whole boiled egg in there, Skye thought.

Skye hissed, 'Stop it. Stop staring at me like I'm a committed celibate who's crossed the line.'

Sun seemed to compose herself, leaning back to get a better view of her floosy sister. 'Fletcher is such a fantastic person.' The edges of her lips twitched as though she was trying to control a gleeful squeal. Skye bet she couldn't wait to tell Lou. And the rest of the family.

'But truly Skye, this couldn't have happened to two nicer people. Fletcher is awesome. And seriously, what were you thinking when you hooked up with Beau? He reminded me of...'

Skye knew what was coming. 'Cal. Seems poor choices in men are my speciality.'

Hipster guy delivered their second order of coffees along with two glasses of water.

'Except for Fletcher,' Sun said. 'I'd think about changing teams for Fletcher. But don't tell him that. And whatever you do, don't tell Lou.'

She guffawed and then her manner became pseudo brusque and business-like. 'What would you like to know about this gorgeous male specimen whom you profess to have no interest in whatsoever? Oh, apart from a casual fling.'

Rather than fire off questions, Skye stumbled through her story of finding the photo of baby Nat Brand, followed by last night's discovery of the airline ticket for a Mr Samuel Brand, a second photo and email from someone in Thailand with a Thai name.

All through the telling, Sun gave sombre nods and sipped her coffee.

'Fletcher's a private person,' Sun began slowly after Skye had finished. 'There's details Lou and I don't know. He didn't tell us he was off to Thailand. We found out this morning when Lou went downstairs to get fresh bread and he wasn't there. The apprentice baker told us he had to rush off to deal with a personal issue and he'll be back in about a week.'

Skye nodded. 'What about the baby? His baby.'

A shadow crossed Sun's face. She leaned on her elbows and cupped her face in her hands. 'We know all about the baby.'

She stared past Skye into the middle distance and then gazed at her. 'I'm only telling you this because I know Fletcher wouldn't mind. He was waiting for the right time to share his story with everyone. But helping Airen took over.'

She sat upright, fidgeted with a stray strand of hair and examined it distractedly before refocusing once more on Skye. 'This is what he told Lou and me.' She paused and blew a little circle, like she was exhaling the smoke from a cigarette. 'He, Fletcher, met a girl a couple of years ago in WA. They had sex. Just the one time. Simple as that.'

Skye leaned forward, arms folded on the bench top, and made an educated guess. 'And what? She gets pregnant?'

Sun gave a slight nod, drew in her eyebrows and pressed her lips together as though sorting out the next chapter of Fletcher's story.

'Yeah. But he doesn't find out straight away. With the one night stand over, they go their separate ways. Then he gets a call from Thailand six months later. She says the baby is his and she needs his help. Financially. So, he sends money. And after the baby is born, he goes to Thailand and marries the girl.'

Skye started. 'Marries?'

Sun shrugged. 'I guess he felt it was the decent thing to do. She's a young woman from a strict family and Fletcher's not the sort of guy who lets people down. I think they went to a registry office so it was nothing special. But it was important to her.'

'And then?'

The expression on Sun's face, Skye had seen it before. An etching of sadness and loss. 'There's no easy way to say this but the baby died. He was four months old.'

Skye's chest compressed and bounced back as though the wind had been knocked out of her. Why didn't she know this about Fletcher? Why hadn't he told her?

She finally found her voice, filled with urgency. 'How did he die?'

'No one really knows.' Sun shrugged again, her shoulders more hunched. 'Possibly SIDS.'

The need to know every last detail about Fletcher's life spurred Skye on. 'Only possibly?'

Sun stared directly at Skye. 'That was the finding after the autopsy. Fletcher went through a horrific time and incredible guilt for not being a good father and for being unaware of his wife's emotional condition. It wasn't a happy relationship.'

Skye couldn't begin to imagine Fletcher's grief or the mother's pain. 'Was it undiagnosed postnatal depression?'

'Yeah, I'm only guessing...' Sun trailed off.

Skye had to ask, 'And they separated?'

Sun nodded.

'Do you know anything about her?'

'Not much. Fletcher managed to keep his personal life low key and out of the media, all things considered.'

Skye had done an internet search for Fletcher King and found nothing except several American-based men with the same name on Facebook. She'd obviously been searching for the wrong name.

'What do you mean? Isn't he a baker?'

A vague memory of *BRW* and the 'young rich list' wafted into Skye's consciousness.

Sun tilted her head and clicked her tongue. 'Amongst other things, Fletcher's a talented baker. He came to Dezzy to find his roots, reinvent himself and escape the glare of the media circus in WA. The land here, where he built the house, was left to him by his grandmother. She made sure the inheritance went straight to Fletch and not his mother.'

Skye was beginning to feel stupid. 'Am I missing something here? I take it he's well known in Perth?'

'Mmm, pretty famous. His real name is Samuel Brand. 'Fletcher' is his middle name and 'King' belonged to his maternal grandmother.'

Samuel Brand. The name was familiar but Skye couldn't place it. Sun helped her out.

'Sam Brand is a hugely successful entrepreneur. He developed heaps of apps before the app boom. He was an early innovator. He saw the trend. The big one was Surf 'N' Snip, a surfing app that went bonkers worldwide after its launch about ten years ago.'

'Doh.' Skye slapped her forehead, realisation dawning. How could she have been so unaware of Fletcher's other life?

'I knew nothing about this. Nothing at all.'

'There's a reason for that. Fletcher is worth quite a few quid. You can understand why he doesn't want share that information with all but a few close friends.'

CHAPTER 30

Skye got the call after she and Sun returned to the office. It was Jasper Raison, her editor at the online newspaper, *The Hunch*.

Jasper's voice boomed. 'When are you coming back to Sydney Skye? We're missing you here but you don't want to leave it too long.'

Skye mumbled something about being back soon but Jasper wasn't listening. He talked over her. 'I'm sure you know the reason for my call. There's an opening in the real estate section for an editor and I want someone with experience to lead the team. I'm offering you the role but I need to know if you're in or out. By tomorrow.'

Maybe this was a sign. Airen had humpback whales and Skye had bombastic male journos. If she was going to focus on advancing her career, it had to be Sydney.

She relayed the very short conversation to Sun.

Her sister gave her a tight smile. 'Sounds like an offer too good to refuse.'

Sun was right. The offer was a now-or-never opportunity.

'I have to give it some thought,' Skye said.

The earlier lightness that Skye had seen in Sun seemed to dissipate. 'There's no time to for that Skye. He wants an answer now.'

Skye chewed her bottom lip. There was so much work to do in the Dezzy community to keep people informed and engaged with the news around town and the hinterland. Sun had a huge job on her hands.

'I think you should take it.' Sun addressed Skye with a steely glint in her eye that said she'd made up her mind on Skye's behalf.

'Why?' Skye asked. 'You need someone here in a senior role.'

'Nah, we'll get by. I've got an old journo mate who owes me a favour. I'm sure I can get him on board.'

As Skye went to protest, Sun shut her down. 'I know you Skye. This has been a dream of yours. If you stayed here, you'd always wonder, 'what if?' You need to do it, get it out of your system.' Two lines creased between Sun's eyebrows above her freckled nose, and she carried on. 'Dad would want that. He'd want you to broaden your horizons.'

'I dunno about that,' Skye said. 'He was passionate about *The Northern Sun*. It always came first.'

Sun nodded. 'Well, I'm not about to let it go. The paper's set to go fully online soon to complement the digital and print editions. We're a bit late on the uptake, there's been a lot of tweaking to get it right, but we're finally moving into the twenty- first century. And I've got the youngsters on the team working on our social media presence.'

Skye dropped her arms and left them hanging.

'I'd love to stay,' she blurted out, shocked at the ferocity of her words and the sudden desire to hug Sun again. 'But you're right. Jasper Raison's a legend in the media world and it's a big deal to get a call from him.'

Then there was another bigger truth she had to speak to Sun.

'And,' she blew out and squeezed her eyes shut as if blotting out her sister's face could make what she was about to say easier, 'I don't think,' she said and opened them again, 'I can face Fletcher again. I need to go.'

Sun went to speak but Skye cut her off. 'He left without leaving a message or giving any indication of whether he thought there was a chance we could... be together, somehow. I didn't help matters by implying our fling was a fling and there was nothing more to it.' Her voice shook, giving away the intensity of her inner turmoil.

'Call him.'

Skye shooed away the idea with both hands. She was terrified of rejection, of the words of dismissal that might flow from Fletcher's mouth or, worse still, that he may not pick up or return her call.

'No way, I know it's odd for a journalist, but when it comes to talking tough, I hate phones. What would I say? 'I lust after you'?'

'That's a start,' Sun half joked. 'Most men'd love that sort of attention from someone as intelligent and attractive as you. What about an email?'

'Not going there. Too much room for misinterpretation.'

Sun gave Skye her 'what are we going to do with you?' look, cocking her head to one side and folding her arms. 'Fletcher's complicated. And I totally get that you're scared about his reaction if you put it out there. A lot of men would run for the hills.'

'Exactly. What if he only wanted a 'friends with benefits' arrangement? I want more than that. I don't want another lopsided relationship. And let's not forget he's the father of your and Lou's soon-to-be-born child. There's a whole other layer of complications there.'

* * *

Skye had to complete one last *House of the Week* real estate feature story for *The Northern Sun* before she left Desiree Bay.

She walked down Sinclair St, past The Old Bakery, until she reached a small cul de sac, Bruce Place, that contained twelve houses all up. She stopped at no.8, outside a cream-coloured brick veneer split-level home, with an asymmetric gabled roof. In a front yard with a neat mown lawn stood a circular trampoline enclosed by a high safety net.

A large frangipani tree directly in front of the house was on the verge of bursting into bloom. Flowers grew from the tips of the tree's stubby finger-shaped branches that oozed a sticky fluid if snapped. They were framed by a cluster of large canoe-shaped leaves. The yellow-centred pink flowers were twisted tight like wrapped lollies, as if waiting for the right moment to reveal their beauty and release a subtle fragrance.

Her interviewee was a childhood friend, Josie Barnett, who, like Skye, had endured the taunts of school bullies.

Josie had done it tougher than Skye. She was one of three children, triplets. And the one least likely to succeed, or so the bullies had teased. The last-born runt of the litter, they taunted. Excruciatingly shy, she'd endured their careless cruelty in a timid tight-lipped silence.

Her sister Elise was the star of the trio. She became a radio news reporter, based in the Middle East. Tragically, she died in a helicopter crash while on assignment around the time of Jonno's death.

Josie and her father, Frank, were now the carers of Elise's five-year-old daughter Juliet. The other triplet, Nicholas, was a landscape architect who lived in the hinterland. Josie was a librarian at the local council library.

Skye's arms tingled as she tapped the door knocker three times.

Death did not discriminate. It swooped into people's lives, often with an unexpected brutality, and out again, sucking the joy of life from those left behind.

Sitting on a couch in a living room framed by high timber-framed glass doors, she and Josie exchanged belated condolences.

From a side table, Skye picked up a framed photo of the triplets – Josie, Elise and Nicholas.

'Do you miss her?' Skye observed the three dark haired brown-eyed siblings with their arms linked, Nicholas in the middle.

Josie, sitting opposite, attempted a smile. 'You get used to it after a while, that weird sensation of emptiness.' She pressed her hand to her heart. 'I carry that around with me every day. But Dad and Nick are a huge help. And of course, we have Juliet. I'm grateful for that, for them.'

Over a cup of tea and a plate of homemade shortbread, Josie explained how the house had to be sold to fund the building of a granny flat behind the house next door, which also happened to be owned by her father.

'Dad'll move into the granny flat and Juliet and I will move into the big house,' Josie said in her small shy voice, adding nervously, 'But don't write that in the story. You know what people are like about money and assets.'

Josie seemed mildly affronted when Skye asked her why she'd stayed in Desiree Bay after all she'd been through.

'Because I can't think of where I'd rather be. Despite some of the people in this town, I love it. And most of the people in Dezzy are the best kind of people. When Elise died, I got messages and flowers and tons of roast dinners from people I hardly knew. The bullies don't worry me anymore. I see them for what they are.'

Skye remembered that Cal was one of those bullies who used to knock Josie's notes off the desk at school and laugh with the others as she scrambled to pick them up. A sense of shame filled her. She'd seen this happen and let it go. Never again.

Josie observed her through narrowed eyes, causing Skye to blush for her weaknesses. 'Overall, Dezzy's the best place to bring up Juliet. It has the ocean, fresh air and nature. The local school's pretty good. They have a strict anti-bullying policy, which I helped draft along with other parents, teachers and community members. And Dad and Nick are here. It must sound boring to you, what with your career and everything, but to me it's home.'

Afterwards, Skye walked back through town and saw it in a whole new light. This place had a future. The shopping precinct was busy and the cafes buzzing with customers. At the weekend, the main drag was crowded with day-trippers, backpackers and families. They were there to enjoy a holiday at the beach before heading back to the reality of life in a larger regional town inland from the coast, or to a major city.

She reached the beach, took off her shoes and stepped onto the sand, warm, soft and silky between her toes. Immediately her gaze flew to The Point. The usual shudder of dread didn't take hold. Today she admired its beauty, its bare-boned resilience against the elements. She recalled the multitude of joyous moments she'd experienced there, in the surf, on her board, feeling free and at peace.

A breeze caressed her face and streamers of sunset clouds glowed vermillion, pink and orange above the horizon. Skye turned away from temptation and trudged back up the beach.

Tomorrow she'd return to Sydney and follow through on her plan to become a successful award-winning journalist.

CHAPTER 31

It had been another long day interviewing real estate industry experts and churning out content on the state of the Sydney real estate market.

Could next year be as exceptional as this year or was the property bubble about to burst? Was it turning from a sellers' to a buyers' market? Was the rental market about to crash because of an oversupply of home units in Sydney and Melbourne? Were overseas buyers less active in the market since the government tightened the rules around lending and foreign ownership?

Skye had been back in Sydney for a couple of months but it felt like years. She was on a treadmill and, like all treadmills, this one was going nowhere. She was writing the same old stories repackaged with different 'clickbait' headlines and intros. A monkey could do her job, maybe even better than she could. Whatever, she was getting paid peanuts for churning out mindless fodder to feed people's paranoia.

She didn't notice the message on her mobile until she arrived back at the studio apartment she rented in inner-city

Potts Point, a street away from Sydney's once notorious red-light district Kings Cross.

The Cross, once the haunt of creatives, society's misfits and addicts - artists, musicians, actors and writers - was slowly becoming gentrified. The art deco apartments and Victorian terrace houses once under threat of demolition were desirable assets guaranteed to hold and increase their value. Bankers, property developers, coal and oil tycoons, well-heeled drug barons, digital and IT entrepreneurs, medical specialists, nightclub owners, stockbrokers, barristers, magistrates and judges outbid the normal folk as the hammer slammed down on the auctioneer's victory cry of 'SOLD'.

Skye couldn't afford to buy in the Cross, not on her meagre salary that hardly covered the rent. And even if she could stretch her finances for a loan on a one-bedder, she wasn't sure how she'd cope in such a tiny space.

The apartment didn't have a balcony. The view from her lounge room (which was also her bedroom) window was of the liver-brick unit block next door. There was no space for a small garden and she couldn't consider a dog, which would be cooped up all day in an area with the dimensions of a king-size kennel.

She managed during the week. After working twelve-hour days, she wanted nothing more than a stiff gin and tonic and a night in front of the telly until the next day rolled in.

But on the weekends, she turned into a caged animal. All her 'spare cash' went on café breakfasts, caffeine and the gym, just to get out of the place.

Since her return to Sydney, Skye had managed to clear her stuff out of the apartment she shared with Beau and sell off the useless objects that once obsessed her. She didn't want them anymore.

She was just holding it together. Waiting. But for what?

Then the call came. 'Skye, call me. It's urgent.'

This time around Skye had a fair idea about the meaning of 'urgent'.

A thrill of excitement charged through her as she pressed 'call back'.

'It's happening.' Sun's voice quivered. 'You have to get here asap.'

'How long have I got?' Skye pressed the phone to her ear as she hauled her suitcase from a built-in wardrobe and flung it on the lounge.

'How the hell would I know, I'm not a doctor. Lou's waters broke about an hour ago so it could be anytime soon but she hasn't gone into labour yet. No contractions as such.'

'As such?' Skye grabbed a bunch of undies from a small chest of drawers and threw them in the suitcase.

'Yes, 'as such'. Skye, this is no time for correcting me. Lou's not having contractions yet but they've got to start sooner rather than later. I'll keep you posted.'

Her sister's bounce-off-the-wall energy plugged into Skye like the pink Eveready battery Energizer bunny in the old TV commercial. Thirty-minutes later she'd booked a flight to the regional centre closest to Desiree Bay, organised car hire, packed and called for a cab to take her to the airport.

To hell with her job.

It hadn't panned out the way Skye predicted. Jasper Raison had gone quiet on his promise of potential elevation through the ranks once the publication grew its readership. Staff members were leaving and not being replaced. As far as Skye could tell, the only thing that had grown in the last few months was her workload. To hell with Jasper Raison.

The spirit of defiance filled Skye with a new determination. She couldn't believe how exhilarated she felt to know she was going home.

This was the moment she'd been waiting for. The excuse to head back to Desiree Bay. To her true calling.

This was it. It was September fifteen, the day before her father Jonno's birth, and she was about to become an aunty for the first time.

CHAPTER 32

The hospital was around ten kilometres inland from Desiree Bay, at the edge of an ever expanding regional town where outlying land was being carved up into new residential estates with names made up by the developers. Skye drove past swathes of barren cleared land, named 'The Breakwater', 'Tree Tops' and 'Summer Shores', that promised buyers an idyllic lifestyle in the heart of paradise. There was no breakwater, summer shores or treetops anywhere in sight.

These sites were denuded of vegetation and sealed roads laid out. To Skye, they were desolate and soulless wastelands, with no infrastructure. The only way to get to a bigger town was to hop in the car. They were soon to be populated by McMansions sitting suffocatingly close together on the low-lying swampy, flood-prone land.

Skye wondered with a stab of imminent dread where the possums, bats, birds, frogs, snakes and insects relocated once their habitat disappeared.

As the radio pumped out hits of the '80s, '90s and 'now', she tried to keep her mind on the soon-to-be-born baby. As much as she could, since Fletcher kept pushing himself into her thoughts.

When Sun called, Skye pulled into a rest stop off the main road.

'It's all happening, Lou's having contractions. Come straight to the hospital,' Sun instructed. 'Fletcher will be here. He'll come out and get you and take you to the birthing suite.'

Sun sounded like she was panting into the phone. Skye almost laughed. Her sister could have been the one in labour.

Her pulse skittered when Sun mentioned Fletcher. Skye had settled on a romantic vision of him; his dreadlocks, surfer's physique, cheeky smile and eyes that glowed with an inner light that made everybody who met him feel welcome.

God, she didn't know what made her more nervous. Being present at the birth of her niece or nephew, or seeing Fletcher again for the first time in months.

She'd workshopped herself through the prospect of being face-to-face with him, in the flesh, again. It was inevitable.

She hadn't heard from him since the night he left for Thailand. Day after miserable day in Sydney she dealt with the disappointment of no phone calls, messages, emails or anything to indicate that he wanted to see her again.

She wriggled in the seat of the hire car as she drew closer to her destination. How would she react when she saw him again? It was like she was a terrified job candidate about to be called into meet the CEO for the final interview.

She thought about compiling a list of dos and don'ts on meeting Fletcher again but scuttled the idea as foolish and immature. What was she? Twelve? Some days she felt like a schoolgirl obsessed with the lead singer of a boy band. Fletcher occupied her mind all day long and in her dreams at night. If she had a photo, she'd get a magnet and put it on the fridge or blow it up to poster size to put on her bedroom door, if she had a bedroom door.

The most important thing was to remain aloof and in control of her emotions when they met. And to emphasise her state of wellbeing, how great it was to be independent and single again. She would maintain a friendly yet cool distance. And there would be no touching. Definitely no touching.

Anyway, this visit to Dezzy was all about the baby, not Fletcher King aka Samuel Brand.

As she turned into the hospital's circular driveway, the car lights spotted trouble with a capital 'T' at the front entrance. Fletcher was already outside waiting for her. Skye gripped the steering wheel. Of course, he looked amazing. Her imagination set off at a cracking pace and her rehearsed indifference scrambled out the window. She was a jumble of nerves, her insides popping like corn on a hotplate.

She clung to her new mantra.

Do not sample the product.

Fletcher King was out of bounds for so many reasons. Analogies clamoured in Skye's head, ridiculous but true. Fletcher King, more tempting than a rich dense chocolate cake, more desirable than diamonds. Sexy as. Just sexy as? Sexy as sex.

She swerved haphazardly alongside where he stood, causing him to jump back, and pressed the button to wind down the passenger-side window. But it was the wrong button. Down came the back passenger-side window. She hastily pulled at the button to lift that up and jabbed the button next to it, all fingers and thumbs.

Fletcher, cool as a cucumber, placed broad strong hands on the car roof and leaned down and stared at her from the passenger side of the car.

She finally managed to get the right button and leaned across her seat, hot and bothered despite the car's air-conditioned comfort.

She coughed out, 'Hi, how's it going?' Inwardly squirming, hoping like hell he didn't notice her agitated manner and her voice way too high and cheerful. Too staged.

'Good to see you again,' he said.

Her head teemed with little red demons. They prodded Skye all over with their sharp prongs. The feeling was delicious and it made her want to jump Fletcher's bones there and then. Forget the baby or becoming an aunt.

A room would be better.

But obviously Fletcher was distracted. *For chrissakes Skye, he's about to become a father.*

'Lou's in the early stages of labour so it's pretty relaxed, no rush.' He bumped a hand on the car roof as he moved back.

Skye pulled herself together and pointed vaguely in the direction of the parking lot, well-lit by flouro lights jutting out from tall steel poles.

She leaned across again. 'I can see a spot. You go back inside. I'll find you.'

Fletcher smiled and Skye nearly bit off her bottom lip at its immediate effect on her erogenous zones. She was so *not* over him.

She drove way too fast into a car space, braked jerkily, and did what she could to compose herself. No use breathing through it. She'd end up hyperventilating.

Unfortunately, Fletcher had ignored her advice and remained standing at the hospital entrance, this long-limbed god she'd vowed to forget because he wasn't her 'type'. Skye stopped a safe distance away from him but Fletcher didn't seem to notice her hesitation. He stepped forward and gave her a brief hug, planting kisses lightly on both her cheeks.

Heat lit up her skin as she inhaled his familiar sun-kissed scent and felt the hard warmth of his arms around her. So much for no sampling.

'You look sensational,' he said, pulling back. 'Sydney must be working for you.'

'Yeah, it's great, I love it,' she lied.

They stood for a moment and Skye got the odd feeling Fletcher was about to say something but changed his mind. He settled on, 'Let's go then.'

They walked together through the sliding doors and followed the signs to the birthing unit. He was dressed in blue denim jeans, an unbuttoned blue-checked flanno over a white t-shirt and a scuffed pair of runners.

'I remember the last time we were at this hospital together,' Fletcher said. 'And the time before that. It's weird, like we're always hooking up here.'

Skye laughed, relieved he was keeping it light. 'Thank goodness this is a happy occasion.'

'Not everyone's here yet but I managed to convince Betty...'

'Grandma's here? I thought she had agoraphobia?'

'It wasn't easy. She agreed to come after I promised her Pepe would be in safe hands - he's with your friend Josie. I had to cover her eyes with one of those eye masks, like the ones you get on a plane, before we left the house. She was freaking out about having to go outside, past her front gate. I got lucky, got a parking space right out the front here so she barely noticed the transition from house to Kombi to hospital.'

They walked to the birth centre reception area as Skye pictured people's reactions to the bizarre sight of Fletcher leading along an elderly woman wearing an eye mask. Maybe nobody noticed? Stranger things had happened in Dezzy.

A midwife, fine blonde-streaked hair in a ponytail and dressed in a hospital-issue pale blue shirt, long pants and sensible shoes, greeted them at the main desk.

Skye recognised her face, round and open with clear brown eyes. Smiling eyes, she thought.

'You were in Sun's year at school,' Skye said.

'Yeah, I'm Jane, the midwife on duty for Sun and Lou. I remember you too Skye. It's nice to catch up for such a beautiful event.' Skye briefly clasped Jane's extended hand before Jane got down to business.

'It's coming along nicely,' she said. 'Lou's dilating at a good pace. At the moment, she's having a warm shower to help her relax. Head in if you like, I'll be there in a minute.'

Fletcher walked ahead of Skye through heavy plastic swinging double doors and into a birthing suite styled for comfort, though there was no disguising the fact this was still a hospital.

Soft wall lights threw a muted glow across two oil paintings on a pale cream wall, one of the beach at Desiree Bay and the other of The Point.

A hospital bed with all the rails down was positioned close to a corner of the room. It was made more homely by a patchwork doona thrown across the end. Heavy dark curtains shrouded the window next to the bed. Skye guessed the room had been decorated with donations from the local community.

As her eyes adjusted to the semi-darkness, she noticed a motionless supine figure on the bed. Grandma, still wearing the eye mask.

Dodging a big bean bag and half-a-dozen large colourful chintz cushions that could have been ashram rejects, Skye grabbed Fletcher's arm and pointed in an exaggerated fashion to the corner.

For the first time she recognised a nervous energy in Fletcher, who flinched at her touch. 'When Grandma wakes up, you might want to have a chat, calm her down,' he said softly, his eyes focussed on the closed door to what must have been an ensuite.

'Your mother and Jimmy are bringing over some crystals,' he continued distractedly. 'Airen's on his way and Lou's parents have chosen the sensible option –they're coming to the hospital *after* the baby's born.'

Skye marvelled at how her family had somehow hijacked the birth and turned it into another gathering. It was as though Jonno was in the room with them, making sure the Summerhayes' clan was somehow responsible for this baby's successful entry into the world. The realisation of her family's innocent yet meddlesome ways made her feel like she had no right to be here.

She leaned close to Fletcher and whispered, 'Maybe I should leave and come back after the baby's born, let you guys run the show.'

Fletcher turned his head slightly, not quite meeting her gaze.

'Don't go, I'm nervous as hell Skye,' he said, shocking her with uncharacteristic candour. 'I've never been through this before. I missed the birth of my first child.'

Skye stared at the floor and wrung her hands together. Fletcher didn't seem to notice her unease. 'I can't do anything to help Lou here today,' he said. 'I couldn't even save my own son.'

'It wasn't your fault.'

His eyes met hers in a candid collision. 'I shouldn't dump my shit on you Skye but I screwed up the first time round. I wasn't interested in my son and I didn't love his mother.'

Skye hugged her waist. Fletcher was hurting and she couldn't think of anything appropriate to say that would ease his pain. So she listened.

'I miss my son every day.' His voice was gruff. 'I should have been there for him. Maybe he'd still be alive if I'd been there for him. And his mother.'

Skye lightly touched his arm. 'You can't change the past but you can be here for this baby that's about to be born. I'm sure you were a great dad and you'll be a great dad again.'

A gentle energy flowed between them as Fletcher's gaze intensified and they became unified in their grief for those they had loved and lost in tragic circumstances.

In that moment, Skye experienced a profound peace. One thing she knew for sure. She could never go back to Sydney.

CHAPTER 33

Jimmy and Oceane moved through the birthing suite with a sense of purpose. Shoeless and dressed in matching purple caftans and loose-fitting cheesecloth trousers, they deposited chunks of rose crystal quartz, amethyst and other gems – coloured from deep green to earthy brown with shots of silver – in seemingly random spots around the room. They popped gems under cushions, on windowsills and around the base of the bed where Grandma lay, her pose scarily like that of a corpse the orderlies forgot to move to the hospital mortuary.

After Jimmy and Oceane completed that task, Jimmy placed seven candles – round, square and rectangular – on a dressing table with a mirror hanging behind it that was next to Grandma's bed.

As he lit each one, Jimmy chanted the same blessing, 'Peace and loving kindness to Lou, peace and loving kindness to Sun, peace and loving kindness to the adorable baby about to be born, peace and loving kindness to Airen, peace and loving kindness to Skye, peace and loving kindness to Oceane and meself...'

He glanced at Grandma's prone form, veiny threaded age-spotted hands crossed over her chest in a vampire-like pose. 'Peace and loving kindness to Betty, grandmother and matriarch of the Summerhayes clan, soon to become a great grandmother. We honour ye and salute yer resilient spirit.'

This well-meant sentiment muttered in an impressive baritone voice with a broad Scottish accent did not rouse Grandma, who remained stiff and inanimate as a plank of wood.

Skye tip-toed to the bed, holding her breath. She hovered over Grandma whose mouth plopped open to release a light snoring like a faulty cord-starter motor on an old Victa lawn mower. Her chest rose and fell in the rhythm of someone in a deep sleep. Definitely alive, Skye concluded, relieved that Grandma had the decency not to steal the limelight by carking it before Lou gave birth.

The enticing scent of vanilla spiked with cinnamon and star anise wafted around the room as Oceane linked her arm in Skye's. Jimmy had curated a playlist on an app, and it was being played through two portable Bluetooth speakers. An otherworldly yodel-cum-chant accompanied by pan pipes, bird trills and trickling water, played on a loop.

Finally, Jimmy completed his ritual with, 'Peace and loving kindness to Fletcher.'

Shortly after, Fletcher emerged from the ensuite with his arm supporting a naked Lou. A bedraggled Sun followed, her clothes wet and dripping on the grey lino.

Skye went to help but stopped. There was nothing she could do but cause a traffic jam. The room was already crammed with too many helpers. She felt like an intruder who'd gate crashed a private party.

She considered relocating Grandma from the bed to a chair but maybe Lou didn't want to be on the bed? Skye vaguely recalled sex education classes and a soft focus video of a woman giving birth on the floor.

Apart from that, she'd only ever watched actors feign labour on TV shows or in movies. The actor was usually on a bed, often with her legs in stirrups and private parts covered by a sheet, with an obstetrician – usually male – coordinating the proceedings with clinical efficiency. Red faced, she grunted and screamed until a baby almost the size of a toddler was brought out from some magical place the viewers never got to see.

Jimmy rushed into the ensuite and out again with a couple of towels. He handed one to Fletcher, one to Sun and got down on his hands and knees and mopped the wet floor around them with another.

Lou swayed in ponderous slow motion, reminding Skye of an unstable baby elephant not quite sure of its footing. Fletcher's arm muscles flexed around her, ready to catch her if she fell.

'Jane, get Jane.' Lou's guttural grunts seemed to come from deep within, no doubt a primal reaction to the pain that must be streaking around her abdomen in a constant assault.

On cue, Jane emerged like an ethereal being from a dark corner of the room and took charge. 'Hey Lou, let's get you comfortable so I can check your progress.'

Skye admired her calm competence and upbeat, but not overly Pollyanna, manner.

Lou frowned and pouted. 'Don't wanna move. Wanna stay here.'

This was followed by a blood-curdling wail that would have set off the neighbourhood dogs if there'd been any close by.

Jane's brow creased, she seemed to assess the situation and made a quick call. 'Okay, you don't have to move from that spot Lou; but here's the deal.' Her vowels were rounded and her consonants clipped to indicate that she was in control of the situation. 'It's fine to stay here but if you do, you'll have to squat, lay down or get down on all fours.'

Lou's belly bulged like a massive ancient gemstone – shiny and distended as though the unborn baby was pushing with its hands and pounding at the uterus with its feet in an attempt to kick its way out.

Skye couldn't begin to contemplate the miraculous event that would soon take place. She glanced down, realised she was clutching at her stomach and hastily removed her hands.

Fletcher had regained control of his own emotions and was starting to embrace his role. Skye didn't want to interfere but she asked Jane if there was anything she could do to help.

'Bring over the beanbag.' Jane said to no one in particular.

Before Skye could get to it, Jimmy dragged over the beanbag.

When Lou sat with her back against the beanbag, Jane knelt on the floor to get a better view of Lou's perineum.

'The cervix is fully dilated,' Jane announced, smiled briefly at the cheer squad standing around her, then focussed on Lou. 'It's time for you to push Lou, but the idea is to take it slowly, counting through the breaths out, because we don't want anything to tear.'

Lou reclined in a semi-supine position, her face and body covered with a sheen of sweat that gave her skin a glossy glow. Her eyes were open and she stared intently at the ceiling.

Skye checked the ceiling too, just because Lou seemed to find it so fascinating. But it became apparent that Lou's focus was inwards, not on the dull white paint, dinner-plate light fitting or plain cornices.

'I want an epidural,' Lou said in a half-whisper and shuffled her feet inwards so her legs were closer to her body.

Like that'll keep the baby inside, Skye thought, and her own pelvic floor muscles clenched in sympathy.

'It's way too late for that,' Jane told Lou with a breezy conviction.

Skye was sure Jane was familiar with that request from women moving into the second stage of their labour.

'Your baby will be born soon and I need you to push when I ask and to hold off when I tell you. That might be really hard to do so you have to help me out here Lou. Listen carefully. Pay attention.'

Lou's expression was momentarily uncomprehending. But the curtain of mist swiftly rose as Jane's words sank in. Her eyes widened and her face contorted into a portrait of terror as she howled 'no' like a wolf at the moon.

Airen strolled in mid-wail.

'Woah,' he said in a stage whisper as he eased himself on to the floor next to Skye, at the base of Lou's feet. 'Beached whale.'

'Shooosh,' Sun hissed. She knelt directly next to Lou, applying a cold washcloth to her clammy forehead.

Airen apologised and appeared appropriately chastised. Resting back on his haunches, he removed an expensive digital camera from his backpack.

Skye watched Airen attach a zoom lens. 'Photos?'

'I'm the official photographer and videographer. Don't worry, it'll be in good taste.' He grinned and raised the camera to frame a shot in the viewfinder.

Skye grimaced. 'The last thing I'd want would be someone filming my fanny with something as big as a watermelon coming out of it.'

Sun glared at them. 'Shoosh.'

'Shuddup, all of you,' Lou shrieked before muttering something in Mandarin that sounded pretty foul.

Fletcher, who knelt on the other side of Lou, cast a sympathetic glance at Sun. His nervous tension hummed like electricity through a wire. Sweat beaded on his brow as his attention swung back to Lou. Her cheeks were aflame, she groaned and grunted, her breath coming in long rasping pants.

Skye found she was breathing in time with Lou, harsh and strong, whooshing out the bad air and sucking in the good. It was surprisingly liberating.

She gazed around her. Everyone in the room was in that zone, their breathing aligned and charged with a positive aggression. Powerful energy swirled around them and Skye understood, in that moment, how all life on the planet could be connected in a universal breath.

After about an hour, a subtle change occurred as Lou slipped out of the rhythm.

Skye sensed it was time.

'I can't do this,' Lou shouted directly at Airen, who had the lens focussed on her, flashing red on 'record'.

Jane murmured encouragement, leaned in close and observed Lou's perineum. She drew back and nodded like a sage.

'The baby's head's moving down the birth canal, so ease off the pushing and make the journey a relaxed one,' she coached Lou.

Lou began to sob. 'I can't fucking ease off, the baby won't let me.'

She shuddered through a powerful contraction and grabbed at Fletcher's hand. 'Help me. Please.' A high pitched whimper.

'How?' Fletcher asked, all gentle concern, though Skye saw the fear in his eyes.

'For a start, turn off that fucking hippy dirge, it's doing my head in.'

Everybody laughed, even Jimmy. It felt like the aftermath of a storm when the temperature drops and a luminous sun tentatively peeks out from behind a black cloud.

Glad to be of some assistance, Skye bolted to her feet and switched off the chant. As she went to sit back down, Airen, still filming Lou's perineum, pulled his phone out of his pocket and thrust it as Skye.

'Put this on, it's a selection of Lou and Sun's favourite songs.'

Skye took the phone with the app open to a folder named 'Lou's birth toons'. It had to be better than generic panpipes in a computer-generated rainforest.

She set up the Bluetooth with Airen's app, and a menacing base guitar paired with tense growling vocals of a demented Mark Seymour from Hunters and Collectors burst out of the speakers. *'The Slab?'*

Sun had been obsessed with the band from childhood and had introduced her siblings to Hunters and Collectors earthy grunge style of Australian pub rock. Skye turned down the volume and asked Airen, 'Have you got anything a bit more low key?'

'Turn it up,' Lou half laughed, half shrieked and dug fingernails into Sun and Fletcher's hands as Jane instructed her to relax 'or at least try' to ease off into a gentle push.

'Woohooeeaaaaaaaa.'

Skye spun on her heel to witness the most incredible moment in her life. As the bass guitar pounded a back beat and cacophonous brass entered into the fray, the baby's head emerged into the world from its watery home of the past nine months.

'Baby's coming, Lou, would you like to feel the head?' Jane's voice was loud over the hammering of drums, guitars and Lou's unfettered whoops that could have been joy or despair.

Lou's expression was terror-stricken. 'No,' she roared and cast non-seeing eyes around the room. 'Just get it out. Now.'

The rest of the baby slithered out in a slippery jumble of gel and blood-coated limbs into Jane's silicone-gloved hands.

CHAPTER 34

It was over in an instant. Skye managed to turn down the volume but otherwise she was screwed to the spot in absolute awe, her whole body shaking, legs unsteady as a passenger on a ship rolling in big seas.

She laughed and cried as Jane lifted the baby into the light.

Sun resembled a statue in relief while Fletcher gulped in air as though he'd just slid out of the womb.

Jane held the baby in both hands, careful not to tug at the umbilical cord attached to the still-to-be-delivered placenta.

Everybody waited.

Skye wanted to snatch the baby and slap its bottom the way it was done in the movies. What was wrong? Why wasn't Jane helping out? It couldn't have been more than a couple of seconds but it felt like an eternity.

Lou asked what they were all thinking. 'Is she okay? Is he all right?'

And then it happened.

The cry shocked everyone into relieved riotous whoops of laughter. Airen put down the camera momentarily to applaud and whistle, top teeth over bottom lip.

The cry was raucous. And, Skye conceded, much like the caterwaul of a distressed feline.

The baby writhed, tiny arms flailing about, trying to find purchase, seeking out that heavenly place it just exited. A creamy white substance coated parts of its body. Skye thought it looked like it had been rolled in a milk and flour mixture and then shaken lightly so only bits of the glutinous mixture remained in the creases of skin.

'He's a goer, this one.' Jane allowed herself a satisfied smile. 'Got a bit of protective vernix left on his skin which is good. It's what we want to see.'

Fletcher appeared not to have heard her. 'A boy,' he said in a monotone. Skye examined his features searching for disappointment or, worse still, a lack of interest in his newborn baby.

But maybe she was reading more into it than she should have? It was a habit of hers when, in reality, his voice and face gave nothing away.

Jane placed the baby on Lou's chest followed by a heated towel over both of them. 'Let him feel the warmth of your body, he knows your scent already,' Jane encouraged.

Lou placed her hands protectively across the top of the tiny body under the blanket and sobbed in what sounded like sheer relief that it was all over. 'He's good,' she said in a tremulous voice and lowered her chin to her chest to get a better look.

Sun touched the baby's damp head with fingertips as light as feathers. 'He's perfect.'

About ten minutes later, Lou pushed out the placenta. As Jane inspected the still pulsating nutrient source, with a liver-like consistency, the size of a dinner plate, Oceane announced that it would be frozen and then defrosted for the next family gathering.

Airen lowered the camera and screwed up his face the way he did when he was a kid forced to drink one of Oceane's healthful concoctions. 'I won't be going to that barbecue.'

Oceane clicked her tongue with a 'tut-tut-tut' as a mother would to an ignorant child. 'Darlin', we're not going to eat it, though there's nothing wrong with that. The placenta is tasty in a stew with carrots, onions and celery.'

Skye clenched her teeth. 'No way. I'm with Airen.'

Oceane didn't hear her or pretended not to. 'I've discussed it with Lou and Sun. We decided to bury the placenta in the garden at Grandma's place. We'll give it time to compost before we plant the cutting of an ancient Wollemi pine next to it. As he grows up, our little boy will witness its growth, nurtured by the nutrients from his mother's placenta.'

Skye couldn't argue with that symbolic gesture.

After Sun cut the clamped umbilical cord, Jimmy popped open a bottle of French champagne and poured everyone a glass, except for Airen, who opted for lemonade.

Grandma, alerted by the sound of the cork, tottered from the bed with the eye mask pulled down around her neck. She cocked her head to one side, as bright as a lorikeet, and observed the baby. His hands as delicate and fragile as rose petals were clenched into tight fists against Lou's chest.

Grandma had to bend down to see his face, with a button nose, eyes squeezed shut as though the dim light was too intense and ruby lips sealed tight like flower buds before dawn.

'Oh, Love, isn't he just the ants pants?' Grandma cooed as she accepted a glass of champagne from Jimmy.

'Who does he look like? Lou? Fletcher? Or both? Too soon to tell.'

She appeared to have missed nothing. Skye was sure she'd taken sneak peeks during the labour.

Jimmy held his glass aloft and they all followed his lead, even Lou who was propped up to an almost sitting position on the floor. 'I would like to dedicate this toast to Lou, who did an incredible job, even with all her cussing and cursing.'

A murmur of agreement ran around their contented circle and Lou, who an hour ago resembled a feverish wildebeest, assumed the serene expression of a saint. Her black hair shone like ebony polished with a soft cloth and her skin gleamed satin smooth as if she'd emerged from a sixty-minute de-stress massage. All that was missing was the halo, Skye thought with a smile.

As they raised their glasses, Skye watched Fletcher. He stood back from the circle, like the shy new boy, unsure of his role in the group. His gaze was fixed adoringly on the baby and a smile hovered at the corners of his lips.

After the baby was swaddled like a mummy, except for his ruddy little face, Skye got to hold him briefly. She stroked his cheek with her index finger, noticing with delight that his mouth formed a perfect 'o' in a reflexive yawn. In that instant, as she balanced the vulnerable sweet-vanilla pod warmth of him in one crooked arm, Skye's heart melted.

She resolved there and then to be a good friend to Fletcher, a sister-in-law who would always be there for him. She would also be the best-ever aunty. If Sun and Lou needed a babysitter, and Fletcher wasn't around, Skye would drop everything for the little tot. That's what she would do. She would become a better woman.

Grandma sat on an old couch near the double exit doors. Skye gently lowered the precious bundle into her arms.

'It's about time we met young man,' Grandma murmured. 'You are the young prince, aren't you? Freshly minted, yes, you are.'

Fletcher was suddenly beside her. 'Pepe will be jealous.'

Skye chuckled. 'Poor Pepe. He'll have to get used to the competition.'

Checking her watch saved her from making eye contact with Fletcher.

It was after midnight. September sixteen.

The baby had been born on the same day as Jonno, just after midnight on September sixteen.

'C'mon Betty, I'm taking you home,' Skye said to Grandma. 'The clock's struck midnight and I don't want you turning into a field mouse.'

Fletcher gently eased the baby up and away from Grandma. He seemed tinier still in Fletcher's large muscular arms. Quietly, Fletcher rocked the baby and sang an old Bob Marley song, Three Little Birds, not quite but almost under his breath.

Grandma gulped the last of her champers and rose to her feet. Skye thought she saw the champagne glass disappear somewhere in the folds of Grandma's house dress but this wasn't the time for a body search.

Grandma held Skye's hand. 'I remember it like it was yesterday, your father humming that tune when you were little. It was one of his favourites.'

She pressed her fingers to her lips and blew Fletcher a kiss. 'I have a feeling everything's gonna to be all right too.'

CHAPTER 35

Two weeks later

Skye sat cross-legged on the beach with her hands resting in her lap and her surfboard by her side. She draped an Indian cotton scarf shot with bright pink and green colour waves, on loan from her mother, around her shoulders to block the sun. Even though she wore a spring suit, it wouldn't protect her bare arms from the damaging rays.

An afternoon breeze infused with ocean salt tickled her cheeks. It relieved the heat of the spring day and added a kick to neat sets of waves running off The Point.

Straightening up her spine, chest proud and head held erect, she slowly eased her eyelids to almost shut. Her world became a fuzz of yellow sand merging with blue sea and sky. She was supposed to be in the moment, meditating on nothing but her breath, but as usual her mind went rogue and her thoughts darted back to the events of two weeks ago.

Edwin Jonno Nathan Summerhayes-Cheng had weighed in at a respectable 3.6 kilograms.

Already Oceane had picked that her grandson was destined for great things. 'Look at those beautiful long legs, they're running legs. And what about those cheeky chubby arms, definitely swimming arms or surfing and lifesaving. And see how alert he is - he takes in absolutely every detail. He'll be a leader of some sort.'

Jimmy had joked that 'wee Ed' had so much hair it could be woven into dreadlocks to match his father's.

As Skye sent the bad energy away on an out breath and invited in loving kindness on an in breath, an image of Edwin's father popped into her head. His dreadlocks were flying and he was being chased by a little boy with locks as bouncy as the springs on an old-fashioned bicycle seat.

Skye twitched her nose, irritated by a strand of flyaway hair. The 'in the moment' moment was lost as she considered her future.

For the time being she was a lodger at Grandma's, having taken on the role of acting editor at *The Northern Sun* while Sun took three months' leave.

She ran her hands through her hair and across her head, where she felt an imaginary itch. She blew out a frustrated breath. How would she ever get anywhere with her meditation practice? Just as her mind slowed down and her breath whispered in her ears like a gentle surf, a thought buzzed into her dream-like state.

Giving up, she'd try again later, Skye opened her eyes and stared straight ahead at the cinematic horizon of a line drawn through aquamarine ocean to the deep blue of the sky.

Her future. The plan was to find a place of her own in the next week. She avoided Cal's real estate agency and approached the new agent in town. Cal's alignment with the pro coal seam gas lobby didn't work for Skye. Making the decision to cut advertising ties with Cal's family's real estate agency had been hard but *The Northern Sun* could no longer have an association with the Sturgess family if it was to remain true to its ideals.

Skye stared at the waves rolling off a bombora at The Point. About half a dozen surfers were out there, hoping to achieve nirvana off the front of a perfectly formed wave.

A light bulb switched on in her head. Surfing would be her meditation. Today, she'd picked a long board for the milder conditions. It would be mentally challenging to get back out there but she was as ready as she ever would be.

Her heart rate increased at the thought of it and her body pulsed with spiked adrenaline. She had to do this. She must do this. She was sick of coming down to the beach to watch others surf, wanting to be out there with them but not quite able to make the leap from observer to participant.

She dreamed about catching fully formed waves, hovering inside curved walls of shimmering glass on the verge of shattering, moving at light speed and shooting out the other side into the painfully blue sky. She dreamed about moments of searing clarity.

Skye felt a presence beside her. Her gaze moved from big tanned feet, along firm calf muscles and up past psychedelic boardies to a broad chest, strong wide shoulders and neck, to a face that set her soul on fire.

The trademark dreadlocks had been chopped to shoulder length and the bristles shaved, which made him look more like twenty four than thirty four years old.

Skye thought his smile had the healing power of morning sunshine streaming down to warm her all over, while his deep sea eyes could see into her soul.

Until now, she had somehow managed to avoid him, visiting Sun and Lou and the baby when he was at work, and steering clear of the bakery and beach at all other times. Except for today. Her sink or surf day.

They were always going to bump into each other and Skye had resigned herself to the fact that, sooner or later, she would have to deal with her crush, to see him again and consciously steer away from the personal. Keep it totally above board, so to speak. Absolutely no sharing of private most intimate thoughts about love and life and the possibility of making something more out of their relationship.

'Long time no see,' Fletcher said, without a hint of irony, though from his raised eyebrows it was obvious that he was aware of her avoidance tactics. Maybe he'd been avoiding her too?

'Mind if I join you?'

She didn't need to answer. He placed his board onto the sand as though it was a rare and fragile object before he lowered himself lithely on to his haunches, heels flat, next to her.

Skye might have imagined it, but it seemed like he'd brought a fresh breeze with him, familiar and salty, a crystal clear aquamarine smell that she could easily dive into.

For a while they watched a man throwing a stick into the ocean, where it was fetched by a dog with patches of caramel-and-white on its scruffy short coat. Dropping the stick at the man's feet, the dog stared at him, and the stick, then at the stick and at him, up and down, up and down, in rapturous attention, until the man flung the object of desire into the fizzing shore break.

The moment the stick was airborne the dog loped into the surf, fearless, somehow able to judge the angle of its trajectory. When the stick landed the dog was at the ready and lunged for it with jowly jaws open. Victorious and fulfilled, the dog paddled back to the shore, prize firmly gripped between its teeth, jowls turned upwards in a doggy smile.

It was nice to sit next to Fletcher and just be with him. To Be. To Be With Him. Skye ran the idea around in her head like a lolly melting as it swirled around her mouth, trying not to get carried away with the delicious possibility of being with Fletcher. Skye broke the silence. 'Dogs are funny.'

'Ya gotta love dogs. They're single minded. Totally OCD.'

Skye grabbed a handful of sand and let it stream through her fingers. 'Where's Occy?'

'It's hot down here so I left him at home to herd the chooks.'

Skye smiled at that. It would be too easy to stay with the light banter all afternoon but there were questions burning inside her that needed to be asked.

'Ed's the most beautiful baby,' she started slowly, picking up another handful of sand, trying not to stare at Fletcher but at the coarse grains rushing to join a beach. 'You must be thrilled.'

When he didn't answer, she snuck a glance. His gaze was lowered too, so Skye could only see his profile, where a smile tugged at his lips as though he was trying to hide his pleasure at becoming a new dad.

Her confidence grew. 'Is he like Nat at all?' She pushed a little further, her *I won't pry* mantra totally discarded. It was an audacious move on her part but she felt she had nothing to lose by going there.

Fletcher shook out the sand and smacked his hands together, before sitting with his knees pulled into his chest.

Skye breathed a quiet sigh of relief when he started to talk.

'Sometimes I catch a glimpse of Nat there. When Ed's sleeping or yawning, I can see it a bit around the mouth and the nose.' His voice was soft. 'But those physical features that are similar in babies change. And temperament wise, he's more laid back than Nat. Ed's got this big smile. I know they say babies don't smile this soon after being born but Ed smiles all the time.'

He laughed as through embarrassed at his own enthusiasm.

'I agree. He's so chilled, so happy, such a blessing,' Skye said, and relished the companionable silence that followed.

Two surfers, both young grommets dripping wet and shaking out their sun-silvered mop tops, strolled past, laughing at something one of them had said.

'I had to go back to Thailand for a funeral,' Fletcher said into the middle distance. Skye tensed. Waiting. If he wanted to tell his story, she would listen.

'Nat's mother died. I'm sorry you had to find out bits and pieces of my story from Sun, and from the stuff I left at the house.'

'S'okay.'

'I don't want to bore you...'

'No, go on, I'm not bored.'

It took another minute before Fletcher found his voice again. Skye drew her knees to her chest and rested her chin on top of folded arms.

He sighed deeply. 'About ten years ago, I met Nat's mother, Samorn, at a party in Perth. We had sex, a one-night stand, whatever you wanna call it.

'Sun might've told you about the app, and there were several other business coups that brought in a shitload of money, really fast. It was madness. I was the golden boy, feted by the tech world and followed around by hangers' on who were there for the ride.'

He twisted around to face her and gave a sad smile.

'I didn't think anything more about Samorn. It was easy to get laid without thinking about the consequences. Back then my life was out of control. There were women everywhere, drugs, alcohol, the whole catastrophe.'

Skye nodded. 'That's why you *get* Airen.'

Fletcher's laugh had a sharp knowing edge to it.

'I totally *get* Airen,' he said. 'He was a young footy player with his star on the rise, tempted by the lure of the dollar. People everywhere telling him how great he was, how much money he could make. Don't get me wrong.' He pushed his hand across his face and tugged thoughtfully at his chin with his thumb and index finger.

'Money has its uses. It gives you choices,' he continued. 'But you have to make them wisely. At the time, I was like Airen. A kid in a lolly shop. Such a douche. Taking, taking, taking. Never giving back.

'I believed what people told me about myself. I was a legend in my own mind. I didn't take any responsibility for my actions. It was all about me.'

He made a squiggly pattern in the sand with his finger. 'Anyway, I should have known that sooner or later my casual 'f-ing' around would catch up with me. Out of the blue, Samorn called me. She was pregnant. She said it was mine. The moment I saw Nat, I knew it was true but I had a paternity test done anyway. I was furious she let it happen. I didn't want a kid. And no way did I want to be with Samorn,' he continued. 'She wanted money. At first I said no. I didn't want to have anything to do with her, or the baby. But I started to think about my own totally screwed childhood and I didn't want that to happen to any kid of mine. I hadn't planned to be a father but I decided I needed be there for Nat. So, we got married, just to keep Samorn's family happy.'

Another pause as Fletcher sighed and shut his eyes.

'Nat died when I was back here, partying and mucking around, seeing other women, pretending my other life with a wife and baby didn't exist.'

The wind had abated and the ocean whooshed like a mother cooing 'hush hush hush' in a baby's shell ear. Fletcher rubbed his hands across his face again. Skye could feel the grief as though his baby son had died only yesterday. His shoulders rose and fell as he drew in and expelled harsh breaths that ended on a shudder.

She had no words. 'Sorry' sounded limp and meaningless, so Skye simply placed her hand on Fletcher's, which seemed to trigger him out of a trance and back to the present.

'I'm sorry, I...' he began but Skye squeezed his hand softly.

'Don't worry.'

'Samorn blamed me, and she was right to. After Nat's funeral I left her for good, moved here to Desiree Bay to my grandmother's place. Reinvented myself. I got rid of Samuel Brand and became Fletcher King. I made no effort to contact Samorn though her brother wrote occasionally. Through him I found out she'd moved into a temple retreat on the outskirts of Bangkok.'

'And that's where she died?'

'Yeah,' the word was a whisper breathed out on a sigh. 'She took her own life.'

Skye barely heard the words. The wind carried them away.

'That's so horrible. Poor Samorn. She lost everything.'

Fletcher squeezed her hand in his and Skye thought about Airen and the small miracle that had convinced him to choose life over death.

'I wanted you to know all this. The name change, that was purely to escape from all the bullshit...'

'I like the name Fletcher King,' she said. 'That's who you are to me.'

They smiled at each other and Skye's heart opened like a rose in stop motion as Fletcher leaned in and brushed his lips lightly against hers.

'Please do that again,' she said firmly.

The next kiss lasted longer, teasing and tantalising with possibilities.

'I'm glad you came back.' Fletcher traced the line of her jaw with his index finger. 'I didn't think you cared at all. About me. And I didn't wanna stuff up anyone else's life so I went straight to Sun and Lou and told them about my feelings for you.'

Skye grabbed his hair and pulled him back to her. After a while, they both came up for air, laughing.

'I was so scared *you* didn't give a bugger about *me*,' she said, and shivered with anticipation as he gently ran a finger across her collar bone.

'I want to be with you.' His voice was gruff. 'You're gutsy, smart and intelligent, beautiful and besides, Occy adores you.'

Laughing their way into a loose embrace, they fell back onto the sand, and Fletcher rolled Skye over so she lay on top of him. She rained kisses across his face and nibbled at his neck, breathing him into her, pressing her hands into the sand to an elevated position where she could stare at his beautiful face.

Now it was her turn to talk. 'I'm not an easy person to be with, I'm OCD, just like the dog with the stick. I resist change. I'm demanding and bossy, I make lists for everything...'

Her self-criticism was brought to an abrupt halt by another mind-blowing kiss. When Skye resurfaced her thoughts were more on getting back to Fletcher's place and into his big comfy bed.

'Hey, hey, what's up?' a voice called out.

Skye and Fletcher scrambled to a seated position, Skye's guilt meter flying to the max as Airen placed his board on the sand next to Fletcher's.

'Have I interrupted something?' Her brother's cheeky grin made it impossible for Skye to be mad with him though her instinct was to tell him to bugger off.

'Not at all mate,' Fletcher said, shaking sand out of his dreadlocks. 'We were having a chat.'

Airen's eyes turned into assessing slits. He could barely conceal his glee.

'Chat, eh? That puts a new spin on it. I knew you'd be down here mate but I didn't expect to find my sister here with you.'

Skye wiped her hands free of sand and tried to readjust everything.

'I was thinking of taking the plunge,' she offered quietly as reluctance and self-doubt seeped into her bones. She hadn't expected an audience for her first foray into the ocean on a surfboard since Jonno's death.

'Let's go in together,' Fletcher suggested.

Airen nodded in agreement but, now she was being put on the spot, Skye wasn't so sure that was a good idea.

'I don't know. I was going to do it on my own. I'm a bit nervous.'

Airen's expression softened. 'Come out with us, it'll be good. I promise. We'll look out for you.'

Fletcher stood up and offered his hands. Skye slipped hers into his and he pulled her to her feet.

All three turned to face the surf and Skye linked her arms with both men.

'I love youse guys,' she said shakily in her best Aussie Ocker accent.

'Love ya right back,' Airen said.

Fletcher gave her one of his billion dollar smiles.

After Airen let out a rallying war cry and count-down of 'One, two, three!' they grabbed their boards and hurtled across the sand and into the surf.

After she plunged through a breaking wave, exhilarated as the cleansing sharp thrill of it illuminated her senses, Skye eased her body up onto the board. Fletcher moved in beside her, going stroke for stroke out to the bombora. Gone was the fear she'd anticipated. With Fletcher beside her, she knew she was safe. And always would be.

Airen was ahead of them, moving forward with the ease of a natural athlete, gliding over the undulating surface towards a pod of locals, floating on their boards, waiting for the perfect wave.

'There's no turning back now,' Fletcher said. 'We're in this together.'

Skye knew he was right.

Heart pumping hard, feeling the exquisite high of life washing over her like some crazy spiritual healing, she gave a jubilant hoot and surged forward, ploughing her arms into the soft velvet water, its cool caress on her warm skin.

'Hey, wait for me,' Fletcher called from a distance.

But Skye was already there.

Acknowledgements

I never thought the day would come when I would be able to call myself a self-published author.

During the writing of this novel, I experienced periods of crippling self-doubt. The loop in my head of 'I'm no good at this, why bother?' threatened to overwhelm me. But constructive criticism from friends and family spurred me on.

Finally, I've done it — but not on my own.

I'd dabbled in writing since childhood but found inspiration in 2004 after attending a Romance Writers of Australia (RWA) conference in Coogee, Sydney. So it's fitting that my first shout-out goes to the RWA, a volunteer-run organisation that supports authors across a vast range of genres, not just category romance.

I've completed RWA courses on conflict, plotting, character development, the hero and heroine's journey and more. I've entered numerous contests, and several of my short stories have been published in RWA anthologies.

Thanks to the RWA, I learned the craft of writing.

I met Anita Joy, who writes under the pen name of AJ Blythe, at an RWA conference, I think it was 2005, and we've been friends ever since. Anita is one of those rare human beings who gives freely of her time even though she leads an incredibly busy life. She's been one of my cheerleaders, and that can be tiring work.

Writing NSW is another organisation that has contributed to my growth as a writer. In 2014, I enrolled in *Year of the Novel*, led by author Emily Maguire for the first two phases and editor and publisher Linda Funnell for the third phase.

I'm a procrastinator. If I can avoid writing, I will. I love the creative process but getting-started and keeping-going are the hardest parts.

This course set me on the right path and by the end of 2014 I had completed the first draft of *Return to Desiree Bay*.

In the early days when the novel was a work in progress, Lisa Thatcher and Cath Jones provided constructive feedback for which I'm grateful.

In 2019, I dragged the manuscript out of the drawer and registered for yet another writing course. I know, when is enough enough?

I met Sandra Groom at author Kate Forsyth's weekend workshop run by the Australian Writers' Centre. Now a published author, Sandra cast her keen eye over my manuscript as it evolved into the final version.

Here's to the nurses, my sister-in-law Patsy Quealy included. A registered nurse and practising midwife, Patsy fact-checked the details in the novel's 'childbirth chapter'. I forgot how it all worked!

And what would I do without my good friend Lisa Chandler, wife of Lewis and genius in her own right who always heads into the surf ahead of me. Lisa is a goddess of many things, and one of her talents is graphic design. Without Lisa's help, I would not have my website which features a bespoke logo of a winged pencil that contains my initials.

Another thank-you goes to publishing expert Joel Naoum for his guidance through the self-publishing labrynth.

The friends I've made through pool and ocean swimming also played a part in getting this novel published, although they don't know it.

One day after a pool squad session, I let it slip that I'd written a novel.

From that day on, they never let up.

"How's the book going?"

"What's happening with the novel?"

"When will your book be published?"

It wore me down.

The novel is set in the fictional coastal town of Desiree Bay which could be any of the beautiful hamlets along the east coast of NSW that stretch from Yuin country in the south to Bundjalung country in the north. Sydney, Eora country, also features.

There is a nod to the far-north coast: Byron Bay (love it or not, it gets under your skin), Lennox Head, Brunswick Heads and Crescent Head. But the town could just as easily be located on the south coast: from Gerringong to Jervis Bay, Huskisson, Mollymook, Milton, Bawley Point and more.

The facade of The Last Post Hotel was inspired by the iconic Marlin Hotel in Ulladulla. Completed in 1948, the Marlin was the first hotel to open in NSW after World War II. I love the pared back art-deco-style building that dominates a corner block as you drive through town along the Princes Highway. It has a solid and reliable presence as the bastion of the old guard.

I wrote the novel in 2014, when life was free and easy (though I didn't think so at the time). My protagonist Skye Summerhayes would have trouble trying to travel from Sydney to Desiree Bay if this story had unfolded in 2021 during an extended lockdown in NSW due to COVID-19.

There's no other way to finish this ramble than by thanking my family — partner John, amazing daughters, Holly and Greta, and awesome step-son Josh.

I am indebted to Greta for her involvement from the start. In 2014, Greta's Higher School Certificate year, we'd often meet at Mitchell Library/The State Library of NSW or Ryde Library where Greta would study and I'd write.

Greta read the first draft of the novel from start to 'The End'. More recently, she provided feedback on the blurb. She has always believed in my writing. That means so much to me.

And how could I leave out Holly, who recently combed through much of the revised version of the novel and provided insightful suggestions. Every single one a gem.

I couldn't ask for anything more.